DIVIDE
&
CONQUER

CUT & RUN SERIES BOOK 4

BY ABIGAIL ROUX

RIPTIDE
PUBLISHING

Riptide Publishing
PO Box 1537
Burnsville, NC 28714
www.riptidepublishing.com

Divide & Conquer

Cover art: L.C. Chase, lcchase.com/design.htm
Layout: L.C. Chase

ISBN: 978-1-963773-10-1

Second edition
June, 2024

Also available in ebook:
ISBN: 978-1-963773-09-5

DIVIDE & CONQUER

CUT & RUN SERIES BOOK 4

BY ABIGAIL ROUX

RIPTIDE
PUBLISHING

For all of those who keep going, even when they can't see the light.

TABLE OF
CONTENTS

CHAPTER ONE

Cued by the station jingle, the lights came up on the television newscast set, highlighting a slim, pleasant-faced black woman in a white blouse and green suit jacket sitting at the desk and tall, smiling man wearing a charcoal gray suit. The station logo appeared on the screen. "This is WBAL TV 11 News at 6. I'm Jeff Barns."

"And I'm Alicia Harrison. Good evening."

The camera focused on Harrison as a photo of a police car on fire appeared over her left shoulder. "Riots shook the city last night following the Ravens' loss to the Pittsburgh Steelers in the divisional round playoff. It was the third riot since New Year's Eve, and the violence continues to escalate. Andrea Gregg has more on the story."

A siren cut to a night shot of a police car burning. People ran in front of it, taking photos and yelling as firefighters worked to douse the flames. The windows in the store behind them were smashed, glass scattered everywhere. A teenager was kicking in a final window in the background.

"For the third time in a month, residents of Baltimore have woken up to a city in ruins."

The sound of glass shards crackling and dragging on concrete accompanied the shot change. An older, balding man was sweeping up glass in front of a store.

"They ransacked the place," the man, identified by the title cards as *Store Owner Steve Vilnick*, said. "This is the second time this month. I'm not sure we'll open again."

As he kept sweeping, Gregg's voice took over. "So far, no one has been seriously injured in the riots, but the property damage now reaches into the millions. Police say they are doing all they can to bring those responsible to justice, but tempers are beginning to fray. Today, city residents showed their frustration in a number of organized protests outside police headquarters."

The shot changed to a demonstration outside the ugly facade of one of Baltimore's many police district buildings.

"They aren't doing enough," a young woman identified as *Jasmine Burke, student*, said. "What have they done to stop it? Nothing. It's getting so you can't go around at night anymore without walking into the middle of a battleground."

"What are we paying them for?" *Roy Monroe, store clerk*, said. "They've made no arrests, got no leads. Man, after they smashed up the store I work in, we had to shut down for a week, and I didn't get reimbursed for that time. Why are we still paying them?"

"I am concerned. Of course I'm concerned," *Bob Smitherman, banker*, said. "Places that have always been safe in the city just aren't anymore, and public events? After New Year's, I'm avoiding them. Too many angry people and too few police."

The shot switched to the Baltimore police chief. "We are, of course, doing all we can to stop the instigators of these riots, but we need the public's help to restore peace and safety to our city. We can't stand strong when we're divided."

A young woman in a light blue blazer appeared on screen holding a microphone. Her title read *Andrea Gregg, WBAL reporter*. A number appeared at the bottom of the screen. "Police are asking anyone with information or photos of rioters destroying property to call the tip line. You can also submit tips anonymously at www.baltimorepolice.org. This is Andrea Gregg, reporting for WBAL TV 11."

The steaming hot water poured down over his shoulders, and Special Agent Zane Garrett groaned, drawing it out as he rotated his head to stretch the tense muscles of his neck. The shower was a pleasure after the two-hour workout this morning that had culminated in another rough-and-tumble boxing match with his partner.

Zane let his eyes flutter shut, laid his head back to soak his hair, and released a long sigh while he enjoyed the pounding water pressure.

This was an old gym, a small one tucked away in the basement of the FBI's Baltimore field office. But Zane preferred it to the newer, shinier fitness center in town that some of the agents frequented. Mostly because this old locker room had wonderfully tall shower heads and he didn't have to stoop—one of the hazards of being six foot five—and half-wall shower stalls, which meant he could sometimes ogle his very handsome partner without too much risk of being caught.

Straightening, Zane opened his eyes, switching his attention from the water trickling down his face to the man not even three feet away on the other side of the tiled barrier.

Special Agent Ty Grady stood with his face turned toward the water and his hands on the tile wall in front of him, his shoulders hunched forward and his back arched. His dark brown hair was cut short, shorter than usual, a necessity after being bleached blond for their last assignment. The water poured over and around his defined muscles, sloughing off the remains of the soap from his body and making the dull gold of his Marine Corps signet ring shine. Winding down in the shower was one of the few times Zane ever saw his partner that still, a true novelty when it came to Ty Grady.

Although if Ty stayed in place for more than a minute, Zane could get his hands on him . . . Zane growled and ducked his head back under the water, reaching to turn down the water temperature before grabbing his bottle of body wash. His ability to keep the lust in check while at work was usually better than this.

When he glanced over a couple of breaths later, Ty was leaning his arms on the partition between them, smirking at him. Zane arched an eyebrow, wondering not for first time if Ty could read his mind.

Ty looked him up and down and then glanced over his shoulder at the otherwise empty showers. "So, I had a thought," he told Zane casually.

"Danger, Will Robinson," Zane commented as he squeezed gel into one hand and started soaping up.

"Don't be like that," Ty told him, his voice sounding hurt but carrying the undertone of mischief Zane was well used to.

Zane snorted and shifted under the water as he washed off so he could look at Ty without craning his neck. "You had a thought," he prompted with a small smile.

"No, you'll have to work for it now," Ty responded with another smirk as he turned back to his own stream of water.

Zane rolled his eyes and chucked his wet washcloth over the divider, smiling as he heard the wet splat against Ty's skin. Ty's infectious laughter, mingling with the relaxing thrum of the water running through old pipes, rewarded his effort. Zane grinned, letting the little spark of warmth spread through him as he finished rinsing off.

He was reaching to shut off the water when a shrieking alarm pierced the soothing peace of water falling.

"Fire alarm. Time to go," Ty announced calmly as he turned the water off and grabbed his towel from the far wall of the shower stall. He didn't even dry off. He just wrapped the towel around his hips and headed for the exit as if there were nothing unusual about it.

Zane winced as he covered one ear. "Ty!" he called out as he snatched up his towel and hurried after his partner. He grabbed Ty's arm when he caught up. "You can't go outside soaking wet and practically naked in the middle of goddamn January!" He started tugging Ty back toward their lockers, where they could at least grab shorts and T-shirts and running shoes.

"Cold is better than on fire," Ty argued, though he let Zane drag him back.

"There's no fire down here."

"You don't know that."

"And the exit is twenty yards away," Zane said as he hurriedly pulled Ty along behind him. "Now get dressed. And shoes."

"Garrett, when an alarm starts going off, I head for an exit!" Ty shouted unhappily. He wasn't panicking, of course. Ty never panicked unless he was trapped in the dark or couldn't find his beloved Bronco in the parking lot. He shucked the towel, pulled on a pair of shorts, and slid his feet into his worn athletic shoes. Then he grabbed Zane's arm and gave him a tug toward the exit, heedless of Zane trying to get into his shorts.

"Okay, damn, give me *one* second!" Zane exclaimed, grabbing his T-shirt and towel after shoving his feet into his running shoes, resisting Ty's yanking as he leaned over to snatch up Ty's T-shirt before letting his partner pull him along.

"Drag your feet later, Lone Star. Either the building's on fire or it's a drill and we'll be doing paperwork until our fingers bleed if we're not out in time," Ty insisted as he pulled Zane along the corridor toward the emergency exit. Ty was notoriously flighty and could be easily distracted, but in an emergency, he honed in on one thing and one thing alone: survival. There was no fighting the iron grip he had on Zane's arm or his insistence that being half-naked and outside was better than any alternative right then.

"I'm thinking we'll get a little leeway since we were *in the showers*," Zane bit off as they thundered up the concrete steps out of the basement and through the emergency door that led outside into the bitter cold and wind.

The morning sun blinded Zane as they pushed through the emergency exit and emerged onto the wet sidewalk in front of the building. The next thing he knew, Ty was ducking in front of him as if taking cover from a projectile, and Zane turned instinctively to check the threat. A shocking slap exploded across his face in a spray of ice water across shower-flushed skin.

Another immediate snap, this one on his upper arm, another on his thigh as something else hit him, and more water splattered across him in the chilled air as he spluttered and wiped his eyes with one hand, striking out with the other at something dark flying toward his face. He felt the brief sensation of rubber on his fingers and then another painful snap like a rubber band, then more water. Zane swung toward movement at his left side. Five heartbeats had passed.

By the time Zane realized he'd just suffered through a barrage of colorful water balloons, Ty was standing again and looking at the rowdy crowd being pushed back behind the snow-dotted barriers on the sidewalk opposite the FBI building. More protesters.

Protesters lobbed more water balloons across the street. Ty deftly caught one, cradling it like a football to keep it from popping. He reared back as if preparing to sling it back toward the crowd.

"Grady!" Special Agent in Charge Dan McCoy barked from somewhere near the main entrance.

Ty's shoulders slumped, making him look like a scolded puppy who was miraculously good at dodging water balloons, and he dropped his ammunition as more landed around them.

Zane wasn't so calm. He angrily batted down the next balloon thrown at him, and it hit the concrete with a smack and splash. The frigid wind bit into his wet skin and sucked the breath from his lungs, and Zane couldn't suppress the shudder, still feeling the sting of busting balloons on his skin. "What the hell?"

"Quit bitching. At least they're full of water and not something worse," Ty shot back at Zane through gritted teeth. He folded his hands over his chest and the white words on his blue T-shirt—"Relax, I'm hilarious"—and hunched his shoulders as he turned to look up at the concrete structure behind them. "Goddamn it, it's not on fire!"

Those around them close enough to hear began to laugh, including some of the protesters across the street. Zane shook his head. How the hell did Ty manage to relate to people without even trying? It would never cease to amaze him.

Another balloon sailed through the air, landing at the feet of a man with a bullhorn who stood near the entrance to the office building. He began to inform the crowd that any further action would be considered an attack on federal property and federal agents, and that arrests would be made. When the words "up to and including deadly force" came out of his mouth, the crowd began to rumble.

Zane had read the memos. But this was the first time he had personally run into an attack. "I guess they figure we won't arrest them for assault," he said with a shake of his head as he watched his breath practically crystallize as he exhaled, it was so cold.

Ty looked around the crowd, his face expressionless. "Couple rubber rounds int-to them should f-fix them up," he decided, his teeth beginning to chatter in the cold.

Zane snorted. "Into the balloons, or into the crowd?" He crossed his arms, mirroring his partner, and took a step back. He glanced at Ty. "Imagine the paperwork."

"Garrett! Grady! Get your asses back inside!" McCoy yelled from across the lawn. "I'm not signing off on the sick leave when you get pneumonia!"

"You say that now, but I'm n-not f-filling out any f-forms!" Ty yelled back, stuttering harder. He was watching one of the agents decked out in riot gear, specifically eyeing the gun filled with rubber bullets. Another volley of balloons, yellow and green and red and blue, pulsing with freezing water, sailed through the air toward them.

If Ty had one of those rifles in hand, he could make an impressive show of those flying targets; that might clear these people out fast. Zane knew that was exactly what Ty was thinking. He also knew Ty wasn't thinking about the PR aftermath. Even when Ty considered the public backlash of his actions, he rarely cared.

"Fuck this," Zane growled. He took Ty by the upper arm even as Ty took an impulsive step toward the man in riot gear. Zane turned them around and started pulling him back toward the building, dismissing the people watching and jeering at them.

"Those little yellow f-forms with the rippy s-sides, and the blue ones th-that ask the s-same questions f-fourteen times, and the goddamn p-pink ones that make your fingers b-blue," Ty rambled as he followed along without protest. He sounded like Porky Pig. "I'd f-fill all those out if I could sh-shoot someone right now."

"This time I'm with you. It would be worth it." Another agent swiped an ID card for them, and Zane opened the side door to the building, shoved Ty inside, and followed, pulling the solid steel door shut behind them and wincing because the alarm was still wailing.

Ty threw his arm over Zane's shoulders and hugged him close. His skin was cold against Zane's. "This is g-getting ugly," he said, not looking at Zane. Zane knew he was referring to the situation at large, the unrest in the city. He continued to speak, lowering his voice until Zane couldn't hear him above the blaring warning.

"We need to go back to the showers. Hot water," Zane said when he shuddered, and not in a good way. "Riot team will clear those assholes out before we leave. And you know whoever pulled that fire alarm is in deep shit."

Ty shook his head. His fingers dragged against Zane's skin as he removed his arm from Zane's shoulders. "Work, work, work," he murmured, shaking his head.

"I'm s-serious," Zane said as the cold really started to set in. "I'm too cold." His fingers were almost numb as he tried to grasp the bottom of his wet T-shirt to pull it over his head.

"I'll warm you up later," Ty promised. It was a nice thought, but not helpful right now. Ty had somehow mastered the shivering and teeth chattering already. He'd once told Zane that the best way to stop the shivering was to consciously relax your body, et voilà, no more shaking. But Zane had never gotten it to work.

Zane turned and led the way back to their lockers, managed to get his wet clothes off, and rubbed himself down roughly with his towel, trying to ward off the bone-aching chill.

The alarm abruptly cut off, but the ringing in Zane's ears still covered any sound Ty might have been making behind him. Then three fingers touched the nape of Zane's neck and dragged down his spine, between his shoulder blades, to the small of his back and across a hip as Ty moved past him. "Eight-hour workday to go, Lone Star. Suck it up," Ty said as he popped open his own locker.

This time the shiver skittering across Zane's skin had nothing to do with a chill and everything to do with finding the patience to get through the day while looking forward to that night.

The blinking light on his phone drew Zane's attention away from the report he was trying to parse. He always muted his phone when he was in the office, especially at times like today when the whole team—like school kids at desks in a little pod shaped like the Pentagon—was stuck slogging through their casework.

He was sitting with Michelle Clancy, Scott Alston, Fred Perrimore, and Harry Lassiter, the other members of their extended Bureau assignment team. Still, it could be a call from one of the other departments, a contact, or another agent. So Zane slid the cell out from under a pile of folders and thumbed off the key lock as he looked at the screen. It was a text message. Frowning a little, Zane hit the key to open the message.

Whats proper workplace etiquette for picking up computer and tossing out window? Open window first or break glass?

Zane blinked and read the text again. Then he focused on the number and realized who'd sent the message. He sighed and set his phone down, going back to his report. It wasn't a message that needed an answer. His partner wasn't more than ten feet away, sitting at his desk, staring at his computer screen and repeatedly tapping the same error key on his keyboard. If Ty wanted a response from Zane, he could just open his mouth and speak. When Zane glanced at him, he saw Ty sit back in his chair and cock his head at the computer. He'd stopped typing, and he looked listless and frustrated.

Ty's computer never worked the way it was supposed to. The team joked that he had electromagnetic pulses going through him, because no matter what he touched, the machine nearly always messed up. The computer, the printer, the fax machine, sometimes even the automatic faucets in the bathrooms. They never worked correctly for him. He also hated paperwork with unusual passion, so it made it doubly funny.

Zane looked down at the files spread across the desk in front of him. He could sit and do detail-crunching all day; it appealed to his analytical brain. Ty, however, made no apologies for being bored by paperwork. He was definitely a man of action. Zane usually tried to at least send him out on errands, but today there wasn't even that to throw in front of him. With one last glance at Ty, Zane went back to reconciling suspected criminal bank account transfer data connected to a series of kidnappings.

Several minutes later, the light on his phone blinked again. Zane stopped typing as he looked at the phone and then across the desks at Ty. He didn't appear to have moved, and his phone was nowhere in sight. He wasn't looking at Zane, and there was no ghost of a smile on his lips like there would have been if he'd been up to something. Zane had seen that smile too many times to miss even a hint of it. He picked up his phone and saw the second text message. Same phone number. He'd never gotten around to programming Ty's name into the contact list.

He debated not even looking at the text; he wasn't sure he wanted to encourage Ty to distract him from work. Then, after a moment, Zane shook himself. There was no reason to be so seriously uptight about this. He activated the phone to read the message.

The last 3 calls on my phone are for backup and pizza and sex. In that order. Cant decide what that says about me.

Zane almost forgot to repress his smile. The night before Ty had called him to say he'd ordered pizza and that Zane should pick it up on his way over. They had intended to watch some football in front of Ty's big-screen TV, but pointless playoff games not featuring any of Ty's favored teams weren't enough to hold Ty's attention for long. After the pizza was gone, they'd wound up in front of the TV all right, doing something entirely different than watching it.

Zane sniffed. He very purposefully did not shift in his chair as he set his phone down without answering or looking up at his partner.

Maybe he'd pick up dinner tonight too.

His phone almost immediately lit up again. Zane hadn't even picked his pen back up. This time he glanced around the desks at their team members—none of them were paying him or Ty a bit of attention—before he poked at the phone to read the message.

You realize I have free texting plan right?

Obviously, ignoring Ty wasn't going to work. But Zane pushed away the phone, determined to do his level best. Simply because the struggle would amuse Ty, if he were being honest with himself. And keeping Ty amused was good for the rest of humanity.

The phone lit up again, and when Zane's eyes cut to look at Ty, his partner was leaning back in his chair, feet blatantly propped on his desk as he held his phone in his hands.

Zane kept typing with one hand as he unobtrusively shifted his phone across the papers strewn in front of him so he could hit the button and read the message without drawing attention to it.

Pop quiz partner. How many letters in the government alphabet?

Biting his tongue, Zane tried to decide what the answer to that would be. It was fifty-fifty that it was a joke. He figured Ty was trying to break him now, to get him to react, maybe even to laugh. As he checked his peripheral vision, he could see Ty watching him, his head lowered just enough to make him look slightly predatory. Zane knew that look too well. Most people who didn't know Ty were intimidated by the glint in his hazel eyes and the slightly malicious curve to his full lips. But Zane had come to learn that Ty only wore that look when he was enjoying himself. And it made his clean-shaven, heart-shaped face that much more handsome, which irked Zane to no end. Irked and aroused.

Just to egg him on, Zane ignored the message, went back to working on the reconciliation, and tried to build up the resolve it would take not to react to Ty's next attempt to break his cool.

The phone lit up again, and this time Ty had returned his attention to his computer when Zane surreptitiously glanced at him. Zane wondered how the hell Ty typed so fast on the itty-bitty phone keypad. He would have liked to have seen it, if it wouldn't have spoiled their game.

He made them both wait five minutes through a discussion of assets with Alston before he hit the key to open the latest text message.

Answer: 19. ET went home on a UFO and the FBI went after him.

Zane blinked several times at the screen as he kept a straight face, though by all rights, that one did deserve a laugh. Who'd have known he'd be tapping into years of undercover experience to hide that he was playing text games in the office? He tapped his pen thoughtfully on the ledger as he stared at it blankly. He was certainly distracted now. He suspected Ty knew it. But they'd both continue to enjoy it if Zane tried not to admit it. He wouldn't have dreamed of goofing off like this at work a year ago. Hell, six months ago. But Ty Grady had done his damnedest to yank the stick out of Zane's ass . . .

The little message icon in the corner of his phone's display began to blink, indicating he had yet another message. He hadn't even seen Ty move. Was it possible to schedule these texts ahead of time? That would take quite a bit of forethought, but it was just the kind of plot Ty would favor. Zane shifted around his stack of folders, took a drink of coffee, and checked the message.

You know you want to laugh.

Score one for Zane Garrett. He looked up slowly, face composed, raising one eyebrow.

Ty was watching him. He winked when Zane met his eyes, but he wasn't fully smiling yet. He still wore that infuriating smirk. Instead of answering in any way, Zane sniffed and turned to his computer. That reaction would surely get another out of his partner. Besides, Zane was intrigued now to see what Ty would come up with that would be enough to get Zane to laugh despite his practiced control.

He didn't have to wait long for Ty's next attempt. His phone lit up, and Zane was able to catch a glimpse of Ty reaching out to set his own phone on the desk. Zane deliberately waited a couple of minutes before turning in his chair to change out files and check the message.

Did you hear about the guy downstairs who lost his left arm and left leg in a wreck? He's all right now.

Zane stared at the little screen really hard for a long moment before he was able to shake his head ever so slightly and turn away from the phone.

He slowly looked around at the rest of the team, wondering how none of them had caught on. Did they really pay so little attention? Or was it that they weren't at all surprised to see Ty texting *someone*, and they just didn't connect him with his partner? Zane knew Ty received about half a dozen text messages from various people on a normal day, but Ty rarely checked them or responded when he was working.

Zane deliberately shoved some files into his outbox and did not look in Ty's direction. He turned his attention to a conversation between Clancy and Perrimore about calling a judge for a search warrant, but he was hyperaware of his partner.

He heard Ty's chair squeak as he moved. Ty's chair always squeaked because he was so damn hard on the thing, always moving around and fidgeting. His chair stayed broken and noisy, just like his computer.

Zane's phone lit up again, and he keyed it with his right hand while answering a question from Clancy.

When she turned away, he finally glanced down at the phone.

What do you call a monkey in a mine field? A baboom.

He had to admit: that one was funny. This time Zane had to close his eyes to keep his reaction under control. When he opened them, he deliberately turned his chin to look right at Ty in an open challenge.

Ty's feet were still propped up, and he was leaning one arm against his desk, fingers strategically covering his mouth as he shook silently. He was watching Zane, and his hand couldn't cover the smile lines around his sparking eyes or the slight dimples that formed when he laughed.

Damn, Ty Grady was a fine-looking man. Even more so when he was relaxed and smiling.

Zane didn't feel the urge to laugh anymore. Instead, he found his thoughts slightly more erotic, thinking about the man sitting several feet away and just exactly how fine-looking he was, both in and out of that suit. Zane pulled himself toward his desk in the rolling chair, just to get his lap under cover. Then he offered Ty an angelic smile.

Ty shook his head and bit his lip to stop his silent laughter, though the dimples were still there as he grinned. Zane stared after him for a few moments, thinking about just how amazing it was when Ty smiled or laughed and his eyes lit up and the hard shell melted away from him.

Ty waved his hand at Zane in apparent surrender as he turned his chair to face his own desk again, still shaking his head and laughing.

Zane doubted that was the end of it and expected another text message within a few minutes, but Special Agent Scott Alston chose that moment to stand up.

"Time to meet with McCoy," he said to Ty and Perrimore.

"Have a good time, guys," Clancy teased as she sipped at her melting smoothie.

Ty stood with a decent amount of grumbling and fanfare, making a show of gathering his files and his suit coat and getting his gun out of its drawer to slide it into his holster. Zane tidied a file, set it aside, and opened another as he watched Ty discreetly. "Say hello for me," he said smugly. He knew that the only thing worse than paperwork, in Ty's opinion, was a multi-departmental meeting where he was expected to sit still.

"Don't break anything playing solitaire," Ty shot back as the three of them headed toward the elevators.

Zane let the smile pull at his lips as he tapped his fingers on his phone and watched Ty walk away.

Ty had his eyes closed and massaged the bridge of his nose as he leaned his elbow on the arm of his chair, slumping slightly. He was listening. Quite attentively, to his everlasting chagrin. But he could listen with his eyes closed.

He was pretty sure he, Alston, and Perrimore had all been summoned to this meeting by mistake anyway. So far they'd been over the escalating violence in the city, in particular a nasty case of arson in which a second explosion had been rigged with the express purpose of injuring or killing firefighters. Everyone was up in arms about it, including Ty. There would be a memorial for the slain heroes next week.

But while escalating violence could possibly be in Ty's job description, arson certainly wasn't.

Next they hit on a bank robbery that had "professional job" written all over it. They'd caught a break publicity-wise with that one, since it had happened on the same day as the arson tragedy and hadn't received much press yet. What's-His-Name from Financial Crimes was told to look for similar robberies in neighboring states over the weekend. Something that organized had probably been run before somewhere and would surely be run again. Soon.

Weekend assignments. Awesome.

And bank robberies weren't Ty's job either.

Then the agenda moved on to the negative image the FBI was being painted with of late and several avenues the PR people had come up with to nip it in the bud.

None of which had much of anything to do with Ty, so he still wasn't exactly sure why he was supposed to be here at all.

"So," Special Agent in Charge Dan McCoy was saying, "we're going to give them what they want so they'll get off our backs for a while. And Grady, the next time you and your partner want to blow something up, at least pretend you're sorry afterward, got it?"

"Yes, sir," Ty said as he opened his eyes and shifted to a slightly less outwardly miserable position. He wasn't sorry, though. That fax machine had deserved what it got. And Zane had laughed his ass off.

There were only thirty minutes left in the work day, and then he was free to go do cartwheels in the parking lot. He glanced at Alston, who was asking another question, and then Ty's pants pocket vibrated. He actually jerked in his seat before he could stop himself, quickly leaning forward to place his elbows on the table and cover the reaction.

"Something to add?" McCoy asked.

"Nothing constructive," Ty admitted with an innocent smile.

McCoy rolled his eyes and nodded. As he continued outlining the plan to make the Bureau more "fan-friendly," Ty leaned back again and pulled his phone out of his pocket slowly. He kept it under the table as he slid it open and pressed the button that would open the text message he'd received. Ty was almost surprised to see that it was from Zane and not one of the usual suspects.

Baby seal walks into a club.

He pressed his lips together tightly and looked up at McCoy as he tapped out his response to Zane's weak opening gambit.

You shouldnt club baby seals. Bastard.

It wasn't a minute before the phone vibrated in his hand again. He quickly set it to silent so no one would hear the vibrations, and then he glanced down at it to read the new message.

Energizer bunny arrested. Charged with battery. Ty's lips twitched as he tapped out a quick response. *Is he being held in a duracell?*

He returned his attention to McCoy just in time. McCoy slid a file across the table toward him, and Ty opened it as he massaged his left temple.

It was a proposal that outlined a plan to pull as many government and municipal service organizations as possible into a softball league and then open up the games to the public. Ty huffed in amusement.

"Think you could get the ball rolling on that if it's the plan we go with?" McCoy asked.

Ty nodded slowly and then looked up at McCoy. "I know a guy who knows a guy," he drawled with an easy smile.

"I thought you might," McCoy said, sounding pleased with himself.

That was why Ty was here, then, because he'd played on the Bureau team ever since he'd been transferred to Baltimore and knew just about everyone. That had to be it, because everyone knew Ty didn't give a shit about public opinion and had nothing to do with bank robberies or fires.

McCoy moved on to the Financial Crimes dude who still didn't have a name but had a whole hell of a lot of opinions, and Ty surreptitiously checked the phone again. The message icon blinked at him, and he flipped the phone open to read it.

Two peanuts walk into a bar. One was a salted.

Ty stared at it for a moment before looking up and licking the corner of his mouth to keep from smiling. Why the hell couldn't Zane have done this when Ty was bored out of his mind and not sitting in a meeting? He was probably out there Googling jokes on his computer.

"Grady, what do you think?" McCoy asked.

Ty looked at his superior for a split-second of indecision, knowing full well he had absolutely no idea what he'd been asked. "I think it's a shit idea," he finally answered confidently.

"Care to expound on that?" McCoy asked him wryly. "Not really," Ty answered, his voice not quite as steady.

"Okay, at least we're all in agreement on that one," McCoy replied as he took a piece of paper that probably outlined another PR proposal and tossed it over his shoulder.

Ty slowly let out the breath he'd been holding and began tapping a response to Zane.

Fuck you zane. Fuck you. So much.

The answer came back quickly. Zane had to have been sitting there waiting.

I'll get you a salami sandwich for dinner. With extra mayo.

Ty looked up and around the table, trying desperately to concentrate on what they were saying as he jabbed at the keys of his phone to respond. Zane's attempts at seductive innuendo were funnier than his jokes.

All Ill get from you is fired.

If you go for an interview at a rubber stamp company, try to make a good impression.

Ty fought not to roll his eyes as he looked up from the phone he was still trying to hide in his lap. He refused to let one of Zane's bad puns have the last word.

He had to sit for a moment, searching his store of bad jokes for an appropriate answer. He hated to sink to Zane's level, but you had to fight pun with pun . . .

He looked up and took the next five minutes to answer questions and try to at least appear involved in the meeting. The idea about the FBI softball team and setting up tournaments with other city and state agency teams that would be open to the public seemed to be taking root. And Ty had become the focus of the planning, so he had to pay attention.

Ty liked the plan, actually. He didn't know if it would work, but it was never a bad thing to put a human face on the big bad blue line once in a while. A downside, as he pointed out, was that they might get backlash if too many people wondered why cops and ambulance drivers were playing softball while the city was being ransacked. But hell, they were already taking heat, so it couldn't hurt.

Ty jotted down a few notes, people he'd need to contact within other agencies to see if they could set something up, city fields and scheduling and things that he really didn't have time to deal with but would anyway. Then the conversation moved on, and Ty leaned back in his chair.

He stared at McCoy listlessly as his mind began to wander again. He tapped out his response to Zane slowly, trying to get the message out and pay attention at the same time.

If a hunter can shoot a deer with either hand does that make him bambidextrous?

Have you seen eagles catch their prey? They're really talonted.

Ty closed his eyes. The puns were too much. They were just too stupid for his brain to deal with at the end of a long day. He decided to raise the white flag and live to think another day, so he eased back in his chair and slowly punched in the last message.

You win. Ill do anything please make it stop.

It took a minute, but Zane's answer finally popped up.

Promise you'll scream for me tonight.

Ty stared at the phone for just a moment too long. When he cleared his throat and looked up, McCoy was watching him expectantly.

Ty smiled at him widely, the smile that said he knew he'd been caught and wasn't McCoy glad he was so good at his job so he didn't have to punish him?

"Care to share?" McCoy asked drily.

Ty looked around at the other people around the table and sighed heavily. Perrimore reached into his lap and grabbed the phone from him. Ty didn't try to resist; that would just have made them even more curious. He'd never been more thankful that he rarely put real names into his contacts list, though.

Perrimore read the last message from Zane out loud, eyebrows raised. "Who's Lone Star?" he asked with a grin as he looked at the name Ty had stored in his phone. "And does she carry a whip?"

"Everyone get out before my eyeballs explode," McCoy ordered as he sat rubbing his temples with the heels of his hands.

Ty snatched his phone from Perrimore and whapped him in the head as they stood to leave. Alston trailed behind them, laughing the entire way.

Zane looked up from the files he was stacking when he heard Ty's voice, low and wry and borderline aggrieved. A smile pulled at Zane's lips. There hadn't been a reply to his last message of a little less than ten minutes ago.

"Hey, Garrett, have you met Grady's latest fling? She sounds like a real piece of work," Alston said as they arrived, chuckling. "Probably has the key to his handcuffs pierced through her tongue."

That certainly wasn't what Zane expected to hear when they came back from the meeting. So that probably meant Ty had been caught. He didn't appear to have that "just outed by his co-workers" look about him, though, and Zane knew Ty nicknamed all his phone contacts, so he was relatively certain they were okay.

"Getting texts at work again, partner?" Zane drawled as he looked over to see Ty.

"Well, you know my type," Ty responded with a saccharine smile as he passed Zane's desk. "No self-control and loads of mental issues." He did sound exasperated, though.

"That's never seemed to bother you," Zane answered as he stood up and lifted his suit jacket off the back of his chair.

Alston laughed and took off with a wave, not bothering to stick around to hear the banter the whole team had become used to. Clancy and Lassiter had departed half an hour ago, and Zane had seen Perrimore detour toward the elevators as the group came back from the meeting. So once Alston disappeared down the hall, it was just Zane and Ty as Ty locked up his desk drawers.

Ty glanced up at him darkly, and Zane grinned. Oh, he was so going to pay for his mischief tonight. The look in Ty's eyes promised as much.

Ty looked around the nearly empty floor as he moved closer to Zane. He held his phone in his hand, overcoat draped over his arm. He stepped closer to Zane, his knuckles brushing against Zane's stomach as he held the coat between them.

"Me scream for you, huh?" he asked in a low voice, his nearly green eyes raking across Zane's features.

"Since you can't take the *pun*ishment," Zane said, feeling himself warm a little under Ty's scrutiny.

"One more, Garrett," Ty warned as he raised one finger. "One more and we'll see who can go the longest in a cold bed."

Zane frowned and huffed quietly. "Fine. You, screaming," he reminded. "I did offer to bring you dinner."

"Dinner later. My house. Bring clothes for the weekend, 'cause you won't be making it home." Ty didn't say another word, just turned and headed for the elevator at a stroll, shrugging into his overcoat as he went.

Zane watched him go, enjoying the sight. "Score," he said under his breath before he grabbed his phone and keys and hurried to follow.

CHAPTER TWO

I t took skill to juggle a small duffel bag, a suit jacket, a large sack of hot food, and a key, especially when standing on a small concrete stoop. But Zane succeeded and pushed the door open with his foot.

"No friendly fire, please," he called out as he crossed the threshold.

The main floor was silent and somewhat dark. Only one light was on downstairs, in the kitchen at the back of Ty's row house. Light streamed down from the upstairs, though, and Zane could hear Ty up there, talking with someone.

"Hold on!" Ty shouted. Then his voice dropped back to a low murmur.

Zane kicked the door shut behind him and flipped on a light switch with his elbow. He walked through the narrow living room and tiny dining area beside the stairs to the kitchen bar, where he dropped his burdens. Hot food on the counter, bag next to it by the wall, suit jacket on the back of a chair, keys in a pocket. Wondering idly who Ty was talking to, Zane moved around the bar into the kitchen to pull plates and glasses out of the cabinet.

He heard Ty's heavy footsteps on the stairs behind him. Not a good sign. The only time he could ever hear Ty moving was when Ty sulked and threw his weight around. Otherwise, Ty was scarily silent.

"No, that'll be just fine," Ty was saying as he came down the stairs, his voice a slightly more professional one than he normally utilized on the phone. "Thank you, sir, we'll be in touch," he said quickly. Then he snapped his phone shut as he reached the bottom step. He spread his arms wide and gave Zane an incredulous look. "What, no blinking neon sex sign to alert the neighbors? Incriminating videos to send to my mother?"

Zane glanced at him sideways as he pulled toasted deli sandwiches and sides out of the bag. "You've gotten caught doing a hell of a lot worse than getting a text message in a meeting," he answered mildly.

"I'll have to stop calling you Lone Star out loud," Ty grumbled as he tossed his phone over his shoulder into the living room. It landed on the couch with a single bounce. "What's for dinner?"

Zane didn't try to hide his smile. Ty sulking could be pretty entertaining if you didn't let him lay a guilt trip on you. "Italian subs. I promised you salami."

"Are they hot?" Ty asked as he rounded the counter and came up to stand beside Zane, pulling the bag of food toward him.

"Yes, dear," Zane placated. "I had them double wrap them in foil."

Ty reached out sideways, throwing his arm against Zane's chest and grabbing him by the shirt front. He shoved him backward until Zane hit the refrigerator, then held him pinned there with his forearm as a dozen or so glass bottles within the refrigerator clanked together noisily.

"So they'll stay warm for a while," Ty said, close enough to Zane that his words were breaths against Zane's lips.

For a wild few seconds, Zane could hardly believe he'd let Ty catch him off guard. Then he caught Ty's familiar scent and the heat of his skin, and the lust that had simmered since the showers that morning started perking toward a boil. "Yeah," he whispered, pulse thrumming as he set his hands at Ty's hips.

The pressure of Ty's arm lessened as he moved his hand across Zane's chest, sliding his palm instead against the side of Zane's neck and gripping him tightly as he kissed him.

It was easy to sag against Ty to try to get closer. Zane wanted those kisses, and he wanted Ty to manhandle him. As incredibly seductive as Ty had been during the undercover case that had ended a couple of weeks ago, playing at being an outwardly docile trophy husband on a cruise ship and taking a devoted ride on the submissive side, Zane couldn't help but crave having Ty take control. It was fucking hot, and Ty did it *so* well. He moaned into Ty's mouth just thinking about it.

This was why he'd needled Ty all afternoon. It worked almost every time: get Ty just a little annoyed with him and plant a few suggestive comments to give him an outlet.

Ty was still kissing him when he reached up to pull at the knot of Zane's tie. "I can't believe you didn't even crack a smile," he mumbled against Zane's lips. "Babooms, man. That shit's funny."

Zane let out a breathless laugh. "Years of practice," he muttered as he chased Ty's lips with his own.

Ty roughly yanked the tie off, tossing it over his shoulder, then reached for Zane's dress shirt. "You've been practicing the wrong things," he growled as he pulled hard. Zane heard material rip, and several buttons went flying. Ty didn't seem to care. And it just made Zane's pants fit tighter.

"What should I be practicing?" he goaded as he leaned to nip at Ty's earlobe.

Ty shoved him back against the appliance, and the contents rocked inside it again. Something toppled over and clattered.

Then Ty yanked him forward again, into the narrow kitchen. He hooked his foot behind Zane's leg and practically tackled him, sending them both to the floor. Ty used his weight to pin Zane to the bare hardwood as Zane gasped for air. He had Zane's wrists in his hands and was kissing him again, right there in the middle of the floor, and Zane could only whisper Ty's name whenever their lips parted.

Zane's fingers splayed as Ty held his wrists against whatever force Zane tried to bring to bear, but he was well and truly caught. He whimpered against Ty's lips, wordlessly begging for more as he pushed his hips against his lover's.

He could tell Ty'd had a plan when he'd started this, perhaps one devised to torture Zane just a little—well, hell, maybe a lot—at first. But now Ty seemed to have lost the more controlled feeling to him. He loosened his hands from around Zane's wrists and moved one to Zane's body to push the remains of his shirt aside and dip under his belt, sliding his rough fingers against Zane's sensitive skin. Zane groaned happily and shifted under Ty's touch, and he reached for his belt buckle to loosen it.

Ty pushed up to give both their hands room to move, helping him with the belt as he continued to hold Zane's other wrist against the ground.

"Fuck, Zane," he grumbled, finally letting Zane's other hand go and pushing himself to kneel over Zane's thighs. "Why are you always wearing so many clothes?"

"Oh, for Christ's sake," Zane muttered as he unfastened his pants and folded over the placket. "Am I supposed to strip down anytime I walk in now?" he asked as he sat up enough to pull the ruined dress shirt and thin undershirt over his head and toss them aside. "Or maybe I'm just waiting for you to tell me what to do about it," he prodded as he leaned back on his elbows, hoping it would push Ty back into action. Zane was hard and visibly straining his briefs. Ty in charge did that to him really damn quickly.

"With your track record, you'll come in playing strippergram and I'll be in the middle of Thanksgiving dinner or something," Ty grumbled. He leaned closer to Zane, putting his hands on the floor beside Zane's hips. "Shut up," he added almost as an afterthought, his lips moving just inches away from Zane's. He was on his hands and knees again, still fully clothed even after bitching about Zane's unsatisfactory state of undress, and he looked down at Zane with narrowed eyes.

Zane looked at him innocently. "What? Do I have to come up with some more puns?"

"You really have no concept of how close you are to not getting fucked, do you?" Ty asked darkly. Zane shut his mouth and watched Ty closely for clues. He didn't think he'd pushed too much, but he could have miscalculated. "That's what I thought," Ty growled before roughly kissing Zane again, forcing him flat on the floor, actually sliding him on the hardwood with the force and barely giving him the chance to breathe as he practically devoured him.

Something inside Zane gave a pitifully grateful cry of thanks as he collapsed under Ty's weight, not even caring that his shoulders and skull hit the floor hard. He was dizzy already, and all his nerve endings sparked whenever Ty touched him.

Zane *craved* this. He *needed* it, like he needed air.

His reaction only spurred Ty on. Rough hands roamed over Zane's body. Hips ground down against him. Teeth scraped against Zane's lips and tongue and cheek and chin and neck. The day's worth of stubble on Ty's face was almost painful against Zane's skin, but Ty so rarely did this to him that Zane wasn't about to object. He wanted to be overwhelmed; it was a hell of a ride when Ty got it in his head to really drive them to another level.

Zane shuddered as it occurred to him that it really didn't seem like just sex anymore. It was *more*, more passionate, more emotional, more energizing, more draining . . . at that moment, he wasn't sure it had ever been just sex between them. He knew Ty loved him, and sometimes he could feel how badly Ty wanted him. Zane moaned and clutched at Ty. "Please," he breathed.

Ty pushed away from him and quickly yanked his T-shirt over his head, revealing the impressive display of muscles Zane had become so familiar with. He tossed the shirt aside as he laid himself back out over Zane and kissed him hungrily, their bare skin catching and pulling as Ty moved.

Zane wrapped his arms around Ty, dragging his fingers down along his spine before spreading his hands and pressing them flat to slide them into the back of Ty's sweatpants. Ty's hand found its way into Zane's hair, one of Ty's favorite handles when he wanted Zane to stay where he put him. His tongue lapped at Zane's, the kiss forceful and overpowering as Zane felt Ty's muscles tense and flex against him. Feeling that remarkable, unbridled power against his body sent another shudder of need through him, and he felt almost smothered by the heat of it.

It was absolute heaven.

"I meant to at least get us up the stairs," Ty gasped with what was probably supposed to be sincerity as he used one hand to push at the sweatpants he wore.

"Fuck me here," Zane begged hoarsely.

Ty's sigh came out harsh. He was obviously arrested by the idea for a brief moment because he stopped moving. Then he bit at Zane's lower lip, licking at it and delving into another breathless kiss. Zane could feel how hard Ty was as he rocked their hips together, could feel the arousal and need coursing through Ty's tense body, like every ounce of him was coiled.

Zane wanted to feel that inside him so badly he could barely stay still. It was like this more and more often, feeling like he just couldn't *breathe* without Ty.

Ty yanked his head away suddenly, as if he'd just heard Zane's thoughts and was offended by them. "Get up," he practically snarled.

Zane gasped for breath and reached out for help. Ty was pushing himself up almost immediately, and he reached down to grip Zane's forearm and haul him to his feet. He pulled Zane to him and kissed him brutally as he used one hand to push Zane's pants down over his hips. Zane moaned happily against Ty's mouth as he toed out of his shoes and kicked his pants off while sliding a hand up to cup Ty's face to encourage him. He had the distant thought that he'd done an awesome job of planning this for a Friday. He was going to be scratched, bruised, and whisker-burned tomorrow.

Zane didn't give a shit. He tried to pull Ty closer as he gave under the onslaught of Ty's mouth.

Ty pushed him back until Zane hit the countertop, and he didn't stop, levering Zane off his feet as he insinuated himself between Zane's legs. Zane let Ty maneuver him, more interested in groping all the overheated skin and keeping Ty touching him than personal safety. He trusted Ty to keep him from falling. He turned his head and chin, angling for another kiss. He could feel his lips throbbing, already swollen from Ty's ravaging kisses. It was intense and consuming, and Zane was hard-pressed to even remember where they were until Ty swept one hand out on the counter next to them, knocking everything there to the floor in a clatter of knickknacks, junk mail, silverware, and sandwiches. He boosted Zane up to sit on the bar, and Zane wrapped his long legs around Ty's hips and shifted back on his elbows as Ty leaned over him. Ty seemed to have every intention of climbing onto the counter after him and fucking him senseless, but instead he jerked his head up suddenly from the trail of licks and bites he'd been working on making down Zane's torso.

"Do you hear that?" he asked as he cocked his head.

"Huh?" Zane wasn't listening to a goddamn thing but the blood pounding in his ears and Ty's harsh breathing.

Ty looked up at him with a frown, turning his head like a dog trying to hear a strange noise. Then it reached Zane's ears too. Distant laughing, growing louder and louder. Soon it became recognizable as the cackling of the Wicked Witch from *The Wizard of Oz*.

"Fuck, what now?" Ty drew out as he looked toward the couch where he'd tossed his phone.

Zane closed his eyes as he let go of Ty, then reopened them to see the ceiling as he ran his hands through his hair in frustration. With a growl he thumped one fist on the countertop. "Damn it. Answer the damn thing so we can get back to this."

"You know who that is, right?" Ty asked breathlessly.

Zane did. He'd heard that ring plenty of times. It always got laughs in the office when Dan McCoy called Ty and the Wicked Witch let her evil laughter loose through the office. "It's like he *knows* when I'm going to get laid," Ty began to grumble as he worked at extricating himself from Zane's limbs.

Zane stared at him for a few seconds as the fog of intense arousal started to clear, and then he groaned in pain as he let his arms slide down so he flopped to his back on the bar top. "I hate Mac sometimes," he muttered.

"Let me get back to you on that. If he's calling us in, I might kill him," Ty muttered. He pushed away from the counter, his hands sliding down Zane's thighs and away. He headed past the dining table for the couch.

"I wonder how much time we'll have," Zane mused. Whether it would be sex or a blow job or hand job—or, God forbid, nothing—would all depend on what McCoy had to say.

"Son of a bitch," Ty agreed emphatically. He got to the phone before it stopped ringing, and his voice was only slightly hoarse when he answered with his usual curt "Grady."

Zane glared up at the ceiling for another few seconds before carefully sitting up and maneuvering off the kitchen counter. He snorted. On the goddamn *kitchen counter*. They'd never tried that one before, but he had certainly liked where Ty was going with it. He shook his head in mild disbelief as he got his feet on the floor and adjusted the fit of his briefs. He stood looking down at the sandwiches, unopened mail, pens, a key ring, and a pile of paper napkins strewn haphazardly across the floor and then crouched to rescue dinner as he heard Ty speak.

"Wait, what?" Ty asked with an obvious frown in his tone. "I never got any file. What courier?"

Zane got the wrapped sandwiches back on the bar and glanced in Ty's direction before starting to gather the clothing they'd shed. Once he untangled his dress shirt from the undershirt, he held it up to survey the damage. Ty had pretty much destroyed it: several of the buttons were gone, now underfoot, and the seams at the shoulders had literally been ripped apart. He'd obviously been very intent on getting Zane naked. Zane shivered and looked over at his lover. Ty hadn't even gotten around to taking off his sweats. Zane thought he would have fucked him with the damn things still around his thighs if they'd been able to get that far.

Zane dropped the clothes in a pile and walked over to Ty, sidling up behind him to wrap his arms around Ty's waist and nuzzle just under his hairline. No reason to waste time he could spend touching. It would distract him from the fact that they, or even worse, just Ty, might be leaving, and the latter possibility made Zane's chest tighten uncomfortably. It had become more and more painful, being apart from Ty and not knowing where he was or whether he was safe or how long he'd be gone. Not being able to watch his back. Ty hadn't been called on one of *those* jobs in a while, not since their ordeal with Ty's family in West Virginia, but Zane still expected a call some random evening.

Zane suspected Ty had gone to Burns to opt out of the odd jobs, but he'd never asked and never planned to. He still held his breath whenever Ty's phone rang, day or night. Zane closed his eyes and rested his chin on Ty's shoulder. He brushed his lips against the warm skin of Ty's neck, and it made him think of the compass rose pendant hidden away at his apartment in the drawer with his T-shirts. He still hadn't found the right time to give it to Ty.

Ty reached his arm behind him to settle his hand on Zane's hip. "I don't understand," Ty said to McCoy in a troubled voice. "No, I'm not being intentionally dense! I just don't get why it has to be us!"

Zane moved one palm over Ty's stomach and started to rub gently, trying to soothe him. After all, it was partly his fault Ty was so keyed up.

Ty turned, pursing his lips into a shushing gesture to tell Zane to be quiet, and then hit the speaker button.

Their boss' voice came out of the speaker and Dan McCoy was audibly annoyed. " . . .because this is supposed to be good PR, and we need to send agents that people will like."

Zane frowned and mouthed the word "like" to Ty with a questioning look.

Ty was silent for a moment, staring at the phone. "And we're the best you got?" he asked, deadpan.

McCoy laughed. "People do like you, Ty. You're a funny guy. And you know how the ladies like Garrett."

Zane opened his mouth to object, but Ty's hand covered it before he got a sound of protest out.

"Granted," Ty drew out, meeting Zane's eyes and smirking. "If we do this, what do we get out of it?"

"You get to keep your jobs, you worthless hack," McCoy answered without any real heat in it.

Ty's face was nearly expressionless as he held the phone up between them. "Yeah okay."

Zane shook his head, giving Ty an obstinate look. He still didn't know what the hell this was all about, but he had the prickly feeling he wouldn't like it.

Ty turned away from him so he couldn't object again.

"Look," McCoy said, "Garrett gives a great lecture on cyber and criminal connections. I've heard it and didn't even feel the need to shoot myself *or* him. With all the Internet crime lately, it's a popular topic. And you have enough of a sense of humor to talk about undercover investigations without getting morbid or scary. I know it's short notice, but there's going to be a whole series of these things—"

"A whole series?" Ty broke in, his voice going higher in distress. "Do you remember how many times you've said I'm *bad* for PR?"

McCoy sighed in disgust.

"Thirty-seven times, Mac."

"You've counted?" McCoy asked without sounding surprised. "Latent OCD," Ty answered, unashamed. Zane pressed his mouth to the back of Ty's shoulder to stifle the laugh that threatened.

"All right, look, here it is straight. You're both personable and competent, but the real kicker is that you're both pretty, and bottom line, it's better to have eye candy in the newspaper than some nondescript drone. Be there at eight, best suit you own. And call Garrett and fill him in for me, will you?"

Ty grunted in outrage, but the phone lit up in his hand, and he pulled it away to look at it. Zane could see the display informing him the call had been ended.

"'Pretty,'" Zane said flatly. It was funny—usually—when Ty teased him about being pretty, but this was too much. "When the hell did we become fashion plates?"

"Eight a.m. on a Saturday, Zane," Ty said through gritted teeth.

"*This* Saturday? As in tomorrow Saturday? We have to give lectures in twelve hours? We're not prepared for that! I can't just pull a cybercrimes lecture out of my ass!" He *could*, but it was the principle of the thing.

Ty nodded and dropped the phone to the couch. He looked Zane up and down and narrowed his eyes, a slow smile forming. "But we're still in for the night," he pointed out.

Zane let the momentary annoyance fade into the background. They could bitch about work later. "Sure you still want dessert before dinner?"

"You're not dessert, Zane. You're the main course," Ty informed him in a husky drawl. "And you have about five seconds to take your pick of flat surface before I do it for you."

One thing about working for the FBI was that sometimes time passed and Ty thought it might be going in reverse. Other stretches Ty didn't even notice until months had gone by. He and Zane did their jobs, whether that included the god-awful boring paperwork and research Zane seemed to enjoy or the actual tracking and chasing of criminals that was more to Ty's taste. Unfortunately, working for the FBI consisted of 5 percent chasing and tracking, 90 percent paperwork, and 5 percent getting your ass handed to you by your superior, a reporter, a nurse who insisted you'd tear your stitches, or your mother.

Ty would much rather run down a guy and tackle him into the Inner Harbor than have to sit and fill out forms.

He'd ruined that suit, but it had been a hell of a good day.

Ty's evenings had gone one of four ways through January and into mid-February: most often they'd be out working, which meant no time with Zane away from work. Otherwise Ty was going to softball practice and then home late to Zane, or suffering through another freaking PR presentation. And then home late. To Zane. Ty still wasn't too sure how he felt about all the extra responsibilities that were taking up his free time, so he mostly tried not to think about it and just go with the flow.

Time passed almost unnoticed when it had so much structure to it, so when Ty went to meet his partner for a late Friday night dinner after a particularly harrowing lecture to a group of high school kids who'd only wanted to know if he was single or if he'd ever killed anyone, he hadn't expected the chaotic mess he'd found. He'd arrived at one of their favorite restaurants to find Zane waiting for him in the parking lot.

The lot was full to the brim and overflowing into the lot of the bank next door. A crowd of people waited outside in the cold February night, some holding little buzzers to alert them when their table was ready, some clutching their coats around them and huddling with their sweethearts.

Ty hadn't even been able to find a spot to park his Bronco. He'd driven up to Zane as he sat on his motorcycle—Ty still couldn't believe he rode the damn thing in the dry winter cold—and was met with a sardonic smile. "Valentine's Day" was all the explanation Ty had needed.

Both had completely forgotten about the date and the holiday weekend. They'd just wanted a nice quiet dinner after a stressful few weeks of barely seeing each other. They were still laughing at each other when Ty let them into his row house on North Ann Street. Some romantic couple they were, forgetting about Valentine's Day and being surprised by the crowd.

"We'll just have to make do with what's in the fridge," Ty told Zane as he shut the door against the freezing Baltimore winter.

Zane stopped dead, beaten-up black leather jacket partway unzipped, and turned around. "You think I'd better go to Whole

Foods?" he asked. He was probably serious. Ty didn't cook much, and they both knew how he kept his kitchen stocked.

"Give me a little credit, huh?" Ty told him, borderline insulted. "I've got . . . stuff in there."

Zane raised an eyebrow. "Bacon, eggs, cheese, milk, lunch meat, bread, Dr Pepper, Mike's Hard Lemonade you pretend isn't there, chocolate chip cookie dough . . ."

Ty tried desperately not to smile, pressing his lips together hard despite knowing it caused his dimples to make an appearance. Zane knew him a little too well. Except for the chocolate chip cookie dough. Zane had bought that for himself and left it here for a snack. He knew full well Ty didn't like chocolate and that it would be safe. "There's also pork chops in there. And there's some emergency canned veggies in the basement," he told Zane with a mischievous smirk. "Next to the bottled water and zombie-piercing rounds."

"Good to know we won't starve when the zombies attack," Zane said as he shrugged out of his jacket and hung it on the hook next to the door, giving Ty a lazy wink over his shoulder.

"Everyone's a critic," Ty muttered as he watched Zane appreciatively.

Since the awkwardness of New Year's, they'd fallen into a comfortable groove, one Ty was happy to stay in. He'd taken the plunge, literally, and told Zane he loved him. Zane had never said it in so many words, but not long after they'd returned from the cruise ship after Christmas, Ty had noticed Zane hadn't put his real wedding band back on. That was enough for him.

That simple gesture had spoken volumes. Ty knew how much Zane's wife had meant to him and how he'd gone through hell after she died. Zane had still been wearing that ring more than six years after she was gone. Seeing Zane's finger bare warmed Ty in a way few things could. He'd never mentioned it, and they'd never talked about what Ty had said that night in lockup on the ship. They were probably better off keeping it all under wraps, anyway. Zane was happy and relaxed. Ty was happy and . . . well, still twitchy, but that wasn't Zane's fault. They were happy.

"So, cook me dinner, and I'll repay you with sexual favors."

"Sounds good to me," Zane said as he arched his back and rolled his shoulders to stretch. "Any idea what you want?"

Ty simply smiled. Zane surely knew if Ty had his way he'd skip dinner altogether.

Zane chuckled. "Food, Grady, food. Or you'll have no energy for sex later."

"Well, then, get to it," Ty grunted at him, ushering him through the length of the narrow row house.

In short order, they were both in casual clothes and Ty's kitchen was lit up and warm with activity. Zane didn't cook often, but at some point he'd picked up better than run-of-the-mill cooking skills and was generally willing to fix up a quick dinner if they were too wiped after work to go out. After foraging through Ty's refrigerator, cabinets, and pantry, he'd come up with barbecue pork chops, green beans, a piece of a loaf of asiago bread from the bakery down the street, and now he was making mashed potatoes. From scratch, which tickled Ty to no end. It seemed such a domestic task for his tough-guy partner.

Chops sizzled on one burner, and Zane was pushing a pile of chunked potatoes to the side of the cutting board and starting on another, the knife moving swiftly and efficiently in his hands. A pot of water boiled on a third burner behind him.

Ty devotedly stayed away, mostly because it was a tight fit with both of them trying to move around each other in the narrow row house kitchen. Also because Ty disliked cooking—too many nights in the desert or jungle losing a game of Rock, Paper, Scissors and being forced to go hunt up dinner for the entire Recon team—and he rarely had time to do it even if he'd wanted to. Instead, he hovered around the other side of the bar, watching. Occasionally Zane would glance up at him, apparently just to check that he was still there.

Ty leaned his elbows on the counter and held his chin in his hands, trying to keep himself from fidgeting. Zane finished chopping the second potato and looked up at Ty as he scooped the pieces into his cupped hands.

"You okay?" Zane asked. "You're twitchy."

Ty laughed and held out his hand. "Have you met me?" he asked, teasing.

Zane shrugged one shoulder as he carefully let the pieces fall into the pot of boiling water. "I guess we have been going full tilt since we got back from the cruise, but I figured you would have relaxed a little, at least. Your hair's grown out again, so you don't have that to bitch about anymore. The cat jokes have finally died off at work. And I know you're enjoying the softball practices."

"It's fun. You should come out to one of the games," Ty answered with a careful look up at his partner. They were about to kick off the softball league that had been organized, this weekend, in fact. It had become a big spectacle, and it took a lot of Ty's time. More than he liked.

Zane picked the knife back up and started chopping again, a slight smile curving his lips. "Come out meaning 'watch', or come out meaning 'play'?" he asked. "I can do watching. Playing, not so much. Me and sports in high school?" He shook his head.

"I thought you were too busy square dancing," Ty drawled, trying not to smile.

Zane chuckled as he pushed chopped potatoes to the side of the cutting board with the back of one hand. "That too," he admitted. He glanced up at Ty. "I did think about joining the team anyway, you know."

Ty smiled, but his brow furrowed as well. "Why? I didn't think you liked it."

"I don't like making a fool of myself in public, no," Zane agreed, going back to chopping. "But between those damn PR seminars and you at practice, we've been lucky to have a couple of nights a week to ourselves that aren't simply crashing into bed exhausted."

Ty shrugged in agreement, pursing his lips. It was true. And annoying. "You want me to quit?"

Zane's head snapped up, eyes wide with clear surprise. "No, not at all. You enjoy it too much. Just thought I might see about learning something we could both do. But I figured that for now, the AA meetings were more important."

Ty's lips twitched, and he raised one eyebrow as he looked at Zane. He didn't touch the subject of Zane's AA meetings. He never did. "I'll take you to the batting cages one night," he offered instead.

Zane's smile reappeared. "Deal."

Ty hummed and idly watched Zane's hands move. After a few silent moments, he looked down at his own hands, turning them over and frowning at the fading tan line on his finger where the fake wedding ring had been. It had been cut off in the end, but he'd kept the band. It sat upstairs in a box, hidden away with all the other bits and pieces he'd kept from cases. The line would be gone soon.

"I don't suppose if I agreed to go to a game that you'd agree to go dancing," Zane suggested as he scooped more chopped potatoes into the water.

Ty looked up and snorted at him. "I don't mind going dancing. It's just the clubs that make me nervous, too many ways to get killed."

"And strobe lights," Zane added, obviously remembering what Ty had told him when he'd balked at the dance club on the cruise ship. "I'd still have your back," he said, looking up to meet Ty's eyes evenly.

Ty stared back at him, feeling a shiver run up his spine as he looked into Zane's dark eyes. It was frustrating sometimes, how one look in Zane's eyes made Ty want to throw everything else out the window. But mostly it was fun.

The shift of his weight to stalk around the bar and steal a kiss was interrupted when the police-band radio he kept in a little-used corner of the kitchen crackled to life, the voice sounding marginally panicked as it asked for backup and the bomb squad.

"10-79!"

Ty straightened as he looked at the radio. The signal was weak enough that it only picked up on calls from his neighborhood, alerting him to anything in the vicinity he might be able to help with. It rarely came to life.

Zane set the knife down and picked up a towel, drying his hands as he turned to listen, a frown on his face.

"10-79," the radio spat again through the static. "501 East Pratt Street."

Another voice answered, also sounding panicky and out of breath. These people weren't making official police calls; they had to be off-duty.

"Jesus, that's the aquarium," Ty told Zane.

Ty stood and pushed away from the counter as Zane turned off the burners. "What is it? Ten, twelve blocks?" Zane asked as he strode to the couch, plucked up his shoulder holster, shrugged into it in a quick and long-practiced move, and slid his gun into place.

Ty nodded as he jogged toward the coat rack by the door and the small table drawer where he kept his sidearms. He hurried to put the shoulder holster on, getting the straps tangled as he did so and not caring. Zane grabbed his keys and leather jacket.

"We'll get there faster on foot in this kind of traffic," Ty told him as he yanked at the front door.

"I'll drive between cars and on sidewalks if I have to," Zane answered.

Ty stood at the front door, momentarily indecisive. He would gladly ride on the back of Zane's deathtrap Valkyrie if he really thought it'd get them through the Friday night traffic gauntlet of Fell's Point to the Inner Harbor faster than he could hoof it. Maybe.

"You ride. I'll run," he told Zane, completely sincere in his belief that he could get there quicker.

"Meet you there," Zane said as he headed for the bike parked in front of the row house.

Ty slapped his hand down on the badge that lay on the table, sliding the chain it hung from over his head as he pulled the door closed and hopped from the top step of his stoop to the sidewalk. He sprinted toward Fleet Street as Zane started the bike with a quick jump and revved the engine. He knocked back the kickstand and got the Valkyrie moving as he shoved his helmet on without buckling it.

Ty watched him weave into the heavy traffic and followed in Zane's path for half a block, but then he did what only a man on foot could do and parkoured his ass over someone's fence and into the alleyway between two buildings. It wasn't just a matter of getting to the aquarium in time to help now—it was a matter of pride. He'd beat that damn motorcycle even if it killed him to do it.

CHAPTER THREE

"**T**his is a WBAL TV 11 News Special Saturday Report. I'm Andrea Gregg."

"A false bomb threat last night had off-duty police officers and volunteer workers scrambling to evacuate a group of children from the Baltimore Aquarium. The aquarium was open late for Sea Life Safari, an educational evening program for kids in kindergarten through second grade. The program was sold out with forty children in attendance."

The visual cut to a grim-faced older man with graying hair wearing a blue polo embroidered with the aquarium's logo. The titles labeled him as a *Facility Proctor*. "We were having a great time," he said. "The kids were really enjoying it. We were spread out all over the aquarium in little groups, to give them more one-on-one attention, but it made it harder to get them all out without panicking them. We didn't want to panic them."

"How did you hear about the bomb threat?" the reporter's voice asked.

"A security guard came up and told me we needed to get the kids out quickly and quietly. He didn't tell me why, just that we had to go *now*. Now, you have to understand, these are little kids, and they're all spread out through the room, and we just had two adults per ten kids, which is normally fine," the man answered, starting to ramble.

The reporter cut in. "So you ordered the evacuation of the facility."

"Security did," he said, starting to look a little nervous. "We did it as fast as we could."

The video cut back to the outside of the aquarium and Andrea. "WBAL News arrived just as the children were being escorted from the building and, we are told, right after the first police car arrived."

The picture changed to a well-lit nighttime scene of the front expanse of concrete along the harbor. For a few seconds, children rambled out through the doors, some skipping and singing, some jogging, others dragging along as the proctors tried to shoo them directly away from the front door. A voice-over started.

Two squad cars sat parked at the curb, blue lights flashing, but the uniformed policemen were fifty yards up the pier toward the museum, moving the children away from the building. At the same time, the rumble of an engine covered the chatter of children's voices.

"As we filmed, several off-duty officers arrived on the scene."

The footage shook and swung around to a man sprinting toward the aquarium through the jumble of concrete and carefully manicured shrubbery between buildings. He leapt over a barrier, using his hand to support him as he literally ran sideways against the wall beside him and then hopped down again, running full-tilt toward the aquarium entrance, jumping over low barriers and concrete planters instead of going around them. The badge hanging from his neck was easy to make out as it bounced around, glinting in the various lights of the harbor.

"Over there!" a crew member shouted and the camera swung again. A cobalt blue motorcycle tore up Pier 3 from Pratt Street to the brick and concrete courtyard and skidded to a stop next to a lamppost. The man's helmet hit the concrete as he yanked it off in his hurry to get off the bike, and the camera zoomed in on a badge hooked onto his waistband before panning to the right to follow him as he ran.

More plainclothes policemen began to arrive, most on foot from the parking lots, and the camera jumped from one to the other, going back to the two who had arrived in such spectacular fashion as they met for mere seconds in the center of the courtyard with a few other policemen and then hurried to the aquarium entrance. The footage remained on the front door for a moment before it was kicked open and an off-duty came out carrying a child under each arm.

"With the help of the officers, the evacuation finished quickly. We are told that the news spread through word of mouth and police radios, though officers are not required to leave their radios on if they are not on call."

"The bomb squad arrived as the evacuation finished and, after searching the building, declared it a false alarm. Despite this, parents and officers are angry that such a threat was made." The camera zoomed in on two men—the motorcycle rider and the parkour runner— as they exited the aquarium, looking distinctly displeased. The runner started to shrug into his jacket he'd shed earlier, but the rider stopped him long enough to reach out and fix a twisted strap on his shoulder holster.

The video quick-changed to the camera and reporter converging on that man who'd run onto the scene: he wore a brown leather jacket, Converse sneakers, and a deep frown on his heart-shaped face, along with more than a five o'clock shadow.

"Excuse me, sir! WBAL 11 TV. Did you run here, sir? How far did you come?"

The man looked like he was going to move to avoid the camera, putting his shoulder toward it and giving the lens a wary look. Then he looked to his companion, whose dark hair was still mussed from the motorcycle helmet he'd discarded. They shared a shrug.

"Can you tell us what agency you work for and why you're here?" the reporter persisted from off-screen, the microphone shoved toward him.

The runner sighed heavily and met the reporter's eyes. He was still out of breath when he spoke. "I'm a special agent with the Federal Bureau of Investigation. My partner and I heard the call over the radio and came to help." His words had finality to them, as if that was all he was going to say. He started to turn away.

"Is this threat linked to the others? What does Baltimore law enforcement intend to do about these continuing threats?" the reporter asked hurriedly.

The man stopped at the last question, his head down, and the camera was briefly filled with his broad shoulders squaring and the face of his partner, who was looking at the reporter over one shoulder with narrowed eyes.

Then the agent turned and looked the reporter up and down before turning his eyes directly into the camera. "Baltimore law enforcement is going to kick this threat in the ass," he answered heatedly, his oddly colored eyes flashing angrily. He pointed one long finger at the camera, as if speaking directly to the bombers who had set Baltimore on its ear. "We're coming for you."

A nearby parent cheered, and several other parents, aquarium staff, and officers broke into spontaneous applause as the man's partner, who was failing to conceal a smile, steered him away with a hand on one shoulder.

Video cut to the Baltimore police chief. "Of course we'll consider this threat as seriously—if not more so—than any others," he said firmly. "Baltimore's children are our greatest treasure, and we'll be working closely with the FBI to find the perpetrator of this heinous hoax."

"'Heinous hoax'? Who talks like that?" Special Agent Scott Alston complained.

"Always attempt to avoid alliteration," Ty said with a straight face. Alston barked a laugh.

"You shut up," McCoy snapped as he pointed a finger at Ty.

The entire department was gathered in one of the auditorium-like lecture halls on the main floor of the field office late Saturday morning. People had still been filtering in as McCoy watched the tape of the news story from that morning again. He pulled at his hair as Ty appeared on camera, and Ty sank lower into his chair, hiding his face behind his hand and trying to make himself smaller. He knew he was in deep shit this time. But he would say it again if presented with the opportunity.

"And you, Garrett! You were right there! You should have known better than to let Grady talk to a reporter!" McCoy added from where he stood on the small stage, clearly working up an angry head of steam.

Ty heard Zane draw in a breath, but nothing else. He turned his chin to see Zane sitting still, staring at McCoy, his lips pressed flat. Ty knew that meant his partner *really* wanted to say something but was stopping himself. Ty would have liked to have heard it. It wasn't often Zane let his temper loose.

To Ty's surprise, it wasn't Zane who finally spoke. It wasn't even someone on his immediate team. A voice in the back piped in. "Sir, all due respect, but it was about time *someone* said it."

A rumbling of agreement passed around the lecture hall.

"We've been getting nothing but shit from the press and people out there since the fall," Special Agent Fred Perrimore added, his deep voice easily carrying through the room. "Then today I drive in, and nobody threw water balloons at my car. They're still yelling that we should be doing something, but it's an improvement."

McCoy began to rub at the bridge of his nose, squeezing his eyes closed.

Ty cleared his throat and sat straighter. He tended to think people needed someone to kick a little politically incorrect ass, and do it loudly, but he wasn't paid the big bucks to make those decisions. He was paid to kick ass quietly. "I'm sorry, Mac," he offered. "I shouldn't have said it, but . . . it can't make things any worse."

"It can make you a target, Grady!" McCoy shouted, obviously at the end of his rope.

Zane finally spoke up. "No more than the rest of us," he said evenly. "If they'd known his name, they would have splashed it all over the broadcast."

"Do you have any idea how many calls we've fielded asking who the two FBI agents at the aquarium were? It won't be hard to find out who you are, and they will eventually. For right now they're calling you 'the Rider' and him 'the Runner.'"

"Original," Alston observed sarcastically with a glance at Ty.

"Catchy," Ty responded with a nod.

"Thought that reporter was gonna pass clean out when you rode up on that hog, Garrett. Good one," Perrimore said with a light punch to Zane's bicep. "Must do you good with the ladies."

Zane just rolled his eyes as he sighed and shook his head. Ty smiled at him before he could stop himself. That Perrimore didn't know the Honda Valkyrie wasn't a Harley probably irritated Zane more than the fact he thought Zane used it to pick up girls.

"One more word from the front row, and I will fire you all on the spot," McCoy threatened. "Now. We have a speaker from Public Relations here to have a talk. You can all thank Special Agent Grady after it's over," he announced to the room, then stalked off the stage and told the guest speaker to go on.

The PR guy started by replaying the news broadcast for them. When Ty and Zane came on camera and Ty spoke this time, his finger pointing at the camera, the room of agents erupted into cheers, whistles, and applause. Ty sank lower and covered his face again so McCoy wouldn't see him smiling and fire him. He felt a nudge of a toe to his foot. A sideways look at his partner earned him an amused wink. Zane had told him last night that he agreed with what Ty had said and the delivery of the message, despite the fact that McCoy would blow a gasket. Zane's prediction had come to pass. There were gaskets galore this afternoon.

"Now, while I must agree that Special Agent Grady's phrasing could have been more diplomatic," the PR rep said, showing off his perfectly aligned, extra-bright white teeth, "I do have to say that the image being presented can only help us. People have been demanding action, and they've just been given some big and bold action."

"Now that is what they should call us," Ty said with a satisfied nod.

"Oh Jesus," Alston muttered.

"And to be frank," White Strips continued, "procedural and agency shows are all over TV and are big hits, and Grady and Garrett here looked just like the rogue agents do on TV."

Zane choked on his sip of coffee, setting off a round of tittering and outright laughter.

"Well," Alston said, just loud enough for Ty and Zane to hear, "McCoy did say you two were pretty."

Ty reached over and flicked him on the tip of his nose. Alston laughed even as he turned his head away.

" . . . and we estimate public opinion of the FBI rose as much as 8 percent after the very first broadcast," White Strips continued.

"Ooh, so Garrett and Grady are sexy TV stars now," Special Agent Michelle Clancy crowed as Zane talked over her, saying, "Those percentages don't mean anything."

"It means, Special Agent Garrett," White Strips said with a smarmy smile, "that due to your sudden rise in popularity, you and your high-profile partner just earned another three months of community class duty."

"Oh son of a bitch!" Ty blurted out with a flurry of hand motions and stomp of one foot, sending another ripple of laughter through the entire conference room.

"I didn't even say anything," Zane objected.

"Your bad-boy biker image did your speaking for you, Special Agent Garrett," White Strips pointed out. "You should have thought of that before zooming however-many hundred feet down the pier on that motorcycle."

"Yeah, Garrett, next time curtail your hotness," Ty sniped. He crossed his arms and slumped in his seat like a sulking child. More classes, more lectures, more dealing with people and being nice to them. He was going to go insane. "And do I get no credit at all for *running* the same distance in the same amount of time that he *rode*? Come on!"

There was a brief chorus of pandering, unsympathetic "awwwws," followed by Alston drawling, "And why is it—"

"We shop at the same grocery," Zane said sweetly, cutting off whatever Alston was starting to spin out.

"Ty doesn't eat real food," Alston observed with a frown.

Ty waved him off.

"Back to business," White Strips insisted, picking up a stack of thick manuals and starting to pass them out. "Time for a general review of agency public-relations guidelines."

Ty groaned inwardly. He hoped the sudden support from his fellow agents would hold after being bitch-slapped with a regulations manual for the next hour. He doubted it.

Zane parked near the ambulance that sat to the side of the softball field and climbed out, leaving the truck running with the heater on. It only took him a few steps to get to the open back doors of the ambulance where Ty sat, looking awfully dejected. He wore a loose blue and gray baseball jersey with the word "Feds" written in cursive across the chest, and he was covered in red dirt almost from head to toe. The number twelve and the name "Bulldog" were stitched on the back where his last name should have been. The jersey had come untucked from a pair of gray baseball pants, revealing a dark blue Under Armour shirt that hugged Ty's torso.

When Zane stopped at his side, he turned his head and gave Zane a sheepish smile. "Hey," he greeted.

After looking Ty up and down, Zane smiled. "How you feeling?"

"Had better nights." Ty's words were slow and careful. Then he held up his right hand, which was wrapped up in white athletic tape. His pinkie finger was almost indiscernible. He held a disposable ice pack in the other hand, pressing it to his ribs. "Got run over by a fireman."

Zane couldn't help but laugh.

An EMT wrapped up in a heavy jacket nodded solemnly. "I'm shocked he remembers it."

"You hush," Ty grunted at her.

"Can he leave?"

"I've done all I can do for him," she answered with a nod and a pat to Ty's shoulder.

"C'mon, your chariot has arrived," Zane said, stepping back and waving the way to his truck. "Did you get the truck's number?"

"What truck?" Ty asked as he slid carefully from the ambulance and trudged around it. He wasn't entirely steady as he stepped past Zane; his cleats dragged through the gravel. He seemed to be moving on autopilot as Zane steered him to the passenger seat.

Zane helped him in, pushed the door shut, walked around to the driver's side, and climbed in. "The fireman's truck."

"He didn't use a truck," Ty answered with all sincerity. "His jersey says he's Tank. I got jacked, man. Dude picked me up and threw me down. Gave me Vicodin," he told Zane with a deep frown, not appearing to notice his thought processes hopping around.

"What'd you do? Break it?" Zane asked, reaching out to try to catch the flailing hand that was all wrapped up.

"They told me what was bruised and cracked. Dislocated finger, maybe a cracked rib. I tried to listen, but the EMT had this . . ." Ty put his hand up near his throat and seemed to search for the right word, his hazel eyes not quite focused. "Really low-cut . . . I got distracted."

Zane pressed his lips together to keep back the smile.

"And they counted the run! I had him out at the plate, though. I held onto the ball. Well, it stayed in my glove, anyway. Glove got knocked off. Should have been like half a run."

"That's terrible," Zane murmured as he looked at the mess of tape that practically cocooned Ty's hand.

"It *is* terrible, Zane! We were only up by one!"

Zane chuckled as he got the truck moving. "Put your seatbelt on," he reminded. "It's a good half-hour ride to your place."

Ty nodded and buckled with difficulty. "Were you busy?"

"No, it's fine," Zane said, glancing at Ty as he drove. "I was just working on casefile details. Slow night." He didn't mention he'd merely been passing time waiting for Ty to get home and call him to come over. The softball season had been going strong for two weeks now. Zane would have gone to watch the games, but he'd been trapped by the latest PR events for Baltimore business professionals. He wrinkled his nose. Yet one more work commitment keeping him and Ty apart. He truly resented not being able to watch Ty in action.

"Can you stay with me?" Ty asked, his brow furrowing worriedly.

"Of course I can."

"I can't be alone when I take these things," Ty told him, waving a small paper packet Zane assumed contained pills of some kind.

Zane frowned, feeling a twinge of worry. "Why not? Besides the whole falling-over-loopy thing." Ty's reactions to drugs ranged from hysterically funny to frighteningly horrific, and Zane wasn't taking any chances. He hated to say he enjoyed Ty when he was drugged, because it usually made his partner sick. But before that he was like a big teddy bear, warm and open and steadfast and sweet.

"Well, that and sometimes I . . . quit breathing," Ty explained in an offhand manner as he looked out the truck's window.

Zane went absolutely cold and gripped the steering wheel so hard his knuckles turned white. "What?" he asked, tone rising and sharp with surprise.

"Just a little, like my body forgets it needs air," Ty offered with the same maddeningly carefree attitude he handled all the possibly life- threatening situations he found himself in. "And usually not for long."

"Jesus fucking Christ, Ty, don't you think that's something I should *know*?" Zane asked, voice coming out harsh with worry. "But I just told you," Ty said in a hurt voice.

"When you've already taken something?" Zane sucked in a breath and forced himself to relax, but his pulse had jumped and was now racing. "Well, now I'm really glad you called me, because the EpiPens are all at your place."

"Sorry," Ty offered sincerely.

Zane sighed as he stopped the truck at a red light and reached out to ghost his fingers over Ty's shoulder. He shook his head slightly. Just the idea of losing Ty threatened to knock Zane over. When they got to the house, he was finding one or two of those injectors Ty had stashed all over and keeping at least one within easy reach at all times. Ty's weird allergic reactions were off the charts when they happened, and Zane needed to be better prepared.

"It'll be okay. The hot paramedic chick gave me her number to call if I needed help," Ty continued, his good hand weakly chasing Zane's. "She plays first base."

"That's nice."

"I'd rather be with you."

Zane struggled to tamp down the worry. "That's good to hear. You'd never tell me that if you weren't drugged, I bet."

"Nope!" Ty told him happily. He looked over at Zane with a nearly serene smile. Zane leaned over and captured Ty's full lips in a quick yet warm kiss before stepping on the gas pedal. "I should tell you more often," Ty whispered, not moving from where Zane left him, the side of his head resting against the seat.

Zane stared out the windshield at the busy street as he drove. After a long silence, he reached out to catch Ty's good hand and pull it around to kiss the dirt-stained knuckles. "I wouldn't mind hearing it more often," he said, the words coming out hoarser than he expected.

When Ty didn't answer, Zane squeezed his hand gently and moved it, noticing Ty's arm was limp. He looked over to see Ty still slumped sideways, dozing, breaths ragged but steady. Zane couldn't help but roll his eyes and smile. He kept Ty's hand in his and set them on his right thigh as he focused on getting them home.

To get into the baseball complex, Pierce would either have to pick the lock or park his car on the street and risk getting a ticket as he climbed over the fence. He knew his crime history. Too many people got caught because they parked in the wrong place at the wrong time. There was one car in the locked lot, an old Ford Bronco with vintage stickers on the windows. Pierce knew who it belonged to: that brazen federal agent who had called him out on the local news.

Pierce did his research. He even knew the man's name. Grady. Tyler Grady. Pierce sneered as he thought about the newscast. Man had one hell of a nerve to talk shit when he didn't even have any leads. But Pierce had plans for him now too. He didn't know why the truck had been left behind, but it would save him the trouble of having to find Grady's address.

Grady wasn't the only thing he'd researched. He'd also Googled how to pick locks, and he was reasonably sure he could do it. The others stayed in the car as he tried his hand at it.

He could hear them growing more and more impatient, heckling him through the open windows as he struggled with the lock-pick set he'd bought on eBay. Finally he cursed and jogged back to the SUV.

"I can't get it," he told his companions. He pointed at Ross and Hannah in the backseat. "You two stay in the car. If anyone comes by, light a blunt and start making out, got it?" They looked mutinous about being left behind, but nodded.

He beckoned to Graham, the last member of their enterprising little group, to accompany him. Then Pierce took the equipment out of the back, handed off one of the bags, and carried the other as they made their way over the barrier into the parking lot and toward the first softball field, where all the municipal league games were being played.

When they got to home plate, Pierce gingerly pulled the homemade bomb from the bag and set it beside him on the ground, smiling at it with no small amount of pride.

"We have to dig it up?" Graham asked. Even in the shadows it was easy to see the sour look on his face.

"We have to hide it," Pierce said glibly. He'd already explained all this, there was no way he was doing it again, not out here in the open when time was of the essence.

Graham grumbled and complained as they went to work, digging up home plate. By the time they had a big enough space under the plate for the device to fit, they were both covered in sweat and a fine layer of red dust. They wedged the device into the hole, both of them straining to set it just so. It had to be perfect, or the pressure switch on the top wouldn't activate unless someone stood on top of it and danced.

It was a large bomb. Big enough to leave a crater where home plate was and kill everyone in a ten-foot radius even if it was underground when it went off. Pierce belatedly realized that they wouldn't be able to hide all the excess dirt, and he frowned heavily as he mopped at his brow. The air was cold against his skin, but the adrenaline was combating the bitter chill. Their plan was working so far, and no one was the wiser yet because he planned ahead. That was why, after the first couple of bombs had gone smoothly, he'd set up the dry run at the aquarium—easy enough, since he worked there part time—to check the city's adjusted emergency response.

"Start putting that extra dirt in the bag. I'll set the switch," he ordered.

"Can't we just spread it out?"

"These are cops, man. They only way they won't notice if there's like ten pounds of extra dirt out here in the morning is if they're high."

"Fine," Graham muttered.

"Hurry up. And make sure the plate's straight. We still have one more thing to take care of," Pierce grunted as he eyed the Bronco in the shadows of the parking lot.

He'd show Mr. Mysterious B. Tyler Grady what it was like to be kicked in the ass.

CHAPTER FOUR

The first thing Ty noticed was that it was hot. The air he inhaled, whatever he was sprawled on, what was thrown over him—including a heavy body that lay against him; it was all stiflingly hot. To add insult to injury, when he cautiously cracked one eye open, it was bright and sunny, because the blinds were only half-drawn.

His head felt like it was full of cotton, and his limbs were heavy and uncooperative. He groaned and began pushing at the covers and the dead weight against him. It shifted almost immediately and rolled away.

"You okay?" Zane said, voice rough with sleep.

"Hot," Ty grunted accusingly. He pushed at Zane again and winced with the pressure on his sore body.

Zane scooted back, and the heat radiating from him faded. He also pushed the blanket down, leaving only the thin cotton sheet over Ty's lower body. Ty kicked one leg out and rolled flat, closing his eyes and lifting his chin, sprawling as the cool air hit him.

"Better," he muttered, though his ears seemed to be buzzing like he was hungover.

Zane shifted around, moving the mattress slightly. "How're you feeling?"

"Like I got hit by a truck," Ty answered plaintively.

"You said a tank, actually." The bed shifted again, and Zane was off the mattress and moving. "Hurting?"

Ty opened his eyes to follow Zane around the room. "A little, yeah," he admitted. He tried to sit up slowly but gave up on it and eased himself back down with a groan. "A lot. Hungover."

Zane stopped at his side. "What can I get you?" He was watching Ty in clear concern.

Ty waved him off and shook his head, then winced. He closed his eyes and rubbed his fingers across his forehead slowly, massaging and trying to make the cotton feeling go away. It was rare that he felt so crappy he didn't even think about groping Zane when he woke up next to him. "What time is it?"

"About nine."

Ty sat up quickly, instantly regretting it even as he kicked what remained of the sheets away and tried to get out of bed. "I'm gonna be late!"

"Late for what? It's Sunday morning," Zane said, stepping back to get out of Ty's way.

"The game! Yesterday was just the first round of that stupid Goodwill tournament." Ty took a step and stopped short as the room wobbled around him. "Whoa."

Zane was suddenly there, hands under his elbows to help him regain his balance. "You're going to go back and play after getting hurt last night?" He didn't sound incredulous or even questioning. More like he wanted to be sure he understood correctly.

Ty shook his head and blinked rapidly, then focused on Zane and nodded as he steadied himself. "I'm not hurt bad."

"I remember hearing the words 'cracked rib.'"

"They'll just stick me in right field or something."

"Your throwing hand is injured."

"So I'll use a leftie," Ty tossed back.

Zane dipped his chin to try to catch Ty's eyes. "It's not the being hurt I'm worried about."

"What?"

"You're a little shaky," Zane pointed out. "Even for right field." He straightened and let his hands slide from Ty's arms. "But if you want to go, I'll take you over there."

Ty had to agree he probably wasn't in any shape to drive just then, but a few minutes of moving around and being awake would help. He wasn't sure a softball game was really Zane's scene. He knew the skepticism was obvious in his eyes even as he nodded. "The games last a few hours."

"I do like to watch sports, Ty." Then Zane winked and gave a slight smile. "Especially the uniform pants."

Ty rolled his eyes and pointed at Zane as he moved toward the bedroom door. "No ogling in front of co-workers," he warned. He turned and grimaced as his entire body protested. He groaned and leaned against the doorjamb, hanging his head for a moment. "Christ, I'm sore," he muttered.

"If you take the Vicodin, you'll be seriously looped," Zane said helpfully.

Ty winced and looked down at his finger, his other hand settling on his sore ribs.

"Ty, look at me," Zane requested.

Ty looked up at him obediently, unable to wipe the frown off his face.

"If you're hurting, take the pills. You don't stress over drinking beer in front of me anymore. Why stress over this?" He was using logic, and he didn't sound upset.

"Are you sure?" Ty asked anyway. He didn't feel right waving prescription drugs in Zane's face. "Maybe I can just sit the game out. It's not like the world will end if I don't play or anything."

"Like that'll happen." Zane shook his head as he chuckled. He snagged a pair of jeans that lay folded on the dresser and walked over to stand in front of him. They were Ty's favorite pair, stolen from their last UC operation. They would fit Zane okay; his two to three inches of extra height were mostly in the torso anyway. After a smile, he leaned down to kiss the corner of Ty's mouth. "Thank you. For caring enough to worry about it. Now go take the damn pill. Or half of it. A whole will put you back on your ass. They're on the bathroom counter."

Ty muttered as he turned and headed for the bathroom. If he took a half now and another half in a few hours, that would get him through the game, and then he'd have the rest of the day to sleep it off before work Monday morning. If he didn't take them, he might be able to gut out the game, but his bruised ribcage was already screaming just from rolling out of bed.

He stood looking at the little packet indecisively for a long moment before reaching for the pills and pouring them out into his hand. He plucked one from the pile, scooped the rest back up in the packet, and then pulled at the pill to try to break it in half. He cursed when he couldn't get the thing to snap in two like it was supposed to, and he pulled out another one and tried to snap it instead.

After trying each of the pills and failing to snap any of them on the line, he growled quietly and cursed. His fingers weren't working like they were supposed to.

Instead of asking Zane to deal with it, he popped a whole pill into his mouth and swallowed with a wince at the bitter taste. One every six hours was the same as a half every three, right?

Not really, but it would do.

He continued to mumble to himself as he hurried to get ready for the game. After a few more minutes, he joined Zane downstairs.

"Need any help?" Zane asked.

"You think you can find my cleats?" Ty requested as he buttoned the gray Feds jersey with fingers that felt too thick.

"Sure," Zane said amiably, and he headed for the front door.

Ty was still tucking the jersey in and adjusting the Under Armour shirt he wore beneath it when Zane brought his dirty cleats to him. Ty could feel that pill beginning to work already. Now he questioned the wisdom of taking it, and he wondered if it was too late to go throw it back up. They usually took longer to hit him.

Zane looked him up and down with a small smirk before gesturing with one finger for Ty to turn in a circle.

"What?" Ty frowned at him suspiciously, but he held his hands out to his sides and turned in a slow circle as requested. When he completed the movement to face Zane again, he saw Zane watching him, biting his lower lip.

"Well, it'll do for a ballgame," Zane murmured as he stood.

Ty huffed at him and inexplicably found himself blushing under the scrutiny. "You're a dick, Garrett," he muttered as he moved to grab his cleats.

"So says the ass in very tight pants," Zane said, half laughing as he grabbed his wallet and keys. "C'mon. Food, then ball field."

The SUV idled near First Maryland Bank. Pierce checked his watch. The first game was set to start in ten minutes. If he had planned it right, and he had, the explosion would take out at least half of the crowd and players. He smiled. Most of them were cops, and any of the others— firefighters, EMTs, or regular spectators—were just collateral damage. It served them right for playing with the pigs or buying into that spectacle. Besides, the more deaths there were, the less likely it was anyone would pay attention to the bank robbery on the other side of town. He hoped someone stepped on the plate during the national anthem. Chaos, panic, disorder, all of the above.

It would be brilliant. He turned up the police band radio, waiting for the inevitable calls for ambulances, fire trucks, and bomb squads. He only wished he could be there to see it explode.

The number of vehicles clogging the parking lots, streets, and even browned grassy areas around the playing fields surprised Zane. Sure, it was a softball tournament on a Sunday afternoon, but wow. There were people everywhere, in various states of winter dress. It reminded him of a county fair with all the fund-raising vendors set up. He almost expected to smell barbecue, but that would have been Texas. Here in Baltimore it would be the sweet scent of fried crabcakes.

"Where'd you leave the Bronco?" Zane asked.

"In the far corner over there," Ty answered immediately, pointing toward the edge of the lot where several large trees with spindly bare branches loomed over the cars parked on the crunchy dormant grass.

Zane tried to find a space near it but ended up going in the opposite direction to park closer to the field so Ty wouldn't have to walk so far. "Let me guess. She's away from the foul balls."

Ty looked across the lot at the Ford affectionately. Zane had never seen anything special about the old SUV except for the fact that Ty loved her, and Ty was adamant that the vehicle was a *her*. She was an '88 Ford Bronco, green with a tan underbelly, and every inch of her was lovingly cared for, if not pristine. From what Ty's brother, Deuce, had told Zane, Ty'd had the Bronco since he was in high school. He'd rescued it from a scrap yard and rebuilt it himself. The front windshield was scarred with the sticky remains of old entry decals, some of them retaining the shape of their former stickers from the Marine base at Camp Lejeune. Decals littered the edges of the back and side windows. Zane had never taken the time to stop and look at them all, but he guessed that there were dozens altogether.

There was one very prominent white sticker in the rear window that said "Semper Fidelis" beneath the USMC eagle, globe, and anchor. There were several smaller decals scattered around that commemorated certain stretches of the Appalachian Trail. A yellow square with a familiar curled snake and the words "Don't Tread On Me." An old peeling sticker that had seen better days was what Zane had been told was a nautical star. There was a Smith & Wesson logo. In various places he could see a New Orleans Saints fleur de lis, an Atlanta Braves tomahawk, a faded Grateful Dead "steal your face" sticker, and a very old M with a circle over it that Zane knew stood for an Ironman Triathlon. A newer decal sported stylized Arabic writing that spelled out "Infidel" with an assault rifle used as the capital I. In direct contrast, on the opposite window, was the Om symbol. By itself in the center of one of the back windows was a black POW/MIA sticker.

The Bronco and its dressings told the tale of Ty's life and offered glimpses into his heart and soul, whether Ty meant it to or not. Zane knew it had traveled with Ty nearly everywhere he'd been, even serving as his home a few times when Ty was transitioning between lives.

"People have gotten to where they aim at her. Try to hit her with foul balls," Ty complained.

It drew a smile out of Zane, and he chuckled. "That's awful," he commiserated.

"I know!" Ty exclaimed with complete sincerity. He leaned forward in his seat, digging through the duffel bag in the floorboard, and pulled out his cleats, which he'd refused to put on before getting into the car.

Zane shrugged, though he was amused by Ty's utter seriousness. "If somebody threw a softball at the Valkyrie, I'd have to clobber them."

"Throwing is different. A foul ball has gravity on its side," Ty explained as he popped open the passenger-side door and tried to swing his legs out before unbuckling his seatbelt. He grunted as the belt tightened, then reached behind him to fumble with the mechanism briefly before it released and he slid out of the truck in a tumble of shoes and equipment, disappearing from sight. "I'm okay," Zane heard him say.

"He's okay," Zane muttered as he grabbed the ball cap off the floorboard, snagged the keys, and got out of the truck as well. He walked around to the passenger side, half expecting to see Ty on the ground.

He'd managed to get himself together, though, and he was bent over, pushing his feet into his cleats. His equipment bag was over one shoulder, the handle of the bat hanging near the back of his head. He tied his shoe tight before standing and giving Zane a crooked smile.

Zane held out the navy blue FBI ball cap. "You'll need this."

Ty took it and put it on, shaking his head. "I've never actually worn it in a game. Facemask," he told Zane. He nodded toward the field and started walking. "You don't have to stay, you know. There's a lot of news cameras here."

Zane frowned as he followed, checking out the press. "I know. Do you want me to go?" he asked tentatively. Ty could be difficult to read, and since throwing the whole declaration of love into the mix, dealing with him was like navigating a minefield for Zane. They hadn't done the traditional *yours* vs. *ours* kind of distinctions, and sharing still wasn't a strong skill for either of them. This was Ty's scene, and Zane wasn't sure he was welcome here.

"No," Ty answered easily. He turned and looked at Zane, then reached up and took his ball cap off again, handing it back to Zane as if he'd forgotten he'd just put it on. "I just don't want you getting bored. Put this on so people'll know you're one of the bad guys."

"One of the bad guys?" Zane laughed as he settled the cap comfortably on his head. It smelled just enough like Ty to make it worth wearing.

"Well, the other teams love to hate us." Ty's cleats clicked on the concrete as he walked, and even though Zane knew he'd taken more medication earlier, he didn't seem overly uncoordinated or goofy.

They threaded through a crowd of fans and various teams, including local law enforcement, a couple of insurance companies, and an area hospital before they turned the corner of the concession stand

and saw the FBI team. Again, Zane was surprised by the number of people involved, especially out here in the cold in mid-February. He'd heard through the grapevine that Ty had been partially responsible for the league organization, calling in favors, reaching out to contacts in various fields around the city. Seeing the spectacle now, Zane had to wonder just how connected his partner really was.

They were suddenly assaulted from the side by a perky young reporter blurting questions and her hulking cameraman. Ty just smiled and waved her off, telling her, "After the game, okay?"

"Jesus, you weren't kidding when you said this had gotten big," Zane murmured as he stuck to Ty for protection from the mob. "Why haven't I heard more about it?"

"Because you work for a living," Ty responded as he messed with the neck of his Under Armour shirt. He was getting twitchier as they moved, though that didn't strike Zane as particularly unusual. He was about to respond to Ty's gentle dig when someone else spoke up to get Ty's attention.

"We were starting to wonder if you were gonna make it, Grady. You missed the national anthem," Scott Alston said as he walked up to them. He was wearing the same uniform as Ty, but his jersey was tucked in and buttoned and his belt wasn't unbuckled. Zane had heard that all of the teams had given their players nicknames, like Ty's "Bulldog." Some were more interesting than others. From the side, Zane could see Alston's was "Tinman." There had to be a story there.

Alston looked at Zane and held out his hand, clearly surprised to see him there. "Not a big deal unless you're slated to fucking sing it, right? Garrett, good to see you."

"Thanks," Zane said as he shook Alston's hand. "Thought I'd cheer for the team. He was supposed to sing?"

"Right." Alston nodded slowly and looked between them knowingly. "He's too drugged to drive, isn't he?"

"Grady? Drugged? Would never happen," Zane answered, meeting Alston's eyes straight on without blinking.

"Sure it wouldn't," Alston said with a laugh. He reached out and took Ty's hand in his, lifting it to look at the tape Ty had wrapped around his fingers. "I see you have a lefty glove today. Broken or just bent?"

Ty took a step closer and yanked his hand away. "Sit on it and spin, Scott," he muttered as he walked past him toward the larger group of players.

Alston laughed heartily and looked back at Zane with a raised eyebrow.

Zane shrugged helplessly. "He said he wanted to play."

"He always wants to play," Alston assured him. "That's what he was saying last night when we peeled him out of the dirt."

"Been there, done that," Zane said drily. "Ty can sing?"

Alston just laughed like Zane was joking, and Zane let it go, feeling stupid for not knowing something like that about his partner. His *lover*. He glanced around, recognizing some other team members and spectators.

"I'm just going to hang out and relax." He paused, peering after Ty. "I should probably ask where the EMTs are. Just in case."

"Don't worry. One of them has the hots for Grady. She'll be all over it if he's hurt," Alston told him as he turned, waving over his shoulder. "Thanks for bringing him!"

Zane waved him off and turned to survey the bleachers now that the team had cleared out. Close to full, but he'd have room to stretch out his legs if he was careful. He had just started toward them when he heard the clacking of cleats behind him.

Ty grabbed his elbow to stop him; Zane turned in place to look at his partner. Ty's hazel eyes were shining in the sunlight, and he smiled crookedly as he let his hand slide away from Zane's arm. "Thanks for bringing me, Zane," he said with an affectionate pat to Zane's belly, and then he turned away and jogged back toward the dugout on the other side of the field without waiting for Zane to respond.

Zane stared after him, rooted to the spot, and it wasn't even Ty's fine ass in those pants that had his attention. No, it was that flash of light in Ty's eyes that struck Zane right in the gut and made his breath catch. He had to try twice to swallow, and his face felt hot in the brisk air. He blinked hard before he realized he was gaping and made himself turn toward the bleachers and sit down about four rows up.

Occasional actions like that totally convinced Zane that Ty was telling the truth about loving him. It bowled Zane over, and he felt a rush of giddiness. Zane closed his eyes tight and opened them again, and Ty came into focus on the other side of the fence—Zane had zeroed in on him without consciously looking.

A young girl, elementary school age probably, abruptly skipped into his line of sight, climbed up the bleachers deftly, and sat down right beside him as if she belonged there. She gave him a cheerful smile. "Hi!"

Zane did a double take between her and Ty before settling his gaze on her. "Hi," he said, a little surprised. He wasn't the type of guy kids just waltzed up to. Quite tall, broad in the shoulders, muscled, dark hair and eyes, heavy leather jacket and boots, sort of imposing. But it didn't seem to faze her.

"I'm Elaina," she said as she stuck her little hand out to shake his. "Are you a friend of Ty's?"

His hand engulfed hers as he shook it gently. "I'm Zane. Ty's partner. Nice to meet you, Elaina."

"Nice to meet you!" she said enthusiastically. She scooted around on the hard, cold metal bleacher seat to settle primly beside him, looking out at the field like she owned it. "Mommy told me to find someone who had FBI on their clothes. Then I saw you talking to Ty, so I knew you would be safe. He and Mommy used to date," she told Zane with all the tact of an eight-year-old.

Zane stifled a chuckle as he watched her, intrigued. "And who is Mommy?"

"She plays second base. Number five." Elaina pointed toward the field, where the FBI team was filtering out, beginning to warm up. Five was an attractive brunette, athletic and tan and smiling. The nickname on her uniform was "Lefty." She was throwing right-handed, though. Zane didn't have any trouble picturing her with Ty.

"You come to all the games?" Zane asked, opting for small talk.

"Oh yeah. We're the best team here," the little girl announced proudly. "Well, maybe tied for the best. But the firemen play dirty."

"Of course," Zane agreed. He ducked down out of the way as a woman carrying a tray of food climbed up the bleachers next to them. "I'll have to start following the scores."

Zane caught sight of Ty standing in front of the chain-link dugout, bent over and strapping his shin guards on, slowed down by his wrapped fingers, as the rest of the catcher's gear sat in the grass next to him. Zane smiled fondly. Ty was so methodical with some things. He wore his Kevlar religiously and nagged Zane about his when they went out on assignment because Zane hated wearing the vest. Ty cleaned his gun every other day whether it needed it or not. And every tie and strap and buckle on his gear had to be just so—if Zane didn't adjust a strap for him first—if he had even close to the time to fix it. It seemed he treated his recreational gear the same way.

Zane shook his head but didn't look away. Ty Grady was a study in contrasts, and the puzzle-like appeal of it was impossible for Zane to resist.

Zane wasn't sure why Ty was suiting up to catch, though. He definitely shouldn't have been, not with a bum throwing hand. But Ty was obviously under the impression that he could throw with his left hand and catch with his right, instead of the other way around. Zane knew he could shoot a gun, throw darts, and shoot pool, all with both hands. Zane had even seen him hurriedly scribble with both hands, though you could never read the end result, no matter which hand Ty used. Maybe he was truly ambidextrous, another fact Zane was somewhat embarrassed about not knowing, if it was true.

Ty was still fussing with the strap to the chest protector as he and Alston walked up to home plate to meet with the umpires and the other team's captains. Zane couldn't hear them, but he could see Ty and Alston muttering to each other as Ty tried and failed several times to hook the strap at his side while using his hurt hand. Finally, Alston reached out and yanked Ty's helmet from under his arm, swatted his hands away from the strap, and bent to clasp it for him as the others gathered at home plate tried not to laugh. Zane shook his head as he watched. As irascible as Ty could be, he sure had a lot of friends, people who seemed to see right through the façade that had so confounded Zane when he first met Ty Grady.

The gathered men all shook hands where they stood in the batter's boxes. They'd step closer as they shook hands, kicking red dirt on the pristine white plate. Zane watched in amusement as Ty carefully avoided the white chalk lines and home plate. The meeting lasted a few minutes as they went over the ground rules, the men scuffing the dirt in the boxes with their cleats, smoothing out the uneven ridges of dirt. Then they parted and went back to their respective dugouts.

Ty took pains to step over the white chalk lines on the field as they walked, but it was hard to tell if it was to avoid them or because that pill was hitting him.

Elaina leaned closer to Zane. "Mommy says Ty's very superstitious," she confided in a whisper. "He wears the same socks every game."

Zane turned his chin to look at her. "Does he wash them?" he joked. He tried to remember if Ty had put on the same socks Zane had stripped off of him last night.

"Mommy tried once, but he saved them and made her promise not to. He locked himself in the bathroom."

Zane laughed and glanced back at Ty. "That sounds like him."

"He also taught me that you never cross your bats in the dugout, you never touch the lines or home plate before a game starts, and only pansies wear batting gloves."

Zane laughed again. "I guess he would know," he said with a shrug. "I never played baseball. Or softball."

Elaina looked at him askance.

"I can play football though," Zane offered in a conciliatory attempt.

She shrugged off that news and looked back out at the field excitedly as the FBI team took the field to a smattering of applause, boos, and catcalls from the crowd. Zane joined in the clapping as most of the players jogged to their positions, but Ty and Alston, who was pitching, both waltzed out as if they had all the time in the world.

Ty had his head down, his glove in one hand and his mask in the other, and somehow he'd already gotten his face and short hair dirty. It wasn't easy for him to saunter in the bulky gear, but he managed to pull off the attitude anyway. The gear fit his frame well, and it only added to the illusion that he was larger than he really was. Zane knew that in most rec league softball games, the catcher didn't bother to wear gear. But this wasn't your average slow-pitch softball league. The pitchers threw overhand, and they played with a regulation-size baseball. The women who were involved were athletes, not out there for show, and there was certainly no one drinking beer in right field.

Ty had sent Zane a text one night earlier in the month, joking that it was *srius bizness*.

As Ty got closer to home plate, he looked up into the bleachers, his eyes almost immediately settling on Zane.

Zane felt his heart beat hard a couple of times, and he had to draw a breath, because for a second, he was short on air. Then Ty smiled that half smile of his, the laugh lines at his eyes and mouth appearing, before he gave a quick wink. Then he ducked his head and slid his mask on, turning his back on the crowd as he stopped behind home plate.

Zane swallowed hard. That wink had been for *him*.

Crystal-clear revelation struck Zane like a bolt of summer lightning sizzling through the chill February air.

He wanted Ty with him, wanted him badly. Needed him as a partner, and not just at work. Craved him as a lover more than he'd ever jonesed over heroin. Connected with him in so many ways that Zane couldn't see a way to untangle himself and didn't even want to try.

Ty loved him. Zane believed it. Zane had also believed he didn't have it in himself to love Ty like he deserved. It wasn't Ty's fault. There was so much pain connecting Zane to the past, a tenuous lingering link between Zane and Becky, his wife years gone now, that Zane had skipped right over the obvious signs. He'd been too busy grappling with letting go of what was gone and wondering if he had any right to grab hold of what was in front of him.

It was important to Zane to understand when craving Ty had become needing him, and when needing him had become caring for him, and if it was possible for that caring to truly become even *more*. Because Ty deserved nothing less.

Zane could see it now. The craving he worried about wasn't an addiction. It was far more wrenching. Something significant enough that Zane was changing his entire life to be worthy of it, and there just wasn't any other possible explanation.

He loved Ty Grady with all there was to give of his heart, and in the end, all it had taken was one wink for Zane to finally come to terms with it.

As he sat dealing with the sudden realization, the world continued on without him. The players continued warming up. Alston had taken just one warm-up pitch, feeding into the cocksure, evil empire image the Feds team cultivated. The fans in the stands around him continued talking and eating and fussing with their various seating options, and Elaina jabbered on beside him.

Ty stood talking with the umpire, his body language clearly saying he was joking around with the man. He was loose and at ease, having battled past the painkiller and his natural inability to be still. Another moment later he stepped away from the umpire and knelt behind home plate as the first batter of the game approached the batter's box. But Ty wasn't there for more than a heartbeat before he raised a hand to call time and stood back up.

A collective groan ran through both teams and the crowd.

"Oh, good grief," Elaina said as she rested her chin in her hand. Zane shook himself out of his thoughts and looked to Elaina before turning his eyes back to Ty. "What?"

"He does this every game," Elaina complained. "He says the plate's crooked!"

A woman sitting behind them laughed. "He says it's latent OCD." Zane frowned. Ty's shoulders were straight and stiff, in total contrast to the loose relaxation he'd exhibited just a couple minutes before. That wasn't OCD. Zane leaned to the side to try to get a better look at what was going on.

Ty and the batter were standing together, Ty pointing down at the plate as the batter nodded. The umpire was shaking his head, holding his mask in his hand and frowning. It was anyone's guess what they were saying to each other, but whatever Ty was saying, he was adamant. Finally, he yanked his mask off and knelt over the plate, pointing to something Zane couldn't see.

"It's not the freaking major leagues, Grady! It doesn't have to be perfect!" someone shouted from the visitor's dugout.

Zane shifted on the metal bleachers as he watched. "Something's wrong," he murmured.

The batter stepped closer and took his bat off his shoulder, pointing it at the plate. Ty reached out and grabbed the end of it quickly to stop him from poking it, then stood and held up both hands impatiently, like he was begging them to listen to him.

He turned to scan the bleachers, his eyes finding Zane quickly. Zane recognized the look on his partner's face and was moving even before Ty started toward the fence backstop and waved to him.

He met Ty at the fence, reaching up to twine his fingers through the chain-link. "What's wrong?"

"The plate's wrong," Ty said under his breath. "It's not crooked anymore."

"Maybe someone fixed it?" Zane asked. He had no doubt that Ty would notice if it was sitting differently than usual. He just didn't know if it was something worth stopping the game over.

"I've been bitching about it for weeks, and they finally fixed it in the middle of the night last night?" Ty muttered as he looked over the crowd restlessly. His eyes met Zane's. Looking at him this close, it was easy to see what the painkillers were doing to him. "It's too high."

The plate was not the only thing that was too high. But what Ty was saying made it sound like someone had wedged something under it. "You really think it's trouble?" Zane asked quietly. "There's plenty of cops around."

"That's what I'm worried about," Ty told him as several people shouted at them in annoyance. Ty ignored them like only he could. "Do you have your phone on you?"

Zane pulled it out of his back pocket and offered it to him. They struggled almost comically to get it through the chain-link as those around them became more vocal with their displeasure.

"Why don't we just take it up and adjust it?" the hitter asked Ty curiously.

Ty finally pulled the phone through and glanced over his shoulder at the man as he flipped Zane's phone open.

"Who are you calling?" the umpire asked, obviously perturbed. "Bomb squad," Ty answered gruffly.

Zane's fingers clenched on the fence. Ty wouldn't joke about something like that. "Better start telling people to clear out," he told the ump evenly. He'd back Ty up no matter how stoned on painkillers his partner was. "Is there a field announcer?"

"Are you shitting me?" the umpire said incredulously. Other players were beginning to drift closer, obviously realizing that something was wrong beyond the crooked plate and Ty's supposed OCD.

Alston came jogging up to them from the mound, and Ty took a quick step and pointed at him. "Stop!" he shouted urgently before Alston could get to home plate.

The tone of his voice seemed to do the trick. They all knew Ty didn't screw around, and he sounded truly scared.

"I'll get the announcer going," the umpire mumbled as he hurried toward the wooden tower near the dugout.

Zane watched silently as Ty quickly gave information over the phone while the players on the field came in to the dugouts to wait. Word hadn't gotten around yet. Zane glanced over his shoulder at the stands. Lots of families and kids were here. His eyes fell on Elaina. She looked incredibly small and innocent sitting there.

The chain-link rattling near his head drew his attention back to Ty. Ty's fingers gripped the fence, and he looked through it to the bleachers.

"Do me a favor, Zane?" he whispered.

Ty looked really worried, which didn't do much for Zane's peace of mind. "Yeah."

"Grab the kid and don't let her out of your sight, okay?" Ty requested as he looked at Zane finally. "As soon as people hear 'bomb', they're gonna panic and scatter."

Zane nodded slowly. There was a story there somewhere related to the "he and Mommy used to date" comment. But it didn't matter. "Yeah, I'll do it. Be careful."

Ty merely nodded and reached up to touch Zane's fingers through the fence before turning away. He picked up his helmet, then jogged toward the home dugout as the speakers blared on.

"Ladies and gentlemen, at this time we ask you to please move in an orderly fashion toward the south field."

Zane took a couple of careful steps backward, still watching Ty, before he turned to the stands to find Elaina. With just a few strides, he was next to her. "C'mon, Elaina," he said, holding out his hand.

"What about Mommy?" Elaina asked as she climbed down the bleachers.

"Ty will get her and the rest of the team," Zane said as she slid her hand into his, and he started walking, almost immediately hitching his steps shorter because his legs were so long compared to hers.

They were almost across the parking lot when the cute brunette from second base caught up to them and took Elaina's other hand. "Are you Garrett?" she asked Zane breathlessly.

"Yes, ma'am," Zane responded automatically. He looked at Elaina and noted the strong resemblance. Dark-brown hair, large eyes so brown they were nearly black. "You must be Mommy."

She laughed slightly and nodded. "I'm Shannon." She didn't offer her hand, though, instead reaching down and picking Elaina up so they could move faster. "Is this for real, or is Ty going off the deep end?"

Zane glanced at her, surprised. "I'd say it's for real." He pointed at the dugout on the far side of the next field. The lower part of it was made of wooden planks, the upper part more chain-link. "That ought to be a good place to hunker down. We're far enough away."

"God, I was hoping he'd just had too many painkillers," the woman said under her breath. She pulled her daughter higher on her hip and quickened her pace. Zane heard sirens in the distance as they reached the other field.

Zane stopped at the steps to let Shannon get into the dugout first, and then he waited as several other people passed by, distractedly offering an arm to help them clamber down the concrete steps, watching for Ty as fire trucks pulled up at the field. He hated being back here doing nothing.

He finally spotted Ty, standing next to the blue bomb squad truck and speaking with one of the techs. He was gesticulating erratically, obviously worked up, and the tech seemed to be trying to reason with him. Finally, two firemen came up to join the conversation, and one began leading Ty away, toward the dugouts. The fireman was larger than Ty by quite a bit, a true hulk, and though Ty didn't appear happy with the arrangement, he went along without fussing until they reached the dugout where Zane stood.

"Does this belong to you?" the fireman asked Zane in a deep, booming voice, scruffing Ty by his jersey collar like a stray dog.

Zane raised a brow at the phrasing but nodded anyway. "Should have made sure he was wearing his tags, I guess," he answered as he tried to judge Ty's condition.

Ty rolled his eyes and shifted his jaw in annoyance. "They don't believe me," he told Zane under his breath. "This is Tank, by the way. He runs people over."

The big fireman laughed heartily and shook his head. His teeth gleamed bright against his black skin. "Gotta lead with the shoulder when a big dawg is blocking the plate. You know that."

"Yeah, shoulder, not front bumper," Ty shot back.

Tank looked to Zane. "Shape he was in last time I saw him, I'm not surprised he's like this."

"You sure knocked him for a loop," Zane confirmed before asking Ty, "Are they checking it out?"

Ty pressed his lips tightly together and nodded, looking at Zane sideways like he knew he'd be in trouble. Tank spoke up when Ty didn't. "He told them if they didn't, he'd go on record saying he put it there himself so they'd *have* to check it out."

Zane snorted. "Jesus, Ty," he muttered, shaking his head. "There were tool marks!" Ty insisted.

"Take it easy, Bulldog," Tank said as he turned and patted Ty on the back hard enough to send him stumbling forward into Zane, who reacted automatically and raised his arms to grab hold of him.

He still had on the catcher's gear, but as Ty wrapped one arm around Zane's waist to keep his balance, it was clear the pill he'd taken had finally gotten the best of him. His body was loose and relaxed, his movements not as controlled as usual.

Ty muttered obstinately as he turned to look at the scene behind them, his body still brushing against Zane's as they stood together. He obviously felt certain he was right about the threat. But it was entirely possible they'd just evacuated a few hundred people in front of the local news because Ty was high. Zane sighed and kept his arm discreetly around Ty's waist. Most of their co-workers would figure Zane was holding him back anyway.

The bomb squad techs directed a small robot down a ramp from the back of their truck, and another member of the team pulled out a bullhorn to address the crowd as the robot chugged away at a snail's pace toward home plate. Besides that, it was hard to see what was happening on the field.

Ty cleared his throat and turned his head to look at Zane. He leaned closer and spoke quietly. "Where are Shannon and Elaina? They safe?"

"They're in here somewhere," Zane murmured. He splayed his hand flat on Ty's lower back against the fabric. "You don't look so good."

"Shut up," Ty muttered as he turned and looked further into the dugout. He kept one hand on Zane's arm to hold himself steady.

Zane sighed and resisted the urge to lay his forehead against Ty's in a bid for support and comfort. This *definitely* wasn't the place, or the time, no matter how much Zane's instincts were screaming at him to drag Ty away from here to somewhere safe so he could take care of him. He'd have to deal with that—and the fallout of the other momentous realizations of the morning—later.

A voice blared over the bullhorn, and Ty startled against Zane before turning to look at the field as the announcer warned people to stay where they were and cover their heads.

"Tyler, get down here before you fall over!" Shannon shouted. She stepped out and grabbed the strap of Ty's chest protector. "What were you thinking, taking something before you came out here?"

"I was thinking, 'Wow, my ribs hurt,'" Ty answered as he stumbled sideways.

Zane released him as Shannon took charge and pulled Ty down into the dugout. "He really wanted to be here."

"Not getting what he wants won't kill him," Shannon informed them both. She shoved at Ty's chest, and he fell back onto the old, scarred wooden bench with a thump and a rattle of protective gear. She pointed her finger in his face and waved it. "Something had better damn well blow up out there," she warned.

"Mommy, I think you need a time-out," Elaina observed, her young voice wry and amused.

Ty merely nodded as he looked up at her with wide eyes. It was kind of funny, really. Zane had never seen Ty act like that around a woman, except maybe his mama. Usually he was all charm and charismatic quips. Zane had to cover his smile with one hand and turn away. When he did, he saw one of the bomb squad team jogging their way. When he got to them, he leaned against the back fence of the dugout to speak to Ty through the chain-link.

"There's definitely something down there," the man told them quietly. "Looks like a pressure switch of some sort."

Ty turned his head, and the man kept talking to him in lower tones for a moment before standing abruptly and jogging back toward his truck. Zane stepped down into the dugout to stand next to Ty.

"Well?"

Ty looked up at him and licked his lips uneasily. "They think it's a pressure switch," Ty repeated for the people around them. "Bouncing Betty type thing. Bomb squad's going to get one of those kamikaze robots out there to poke it," he told Zane in a lower voice.

Zane sat down next to him. "The games were here yesterday, right? So this had to have been done overnight?"

"Had to be. I was practically laying on the damn thing last night," Ty muttered. "And it was crooked."

"Jesus, Grady," someone from close by said. "I'm never making fun of your superstitions again."

"Told you touching home plate before the first pitch was bad luck," Ty responded under his breath, looking away from Zane as he spoke.

Zane propped his elbows on his knees as he listened to the circus of bomb squad, firemen, news cameras, and cops circling the other ballfield. He didn't want to think about how close Ty had been to bodily harm. He could wish Ty had been in the outfield, but he wouldn't lay odds on someone else noticing the problem with the plate. He sighed and dropped his head, shaking it.

Ty's shoulder brushed his, and Zane could feel him thrumming with nervous energy.

"Are we safe here?" someone asked. "Should we get further away?"

"We're good," Ty assured them curtly. "If it does blow before they can disarm it, they say it's not packed, so there won't be any shrapnel. Unless it blows the arm off the robot or something."

"I've seen that happen," an unfamiliar voice said from further down the dugout.

"Bullshit," someone else responded with a laugh.

"God's honest truth. Arm flew through the air and landed like a damn lawn dart."

"Would it reach us if that happened?" a worried voice asked.

"The robot is made to blow shit up," Ty answered in an annoyed voice. "The articulating parts don't blow off," he snapped. On the surface, his tone of voice said he was talking to a civilian who was getting on his nerves, but underneath that Zane recognized his partner was badly shaken. Zane straightened and leaned back, and when he scooted—not a big deal, since people were crammed onto the bench anyway—he slid enough so their legs touched from hip to knee.

"Everybody down!" someone called from somewhere behind Zane.

Ty's hands were immediately on Zane, tugging at him and pulling him down with everyone else onto the packed dirt. Zane hit the ground hard on his knees, shifting his weight back just in time to avoid falling straight forward onto his face. Ty pulled Shannon and her daughter closer and huddled them all together, wrapping his arm over Zane and pressing him down into the dirt. His chest protector dug into Zane's side as he tried to shield all three of them from the coming blast that supposedly wouldn't reach them.

Sirens blared across the parking lot, and someone shouted into a bullhorn to make certain the area was clear. The scene had to be easier to handle than most, considering everyone there was involved with the city and knew emergency procedures in some fashion. Hell, half of them probably would have been working the scene if they'd been on duty.

It was a long, drawn-out ten seconds of what seemed like pure silence before the explosion sounded. Obviously disarming it hadn't gone well.

Zane winced. It was really, really loud for a bomb little enough to fit under home plate.

A whoosh of dirt and small pieces of trash filtered through the chain-link to flutter over them, and Ty curled above him protectively as the air wafted past. He waited a long moment, his fingers digging into Zane's shoulder as he held him, his breaths harsh in Zane's ear. Zane closed his eyes, thankful that Ty was here next to him rather than across the field. He slowly started to sit up.

Ty pushed himself up when he felt Zane moving, and he raised his head and looked around to survey the damage. People around them were coughing and scrabbling around on the ground of the dugout, everyone trying to gain their feet at the same time. Ty pulled himself up unsteadily and looked through the fence as he offered his hand to help Zane or Shannon up.

"Oh God," he said suddenly, his hand going limp at his side as he pulled his face closer to the chain-link.

Zane got to his feet next to him and looked out across the field with a frown. "What?"

"Garrett," Ty practically whined as he grabbed at Zane's shoulder. "The Bronco!"

The green Bronco rocked as the robotic arm of the bomb robot rolled slowly off the hood. The dent it left behind was massive, giving the distinct impression that the grill was scowling.

"Ouch," Zane breathed.

"My truck," Ty whimpered.

"Oh, Ty," Shannon said sympathetically as she stood and peered out into the parking lot.

Someone else down the dugout gave a low whistle, and several of the other agents began laughing. "The articulating parts don't blow off, huh?" someone asked in a teasing voice.

"My truck," Ty repeated pitifully.

"I'm sure that'll . . . buff out, man," one of them told Ty in a voice that was attempting to be consoling but only managing to waver as the man tried not to laugh.

"In three years, nothing has ever landed there!" Ty cried suddenly. Everyone in the dugout began to laugh.

Zane moved slowly, deciding that turning to face Ty and standing between him and the dugout exit was probably not a bad idea. With Ty's state of mind, he was liable to run out there and lay himself out over the truck to protect it. After another look at Ty, Zane took hold of his forearm. Just in case.

"Who the hell thinks that shit's funny?" Ty shouted at everyone. "Where's my gun?" he demanded with all seriousness as he began to pat himself down.

"Who are you gonna shoot? The robot?" Zane asked with a sigh. He saw one of the bomb squad men give the all clear sign, and he tugged at Ty's arm. Reporters began to crowd toward the cordoned-off area as people began to stir. "Come on. We'll go check the damage."

Ty swung out of the dugout and began stalking toward the Bronco, muttering angrily as he started shedding his catcher's gear. Zane jogged after him, dodging the shin guards and chest protector as they bounced to the ground.

"I can't fucking believe this," Ty exclaimed. "What's the likelihood of that shit, huh?"

"Special Agent Grady!" a reporter called out, and Zane turned to see her running after them in an impressive pair of stilettos.

Ty turned to her and flopped his hands. "Seriously?" he shouted angrily.

"Is that your car, Agent Grady?" she yelled after him, microphone out as she and her cameraman continued hurrying toward them, trying to catch up from twenty yards behind. Zane wondered how she knew Ty's name.

Ty turned to look at the Bronco, waving his hand at it. "Yes, it's mine! Look at it!"

He took one more step toward the frowning Bronco, and the hood blasted upward, belching flames. The sound followed, a scream of metal and machinery, like a terrified mechanical plea for help, and the old Bronco jumped into the air, flame and heat blasting out of it as the gas tank exploded. The concussion of the explosion knocked Ty and Zane backward and to the ground, heat whooshing over them with what Zane would have sworn was a pained groan from the vehicle.

The dying breath of Ty's beloved Bronco.

Ty rose slowly, looking with absolute horror at the flames that licked at the tree branches above. He suddenly pushed himself up and made to run toward the wreckage. Zane grabbed for him, tripping him up and then tackling him to the ground. Zane had no doubt Ty would try to put the flames out himself and probably go down in a fiery blaze of glory trying to save the damn thing.

"She's burning, Zane!" Ty yelled, in a panic, voice full of anguish as he tried to squirm out of Zane's grasp.

The sound broke Zane's heart. He had to wrap both arms around his partner and put all his weight into him to keep Ty from lashing out blindly as firemen ran past them. "Ty, *stop*," he said firmly.

Ty tensed like he was going to lunge again, but then he relaxed beneath Zane as if someone had let the air out of him. He didn't make a sound, and he seemed to be holding his breath as he craned his neck, staring at the crackling flames and pillar of black smoke.

The cameraman skidded to a stop beside them, filming the burning Bronco, filming the firemen trying to stem the flames with extinguishers, and filming them as Ty lay beneath Zane and watched his oldest friend burn.

CHAPTER FIVE

Z ane jogged down the stairs to the living room and stopped, looking around to find Shannon. She'd given them a ride to Ty's house, since Zane's truck had been behind the cordoned-off safety line. They had decided they needed to get Ty home, away from the television cameras that seemed to love to torment him, where he could fall apart in peace.

He found her sitting in an armchair, and Elaina was crashed out on the couch, so Zane moved to join them.

"How is he?" Shannon asked dubiously. "I know how he felt about that truck."

Zane shook his head as he stripped out of his heavy sweatshirt before sitting down. "He's still in shock. Not pacing or ranting or anything else I would expect out of him. I'm not sure which is better." He glanced up to the ceiling. "He's supposed to be getting in the shower."

"Silent and still is not a good sign," Shannon advised as she straightened and put her hands on her knees. She stood and glanced up at the ceiling as well. "You want a beer? I think we all deserve one after today," she said quietly as she headed for the kitchen.

"Dr Pepper is fine," Zane said. "I was thinking about suggesting we order in some food. I want to keep an eye on him after the reaction he had to the painkillers."

"It's not the painkillers I'm worried about. He talks about that truck like it's a person. He just lost his oldest friend out there."

"I know," Zane said grimly.

"The pills will just make it worse. How many did he take, anyway?" Shannon asked as she rummaged in the refrigerator. She certainly behaved like she'd been there before. Zane had to force himself not to wonder how long it had been. He'd never heard Ty speak of her, and he'd never seen her before.

She let the door swing shut as she moved back toward Zane with a bottle of beer and a can of soda.

"I didn't see him take the pill. After the shape he was in last night, I'd say he took a whole one today, which makes me think I should smack him upside the head," Zane rambled, accepting the Dr Pepper with a quiet thank-you as he thought about how sick Ty would be tomorrow.

Shannon laughed at him quietly and sat down opposite him. "You two are funny," she commented with a shake of her head.

Zane blinked and focused on her, thinking back over what he'd just said and deeming it safe. "Why do you say that?"

"I mean, don't take offense or anything," she said quickly, keeping her voice down as Elaina snored beside her. "You just don't take any of his bull. And seeing him today, he obviously trusts you. It's just . . . unusual to see him show that much real emotion around anyone."

Zane studied her for a long moment before relaxing back into the chair. "Well. We've been through a lot together."

"So I hear," she acknowledged with a slow nod. She licked her lower lip and looked down at the rug, tapping her finger on her beer bottle uneasily, as if she'd run out of things to say and couldn't seem to decide on a safe new topic.

Zane resisted the urge to smile. She wasn't a field agent; she was too easy to read. "And what have you heard?" he prompted, curious about her. "I'm guessing you're assigned here at the Baltimore office, but I've not seen you before today." He gave her an honest grin. "I'd have remembered."

She snorted at him and smiled wryly. "You can't charm me, Agent Garrett," she warned, pointing upward to where they could hear Ty moving around. "I've been baptized by fire."

"Please, call me Zane," he requested. He was starting to see why Ty had been drawn to her. Not only was she attractive, she was smart and straightforward.

She smiled more and nodded in thanks, then looked down at her hands as she played with the peeling label of her beer. "I'm an analyst focusing on the Middle East. That's how I met Ty. A couple years ago I needed a native speaker for a recording, and someone pointed me to him for help."

Zane continued to watch her. "Elaina told me you and Ty used to date." He glanced up at the ceiling again as he heard the water turn on in the shower upstairs.

She cleared her throat and nodded, gazing at her daughter before looking at Zane. "We were together for a few months. Nothing really serious, more . . ." She shrugged and shook her head, searching for the right words. "Like duct tape on a window. You know it'll fall apart eventually, but at least you can make interesting patterns in the meantime."

Zane laughed softly. "That's an odd description."

"But apt, isn't it? With Ty? I don't mean it as an insult. He was good to me. He still is. We parted on good terms. And he was like a godsend for Elaina when she really needed someone. He still makes an effort to spend time with her when he can. He's just not the type you bring home to Mom, but he's a good guy," she asserted with a self-conscious laugh.

"One of the best I've met." Zane looked over Elaina and thought about Ty's family. "I'm not surprised he spends time with her. She's adorable."

"Thank you," Shannon said with a smile. The water turned off upstairs with a heavy clank, and she glanced upward. She looked back at Zane, and her smile faltered.

Zane shook his head, wondering what had her anxious. Then it occurred to him. She was waiting for him to excuse himself. "Ah, I don't live far, but it's pretty cold to walk it. I can't leave until I call a cab," he said, hinting at leaving to give her time with Ty. Now to see if she'd take it.

She began shaking her head quickly. "No, there's no need for that, I can take you home. I just . . . he really shouldn't be alone tonight. But . . ." She stopped and held her breath for a heartbeat before letting it out in an irritated rush as she smiled and laughed at herself. "When he's all pitiful and drugged like this, I just really shouldn't be around him," she admitted as she blushed furiously. "Could you maybe stay with him?"

Zane didn't even try to hide the grin. Yeah, she was spunky. "Well, that being the case, yes, if you can run me to my truck so we're not stranded." He shrugged and took a drink from the half-empty can in his hand.

"Of course," she agreed gratefully.

They could hear Ty moving around upstairs again, which was an altogether good thing, since he'd been practically catatonic earlier. A few moments later, he thumped heavily down the stairs and padded barefoot into the living room, hair still damp and mussed. He wore a pair of sweatpants and a thin, faded T-shirt that had once had writing on it, and he'd taken the time to tape up his fingers after the shower. He looked awful, like someone had just put his puppy on a spit roast. He glanced at them both sheepishly as he joined them, but then he waved a hand at Shannon's beer and snorted.

"Make yourself at home, sweetheart," he joked quietly.

Shannon huffed back at him. "At least it's real beer and not hard lemonade."

"He's probably got that too," Zane commented before draining his soda can. He pointed at Ty. "But none for you at all."

"What's wrong with hard lemonade?" Ty asked, clearly offended.

Shannon laughed as she stood and set the bottle on the table beside the couch. "Are you okay?"

Ty shrugged uncomfortably, obviously searching for an answer that was somewhat honest. Zane looked between the two, deciding it would be best if he stayed out of this conversation. He'd have his own version with Ty later.

"Well," Shannon murmured, obviously knowing Ty well enough to know that he wasn't okay. She stepped closer and hugged him tight. "I'm going to take Zane back to get his truck, okay? He's going to stay with you tonight to make sure you don't throw yourself off the balcony."

Zane stood and moved away, giving them some space, wondering if Ty was feeling as awkward as he was. Zane had never met one of Ty's old girlfriends. He hadn't realized Ty *had* old girlfriends.

Ty merely nodded as she let him go. He made an effort to give her a smile, but his heart obviously wasn't in keeping up a façade. It was interesting that he didn't seem to feel the need to bother with her.

Shannon retrieved her purse from the kitchen counter, and Ty glanced over at Zane and met his eyes. Zane tipped his head to the side in question, raising one brow. Ty responded with a helpless gesture that wasn't quite identifiable, other than to say he was indeed uncomfortable and probably heartbroken.

Ty cleared his throat and stepped over to the couch where Elaina still slept peacefully, and he bent and gathered her carefully in his arms before easily lifting her. She murmured sleepily and snuggled up against his shoulder.

"Let's get you to the car," he said, and Shannon watched them with a sad smile as Ty carried the girl toward the door.

She looked to Zane. "Ready?"

Zane nodded, watching Ty closely, but he figured he had to trust Ty to know if he'd trust himself enough to carry the little girl. Seeing him with her, so careful, almost loving . . . it was a totally different side of Ty, even from what Zane saw in him, and he doubted he would ever see all the sides of the man he called his lover.

Ty sat in his living room with all the lights off and the blinds drawn, staring at the outlines of the furniture in the dark. His head was pounding, but it was from anger and anguish more than the pill he'd taken several hours ago.

Not only was someone trying to kill as many Feds, cops, firemen, EMTs, and civil servants as they could, they were setting bombs in public places where anyone could stumble over them.

And they had bombed his Bronco.

Ty closed his eyes as a wave of nausea passed through him. He knew it was silly to be sitting in the dark mourning a vehicle, but he didn't care. That Bronco had been part of him. He'd had her for half his life. Rescued her from the scrap yard and rebuilt every piece of her with his own two hands. Why the bomb had gone off when it did was anyone's guess, but Ty firmly believed the Bronco had done it—no matter how silly that sounded. She had been a loyal companion, and now she had taken the hit for him. Thrown herself on the grenade.

He knew he had tears streaming down his face, but he didn't care. She *deserved* to be mourned.

The scratch of the key in the lock of the front door didn't even faze him. Zane entered in a splash of sunlight and a rush of cold air, quiet besides a rustling of plastic and paper. He closed and locked the door behind him and stayed in place. Probably letting his eyes adjust to the dark.

"I brought some lunch."

"Ugh," Ty responded automatically as the thought of food made his stomach protest.

"Yeah, I figured that would be your reaction." Zane's voice held a hint of amusement. "So I got chicken, mashed potatoes, and biscuits. Plain stuff to settle your stomach." He started moving toward the kitchen bar.

Ty swallowed heavily and watched him go, trying to think of something to say that didn't involve food, bombs, cars, women, or him sitting there by himself in the dark and wiping tears off his face. He watched Zane set a couple of bags on the bar along with his keys, wallet, and badge. After turning on the small work light under the microwave, he came out of his heavy leather jacket, and his gun joined the pile. Then he turned and leaned back against the bar, hands in his pockets, looking toward his partner.

"Vicodin worn off?"

"Oh yeah," Ty answered as his stomach flip-flopped and nerves inexplicably assaulted him. He didn't know why he was nervous. Hell, he hadn't even done anything wrong this time. Much.

Zane watched him for a long moment before walking over and standing in front of him. "Can I get you anything?" He sounded—and looked—honestly concerned.

Ty looked up at him as the vise around his chest eased some. He smiled wanly and reached out to slide his fingers against the back of Zane's hand.

Zane squatted down in front of him, catching his hand and lifting it to kiss his knuckles. He sighed. "I'm sorry, baby. I hate that you're hurting," he added quietly.

The words hit that now-familiar chord in Ty's chest that made it twist and tighten. He shook his head to rid himself of the painful feeling that the attack and subsequent loss had caused and reached out to pat Zane's cheek. "I'm okay. I'll wake up in the morning ready for revenge, and it'll all go back to normal."

The grunt Zane gave in response didn't sound too sure, but he didn't comment. He turned his face to kiss Ty's palm before shifting his weight to stand. "C'mon. At least eat some mashed potatoes for me." He pulled at Ty's hand gently. "Then we'll go to bed, watch movies, and be lazy the rest of the day."

"Okay," Ty said suspiciously as he stood. He knew Zane well enough to know when he was keeping something from him. But he also knew Zane would come out with it in his own sweet time and not before, unless Ty dug hard for it. And he didn't want to dig. He just wanted to sit and cry and have the day be over. "Can we just skip food and go to bed?"

The lines of Zane's face softened visibly. "Yeah. I'll put the food in the fridge. You go on upstairs. I'll bring some water."

Ty nodded as he moved past Zane toward the steps in the center of the narrow row house. He let his hand slide down Zane's forearm and across his belly as he went, then put his head down and climbed to the darkened bedroom on the second floor. He supposed it was normal to feel like something was amiss after nearly being blown up and then watching your oldest companion and most beloved possession go up in smoke as people around you filmed it. Not to mention the fact that he was now officially a target. He'd become the poster child for shit that needed exploding in Baltimore.

It was only a few minutes before he heard Zane's footsteps on the stairs, and then Zane appeared in the doorway, small duffel in one hand, gun in the other, two bottles of water in the crook of his arm. The gun and bottles went on the nightstand, the duffel on the floor next to the dresser. He probably had more clothes stashed in Ty's spare room now than he had at his own apartment. Ty often wondered how it would go down if Zane chickened out and ended it. Would he get to throw all of Zane's shit off the balcony and make a scene? That was really the only thing about the end he looked forward to.

He sat on the bed, frowning at Zane's shoes as he thought about it. Then the mattress dipped next to him.

"Thinking awfully hard for someone who was blitzed on painkillers all morning." It was a gentle tease.

"Don't ever let me take another one of those things." He knew he'd need one in the morning, of course.

"If that's what you want, all right. You can stick to Tylenol and beer," Zane replied.

Ty reached out and patted Zane's knee, letting his hand rest there as he finally forced himself to look up and meet Zane's eyes. "Thank you for believing me today," he said roughly. "No one else did."

"I trust you," Zane said simply.

Ty's hand tightened for a moment, and then he looked away and let his fingers slide off Zane's knee.

"Ty, I . . ." Zane's voice trailed off, and he took a shaky breath before trying again. "How about you lie down? You look like you're about to fall asleep sitting there."

"Yeah," Ty agreed sedately. He pushed himself back and rolled into the middle of the bed, moving the sheets around and kicking them to the bottom of the bed. "What's on your mind, Zane?"

Zane leaned back on one hand as he turned to look at Ty. His eyes told Ty he didn't plan on answering. Ty let his hand fall to the side, his palm landing against Zane's back just under the shirt. Zane gave him a half smile over his shoulder before pulling his shirt over his head, exposing his scarred back to the light of the lamp in the corner. He got up, kicked out of his shoes and jeans, and was soon crawling into the bed next to Ty in just briefs.

Ty reached out and let his forearm fall across Zane's chest, then turned and slid his other arm around him, pulling him closer and curling against him gratefully. Zane settled on his side, closing his arms around Ty and sighing. Ty felt the words on his tongue and consciously held his breath, warding them off. He knew Zane was uncomfortable with the words "I love you," though he didn't exactly understand why. It wouldn't do either of them to beat it into the ground. Ty knew Zane loved him, in his own way.

And he hoped Zane knew the only thing Ty had loved longer than him was that Bronco.

It felt like Ty was awake for a long time before his mind actually realized it. He was aware of being in bed. He was aware of the very early morning sunlight hitting his face. He was aware of his entire body being sore and borderline painful. He was aware of a solid ache in his heart that was shaped like a green and tan Ford Bronco.

He just couldn't seem to convince himself to move or open his eyes. But finally, he turned his head and cracked an eye open with a soft groan.

Zane lay on his side next to him, his hand extended to rest on Ty's chest. He looked relaxed and deeply asleep, though Ty knew better. Zane still slept lightly, albeit better the few nights a week they slept together.

Ty remained still for a long time, trying to piece together yesterday and trying to decide just how badly he hurt this morning. He felt like he'd been hit by a tank. Again.

Finally, he had to shift and roll. He gasped in surprise as he did so, not expecting the stabbing pain in his side.

Zane's eyes snapped open, and he pushed himself up on one elbow. "Careful, you're bruised as hell."

"Sorry," Ty gasped as he tried to decide which way to move. Because after he settled, he wasn't going to move again. Ever.

"Need to get up? Might be a good idea. I bet you're stiff."

Ty grunted and nodded, pushing himself up carefully. He looked at the tape on his fingers and grimaced as he sat up fully. Zane stayed where he was, watching silently. He was still warm and sleepy, and he looked it too.

"Sorry I woke you," Ty offered pitifully as soon as he was sitting. Zane shrugged and slid back down, pulling his pillow to his chest. "Got any Tylenol?" Ty asked him with a wince. He rubbed gingerly at his ribs.

"Yeah. I've not flushed the Vicodin yet, if you want it," Zane said quietly.

Ty turned and looked at Zane in surprise. Zane raised one brow but didn't say anything else. Ty gave him a grunt and gingerly laid himself back down. He reached out wordlessly with his good hand and slid his fingers into Zane's as he closed his eyes.

Zane remained still after curling his hand around Ty's, and a quiet minute passed before he took a deep breath and let it out loudly before sitting up. "I'm going to get you something. You have to be hurting pretty bad."

Ty didn't argue. He'd had so much worse than this, but in recent years his motto had become something like "why hurt when you don't have to?" He opened his eyes and watched Zane appreciatively but didn't try to sit up again.

Zane smiled, apparently not surprised by the response. "I'll be back." He walked out of the bedroom, disappearing down the hall. When he came back, he set the tiny envelope in Ty's lap before reaching for a bottle of water from the nightstand and offering it to him.

Ty looked at the packet of Vicodin in distaste as he accepted the bottle. "Think it would hurt me any more to take another one?" he asked uncertainly.

"Are you planning on going anywhere? It is Monday, you know," Zane said. "You might at least consider going into work, although . . ." He shook his head as he looked over all the bruises.

"I have to go into work. I'll catch all sorts of shit if I call in."

Zane shrugged. "Your choice. You can man up, go to work, and be miserable all day, or you can stay here, chill out, and deal with people's shit tomorrow." He started pulling clothes out of the closet. "You're probably all over the news anyway. Again."

Ty sighed and started trying to get out of bed. "When you put it that way," he muttered as he stood up.

Zane picked his duffel up and tossed it on the bed. Then he stopped and looked up at Ty. "Would you at least take the Tylenol? Because you look like shit and it hurts watching you."

Ty cocked his head and grimaced again. "Do I look too bad to go in?" he asked with real concern. "I mean from the drugs, not the bruises." He would be damned if word got around that he was hungover or high this morning, not after the scene he'd made yesterday.

Zane shook his head. "No, you just look like you're really in significant pain. Of course, other people might not recognize that on you and think you're being your normal grumpy self."

"I can deal with that," Ty said with a satisfied nod. He winced once Zane turned away from him and headed for the spare bedroom, where a couple of Zane's suits hung in the closet. "Wear the gray one," he called out on impulse, hoping Zane would do it just to humor him. He loved Zane in that charcoal suit—it made his dark coloring that much more striking. Zane might argue against being pretty, but he was wrong.

"Yeah, fine," Zane called back.

Ty smiled, then sighed as he looked at the pills in his hand. Opening the flap on the packet, he shook the tablets out into his hand and contemplated them sourly. Zane came back down the hall just as he popped a pill and chased it with a few gulps of water.

"Guess I'm driving, then," Zane observed before he turned into the bathroom.

"That's not funny, Zane," Ty shot back at him.

"Wasn't meant to be, Ty."

They got dressed quickly. Ty gave Zane one of his better ties to wear because the one Zane had left there had been ripped off at some point and was mangled beyond repair. Ty preferred the narrower style of ties, and though it looked good on Zane, people might notice it wasn't his. They'd have to deal with it, though. What with all the PR hype, the Bureau had cracked down on the dress code; ties were a must in the office.

Ty stepped out into the hallway carrying his shoes under one arm and picking at the medical tape on his fingers. He pulled it off carefully to check his finger. The joints were blue and swollen, and it hurt like hell to move it. He was beginning to suspect it actually hadn't been fixed properly.

He sighed and balled up the tape. He'd have to raid the first aid kit when he got to the office.

"What do you usually do for breakfast?" he asked Zane in a loud voice. He realized Zane had never actually stayed here for the morning before work. On the weeknights he stayed over, he got up early and went back to his apartment to get ready for work while Ty went for his morning run, and then they met up at the office. It was an odd feeling, having Zane here. Kind of nice.

Zane appeared in his bedroom doorway, working on his tie. "There's a good bakery and deli on the way to the office from my place. I stop and get coffee, at least." He fussed with the knot and then pulled the ends to loosen it and start over as he turned back into the room.

Ty moved toward Zane and reached out to grip his shoulder. Zane relaxed as Ty reached around him to take hold of the tie from behind. He had tried before, but the only way he could fix a tie was if he was wearing it. He tied the knot deftly with his arms wrapped around Zane, and the warmth of Zane allowing the simple action sank deep into him.

When he was done, he placed his hands flat on Zane's chest and hugged him, then backed away before the moment could get too saccharine.

"I'm going to need food or I'll get all . . . zingy," Ty told him with a frown as he turned away.

"That would go over well in the office," Zane said wryly. "I'd kind of like to see it."

Ty nodded and muttered wordlessly and headed for the stairs, thumping down to the living room to put on his shoes. It was going to be a long day.

Zane parked his truck on the curb next to a government-issue unmarked SUV. "Why don't you stay here? There's an extended team in there already; it's not like I'll be alone."

Ty nodded as he looked out at the array of Baltimore PD uniforms and FBI windbreakers already on the street. They had been called in to investigate a suspicious package reported at an upscale shopping area in the Inner Harbor. Patrons and employees clogged sidewalks that were being barricaded off—the building had already been evacuated as a precaution—and reporters elbowed their way through willy-nilly. A lot of reporters.

"Don't have to tell me twice," he muttered. The morning's brief zing from the Vicodin had worn off quickly, leaving him achy and nauseated and altogether miserable, just as Zane had predicted.

Zane unfastened his seatbelt and offered Ty a half smile. "Take it easy. I'll be back soon, and we'll get an early lunch and I'll take you home." He climbed out and shut the door, walking over to a group of agents as he tugged a matching navy-blue FBI windbreaker over his head. Ty belatedly thought he should have told Zane to put his vest on. He never wore the damn thing unless Ty nagged him about it.

Ty scooted down in his seat and put his sunglasses on so that no one would notice if he went to sleep sitting there. His stomach was unsettled, his head still pounded, and he felt . . . floaty. He was sure there was another word for it, but that was about as close as he could get to describing the feeling. It was entirely unpleasant. He probably should have called in and just stayed at home. On the plus side, his ribs didn't feel like they were about to snap anymore, so he might be able to flush the rest of those pills when he got home. And Michelle Clancy had taken one look at his finger that morning, grabbed his hand, and yanked the offending digit into place before he could scream for help. It had hurt like a son of a bitch, but now the pain had subsided to a dull throb, and he thought it might be okay.

He watched as Zane walked into the shopping complex with a mixed group of agents and cops, following the bomb-sniffing dogs, and then looked up at the face of the glass-walled building, trying to decide which part they were heading for and wondering why they were going up with the bomb techs at all. Protection detail, maybe? Backup for continued evac? If he remembered correctly, there was shopping on the second and third floors. He'd been in the food court a couple of times.

Ty groaned at the thought of food and shut his eyes. He should have just taken the Tylenol and bitched about being sore all day. If he started throwing up, his ribs would hurt again.

He unbuckled his seatbelt and slumped further in his seat, practically lying flat with his legs extended onto the driver's side dashboard. He watched the building idly, waiting for Zane to come back and drive him home, where he could wallow in misery for the rest of the day.

He zoned out for awhile, drifting in and out, but his eyes were open when all the windows on the far corner of the building's third floor blew out in an explosion that sent flames licking out of the casements.

Ty was moving and out of the truck, feet pounding on the concrete, before he realized what he was doing. He and other agents who'd been loitering around outside ran toward the building as the flames receded back into the windows and alarms began to blare. First through the doors, Ty took off toward the stairs with several others on his heels. He took the stairs two at a time, the other agents falling behind by the time he reached the third-story fire exit.

When Ty pushed through the door, it was face-first into a fine mist the sprinklers spit and sprayed over him, the water working to put out the flames. Smoke choked the shattered concourse; smoldering and dripping debris littered the once-shining marbled floors, and scorch marks blackened the walls.

"Garrett!" Ty called out as he covered his mouth and nose with his sleeve and moved into the cluttered space.

"Fire and rescue's on the way," an agent told him breathlessly as he came through the door behind Ty.

"How many we got up here?" Ty demanded.

"Ten, at least," the man answered, "not counting BPD." Ty began picking his way down the ruined hall, staying low and watching the ceiling for falling tiles. He heard a dog whining and followed the sound.

"Garrett!" he called out again before coughing.

Thick, ugly smoke billowed through the once-clear hall, drawn by shattered windows acting like a flue, making his eyes sting. Whole walls had been blown out of several ritzy boutiques, sending merchandise flying like the building was an ashy snow globe turned over and shaken violently. The blast pattern fanned so far out—all the way to the exterior walls in places—that it was impossible to tell where their people could have been. Then Ty found two agents in windbreakers leaning on each other, one limping heavily, struggling through the mess.

Ty grabbed one by the shoulder, looking them both over for obvious injuries. He could see a broken arm on one; the other appeared merely bruised and battered. "You okay?" he asked, raising his voice in anticipation of both men being nearly deaf from the concussion of the blast.

One glanced up and nodded, although he grimaced. "Two storefronts that way," he said hoarsely as he pointed. "Some of our guys are down."

Ty took off the way the agent had pointed, moving over the debris with less care than he should have. He clambered over a grisly burnt and melted mannequin and half a wall of shredded clothes blown out of one of the stores. At the sound of a sharp crack, he looked down to see a now-crunched pair of aviator sunglasses. More glass from the storefronts covered the floor like scattered diamonds glinting in the rain still coming down from what sprinklers were intact. Getting around a collapsed metal gate took precious seconds he didn't have, and then he stumbled upon a group of agents with various injuries, some worse than others. A dog hunched over its master, whining mournfully and periodically pacing away as if trying to decide whether to go for help or stay.

An agent turned and waved Ty over. "We need EMTs," the man said, his voice overloud. He pointed down at the woman in an FBI windbreaker. She grimaced, the soot streaks on her face emphasizing how she was white with pain, holding onto her broken leg while another agent tried to splint it to hold it still.

Ty took out his phone, though he was certain paramedics had already been called and were right behind him. He moved toward them as he made the call anyway. Why hadn't he done that first? Or at least told someone else to do it? He wasn't thinking clearly.

"How many?" Ty asked the man, who seemed unharmed.

"Four down here, two unaccounted for. They were in the store, checking the back rooms." The man pointed to a couple of agents frantically laboring to push aside burning debris where some interior walls had collapsed in. "They were closer to it," he said, dread clear in his voice.

Ty moved to help and ended up ordering one of them to head toward the exit because his head was split open and bleeding.

His training was kicking in, so he wasn't panicking about Zane just yet. He knew that later, when the adrenaline wore off, he would be sick no matter what happened.

They moved chunks of plaster and torn wood, tossing them to the side as they dug around. "Garrett!" Ty called again as soon as they'd made a dent in it. Later, he wouldn't remember how much time had passed.

Some of the plasterboard on the floor shifted further in, and the other guy digging yanked it off to reveal an unconscious agent with terrible burns on her face and hands. He knelt down and checked her neck and back, then swung her into his arms before nodding at Ty to keep going, then heading out of the ruined storefront.

Ty stuck his head into the hole they'd made, but there was nothing else in there but more plaster and cement block.

"Fuck," Ty breathed as he pulled back out and looked around a little wildly. Out in the concourse, the way he had come, he could see two firemen in their bulky yellow suits working their way toward him. It had been at least six minutes, then, counting on standard response time. It seemed like it had been so much longer. A lifetime longer. Ty turned and looked deeper into the store filled with dull smoke and shifting shadows.

"Garrett!" he yelled as he headed that way. It was dark where the lights had all been blown out, and most of the debris was unidentifiable. He ducked under a fallen ceiling support, forced to crawl across the soaked carpet to get under it.

The rubble blocked so much of the floor that he had to climb on it rather than pushing it aside. As he got closer to the back, the smoke cleared, blown by a cold breeze from the outside. And then he saw it: a bright splotch of red against a charred gray wall. The blood streaked in vertical lines like someone had tried to wipe it down the wall, and a thick, scorch-marked metal door lay at an angle under it, blocking the corner.

But one long leg ending in a familiar dress shoe extended out of the mess of splintered particle board into what used to be the entrance to the storeroom.

"Zane," Ty gasped as the feeling in his entire body seeped away. He moved as fast as he could, batting away the light pieces of wallboard and shoving the still-hot metal door over and out of the way. Ty knelt beside him. "Zane?" he whispered. His voice wavered as he ran his hand over Zane's face.

He wasn't cut up or burned; the metal door had saved him from the explosion. One shoe was scorched, but even the laces were still intact. He didn't look like he was injured at all, other than the garish bloodstain on the wall behind him from his impact and slide to the floor under the door that had shielded him from the blast.

But Zane didn't move, didn't twitch, didn't open his eyes when Ty tapped his cheek. Nothing.

Ty's stomach turned. He pressed his fingers to Zane's neck, feeling for a pulse. His other hand ran through Zane's hair as he did so.

The pulse was there. Ty gasped in relief, leaned down, and pressed his lips to Zane's forehead, heedless of who might see, and then he looked back into the store for help. He knew without a doubt he couldn't carry Zane out of there.

"Hey!" he called as he saw a beam of light playing through the swirling smoke. "Man down!" he called to the fireman desperately.

As the fireman came closer, hacking his way through the wreckage to clear a path for his retreat, Ty recognized him just by his size.

"I could kiss you, man," he told the large black man he knew only as Tank. The man handed his axe to the other fireman and knelt down at Zane's other side.

"Not on a first date," Tank answered. He checked Zane over quickly for injuries, then hefted him onto his thick shoulders with a grunt. "You hurt?" he asked. Ty shook his head. "Shake a leg, then, Bulldog. Building's not stable," he said as he turned and carried Zane into the smoke.

Ty stood there, unable to make himself move. His entire body shook as he watched them disappear.

The other fireman gripped his arm. "Come on. We gotta get out of here," he said. "The ceiling's starting to come down."

Ty nodded and forced his feet to move. He followed the man along the path Tank had cut through the devastation.

By the time he got out of the building—wet, filthy, half-blind, and coughing—the ambulances had cleared out and the firemen were trying to put out what was left of the flames.

What remained were the television cameras. Reporters saw him as he emerged, and Ty could see the recognition sweep through them as he wiped the soot off his face. They began shouting questions over the barrier that had been hastily set up.

Ty ignored them and stalked toward the milling emergency workers.

"Hey," Ty called out to a young agent in a pristine windbreaker standing and staring at the building. The kid looked at him with wide eyes, apparently recognizing him. Ty had earned a reputation with the rookies, not necessarily by deed but through word of mouth. They were all too terrified of him to realize most of the stories were exaggerated. Right now Ty didn't care. "Where'd they take the wounded?" he demanded.

"Uh, I—"

"Where?" Ty shouted angrily. "UMMC," the kid stammered.

"You're driving," Ty told him as he pointed at Zane's truck.

CHAPTER SIX

I t felt like it took forever to get through traffic to the University of Maryland Medical Center, even though it wasn't even a mile away from the Inner Harbor. On the ride there, Ty sat tense and silent in the seat next to the rookie he didn't know and didn't give a shit about right then. When they arrived, Ty tersely told the kid to head back to the office and that he'd pick up the keys later. Despite the rookie's stunned gape, Ty jogged inside the ER without a glance back.

He was at the information desk asking for Zane's location and status when he heard a familiar voice behind him.

"Grady, I'm glad to see you." McCoy stood behind him, looking somber and worn.

Ty turned in surprise, but any formal greetings to his immediate superior were lost on him. "Have you seen him, Mac? Is he okay?"

McCoy slid his hands into his pants pockets and tipped his head to one side before answering in a tired voice, "I don't know anything yet. I just got here. Where were you during all of this?"

"I was in the truck, sick from a Vicodin I took this morning," Ty answered immediately. It didn't even cross his mind to gloss it over.

McCoy's eyebrow jumped, but he didn't otherwise comment. "I've got six agents in this hospital tonight, Grady. Are you going to be able to work?" he asked bluntly.

Ty nodded jerkily. McCoy just looked at him, not breaking eye contact. "I'll do whatever you need," Ty insisted in a hoarse voice.

McCoy nodded slowly. "For right now, I need you to go home." He raised a hand when Ty opened his mouth to question him. "Seriously. You look like you just got spit out by a giant drooling dog, and I've got to muster together a group to investigate what happened."

Ty looked down at himself in consternation. He didn't look *that* bad. "But I can help—"

"Not when you're being targeted. I can't afford to put a team on you to protect you, so I want you off the radar. This may have been a second attempt, for all we know." He turned his chin as an agent appeared at his elbow and murmured in his ear. McCoy turned his eyes back to Ty. "All right. They're asking for you in the Shock Trauma Center. Fifth floor. Get me a status report, then go the hell home. Do not sit here with Garrett and make yourself *and* him a target, understood?"

"Yes, sir," Ty said mutinously. "Anything else?" He wanted to dart to the elevator and get up there as fast as he could, but he had to at least pretend he still gave a shit about the case.

"Go on," McCoy answered, nodding his head toward the elevator. Then he started talking with the other agent, who held an armful of file folders.

Ty's mind whirred the entire ride up the elevator, throwing all sorts of grim scenarios at him that he tried hard to ignore. He'd no sooner gotten to the nurses' station than he heard his name again.

"Special Agent Grady?"

Ty turned to meet the doctor who'd called his name, abject terror clogging his throat.

The doctor was a younger man despite his nearly white hair, and he projected an air of knowledge and experience around him. "I'm Dr. Jameson," he said, holding out his hand. "An agent downstairs called up to say you were on your way."

Ty shook his hand automatically, not bothering to try to be polite.

"Special Agent Garrett has you listed as his emergency contact. Does he have any family? Wife or children?" Jameson asked, his voice dropping to a tone that was probably supposed to be soothing.

Ty's mouth went completely dry, and he had to work just to swallow hard enough to get words out. "He has family in Texas," he said hoarsely.

The doctor nodded. "His next of kin will need to be notified, of course."

Ty stared at the man, trying to take in what he was implying as he felt tunnel vision threatening. It just wasn't making it through. He opened his mouth to respond but couldn't manage it.

"Special Agent Grady? Are you all right?" Jameson asked in concern. "I was told you weren't injured. Your partner will need someone with him until his family can arrive."

Ty closed his eyes and cocked his head to one side, trying to maintain control for just a little while longer. "You saying he's alive?" he managed to ask shakily.

Jameson's jaw dropped. It would have been comical under other circumstances. "I'm so sorry—I thought you'd already been informed. Special Agent Garrett is in serious but stable condition."

Ty took a deep breath and balled his hand into a fist, telling himself that throttling the doctor would get him nothing but jail time. "Can I see him?" he asked through gritted teeth, glaring at the doctor dangerously.

"Of course," the doctor said immediately, apparently realizing how upset Ty was. "This way." He turned and led the way, punching in an access code at a secure door, which he held open for Ty before leading him through a maze of bays to one only dimly lit. The doctor stopped at the entrance by the glass door. "You should have some time. We're taking him for a CT scan soon."

Ty stood at the doorway, looking in at an all-too-familiar scene. They were going to have to make a deal about staying out of hospitals for a while. It was beginning to wear on his nerves.

"Thank you," he forced out to the doctor before he moved into the darkened bay.

"He has a concussion," Jameson said. "We don't know how serious yet. He hasn't woken up, but the swelling inside his skull is already subsiding. I think he'll be okay."

"You *think* a lot of things, Doctor," Ty said coldly without looking away from the bed. "What do you know?"

Jameson spoke after an awkward pause. "Special Agent Garrett has a hell of a hard head," he said frankly. "I expected several skull fractures, but I only found bruising and a split scalp that we stitched up. As it is, his brain got rattled. We're focusing on trying to reduce the swelling, and my hope is that we won't find any internal bleeding.

There's no evidence of any so far. That doesn't rule out other injuries or blood clots. But overall? Your partner is a very, very lucky man." With that, the doctor nodded uncomfortably when Ty glanced at him, and he left.

Ty watched him go, then looked back down at Zane with a sickening lurch of his stomach. He moved closer to the bed and leaned over him, looking at him closely. "We've done this before, Zane," he whispered to his partner. "You need to be more creative with your near- death experiences."

There was no reply. Zane lay absolutely still, the rise and fall of his chest only barely visible under the cotton gown and sheet. He was hooked up to three different IVs, and his head was wrapped in enough gauze to make a turban.

Ty gave a sniff and looked up into Zane's face again. "Fine, copycat. Don't talk to me, then. I'm not leaving," he said stubbornly as he dragged the heavy chair over from the corner of the bay and sat next to the bed. He crossed his arms over his chest and resolved to sit there until Zane woke, McCoy's orders be damned.

He was still sitting there when two orderlies arrived almost an hour later to take Zane to the CT scan.

Ty stood to the side and watched them prepare Zane to be moved. He knew they wouldn't let him go along, even if he flashed his badge around. He smelled of smoke, and his suit was damp and dirty and probably ruined. His entire body ached from head to toe, and he couldn't decipher which injuries had come from his run-in with Tank on the softball field and which ones had come from his foolhardy headlong search through the bomb debris.

He also noticed as he glanced at his reflection in the stainless steel paper towel dispenser that his face was smudged with smoke and dirt.

McCoy had been right: he looked like hell. It would do Zane no good if he woke up to find Ty sitting there looking like this.

He cleared his throat and touched one of the orderlies on the arm to get his attention. "If he wakes up, will you tell him his partner will be back?" he requested in a hoarse voice.

The orderly glanced at him, looked him up and down, and then smiled. "Sure thing."

"Thank you," Ty murmured as he gave Zane one more glance and then went to call himself a cab.

"It was him!" Pierce shouted, eyes bright with excitement.

Graham raised an eyebrow, more and more convinced that his buddy was losing his mind.

"Who was him?"

"That asshole FBI agent from the aquarium! He made me drive him to the hospital!"

"What'd he do, hold a gun to your head?" Ross asked drily.

"No," Pierce answered, sounding more excited than angry. "He just pointed at me and told me I was going to do it, and I had like this physical response where I had to do what he told me to! It was awesome!"

Graham frowned. "That doesn't sound awesome."

Hannah rolled her eyes at them all. She was beginning to grow tired of the game; Graham could tell from the constant sighs she emitted lately. Soon she'd be back under a football player from school.

"The FBI guy from TV was hot. He could tell me to do anything," she told them as she counted out stacks of money from their last robbery.

"So why is this exciting?" Graham asked, ignoring her comment. Pierce grinned manically and dug out a pair of keys from his pocket, holding them up and letting them dangle. "Because he left his keys with me."

"That was kind of stupid of him, but I still don't get it."

"He's a fucking monster—he's got to be like six and half feet tall and eats nothing but steroids and babies."

"Dude."

"He's like Moby Dick and I'm Captain Ahab," Pierce continued with relish.

"Third-year AP English," Hannah grumbled. Graham frowned. "Did you finish that book?"

"No, why?" Pierce answered distractedly.

"No reason."

Pierce nodded, looking smug. "I'm gonna kill him," Pierce said as his eyes lost focus.

"Wait, what?" Hannah exclaimed, sounding just as alarmed as Graham was.

"Come on. We've got work to do," Pierce said to Ross, and the two of them left together, strutting out of Graham's kitchen.

Graham and Hannah shared a look. Graham wasn't sure when it happened, but somewhere along the line, the bombings had become more important to Pierce than the robberies. And now he wanted to kill someone?

Graham frowned as Hannah bit her lip and looked away. Neither of them had the nerve to buck Pierce, and they both knew it.

When Ty returned less than an hour later, just after the lunch rush, he proceeded immediately up to the fifth floor, punched in the code he'd seen the doctor enter to get access to the secure area, and walked straight to Zane's bay, hoping he'd be back from the scan. The last time Ty had suffered holding still for one of the damn things, it had only been about ten minutes, all told.

When Ty arrived, there were two doctors—neither Dr. Jameson—and a nurse already in the bay.

He hung back, practically vibrating with the need to get information and see how Zane was doing. Then he saw Zane slowly turn his head away from the door toward one of the doctors, who was talking to him in low tones. Zane was *awake*.

Ty held his breath and stepped into the bay. The nurse must have seen the movement out of the corner of her eye, because she turned to look at him in alarm.

The doctor turned as well. "And you are . . .?"

Ty merely flipped his badge open to show it to the doctor. He could be an officious ass too.

The doctor wasn't impressed. "Unless you're Special Agent Garrett's family, you shouldn't be here, sir. I've been informed of no guard assignment."

"Consider yourself informed," Ty said to him in a low voice. "I must insist—"

"Ty?"

At Zane's soft word, the doctors and nurse turned back to their patient. Ty stepped closer to the bed, looking at Zane with a mixture of relief and guilt. "Hey," he responded weakly.

Zane's hand shifted and his chin turned, but he just blinked lazily and stared out into the bay with unfocused eyes. "You okay? You were in the truck," he said. The words were so garbled it took Ty a few beats to decipher them.

"Yeah," Ty answered carefully as he studied Zane. He knew that look. It took him a long moment for it to register, but he knew it. It was the same one his great-grandmother had always had when he'd been little, staring past him as she listened to the sound of his voice. "You can't see," he blurted.

"Excuse me," one of the doctors interrupted. "Special Agent Garrett, is this man okay to stay with you? Do you know him?"

Zane blinked slowly. "He's my partner," he said, the words coming out a little more clearly, though still labored. "Tell him. He was in the truck."

"Tell me, my ass. He can't see," Ty grunted to the doctor as he pointed at Zane accusingly.

The second doctor spoke. "You are correct, Agent . . .?"

"Grady," Ty told the man in annoyance. "Why can't he see?"

"Ty," Zane said softly, the tone clear, asking Ty to calm down and let the doctors explain.

The first doctor flipped a page on the chart. "As we were just explaining to Agent Garrett, there was a lot of swelling from the blow to the head. While most of it has subsided and we've confirmed there is no further internal bleeding, we think there was enough to form a few blood clots. We started him on the appropriate drugs, and in a couple of days, we'll run another CT scan to determine the extent of the damage."

"The clots are very near the optic nerves, possibly even inside them," the second doctor said. "That's why he can't see."

Ty stared at them, trying to decide if he was justified in hitting one or both of them. He didn't suppose he was. "Clots," he repeated. "So it's not . . . permanent, right? It can be fixed?"

"We chose a very successful drug for dissolving clots," the first doctor said. "Once we have a chance to repeat the CT scan and run a retinal exam, we'll have a better idea, but I would say it's only temporary and won't require surgery to resolve it."

Through this conversation, the nurse was changing out an IV, and Zane didn't even flinch as she set in another port. "Can I get you anything, Mr. Garrett?" she asked. "Are you in any pain?"

"Headache. I'll live," Zane slurred.

"Well, Agent Garrett, try to get some rest," the first doctor said. "You may find it easier to just keep your eyes shut. I hesitate to cover them until we know more about your condition. We'll be back to evaluate you in a few hours." With that, the two doctors nodded at Ty and left.

The nurse slid the call button cord inside the curve of Zane's arm. "If you need anything, just buzz, and I'll come running. My name's Bree." Then she left them alone.

Ty stood in place, uncertain of what to do. He couldn't fight the feeling that this was all his fault somehow. If he'd just gone in with them . . .

"Stop it," Zane murmured.

"What?" Ty asked defensively.

Zane turned his face toward Ty. "Stop beating yourself up. Are you okay? You were in the truck," he repeated for the third time, his voice low and exhausted.

"You really do have a concussion, huh," Ty murmured. The heavy chair he'd sat in earlier had been put back in its corner, so he moved to the bed instead and perched on the edge. "I'm sorry," he offered lamely. "I should have been in there with you."

Zane shifted his hand against Ty's thigh. "Both'd be here." His tone conveyed that it would be a bad thing.

Ty didn't respond other than to lower his head and look at Zane's hand. "Does it hurt?" he finally asked.

Zane grunted. "Headache. I'll live."

Ty would have smiled at the absurd repetition, but he knew Zane couldn't help it after that hard of a knock on the head. He nodded silently, belatedly remembering that Zane couldn't see him. "You can't see anything?" he asked tentatively. "No shadows, nothing?"

Zane was silent for a long moment as he blinked his eyes over and over. "Nothing," he whispered.

Ty reached down and took his hand, squeezing it hard. McCoy had ordered him to go home, but what good was he there? On the other hand, Zane needed nothing but medical care, and Ty knew that when he was in the hospital himself, he hated having people with him. "What can I do?" he asked, feeling helpless and useless.

Zane licked his bottom lip and opened his eyes, turning his face toward Ty. "Don't leave me alone." His voice actually shook.

Ty looked at him worriedly, and he put his other hand on top of Zane's, holding it with both of his hands and letting his fingers slide up his arm. "I won't go anywhere," he promised.

Zane nodded; it was a jerky, uncomfortable motion. He squeezed his eyes shut as if it would help. "I'm a little rattled," he rasped.

Ty petted his arm ineffectually. He had no idea what else to do. "We're going to have to find a third wheel to take care of us when we get hurt," Ty suggested. "We're not very good at this."

"*Too* good. This is new," Zane said with a soft huff. "Headache."

"Hey, I prefer my run of unlikely finger injuries," Ty responded as he ran his thumb along Zane's wrist. "And it's not new, it's just more epic than what I did in New York."

Zane snorted and seemed to shrink into himself as the silence lengthened. "Sucks," he finally muttered.

"Think of it as . . . special training for your other senses," Ty instructed, faking cheerful.

Zane frowned and took a steadying breath. "If I could see you," he enunciated, "I would slug you."

"Must be my lucky day then," Ty responded wryly.

Zane opened and closed his fist between Ty's hands, flexing his fingers before letting them rest, curling around Ty's wrist. "What now?"

Ty opened his mouth to respond, trying to find either a joke or a silver lining or a nice whitewashed lie. But he could only manage a few soft sounds before closing his mouth again and shaking his head. "I don't know," he answered instead. "I guess we just wait it out."

"Wow," Zane murmured tiredly, head lolling back against the pillow. "You're scared shitless if that's the best you got."

Ty pressed his lips together and looked at Zane helplessly. He met Zane's eyes, knowing Zane couldn't see him. He was glad for it, though. Zane didn't need to see his fear. If he was this scared, he couldn't imagine how Zane was feeling.

Being completely in the dark had taken on a whole new meaning.

This wasn't just dark; it was pitch-black, no relief, no gray, no hint of light under a door, no bare twinkle of stars in the sky. It was utter nothing.

Each time Zane woke up from dozing—no real sleeping, the nurse insisted, waking him up every fifteen minutes—it was easier to think, and his first thought was always that when he opened his eyes, he'd be able to see. But then he did and . . . didn't.

If it weren't for being able to always hear something in the hospital room, he would have totally freaked out.

With a sigh, he shifted a little in the bed, very carefully, not sure if something somewhere would hurt when he moved. He heard Ty gasp suddenly and felt him jerk.

"What?" Ty asked in a hoarse, sleepy voice. Zane frowned. "Ty? Were you asleep?"

"I'm not sure," Ty answered in a voice that told Zane he had definitely been asleep and was still in the process of trying to remember where he was. Zane felt Ty's hand brush against his chest, as if making sure he was actually there and he wasn't dreaming. He raised his own hand to cover Ty's for a moment.

"Sounds like you were," Zane murmured. He shifted his eyes to look around even though there was nothing to see. "What time is it?"

"Late," Ty answered, his voice sounding as if he had turned away. "Can you . . . can you see anything?" he asked tentatively.

Zane shifted a little more onto his side, facing Ty, letting his cheek settle on the pillow. "No," he whispered. His fingers moved slightly on Ty's hand. While he'd never been touchy-feely, now that he couldn't see, touching was much more important to his state of mind. He wondered how long Ty would tolerate it.

"Damn," Ty sighed. He gave Zane's hand a squeeze and pulled away as he stood, just like Zane had known he would. "You need anything? I'm going to go find caffeine. Maybe some real food."

Zane resisted shaking his head slightly. It hurt and made him queasy. "No. Have you been here the whole time?"

"Yeah," Ty answered in a surprised voice. He almost sounded offended that Zane had asked. "Why?"

"Chill, okay?" Zane said with a sigh. "I figured you had, which means you've been here awhile without a break. When did you eat last?"

"Lunch," Ty answered as he moved away completely. "Want me to fi . . . doctor and see . . . get some food?" he mumbled, his voice going in and out of earshot. Zane thought he might be looking around the room for something or possibly putting a jacket on. He might have detected some rustling of fabric.

"Yeah," Zane said, swallowing on the hint of dread that hit him in the chest. He bit his lip and shifted more onto his side and pulled the pillow hard against his chest like he did at home. Damn, he hated this. And he hated even more being scared about it. He squeezed his eyes shut hard.

"What's wrong?" Ty asked as his voice moved closer again.

Zane reminded himself he was a grown man who'd faced all sorts of dangerous and really frightening challenges in his life and tried to relax, with only a bit of success. He cleared his throat. "You'll come back, right?" he finally asked. He winced. Damn, he sounded like a baby.

There was silence in response, but Zane could still feel Ty's presence beside his bed. Finally, Ty moved, and the denim of his jeans scraped softly. He reached out and put his hand on Zane's forehead. "It'll be okay," he assured him, then removed his hand.

Some of the tension melted, enough that Zane could breathe easily again. He nodded against the pillow. "Go on. I'll be here."

There was no response, no sound of Ty moving, but it felt like the warmth had left the room, so he knew Ty was gone. Zane's jaw clenched, and he pushed his face into the pillow. This blind shit had been easier to handle when he was mostly unconscious and unable to focus. With nothing else to do, he started listening, closing his eyes and really *listening*.

After the claustrophobic hell that was the hospital's crowded food court, Ty found himself rattled and unkempt as he made his way to the elevators. He didn't smile and nod at people as he passed by; he didn't even *see* the people he passed by.

He kept his head down, face set in a frown as he fretted over what needed to be done. He'd talked to his mom for at least half an hour as he'd waited in line in the café, trying to convince her that no one had died and that he and Zane both had all their parts intact. When he'd hung up, he'd told himself to appreciate the fact that she cared, remember it was out of love, be glad your mom is still around. Zen, Ty, Zen.

Then the thought that Zane had a mother had hit him like a truckload of panicking chickens and he'd needed to sit down. He'd lost his place in line. Fuck the line.

He was listed as Zane's emergency contact, which meant the only notifying of family was going to be done by *him*. The prospect of calling Zane's parents to tell them he was seriously injured, and oh, by the way, I'm your son's partner who let him go by himself into the building that blew up, nice to meet you, has he told you he likes cock?

Ty closed his eyes and shook his head, surprised to find himself riding the elevator up already.

He took in a deep breath and blew it out carefully. This was merely lack of sleep and possibly a little trauma getting to him. He'd be okay. Zane would be okay. It would all be okay.

"Okay," he said under his breath.

When he got to Zane's room, he was almost good again.

Then he saw Zane, his partner, *his lover*, lying there in the bed, pale and still, somehow managing to look fragile despite what a tall and muscled man he was, and "good" went out the window, down three stories, and splatted on the asphalt.

Ty edged into the room, wondering if he should stay or go, since Zane appeared to be sleeping. Fuck that—if he had to suffer, so did

Zane. He crept closer, eyes passing over the machinery around the room, and he sat gingerly on the edge of the bed.

The corner of Zane's mouth tilted up. "Old Spice," he murmured.

The words warmed Ty more than he was willing to admit. He leaned closer and sniffed loudly at Zane. "Desperation?"

Zane turned up his nose. "Mouthwash. Nasty shit." He shifted his closest hand to touch Ty. There was a small bandage, white against Zane's skin, where the IV had been earlier in the day.

Ty gripped his hand and squeezed it. "You doing any better?"

"Not hurting as much," Zane admitted. "They took away all the wires and gave me ginger ale. I hate ginger ale." There wasn't a lot of force behind his words, but at least it was more than the dull yes and no and "you were in the truck" of early that afternoon.

Ty nodded, not sure what else to say. His mind was still racing, a duck's legs kicking furiously under the smooth surface of a pond. He was pretty sure if Zane could see he'd have mentioned it by now.

"I talked to Ma just now. She said to say hello," Ty tried, grasping for a thread to hang onto before he started going off the rails again. He'd have to take a nap when he got home.

"I could go for some pie right now," Zane said, visibly brightening even though his eyes remained dull and blank.

"I'm sure she's baking furiously," Ty muttered. He looked down at the hand he still held in his. "Do you want me to call your folks?" Please say no, please say no, please say no—

"No," Zane said immediately. Thank God!

Ty cleared his throat and kept talking despite his relief. "Are you sure? It seems like something maybe they should know."

Zane's nose wrinkled, and he frowned before sighing a few moments later. "I guess I might call Annie. But not my parents. We don't . . . we're not really in touch."

Ty winced but didn't push further. He couldn't help but ask, though. "Who the hell is Annie?"

Zane actually smiled and turned his head on the pillow. "My little sister."

"Ah. Am I going to have to call her?" Ty asked, unable to keep the displeasure out of his voice.

"I wouldn't do that to you," Zane assured him, rubbing Ty's thigh soothingly. He'd clearly picked up on Ty's tone of voice. "She does know who you are, though."

"She's knows I'm the partner that let you run into the exploding building alone and that you like cock?" Ty asked without even thinking about turning around to see if anyone was within hearing range.

Zane's eyes widened comically before he blinked several times and shook his head. "That you're the partner who's saved my life multiple times," he corrected evenly. "And yes, she knows I switched teams."

Ty's racing mind finally came to a grinding, screeching, painful halt. "Wait, what?"

"I don't even have to see your face to know you're about to freak out." Zane sighed. "She knows we're partners at work. That's all. I don't share details about my private life with her or anyone, but she does know in *general* terms that in the past I've slept with both men and women. Okay?"

Ty closed his eyes and squeezed the bridge of his nose to ward off the squirrels trying to chisel their way out of his brain. "Zane," he groaned in complaint. "When do you get out of this place? I need to fucking sleep before you drive me crazy."

"I don't know," was the quiet reply.

Ty looked down at Zane, really looked at him, taking in the gauntness of his pale face, the worry etched in every line. It had been a while since Zane had looked this bad. It made Ty realize how much better he'd gotten since Christmas. He reached up and fluffed Zane's hair with the tips of his fingers, not willing to make a public display of his affection but wanting to comfort Zane somehow. "Do you want me to go ask if you can come home?"

Zane got this odd, pained look on his face for a moment before he shrugged. "I don't know what to do. I'm not sure . . . how I'll manage."

"You have me." Ty pressed his lips together hard and felt himself flushing. He opened his mouth to add some sort of qualifier to it, but he supposed after you'd told someone you loved him and dropped to your knees as many times as Ty had for Zane, you were past being embarrassed when you spouted off Hallmark card material.

The small smile on Zane's face softened the worry lines. "I know." He rubbed his fingers over the fabric of Ty's pants. "But you have to work. And play softball. And *sleep*," he emphasized with a gentle poke.

"You saying you don't want me to stay with you?" Ty asked in the most neutral voice he could muster. He wouldn't blame Zane if he didn't. If their positions were reversed, Ty would send Zane away in a heartbeat. And Ty knew that saying he wasn't the most ideal candidate to care for someone would be quite an impressive understatement. But he wanted to be there for Zane all the same. He wanted Zane to know Ty was behind him, no matter what.

"No. I want you with me all the time. But I know us. That wouldn't work."

Ty was on the verge of agreeing, because shit *no*, it wouldn't *work*. They'd be at each other's throats a day in . . . although he had begun to miss Zane quite a bit in the last several busy weeks. He looked into Zane's sightless eyes. The impulse to ask was about so much more than being a nursemaid. "Will you give me a chance?" he pleaded.

The ripple of emotion across Zane's face was indefinable; at first Ty thought he identified surprise, then happiness, then maybe hope. "Yes," Zane answered.

"Good," Ty sighed. He patted Zane's knee. "I'll go hunt down a doctor and threaten him until he lets you go home."

"He'll probably agree. He's not too happy with me as it is," Zane said.

"Why not?"

Zane squeezed his eyes shut and blinked several times after opening them. "Declined pain treatment," he muttered.

Ty nodded, forgetting for the moment that Zane couldn't see him do it. He petted Zane's belly as he stood. He wasn't going to comment on the drugs, just like he had stopped commenting on anything else that touched on any of Zane's vices. It wasn't worth the angst.

"Be right back," he muttered, and he set off to find an unsuspecting doctor to bully.

"Agent Garrett, how are you feeling?" a man's voice asked as someone walked into the room.

Even though he was expecting it, Zane still tensed. He opened his eyes out of habit and sat up. "Pretty good, except . . ." He waved one hand somewhere beside his head.

"Still no vision?" the same voice asked with an audible frown. "Well, that's to be expected. We'll start your discharge papers going, and you should be able to get out of here," he said as papers shuffled.

Zane squeezed his eyes shut and gripped the blanket in one fist. He wasn't so sure this was a good idea, even if he didn't want to be here.

"Unless there's a new problem?" the doctor asked, voice tinged with concern.

"A problem?" Zane's voice got a little high and thin there at the end. "I can't see!"

The doctor cleared his throat. "Agent Garrett, it is a temporary side effect," he assured him. "Now that we know there's not a critical injury, there's no reason for you to remain here. I'm sure you'll be more comfortable at home."

Zane swallowed. "At home. Alone."

"Are you saying you want to remain in the hospital?" the doctor asked him in surprise. "That's not really an option, Agent Garrett."

"No, I suppose it's not," Zane murmured, dropping his chin.

"It'll be about an hour," the doctor told him, sounding relieved that he wouldn't have to talk Zane down out of the proverbial tree. "We'll just get that started for you," he said. His shoes squeaked as he turned away.

"Hey," Zane said abruptly. "Is there anything I should be doing while I'm at home?"

He heard the doctor stop and turn around. "Don't run into things," the man advised after a moment of thought.

"Yeah, that'll be a piece of cake," Zane muttered.

"Rest. Relax. Let someone take care of you," the doctor told him seriously. "The nurse will be back soon," he added. Then slightly squeaky footsteps faded away.

"Relax," Zane said as if someone were standing there. He wasn't all too sure someone else wasn't, actually. "He says relax." He groaned and rubbed his hands over his face.

With a sigh, Zane pulled one leg up and wrapped an arm around his knee as he sat there wondering what the hell he was going to do. He'd already made up his mind not to call Annie. He was sure his sister would fly out here if he needed her, but there really wasn't anything for her to *do*. There wasn't really anything *anyone* could do. That was what was so goddamn frustrating.

A few minutes later there was a soft knock on the door frame of his room. "You want Cheetos or a Snickers?" Ty asked in a disgruntled tone.

Zane turned his chin as soon as he heard the knock. "Snickers will be easier," he said. Although the Cheetos sounded good, Zane knew better than to fight Ty for them.

He could hear Ty unwrapping the candy bar as he moved closer.

"Hold out your hand," Ty ordered when he got to the side of the bed.

Shifting slightly toward Ty, Zane did so, palm up. Ty placed the Snickers in his hand without a word, and then Zane felt him move away and heard him flop into a chair of some kind. The springs squeaked.

Zane lifted the bar tentatively to his lips, surprised when he found it difficult to hit his mouth. He took a bite and chewed slowly. "Doctor was here," he said as he savored the chocolate.

"That was faster than I expected. And?" Ty asked eagerly.

"They're sending me home."

"That's good, right?" Ty asked. "When can we leave?"

"He said an hour." Zane wasn't sure about answering the first question.

The chair creaked as Ty leaned forward. His voice was closer when he spoke. "We talked about this. You don't want to go home?"

"Yeah, I want to go home. I hate hospitals. It's just . . ." Zane frowned.

"You wish you could see," Ty provided matter-of-factly.

Zane nodded. He carefully took another bite of the Snickers. "Don't know what the hell I'm going to do with myself. It'll be a whole new level of staring at four walls."

"Well," Ty murmured thoughtfully. "Man up, Zane. Shit happens, you know? We'll get out of here and get some real food."

Zane sat startled for a long moment and then actually chuckled. "Welcome back."

"What?"

"You sounded a lot more like your normal grumpy asshole self," Zane explained. "Rather comforting, actually." Something about that just made Zane want to laugh. "Yeah, you're going to make a great valet."

He was surprised by a thump on the tip of his nose. He hadn't even heard or felt Ty move. He swiped out with one hand in a belated reaction. "Hey! I've seen you use an iron. That is damn impressive."

"Marines either know how to use an iron or they get married," Ty advised through a mouthful of Cheetos. "The iron is less dangerous."

Zane snorted and almost swallowed the chunk of candy bar in his mouth without chewing it up. "That's actually pretty funny."

"I try."

CHAPTER SEVEN

Zane felt the cab come to a stop. He'd lost track of the twists and turns a while back, and he had no idea if they were at his apartment, Ty's house, or somewhere altogether different. He'd already decided there was no way he'd be saying the words "Are we there yet?"—Ty would go ballistic.

So he sat quietly, face turned toward the window, chin down.

He was wearing scrubs from the hospital; his suit had been trashed. He knew he wasn't bloody, despite the bruises everywhere, so he figured he didn't look too bad.

"We're here," Ty told him. The door on Ty's side opened. "Hold on. I'll come get you," he said before the door slammed shut.

Zane didn't move. He knew this was going to be tough, trying to get around, and he certainly wasn't looking forward to it. He'd barely said a word the whole drive over, just thinking about what he would be facing if he wasn't able to see again. He knew it was too soon to start worrying and planning, but fuck all, he'd only just gotten a bunch of shit in his head straightened out, and now this?

The door at his side opened up, and Ty took his elbow gently. "Watch the curb when you step down. It'll come up fast," he mumbled, sounding as if he was looking down at the ground as he spoke.

Zane turned in the seat and set one foot down. He could feel the soft decline of the curb and shifted his foot a little farther forward before pushing himself out of the seat to stand. Ty got him onto the sidewalk, gave him a pat on the shoulder, then removed his hand from Zane's elbow. Zane heard Ty talking briefly to the cabbie.

Shifting carefully, Zane moved further away from the car and waited. He could tell by the familiar smell of Italian restaurants in

Little Italy that they were at his apartment. He also knew which way the front door to the apartment was, but he didn't know how far away it was. And there were steps and a railing and a bench and some broken concrete in the sidewalk and what if it was almost garbage day and there was a trash can at the curb? Zane groaned. His battered brain was channeling Ty.

"Here," Ty said, surprising Zane out of his circling thoughts. Ty took Zane's hand and pressed something into it. "Use that," he instructed as he held Zane's hand around a curved wooden grip.

Zane realized it was the umbrella he kept beside the door to his apartment. He frowned and curled his fingers around the handle, moving it slightly in front of him. It definitely wasn't a cane, but he figured if he moved it in front of him it would hit something before he did. "Good idea," he murmured.

"I know," Ty responded easily, a smile evident in his voice. He took Zane's elbow and turned him. "Take your time, shuffle your feet when you're not certain. If you hesitate or anticipate, you're more liable to trip over nothing," he advised.

Zane grimaced. "Right," he murmured as he took a breath and took a couple steps. He could feel the hard surface under his feet, so at least he was on the walk. Although he felt like a complete idiot, he swung the umbrella carefully in front of him, the end down around his knees. When he hit something metal that clanged, he stopped in surprise, trying to remember what it could be.

"Just the railing," Ty said at his side. "Steps," he added as his grip tightened on Zane's elbow.

Zane still paused. "How far? Step up now?"

"Yes," Ty answered curtly. "Kick out with your toes to find it."

Zane lifted his foot, kicked, finding the front of the step, and then he put his foot on it, somewhat surprised when it worked. He repeated the motion two more times and stopped. "That's all, right?"

"Yep," Ty answered, and he let go of Zane's arm. The sound of the keys in the door followed, and the door squeaked as it opened. Ty took his arm again, but he didn't pull him. "Come on," he instructed. "Don't drag your feet, there's a doorjamb."

"You've done this before, haven't you?" Zane said, following the directions and getting inside without a problem.

"When I was little," Ty answered in a softer voice. "We'll use the umbrella until I can find something better."

Zane frowned again and placed one hand against the wall he knew was to his right side. "No one in your family is blind."

"My great-grandmother. She died when I was fourteen."

Zane nodded and started moving, letting his hand skim along the wall. He knew he had several feet until he got to a bookshelf. He was on the main drag through the apartment. It led to the kitchen in front of him. He was in the living room, and after the bookshelves there was a hallway to the right with four doors: two bedrooms, a closet, and a bathroom. He didn't really have much furniture, so what trouble could he get into?

"At least I know where stuff is in my own house," he murmured as he walked until his hand met the wood of the shelves.

"That's kind of the idea, sport," Ty murmured from somewhere in front of him.

Zane deliberately closed his eyes to visualize the couch and chairs, and then he swept the space in front of him before taking two careful steps to stop right behind the sofa. He trailed his fingers over it as he walked around the side, and with a sigh of relief he sank down onto it.

Ty patted him on the head as soon as he was down, like he would a dog who'd performed a trick correctly. His voice was the only way to tell where he was. He didn't seem to make any other noise when he moved. No footsteps, no swish of clothing, no cracking bones or creaking joints. Nothing. Eerie. Vintage Ty.

"Want food? It's not too late yet," Ty asked as he moved away.

"Yes," Zane said fervently as he lightly batted after Ty's hand. "There was nothing wrong with me and still they wanted to feed me broth and Jell-O."

"Jell-O's good," Ty argued from the kitchen.

"Not when you're starving, it's not," Zane shot back. He kicked off his shoes, making sure to carefully push them under the old coffee table before he stripped off his socks and propped his legs up. He leaned his head against the back of the couch. With his eyes closed, he could almost imagine it was a Sunday afternoon and he was just being lazy instead of it being Monday night after the day from the third ring of hell.

"Well, what do you want?" Ty asked in something close to annoyance. His voice had moved. He was standing right in front of Zane.

Zane twitched in surprise and his eyes flew open. "Christ, Ty," he complained.

"What?" Ty asked defensively. "I'm hungry!"

"It's a good thing I've calmed down recently," Zane told him. "If I'd had my gun, I'd have pulled it."

"What are you talking about?"

Zane shook his head and wiped one hand over his face. "Order deep dish from Isabella's. They should still be open."

Ty pressed a phone into Zane's hand. "Here. I need ibuprofen," he said as his voice trailed away.

"Kitchen cabinet next to the sink," Zane said distractedly as he ran his fingers over the buttons, trying to figure out how to do this. It was easier to do with his eyes closed, even though he couldn't see anyway. After two aborted attempts, he got the number he had memorized into the phone and made the order for delivery.

He could hear Ty banging around and rattling the bottle of ibuprofen. He heard him open and close the refrigerator. Then he stopped making noise again. A few seconds later, Zane heard the pop and hiss of a carbonated drink being opened just a few feet away.

Zane turned his face that way. "You know, I knew you could be scary. I just didn't realize how fucking scary. I didn't hear you move. At all."

"What?" Ty asked in the same distracted, slightly confused tone of voice he'd used earlier. "You want a drink?" he offered belatedly.

"I'll wait for pizza. I said, you're so quiet when you move I didn't hear you at all. Even footfalls in the carpet, and I know how to listen for those things."

"Oh," Ty said abashedly. "Sorry."

"It's okay. Just confirms that you don't even have to think about it." Zane tipped his head, turning an ear toward him. "You going to stand there 'til the pizza gets here?"

"Thought about it. Kinda hurts to sit," Ty admitted.

"Still hurting a lot from the baseball game?" Zane frowned. "You didn't go into the building and get hurt, did you?"

"Nope," Ty answered as he sat down. The couch beside Zane shifted as he got comfortable.

Zane still frowned, listening to Ty's voice carefully, but there was nothing there to clue him in. "I'd like to know what happened. One moment I was walking through this store to check the storeroom, the next I'm waking up to total black."

"There was an explosion," Ty told him. He grunted heavily, and the next thing Zane knew, Ty's head was resting on his thigh. "About a dozen agents and cops were injured. Six of ours in the hospital. No fatalities, as far as I know."

Zane's frown faded, and he moved his hand to gently settle atop Ty's head, stroking lightly. "You saw it from the truck?"

"Yeah," Ty answered softly. He stretched, set his drink on the table, then settled back against Zane. "You were carried out by a very large fireman named Tank," he informed Zane in amusement.

"Tank?"

"That's the guy who ran me over."

"Oh yeah, met him at the field briefly." Zane slid his fingers down over Ty's cheek. "Got about half an hour on the pizza. Why don't you catch a quick nap?"

"You gonna be okay?" Ty asked him, not even trying to argue.

"I'm staying right here," Zane said, his hand settling on Ty's shoulder so his fingers flickered along Ty's temple through his hair. He felt Ty's arm move, and he imagined Ty was probably putting his forearm over his eyes like he did when he was worn out.

"Wake me if you need anything," Ty mumbled.

"Okay," Zane murmured as he rested his neck a little more comfortably along the back of the couch and closed his eyes. He tuned into Ty's breathing as Ty relaxed, smiling as he *felt* Ty go to sleep, and after a quiet minute, Zane carefully shifted, pulled out the cell phone a helpful nurse had saved from his suit, and activated the voice command function.

"Call Deuce Grady."

Did you say "Call Deuce Grady"?

"Yes."

Dialing.

Zane took a deep breath and tried to let it out slowly as the phone rang on the other end, somewhere in Philadelphia. Ty didn't even twitch in his lap.

"Hello," Deuce answered after the second ring. There was nothing terse or clipped in the way he answered the phone, just another trait of Deacon Grady's that was wildly unlike his brother.

"Hey, Deuce," Zane managed, pretty happy that his voice came out sounding mostly normal.

"Hey, Zane, how's it going?" Deuce responded easily. Zane swallowed. "Not so great," he admitted.

"What's wrong?" Deuce demanded, his voice losing the laid-back quality and becoming more urgent. "Is Ty hurt? Are you hurt? Why didn't Ty call me to tell me? Is he even conscious? What happened?"

Zane resisted the urge to laugh as he gently petted Ty's hair. "Ty is fine. He's asleep. He wasn't the one hurt this time."

"Oh," Deuce muttered, not sounding at all embarrassed over his outburst. "But you're hurt? Are you okay? What happened?"

"An explosion happened. A surprise one," Zane answered. "I'm okay. Mostly. No limbs missing or anything," he tried to joke.

"A surprise explosion," Deuce repeated slowly. He sounded like he might be writing that down. "Interesting," he drew out under his breath. "As opposed to a not-surprise explosion. And it did what, exactly?"

"Apparently some of the parts in my head got a little scrambled," Zane said awkwardly. "I can't see."

"You can't see what?"

"Anything. I can't *see*. I'm blind." Zane was pretty proud that his voice didn't shake or break upon saying it out loud like that.

"You've lost your vision," Deuce summarized in a clinical tone, not an ounce of pity or apology. "Is this a permanent thing?" he asked more carefully. He seemed to be wavering between psychiatrist and friend as they spoke.

Several seconds passed before Zane realized he hadn't answered. "They don't know," he murmured, recalling bits and pieces of what the doctors had said.

"I see." Deuce was silent for a long moment. "Let me ask you this, Zane: are you calling because you need a friend or because you need a shrink?"

"I want to talk to you, Deuce, not Dr. Grady," Zane said, knowing he sounded a little plaintive. "I know we've sort of blurred the lines along the way."

"Then let me just say: dude, that sucks," Deuce drew out with feeling.

Zane cracked a grin and laid his hand on Ty's chest so he could feel it rise and fall evenly. "No shit, man."

"Are you with Ty or are you staying alone?"

"We're at my apartment. I know my way around here," Zane said. "I just got out of the hospital. I don't even know what time it is."

Deuce hummed thoughtfully. "Did Ty tell you our great-grandmother Elsie was blind? She had this watch that you could flip up and feel to tell time. Ty might have it. But then, that was twenty years ago. There's also a button on your phone that will do that, I think."

"We've not had much chance to talk. I was really out of it for a while. It's still . . . sinking in," Zane said slowly. "The panic is starting to creep up on me, and I'm trying to let him sleep a little."

"I can imagine," Deuce said sympathetically. "Doesn't do any good to tell you not to panic, either."

Zane's laugh had a little edge to it. "Right." He blinked several times, resisting the urge to rub at his dry eyes. The doctors had said over and over that it wouldn't help and would probably hurt. But he wasn't sure where the bag from the hospital was, and even if he did know, he wasn't going to wake up Ty to get to it. "This . . . isn't good," he said, and his voice definitely shook.

"What can I do to help you, Zane?" Deuce asked in a gentle voice.

"I just . . . not much scares me anymore, you know?" Zane tried to explain. "But this . . ."

"You don't deal well with uncertainty," Deuce observed almost clinically. "Not many people do. *Why* does it scare you?"

"I can't work if I'm blind. What am I going to do with myself? I couldn't stand the idea of someone having to—" Zane cut himself off before his voice rose any further. He wouldn't be a charity case. He just couldn't stomach it.

"Take care of you?" Deuce finished for him. "Are those the only reasons? Your job and your pride?"

"No," Zane murmured as he spread his fingers over Ty's chest. "Those aren't the only reasons."

"Spill, Zane," Deuce ordered. "Get it out now."

The words balled up in Zane's throat. He was talking to Ty's brother, for heaven's sake. "I'm afraid," he whispered. "I'm afraid it'll change things."

"What things?" Deuce asked. "Relationship things?"

"Oh yeah," Zane answered in a rush.

"You think my brother will dump you because you're blind," Deuce surmised in a troubled voice.

Zane hesitated. "I don't want to think that. It's . . ." He grasped for a word. "Disloyal."

"Disloyal," Deuce repeated curiously. "To whom? To Ty?"

"Yes, to Ty." Zane frowned. "Who else is there?"

Deuce hummed thoughtfully. "There's you, Zane," he continued after a pause.

"Me?" Zane shook his head as he inhaled deeply and sighed. "I don't follow."

Deuce sighed, long and loud. "If there's one thing my big brother taught me, it's that sometimes you have to look out for number one. Don't worry so much about what he'll do or what he'll think."

Zane sighed. "Well, until just recently I was the only one looking out for me, so I'm kind of used to that part of it."

"Tell me something, Zane," Deuce said in a sly voice. "Is that really the biggest thing you're worried about right now? That Ty might leave you?"

Zane pressed his lips together hard. The tone of Deuce's voice made him a little suspicious. But Deuce was never cruel, even if he did like to tease sometimes. Zane was worried about so many things he couldn't even start to rank them, but Ty—and whether Ty would still want him after such a radical change—really stood out. Zane figured it was a reflection of how much their relationship had developed. The next words were out before he thought them through. "He said he loves me."

"I know he does," Deuce assured him with a laugh. "I'm surprised he told you, but I'm glad he did. So, keeping that in mind, I'll ask you again: is that really the biggest thing you're concerned about?"

Zane closed his eyes, even though it made no difference in the darkness, and really considered the question. What did he really have? His job, and Ty. If it came down to it and he lost his job, he was relatively sure he could flounder his way into something else to do, somehow. But if he lost Ty, Zane just wasn't sure he'd care about anything else. The slight pangs of pain he felt whenever he caught Ty looking at him in a particular way came more often now, and it was starting to make him want things he wasn't sure he could handle. "Damn it," he swore under his breath, hoping Ty really was asleep. "Yes."

"Well, I'd say that's pretty good, then," Deuce said happily. "I mean, as far as problems go. Ty's too stubborn to leave you if he loves you."

Zane let out a groan that reflected both frustration and relief. It helped so much just to hear that. "So I'm stressing over what's probably nothing. Paranoia."

"I wouldn't call it paranoia. More... spinning your mental wheels. I mean, has he given any indication that he might leave now? What's he been doing?"

"He's been great, not that there was anything he could do in the hospital. But he didn't leave me alone," Zane said. "Was there when I woke up, sat with me there, got the doctors to let me leave, and got me home. All that aside, I really don't know what to do with myself. In theory? It's temporary. I could wake up tomorrow just fine. Or it could be permanent. Not one doctor of five could tell me anything more than "We just have to wait and see,'" he muttered, "which was kind of cruel in itself."

"Wait and see. Makes you wonder what they tell deaf people," Deuce muttered. "Oh God, that was horrible. Forget I said that."

"You know how many idioms there are that have something about 'seeing' or 'sight' in them?" Zane asked, letting a little waspishness into his voice. He groaned aloud to punctuate the annoyance. He could hear Deuce trying not to laugh. "I'll go nuts if I have to sit around here doing nothing," Zane added. "It's not even day one, and I'm already antsy. And that's with being worried about running into a wall."

"So do something," Deuce suggested. "Who blew you up? Can't you plot revenge or something? Any open cases you can mull over?"

"We were investigating a report of a suspicious package," Zane said as he started thinking over their caseload. "Although I wouldn't be averse to a little plotting. As for cases, it's not like I'm assigned to Financial Crimes, tracing forgers or art thieves through paperwork. Criminal involves more than a little legwork."

"So . . . why was there a bomb there?" Deuce asked.

Zane shook his head, belatedly remembering he had to speak. "No idea. And I've got no information after being in the hospital. I'm sure Ty will find out what he can while he's at the office."

"No, Zane. I mean, *why* was there a bomb *there*? Who called it in? Was it a trap? Think about it. Come up with a theory."

"Yeah, okay. I can do that." He shook his head. "Hey, Deuce?"

"Yeah?" He sounded amused.

"Why are you surprised?" Zane asked, giving into the curiosity niggling at him. "Is it that he told me, or that he feels that way to start with?"

"I knew he was in love with you when we were in West Virginia, Zane. I'm surprised he figured it out. And yeah, I'm surprised as hell that he told you."

Zane barely stopped himself from sitting up and dumping Ty on the floor. "In West Virginia? That was almost four months ago."

"That surprises you?"

"Deuce, if I hadn't been scared out of my fucking mind when he told me, I would have fallen over from the shock," Zane said with some amount of surety.

Deuce began to laugh softly. "And then he shoved you over the edge of a balcony or something, I know. Very romantic." He began to laugh harder.

"It was a three-story drop!" Zane growled in outrage. "I didn't even get a chance to say anything because the ship security guys were waiting for us!"

The laughter trailed off, and the line was silent for a moment. "What would you have said that you can't say now?" Deuce asked, voice neutral.

Zane literally flinched, flashing back to the confusing coil of emotions that had rocked him in that not even two minutes of revelation, jumping, and falling after Ty had said "I love you." But now, he wasn't remembering the literal fall from three decks above a cruise ship swimming pool. He was feeling the echoes of his more recent emotional shock in the stands at a fan-filled softball tournament: The fall wasn't coming. It was already over. He just had to figure out how to find words of his own. The honest words. "I don't know," he got out in a strangled whisper.

Deuce hummed again. "Maybe you should use some of your free time thinking about that. 'Cause if I know my brother, he'll stick with you through just about anything, including going blind. But I don't know how long he'll stick around if he's the only one thinking he's in love."

Zane frowned but had nothing to reply, and they sat there in silence, Zane with his mind buzzing in circles, for almost a full minute before he cleared his throat quietly. "Thanks for the talk, Deuce. I really appreciate it."

"Any time, Zane. You know that," Deuce told him with confidence. "Say hello to my brother, huh?"

"Yeah, I will," Zane agreed, smoothing his palm down over Ty's belly. "Talk to you later." He hit the end-call button out of habit; he didn't need to see the phone to know where it was. "Well," he muttered, "that was full of up and downs, wasn't it?"

Ty grunted as if in answer and fitfully rolled onto his side.

Zane smiled. He did feel better, though after that last bit of conversation, he wasn't sure he should.

When the phone rang, Zane startled and sat up in a rush, his left hand reaching out to fumble for his phone. He hit solid, warm skin, and he paused in place. He was on the wrong side of the bed, and he could tell by the bustle of sound from the street that it wasn't the middle of the night. He still couldn't see. The disappointment and fear welled into his throat.

"Ow, Zane," Ty grunted in a monotone, sleepy voice as Zane pawed at him. He pushed Zane's hand away, and the bed dipped as he rolled over. Zane heard him smack his hand onto the table where the cell phone rang. "Grady," he grunted in answer to the call. He sighed in annoyance. "Now?" he asked whoever was on the other end of the call. "Well, why don't you come here and get it from me like all the other witnesses?" he asked petulantly. "Fine. I'm at Garrett's place."

Then he clicked the phone closed and groaned plaintively, rolling around again. Zane knew him well enough to guess he was burying his head under his pillow in protest.

Zane sighed and lay back down, facing toward Ty, dragging his own pillow under his chest. "Work?" he murmured, wide awake now, although the scare was fading.

"Sort of," Ty mumbled as he lifted up and then rolled out of bed, barely disturbing the mattress. "They want a witness statement from me," he said as his voice trailed off toward the hallway. "They're sending a car."

Zane missed the warmth of Ty's body immediately. He stretched his hand out to rub his fingers across the still-warm fitted sheet. "About the bomb at the baseball field?"

"That and the other. And I've got to go in and find that damn kid and get your keys back."

"Not like I need them," Zane muttered.

"You will soon enough," Ty told him. The water began running soon after.

Zane stood to walk to the bathroom, but his phone's low chime stopped him. He felt his way back to the nightstand and answered with a hint of trepidation. "Zane Garrett."

"Special Agent Garrett, this is Dolores from PR at the Bureau."

"Okay?" Dolores worked for White Strips. He wondered if her boss made her stock floss.

"We've received a large number of requests for interviews, and I wanted to check to see when you thought you might feel up to giving some."

"Giving some . . . interviews? About what?" Zane slowly sat down on the edge of the bed.

"Some are speaking requests from community leaders who attended the classes you've spoken at recently. But we've also had several requests since the press somehow connected you to the aquarium bomb scare. You're quite the celebrity now," she said cheerfully.

Zane didn't know what to say. "I'll think about it," he said weakly.

"Do you still plan to give your talk at the community class this coming Saturday?"

"Do you know what happened to me yesterday?" Zane asked carefully.

"Yes, and I'm very sorry," she said, her voice softening. "The SAIC said that it's your choice about Saturday. Can you let me know by tomorrow if you're going or not?"

"Yeah, okay," Zane said. He ended the call and set the phone back on the nightstand as he heard the water cut off. Zane felt Ty moving around the small room very shortly after.

"You okay?" Ty said in a low voice, much closer to Zane than he'd expected. Ty patted his shoulder and sidled past him.

Zane reached out just in time for his fingers to drag down the damp skin of Ty's back. "Yeah."

Ty hummed in response, the sound coming from the general direction of the end of Zane's bed. "Have you seen my blue tie?" he asked distractedly.

Zane chuckled before he could help it. He stood up, moving away from the bed. "Ah. Maybe hanging with the other suit in the dry- cleaning bag." They'd gotten into enough messes the past few months that now they each kept a suit or two at each other's place.

Ty grunted and made an apologetic noise. "Sorry. Forgot about the . . . seeing thing."

"Guess I'll get used to it fast," Zane said as he tried to figure out by listening what Ty was doing. "Did they say how long this would take?"

"Hour or two. Means probably four." There was rustling and the occasional whiff of Old Spice, and Zane figured Ty was putting on clothing, waving his shirt or jacket through the air as he put his arms into the sleeves. "Do you need anything before I go?"

Zane reached out to touch the chest of drawers in front of him. He might as well get dressed if Ty was going to be gone. "No, I don't guess so."

Ty's hands suddenly slid up Zane's sides, moving to hug him as Ty's chest pressed against his back. He was fully clothed—the soft material of Ty's Tom Ford suit was unmistakable. Zane could feel the knot of his tie, the telltale quality of the material. "The blue suit," Zane murmured. Close fit that hugged his shoulders and body, blue wool, silk overcheck, broken herringbone pattern, single-breasted peak lapel. Ty looked incredible in it. As much as Ty loved to dress down—ratty T-shirts and busted-down jeans—he knew how to look good too.

"Yeah?" Ty replied, lips moving against Zane's shoulder.

"Your favorite. You like the material. Pants fit right. Slim fit in the jacket." Zane lifted his hands to touch Ty's and slide up over the suit jacket sleeves to Ty's elbows. "Makes your eyes brighter," he said before really thinking about it.

"Is that so?"

Zane ducked his head, glad Ty was behind him and not looking at his face.

"I don't think anyone at the office is concerned about the brightness of my eyes. Except maybe that fucking PR guy. But thank you, all the same," Ty tacked on slyly.

"Yeah, well," Zane murmured. That wasn't the kind of thing he said to Ty. It just wasn't. "I think I feel like an idiot now."

Ty squeezed him hard. "You feel pretty good to me," he whispered. Then his hands were sliding off Zane and he was stepping away.

Zane swallowed hard as he lost touch with Ty's warmth and had to grasp for something to say. Ty was going to think he'd lost his mind. "I think I'll go back to bed for a little while."

"Might be a good idea." Ty's voice was moving away. "Get some sleep, Garrett. Call me if you need anything."

Zane listened to the front door shut firmly and sat down hard on the edge of the bed. He felt hot and goddamn *tingly* all over, and it wasn't from anything but what would probably qualify as sweet nothings on the open market. Flopping back on the bed, Zane rolled, pulled Ty's pillow under him, and buried his face in the sheets. It was time to do some serious thinking; he figured he might as well be as comfortable as possible to do it.

"Thanks for coming in, Grady. You weren't injured, right?" Scott Alston asked.

"Like you care," Ty grunted at him. "Let's get this rolling, huh?"

"Don't be a jerk," Alston shot back. "We're all worried about Garrett, and there're others hurt too. Wilkinson's in the hospital with a compound fracture of her right leg, and three others are still there too."

Ty held up both hands in surrender, closing his eyes. "I'm sorry. Sorry."

Alston sighed and sat down. "Yeah, well… it's been a shitty couple of days." He shuffled through some papers. "All right. I need to bend your brain about both bombings, the ballfield and the boutiques."

"We talked about the alliteration, Scott," Ty mumbled, not even managing a smile.

Alston glared at him, then ignored the words. "So far we've found only four agents who were in both places. That includes you and Garrett."

"Who are the other two?" Ty asked as he settled into the seat across from Alston. It was uncomfortable and too low, forcing him to look up at the other man. Classic psychological tactic to make someone being interrogated feel inferior and uncomfortable. Fucking asshole Feds…

"Waller and Carmichael, both from tech ops. They were on the street. As were you, right?"

Ty sighed heavily and nodded. He spent the next hour telling Alston everything he'd done, seen, felt, heard, and thought at both scenes, culminating in a ten-minute rant about his Bronco being melted and who the hell was going to pay to fix an old Bronco that was worth more as evidence than it was on the street and when the hell was he getting his Bronco back exactly?

After Alston managed to quiet him down, Ty was forced to sit there in the uncomfortable chair for another fifteen minutes as Alston got papers together for him to sign. By the time the man returned, Ty was calm again, concentrating on breathing in, breathing out, making the fucking Om sound in his head.

"Okay, Grady," Alston said after Ty was finished running two pens out of ink. "There's good news and . . . well, other news. What do you want first?"

"Scott, don't make me hurt you," Ty muttered dejectedly.

"You're done here, Ty, no more paperwork," Alston said sympathetically. "But . . . you're also done for the rest of the week. Mac's orders."

Ty stared at him, not truly surprised but still disgruntled over being benched. But who was he kidding, really? He was mangled from trying to stop a fireman the size of a refrigerator from scoring in a softball game that was basically a PR stunt, his Bronco was smoldering in an evidence yard somewhere, and his partner had been blown up and was helpless at home. Ty didn't want to be here when he needed to be there.

"Yeah, okay," he mumbled, looking down at his hands and picking at the medical tape around his fingers.

"It's not just you, Ty," Alston said, sounding surprisingly reassuring. "We've locked down Waller and Carmichael, too, and, well, you know about Garrett. We know you're a target. Your face has been all over the news. They're still running that sound bite of yours, and those bastards went after your truck. Now we need to figure out if Garrett was a target as well, and we want you off the field of play. You'll also have a skeleton crew checking on you, just in case." He sighed. "I'll call you as soon as we answer some of the metric ton of questions, okay?"

Ty just nodded and stood. "Are we done?" he asked tiredly. "Or am I due for a full rectal exam today too?"

"Go on. You're looking rough, even for you," Alston said. "Nice suit though."

"Shut up."

Alston smiled. "We'll hold down the fort. Let me know how Garrett's doing when you hear from him, would you?"

"Yeah." Ty turned and practically trudged toward the elevators. Intellectually he knew why he was being sent away. It still didn't sit well with him. He wasn't used to being shooed away to safety when things got too hot. He told himself to look at it as some much-needed time off from work to be with his lover, but even that held a sour note. He tried not to think about Zane's sight and when or if it would return. He told himself not to think of anything as he rode the elevator down.

Zen, Ty, Zen.

Zane heard a key in the lock, and the door complained loudly as it was opened. "Honey, I'm home," Ty called out in a less-than-enthusiastic voice.

His eyes closed against the utter darkness, Zane could see it: the battered metal-core door opening and Ty stepping inside from the stoop, short hair ruffled from the cold wind Zane could feel sweeping in behind him, dressed in a dark wool overcoat, that incredible blue suit, holster at his right side, badge clipped on his belt, displayed whenever Ty set his hand on his left hip in a gesture of mild annoyance. From the sound of his voice, Ty was frustrated now, which meant the tie would be askew—if it was still on at all—and first thing, his jacket would be off, maybe even his shirtsleeves rolled up. Ty had long muscled forearms sprinkled with fine dark hair, and surprisingly trim wrists. Zane had more than once closed his hand all the way around one of those wrists. And Ty's fingers were snub-ended but nimble, for all that several were various amounts of crooked from all the breaks.

He wondered if Ty was frowning. It furrowed his forehead, two lines darting between dark eyebrows, and his usually bright hazel eyes would be somewhat shadowed, trending to brown or dark green. When his full lips pressed into a firm line, it caused dimples to appear in his perpetually tanned cheeks. Zane had caught himself several times in the office looking at Ty's mouth. It got his pulse up when Ty chewed thoughtfully on his bottom lip.

"Garrett?" Ty said in a flat voice. "You still in there?" He put his hand on Zane's chest, leaning over the back of the couch to do it.

Zane actually startled out of his imagining with a sharp inhale. "Oh, sorry," he said, lifting one hand to cover Ty's. "Are you frowning?"

"What? I am now—what the hell kind of question is that?" Ty muttered as he pulled his hand away.

Zane could hear him continuing to mutter as he moved away.

"You sound frustrated. What happened at the office?"

"Benched," Ty groused. "Didn't tell me shit except that I was to go home until they're sure we're not targets. We'll also have a protection crew tailing us."

Zane frowned and sat up. Ty sounded almost angry. "Hey, come here," he requested quietly. Something heavy, probably Ty's overcoat, flopped onto the back of the couch. He felt Ty's weight on the couch beside him, and soon Ty's hand ran into his hair affectionately, carefully avoiding the small crooked line of stitches along the back of his skull.

Zane relaxed and leaned into the hand, moving his own to bump against and slide up Ty's thigh. It was reassuring, having him this close, and if Zane needed anything right now, it was peace of mind. He turned his head to press his cheek against Ty's palm, and Ty's lips touched his gently. Only bare seconds passed before the hip that leaned against Zane's body began to ding and vibrate, but Ty ignored the cell phone in his pocket in favor of the kiss. It warmed Zane, something so insignificant as Ty choosing him over a cell phone call. Silly, maybe, but he was taking all the feel-good karma he could get at the moment. Wanting to be a little closer, he slid one hand to cup lightly around the back of Ty's neck as he gave under Ty's lips.

Ty sat up after the phone went quiet, running his hand through Zane's hair again as he leaned against him on the edge of the couch. "They gave me the rest of the week off," he announced suddenly. "I'm probably a target. They want me to lay low, not come back 'til Monday."

"The likelihood of us being targets is really damn small," Zane murmured, rubbing Ty's back with one hand. "Even with the bomb in the Bronco, it was the only car there overnight. Small chance anyone could know it was yours. And down at the shopping complex? We weren't even supposed to be there, really. We got sent last minute to help out. More likely they want you out of their hair."

"Mac doesn't have any hair left. He pulled it all out," Ty muttered unhappily. "I got to check this," he added, and Zane could feel him pulling his phone out of his pocket. Zane relaxed back, keeping his hands on Ty, just for that connection. Despite the encouragement from talking to Deuce, Zane still felt pretty damn pitiful and lost.

Ty snorted at whatever he was reading on his phone, and Zane heard him snap the phone shut a moment later.

"What's up?" Zane asked.

"It's just my buddy Nick," Ty said as he leaned against Zane again. "He's a cop, on the last hour of an eighteen-hour shift, and he's trying to stay awake by driving me fucking crazy."

"So he's the one who texts you all hours of the day and night?" Zane asked as he rubbed at his temple. The raging headache he'd had in the hospital was still hanging on as a dull ache.

"Mostly, yeah. Why, does that bother you?" Ty asked with a hint of concern. He took Zane's hand as he spoke, his fingers rubbing at the base of Zane's thumb until he found the pressure point between the fingers and squeezed hard.

Zane groaned as the headache began to dull. If Ty knew one thing, it was how to use and abuse a pressure point. "No, it doesn't bother me." He scrunched up his nose on purpose. "You haven't texted me since you got caught with your girlfriend," he lamented, but then he ruined it with a little laugh.

"I still owe you for that," Ty told him wryly. He let off on the pressure point just a little, and the throbbing ache in Zane's head began to subside almost to the point of being gone. "You're right here next to me. I don't need to text you."

"Still."

"You want to hear some of the crap he sends me? Then you won't be jealous."

Zane smiled slightly. He suspected Ty kind of liked that he might be jealous. "Sure," he said amiably as he slid his arm between Ty's back and the couch to pull him closer.

Ty shifted around to reach his phone again, and Zane heard him flip it open to find some example texts to read out loud. "The one he sent me on the way home said, *at my funeral it'll be your job to throw yourself on my casket and weep.*' And the one he just sent me, he says, *false alarm, still invincible.*' No idea what he was doing that he thought he might die. The one before that was *for future reference a lint roller appears to be the best way to get glitter out of a beard.*"

Zane chuckled. "That's some quality conversation there. Is Nick one of the Recon guys? The one I talked to on the phone in New York?"

"The one you talked to on the phone?" Ty repeated in obvious confusion. "Oh! Yeah, the one that called and cussed me out for getting blown up. Yeah, that was Nick. He was Recon, but he was also with me pretty much from the bus to Parris Island."

"So you two go way back," Zane murmured, lifting his hand to rub Ty's belly through the soft dress shirt. Zane idly wondered what color it was.

"Yeah. Tried to get him to join the Bureau with me and Sanchez, but he was being stubborn and disillusioned with The Man. Went home instead. We sort of fell out of touch for a while, when I was undercover. But ever since New York, he's called or sent me a text almost every day."

"He's not around here, then," Zane concluded. "Else you'd be barhopping with him."

Ty laughed softly. "You have that low an opinion of me, huh? Barhopping," he joked in a warm voice as he leaned more against Zane. "He's in Boston."

Zane grinned. "Would he have gone bar*maid* hopping with you?"

"He has in the past."

Zane poked at Ty's ribs gently.

Ty flinched and jabbed back at him. "Quit that," he hissed. Zane could feel him rubbing at his ribs as if it had tickled, but he belatedly remembered Ty's run-in with Tank and the bruising his ribcage had taken.

Zane patted Ty's thigh in apology. "That's great, still in touch with a friend from that far back."

"I'm thinking you'd probably hate him," Ty said thoughtfully, and then he laughed. "About as much as you hated me at first."

"And that was a lot," Zane agreed. "He'd probably hate me too."

Ty made a dismissive noise and stood, taking a step away from the couch. "Are you hungry? I'm going to start fidgeting if I don't find something to do soon."

"I could eat," Zane answered, feeling the cool rush in after the warmth of Ty's body disappeared. "There's not much here, though."

"You want to go out?" Ty suggested, his voice so even that Zane couldn't determine Ty's preference from it. Zane had always thought Ty's emotions were easy to read. But obviously all those cues came from his body language. "Might do you some good. You pick. I'll take you there."

"How about Chiapparelli's? The food's really good."

"That the Italian place you're always going to?" Ty asked.

Zane nodded. "They've got a pretty good selection, and you've seen my lunches. The people there are really nice. It's a family business."

"And I guess you'll know the layout since you're there a lot, huh? Well, you look good enough. Let's go eat."

Zane got up and self-consciously patted his hair after Ty riffled it in passing. He carefully edged along the couch and around it, then took one step to the bookshelf along the wall and touched the books, trailing his fingers along the spines until he reached the shelf with the dish where he left his wallet and keys. "I need a jacket," he said.

"How far is it? Can we walk?" Ty asked.

"Go out the front door, turn right, cross the street, go to the end of the block, turn right, and it's on the right at the end of the block," Zane rattled off.

"All righty, let's go, then," Ty said.

CHAPTER EIGHT

"There are a few steps up just inside," Zane said as they stopped outside a full plate-glass door under a blue awning hanging off a red brick building. "Four, maybe? It's not like I've counted before."

"You don't have to tell me, baby. I can see them," Ty reminded gently.

Ty pulled the door open and guided Zane through. They went up the steps slowly, and Ty cast a critical eye around the restaurant. He'd never been there, but Zane was always producing leftovers in brown paper bags and seemed to enjoy the food.

It was definitely an old building: exposed brick walls had been kept intact inside. The carpet was brown and red and sort of ornate floral in a vintage Italian style. There was a dining room full of patrons in front of them and another to the right. The furniture was dark, heavy wood, including a full wine case directly in front of them where an array of takeout menus, business cards, and a bowl of mints sat. The waiting area was quite small; maybe a dozen people could stand around, and it would be tight. Even the five people already there waiting made it difficult to look around.

An older woman, slight and gray-haired, dressed in the black waitstaff uniform, walked out of the dining room to the right. "Good evening, gentlemen. Two for dinner?" Then Zane turned toward her, and she added, "Oh, Mr. Garrett, lovely to see you again." She had a thick accent.

"I wish I could say the same, Leticia," Zane murmured with a vague wave at his eyes.

She broke out with a sharp question in a language that Ty definitely recognized as Italian. It made him flinch like one of Pavlov's dogs waiting to be hit with an ostrich leather hobo bag.

Zane shrugged in answer to her. She tut-tutted him and turned to Ty. "This way, please. I have a table for you now," she said, ignoring the other customers waiting who had been there first.

Ty looked after her, then turned to frown at Zane. "You speak Italian now?" he asked dangerously. It was still a touchy topic, even almost three months after the cruise ship assignment where not knowing Italian had almost gotten him killed.

"I have no idea what she said," Zane said under his breath. "But it didn't sound good, now did it?"

"I was about to smack you," Ty grumbled. He kept a loose hold on Zane's elbow as the woman led them to one of the tables near a wide window. They didn't even have to weave around many tables to get to it.

Ty glanced around the dining room as he took off his jacket. It was an okay place, but the food had to be spectacular for Zane to eat here three times a week. Ty much preferred his pub; it had character. And a bottle of Grand Marnier with his name on it behind glass over the bar. One-Eyed Mike's was four blocks from his house and almost halfway between his house and Zane's apartment. Much less classy and much more comfortable. He shook his head as he slid into one of the seats.

Zane tentatively reached out to his side, and his fingertips brushed the glass window. "Okay, I know where I am," he said, sounding satisfied as he shrugged out of his jacket.

Leticia whisked by again, dropping off glasses of ice water, a basket of what looked like fresh-baked bread, a dish of real butter pats, and two large single-sheet menus printed on heavyweight paper. After a pause, she took Zane's menu back and patted him on the shoulder. "Ryan will be right out," she announced before leaving.

"Well. I guess it's pretty obvious I can't see, huh?" Zane commented.

Ty looked up from the menu. He narrowed his eyes, leaned forward to look at Zane closer, then reached out slowly and waved his hand in front of Zane's face. Zane didn't even blink. "It's . . . pretty obvious," he said apologetically. He sighed and looked down at the menu again. When he and his brother had been little and gone to visit their great-grandparents, they had amused themselves by blindfolding each other and attempting to navigate various obstacles, just to see how Grandmother Griffin had done it.

But there was a difference between closing your eyes and being blind. Even with a blindfold, there were still variances in light that could give you hints as to where you were and what was going on.

Complete and total darkness—blindness—could be a lonely and frightening thing. Zane was taking it pretty well, considering.

Ty returned his attention to the menu full of Italian dishes and grimaced. "You come here three days a week? Every week?"

Zane edged a shoulder up. "It's right here by my place, and I love Italian food. There's plenty of choices if you don't want traditional red sauce. Sometimes I just get the Baltimore salad."

Ty looked up at him dubiously. "I don't get what's so special about . . ." He trailed off as he saw a waiter come around the corner and head for their table.

The man was dressed all in black like the others, and he was impressively fit. The black T-shirt might as well have been painted over well-defined muscles. His shoulders were broad, and he was trim through the waist. He had dusky skin and sharp, defined facial features, and his hair would have been dark if it hadn't been shorn down practically to the scalp. It made him look sleek.

"Oh," Ty muttered dejectedly.

"Hmm?" Zane asked as he messed with his napkin. Ty shook his head and squeezed the bridge of his nose, trying not to laugh.

The waiter stopped at another table briefly, then hurried over to them. His lips were pulled into a worried frown. "Zane," the man said as he took the last couple of steps to the table. "Leticia told me something had happened." When he stopped, he put a hand on Zane's shoulder.

To Ty's mild surprise, Zane didn't flinch away. "You could say that," he replied as he waved a hand at his eyes. "Work hazard. Got caught a little too close to the explosion at the shopping complex," he added in a very short explanation.

Ty watched Zane and the handsome waiter converse, knowing he had one eyebrow raised and his mouth hanging open. He couldn't help it.

"That's terrible!" the man exclaimed. "You can't see anything?"

Zane shook his head. "Nothing at all. So I have to have help to get around." He gestured across the table at Ty. "Ryan, this is my partner, Ty Grady. Ty, this is Ryan Morelli."

"Hi," Ty said unenthusiastically.

"Welcome to Chiapparelli's," Ryan said with a pleasant smile. "Thanks for bringing Zane by. If I don't see him every few days, I wonder if he's sitting at home starving."

"Gee, thanks," Zane muttered.

"That's . . . that's . . . nice," Ty managed to get out. He cleared his throat and reached for his napkin.

Ryan laughed and pushed at Zane's shoulder. "I've seen that kitchen. It's a travesty. Mine is much better. Now, what can I get you gentlemen for dinner? Zane, we've got the gnocchi today," he said, clearly trying to tempt him.

"So it's either sit at home and starve or eat here and spend an extra hour at the gym every night to work off the calories," Zane said ruefully. "Yes, the gnocchi sounds good. And some fried provolone to start."

"I'll bring you some iced tea." Ryan turned his attention to Ty. "Can I bring you a drink? We have a wine list and a fully stocked bar. And I'm happy to describe anything on the menu for you."

Ty was glaring at Zane, and he had a hard time wiping it off his face before he looked up at the waiter. He smiled woodenly and nodded. "You have Guinness?"

"Yeah, we have to cater to the other Europeans too," Ryan said with a grin. "A pint, then?"

Ty nodded and shot another glare at Zane, irritated that his partner couldn't even see it.

"We've got all your traditional Italian favorites," Ryan said, gesturing at the menu. "We also got in fresh fish today, if that sounds good."

Zane chuckled quietly and covered his mouth with his hand, probably to hide a grin. Ty hadn't been fond of fish since the cruise debacle.

Ty cleared his throat again and offered the waiter another smile that probably came across as more of a snarl. "Anything with white sauce," he ordered as he handed the man his menu.

"Can do. That comes with our house salad, unless you'd like to substitute?" Ryan asked. He glanced at Zane briefly for about the third time.

Ty bit his lip and shook his head. He offered the man another forced smile, then returned his death glare to Zane.

"Okay, then," Ryan continued. "I'll be back with your drinks and appetizer." He patted Zane's shoulder again.

"Thanks," Zane said, tipping his head back to smile in Ryan's general direction.

As soon as Ryan moved away, Ty leaned his elbows on the table and kicked Zane's shin under the white linen tablecloth. Zane yelped and jostled the table, setting the ice water in the glasses to rocking. "What's that for?" he asked, a wounded look on his face.

"You eat here three times a week," Ty said through gritted teeth.

"Sometimes," Zane said, brow furrowing. "So?"

"So? Jersey Shore over there is awfully pretty," Ty grumbled. "'My kitchen is better than yours,'" he mimicked under his breath as he reached for his water glass.

Zane tipped his head to one side, looking thoughtful. "He brought my carry-out a few weeks ago when I called in an order and then forgot because I was talking to Freddy about a search warrant."

"How thoughtful of him," Ty said drily.

Zane shrugged. "He's a nice guy. I guess I've been a pretty good customer lately."

Ty continued to glare at him evilly. And Zane continued to be oblivious, since he couldn't see it. Damn him. "That's not why he did it. You're lucky I feel sorry for you right now or I'd kick your ass," he muttered as he looked out the window.

Zane stopped picking apart the bread he had in hand. "What for?"

Ty continued to grumble at him as he sipped at his water. Although Zane couldn't see, he was sitting right across from Ty, so it looked like his partner was peering right at him.

Then Zane blinked a couple of times and sat back. "Okay, I just caught up with the 'pretty' comment."

"Little slow on the uptake?" Ty challenged.

Mischief chased across Zane's face before he cleared his throat and hid it. "You'd probably kick me again if I said the scenery here was as good as the food, huh?"

"Zane," Ty said warningly.

Zane rolled his eyes and shook his head. "The food really is good," he insisted.

"It better be," Ty warned. He peered at Zane, letting himself investigate the feeling rippling through him. It wasn't that he suspected anything was going on, because he knew Zane better than that. But the sensation of being jealous, no matter how slight it was, was something foreign to Ty. He almost liked it, safe in the knowledge that Zane was completely unaware of the attention.

"He delivers, huh?" Ty said to Zane quietly. "I'm burning every little brown bag I find in your fridge from now on."

Zane just smiled innocently. "Even the cheesecake?"

Ty liked that damn cheesecake; of *course* it came from here.

"Don't push me, Stevie Wonder," he growled.

"Yeah, I understand," Graham whispered into the cell phone, trying to cover his annoyance. Pierce was getting on his nerves with all his damn orders, and in Graham's opinion, he was taking this shit too seriously.

It was one thing to steal money from big banks to pad his wallet. The banks were insured. It didn't hurt anybody. But the bombs were real now and getting bigger and meaner. Pierce liked the destruction. He wanted to hurt people, especially cops. He said they were making some kind of statement now, not just creating a diversion to keep the cops distracted. It was making Graham and the others nervous. He hadn't signed up for a manifesto; he just wanted the extra cash.

"This is the big one, man. We need all hands on deck," Pierce was saying furtively. "The best way to expose society's corruption is to split it open bit by bit and show everyone—everyone!—just what we're dealing with here. The government pigs—"

Graham rolled his eyes. Who talked like that? "Yeah, yeah, I get it. I'll be there, okay? I have to go or I'm gonna get fired." He hung up before Pierce could start into his "manifesto" again.

He peered through the kitchen door to see if table three was clear yet. He could see Ryan out there talking to two big dudes who looked vaguely familiar. Graham belatedly recognized the darker one. Mr. Garrett. No, Agent Garrett. He was some sort of government guy, always smiling and friendly, didn't make a fuss, always left generous tips. He seemed like a decent guy, for a Fed.

Graham looked at them closer, wondering why Garrett looked odd. He wasn't exactly looking at Ryan when he spoke to him, nor was he looking at the pissed-off guy in the blue suit across the table from him. He seemed to be staring off into the middle distance.

When Ryan left them and came through the door, he looked troubled. Graham nodded at the table. "What's wrong with him?"

Ryan looked back at the two men. "He said he was one of the agents caught in that explosion down at the harbor shops. He lost his vision." He gave them one last sympathetic glance and then was gone, off to the kitchen to put in an order.

Suddenly Graham recognized them: the two agents from television that Pierce had the vendetta against. The other man's name was Grady, and Pierce had yet to stop talking about him.

Caught in the explosion. Graham stood looking out at Agent Garrett. The explosion *they* set in the shopping mall. The bomb Pierce insisted needed to be bigger and better.

Graham had been sitting beside Hannah when she'd reluctantly called in the tip that sent the cops and FBI to that building. He had helped lure Agent Garrett into that building. Because of him and his friends, that man, a decent man, a man he knew, was now blind. How many more people like him had they hurt? Or *killed*?

Graham's stomach turned. He ran and took the stairs two at a time, trying to get to the bathroom before he was sick.

Zane sighed as he shut the front door and leaned back against it. While dinner had been great—the food at Chiapparelli's always was— he'd been tense, even in those familiar surroundings, all too aware that someone could walk up behind him at any time. Having Ty there had helped, but Zane was still glad to be home.

"Will you put my leftovers in the fridge?" Zane asked as he held out the brown bag holding the plastic and tin container, stifling the laugh that threatened.

Ty snatched it from him with a grunt. A moment later Zane heard the bag hit the floor, and without warning he was slammed against the door behind him. Ty held him there by both shoulders, fingers digging in hard. But he ghosted his lips along Zane's in gentle contrast to the rough treatment. Zane caught his breath, surprised by the dichotomy and immediately interested in more.

Ty pressed against him, licking at his lips. "I think you should find a new favorite restaurant," he murmured before dragging his teeth across Zane's lower lip.

Zane swallowed hard. "But I like that one." He settled his hands on Ty's hips, his fingers sliding on the soft, fine fabric of Ty's trousers.

"That's what I'm afraid of," Ty growled playfully. He pushed Zane against the door harder and forced his tongue between Zane's lips, running it along the inside of his teeth. He crowded against Zane in an unspoken demand.

Heat flushed through Zane in a sudden wash, and he felt the urgent need to beg for more. He'd been handled with kid gloves for two days now. He *needed* Ty all over him—the rougher the better. When their mouths finally parted, he deliberately fanned the flames. "Lots of reasons to keep going there," he said, breathless.

"Are you *trying* to make me jealous?" Ty asked in a low voice. It was almost a purr with Ty's rough mountain twang.

Zane let out a shaky breath as he felt his body react to the arousal starting to spread through him. "Seems to me you already are." He dug his fingers in where his hands rested at Ty's waist.

Ty pushed his face closer to Zane's, causing his lips to move against Zane's when he spoke, his voice dropping to a growl. "I am," he admitted shamelessly. Zane could feel him smiling. Ty might have been telling the truth, that he really was jealous, but he was also enjoying it. "I think you should start liking seafood instead of Italian."

Zane opened his mouth to answer, but a shaky moan came out instead. He had to stop and take a breath and try again, and he pulled Ty's dress shirt out of his waistband while he was at it. "I do like seafood. They have that there too," he drawled, shifting his groin against Ty's thigh.

"Damn it, Zane," Ty snarled before he kissed Zane again, with no regard for soft lips caught against teeth. He reached between them to yank at Zane's belt, then shoved at his jeans, pushing them down his hips. He forced his tongue into Zane's mouth hungrily and ground their bodies together.

Zane's gut clenched; hearing and feeling Ty this worked up was a hell of a turn-on. And the fact that it was because Ty was feeling possessive . . . Zane's head spun with delight, and he tried to give as good as he got. Ty pulled back from him just long enough to shuck his suit jacket and yank his shirt and undershirt over his head. Zane could feel the bare skin under his fingertips, soft and warm, shifting over muscles he could trace with his eyes closed. Then Ty was on him again, hands all over him as he tugged and yanked at Zane's clothing, biting at his lips and his chin and his neck, sucking on his earlobe and growling, "You're mine. Jersey Shore can get his own."

The arousal ripped through Zane so quickly that his knees went weak, and he sagged against the door with a soft moan, Ty's body pinning him there. "Baby," he gasped helplessly.

Ty finally managed to get Zane's shirt unbuttoned, and he pushed it down Zane's arms and left it there, tangled at his wrists. He dragged his hands up Zane's hips and around his waist to delve under his briefs and grab his ass possessively, then squeezed hard as he thrust his groin against Zane's and kissed him. Under Ty's hands, Zane could do nothing but writhe against the door and try to return the kisses best he could. He had to struggle to get the sleeves of his shirt untangled from his hands, and Ty didn't help him at all. When he finally got loose, he clutched at one of Ty's shoulders for support.

Ty moved his hands, fingers digging into soft flesh as he pushed Zane's briefs down. "Don't fucking move," Ty growled against his lips. And then he was gone, pushing away from Zane and disappearing into silence. Zane almost flailed as he lost his hold, and he flattened himself against the door, trying to keep from sliding to the floor along with his underwear. He sucked in deep breaths, trying to calm down a little. His cock was hard and aching, near-rigid against his abdomen, and he almost reached down to try to relieve a little of the pressure, but Ty's words echoed in his ears, and *no way* was he going to disobey an order like that. He moved just enough to kick out of his jeans and briefs.

He distantly heard the sound of a drawer opening and shutting, and after a few short moments, Ty was back. When he touched Zane, it was obvious that he'd stripped off the rest of his clothes while moving. They'd be tripping over Ty's blue suit all the way to the bedroom. If they got that far. When Ty pressed against him, it was all hard muscle, smooth skin, and rough hands. He grabbed at the backs of Zane's thighs and tugged, pulling Zane's feet away from the door and almost off the floor. It lowered Zane to Ty's height, and Ty rubbed his hard cock against Zane's as he licked and sucked and nipped at Zane's lips.

Zane grabbed for Ty's shoulders and held on tight. Ty was hot and hard all over, and Zane needed him badly. "Baby, please," Zane groaned.

"Oh, now I'm 'baby', am I?" Ty asked gruffly, his voice husky and strained. "What happened to making me jealous? Teasing poor Ty with the hot waiter?" His hand grabbed Zane's ass again and squeezed hard; then he pulled at the back of Zane's thigh and bent his knees, lowering himself enough to yank Zane's left leg over his hip.

Zane shifted his weight to his right leg, reached out to grab the doorknob with his left hand, and hooked his other arm over Ty's shoulder, needing some kind of leverage as Ty manhandled him. "Need you too much to tease," he got out between breaths. "Didn't plan it, really didn't."

Ty hummed disbelievingly. Zane heard the distinctive pop of the cap on the tube of lubricant, and then Ty's hand was between them, squeezing the cold gel out onto his own cock and onto Zane's. He tossed the tube away, and Zane heard it land somewhere as Ty's hand wrapped around both of them and began to jack them slowly.

His lips came to rest against Zane's for a moment before moving. "I'm going to fuck you until you can't remember your name," he promised in an oddly intimate voice. He pulled Zane's lower lip between his and dragged his teeth along it.

Zane clutched at his lover desperately as Ty's hand squeezed. Fuck, he wanted that. "Please . . . please, Ty."

"Nobody likes a beggar," Ty whispered. He hiked Zane's leg up higher and reached behind him with his slick hand. His fingers were hot as they massaged at Zane, teasing at him, taunting him by dipping deeper and twisting. They fucked often enough that it didn't take much preparation, sometimes nothing but lubricant. Ty was doing this now because he wanted to tease Zane, not because Zane needed it.

Zane gasped out a laugh. "You love it when I beg."

Ty growled again, biting down harder on Zane's lip as he moved with alarming speed and power. He hooked his arm under Zane's leg and hefted him farther up the door, getting a gasp of surprise out of Zane. That leg now rested in the crook of Ty's arm, and Zane's balance on the other was threatened when Ty slammed Zane against the door, holding him there with the weight of his body and the strength of his arms. His hands tugged at Zane's hips, bowing Zane's back, and Zane could feel the head of Ty's cock, rock hard against his ass.

A wild, needy keen tore from Zane's throat as his fingers scrabbled for purchase on Ty's skin. He would have given anything to see Ty's face right at this moment. He could imagine it: hazel eyes sparking, brow furrowed and full lips pursed with concentration and intent. The amount of pure brute strength and violent desire it had to take for Ty to practically pick Zane up and hold most of his weight was incredible.

He jostled Zane some more, grunting and sucking air through his teeth as he struggled to get them in position. It took a few attempts as Ty fumbled and kissed him messily, but he finally forced himself inside Zane as he let gravity pull Zane's body down. By the purr that echoed through them both, Zane could tell Ty was savoring the slow slide, and when the head of his cock pushed past Zane's tight muscle, he punctuated it with another violent exploration of Zane's mouth and a hard thrust of his hips.

Zane's cry of pained pleasure was muffled by their kiss, and he dug in his fingers and tensed his leg, trying to hold onto Ty. It was uncomfortable and precarious and unbelievably fucking hot. Zane thought he might come at any moment, come all over Ty and himself right there, just as Ty was getting started. He would have been embarrassed if he didn't want it so badly.

"Fuck," he gasped as soon as their lips parted. "Oh fuck . . . *Ty*."

Ty didn't respond other than to bury his face in Zane's neck and thrust up into him again, over and over. He occasionally hitched Zane higher, the sensation of being picked up and then pulled down onto Ty's cock entirely different from anything Zane had experienced before. Ty panted heavily with exertion and bit at Zane's shoulder as if he wanted to simply devour him. Zane *wanted* to be eaten alive. He held on as the pleasure racked him until he couldn't conceive of anything but Ty's hands and teeth on his skin and riding Ty's cock.

A low growl started in Ty's throat, and the thrusts of his hips began to slam Zane erratically against the door. He tightened his hold on Zane's leg and ass and lifted him higher yet again, putting Zane on the toes of one foot, and Zane gasped as the warm skin of his back skipped on the weather-chilled painted metal of the door, catching and pulling. Ty's growl became a tortured, brutal shout as he fucked Zane painfully hard, without any regard for either of their bodies.

It only took a few of those thrusts to force a broken whine out of Zane as the tension in him snapped and he slammed into climax, coming in pulses with Ty's thrusts, his come smearing between them. Zane's entire body tensed and strained in Ty's arms, helpless. All he could do was trust Ty to keep him from falling and ride out the pleasure that was blotting out absolutely everything but his lover moving inside him, prolonging the orgasm.

It was a few more glorious seconds before Ty's movements froze and his body arched. He was silent as he came inside Zane. When his body uncoiled, he was gasping for breath, his forehead resting against Zane's shoulder. His skin was damp with sweat, and his arms and shoulders trembled as he pulled out of Zane quickly and lowered Zane's feet to the ground. But Zane's legs were far too wobbly to support him, and he grasped at Ty as he started to slide down the door to the thin carpet. Ty huffed a laugh, and they sank to the floor together. Ty shifted and sat down with a thump beside Zane, his back to the door and their shoulders brushing. He was breathing hard from the exertion, still gasping for air.

Zane leaned sideways and laid his head against Ty's shoulder. "What's my name again?" he murmured, still spinning. It was really hard to stop being dizzy when he couldn't focus his eyes on something to halt the motion.

Ty began to chuckle, though the sound was an exhausted one.

"That'll learn ya," he drawled, obviously pleased with himself.

Zane reached up to pet Ty's thigh and then splayed his hand in the curve of Ty's elbow just below where he rested his head. Ty's arm snaked around his shoulders and squeezed him tightly. He pressed a kiss to Zane's forehead, then buried his nose in Zane's hair and inhaled deeply.

"You know I don't care if you eat at that damn restaurant, right?" Ty murmured, his voice low and affectionate and oddly gentle after what they'd just done.

Zane turned his chin enough to press a kiss against Ty's collarbone as pleasant warmth filled him. "You know I've never even looked at him, right?"

Ty was silent for a long moment. Finally he turned his head and said, "Appropriate time for a blind joke here, or is it too soon?" Zane snickered and jabbed at Ty's ribs. "Jerk."

Ty laughed quietly, the sound warm and reassuring, as he nuzzled his nose into Zane's hair again. When the laughter ebbed, Zane realized Ty was holding his breath, and something about the slight tremble to Ty's body made Zane feel that Ty wanted to speak again. It wasn't the first time Zane had noticed it, and suddenly Zane realized what Ty was keeping himself from saying in moments like this:

I love you.

Zane squeezed his eyes shut and kissed Ty's shoulder again, resisting the urge to crawl into Ty's lap and do whatever he had to in order to get Ty to say it again. He wanted to hear it again, just once, after all these weeks, now that it meant so much more, now that Zane had acknowledged to himself that he knew what the leaden weight in his chest was. Now that he might be able to believe what he felt for Ty was real and not just a result of circumstance and proximity. Now that Zane needed courage he couldn't quite find to take that final step and deliberately *fall*.

"You okay?" Ty asked quietly. "I didn't hurt you, did I?"

Zane actually wasn't sure, but he shook his head anyway. "Floor's cold," he whispered as he shivered, and he recognized the source of that reaction. He was scared. There. He'd admitted it. He was scared, terribly scared, because Ty loved him and Zane didn't know how to handle it when he couldn't even explain how he felt himself because he was still digging through fear and guilt about the past and trying to justify reaching for the future he so desperately wanted . . .

"Yeah," Ty agreed contentedly. His fingers played with Zane's hair, his body relaxed against Zane's. He seemed perfectly happy to just sit there and hold Zane for the rest of the night. He cleared his throat and moved his chin to rest it on top of Zane's head. "We're never going to find that lube," he muttered in wry amusement.

"We'll get more," Zane murmured, gears still spinning as he tried to deal with the questions and uncertainty crashing down on him. Somewhere in it all was a pang of upset: wasn't loving someone supposed to be a happy thing? He cursed his innate habit of analyzing everything to death and turned his face into Ty's arm. "How about bed?" he suggested quietly. "I'd . . ." He shivered again.

Ty's chin moved again, and Zane got the impression Ty was peering down at him. "You'd what?"

Zane bit his lip for a moment before answering. "I'd really like you to hold me for a while," he whispered. It felt odd to say it like that, something so innocuous yet meaningful.

"I don't know . . . you're all sweaty," Ty said with mock distaste. He pressed his mouth and nose to Zane's cheek and smiled so Zane could feel it. He inhaled deeply, growling on the exhale. "You smell good, though."

The weight on Zane's chest let up a little as Ty kept his response light. Zane wasn't sure what he'd been expecting. He reached out to drag his fingers down Ty's chest to his belly, where Zane's come had smeared between them. "Could shower first," he offered.

"No point in that," Ty murmured. "Yet."

Zane grunted inquisitively.

Ty smiled against his cheek again, then pulled his arm away and pushed himself to his feet with a groan. "Oh my God," he bemoaned. "I'm too old for that."

"Ha!" Zane scoffed from the floor. "As the man eight-plus years older than you who just got fucked to the point of not being able to remember to breathe, I disagree."

Ty's hand found his and pulled him to his feet. He pulled Zane closer despite both of them still being sticky and kissed him chastely. "Are you complaining?" Ty asked seriously.

"Not even a tiny bit," Zane murmured as he found his physical balance. He leaned closer into Ty's arms, seeking the comfort he craved and needed for his emotional balance, which felt like an unbolted teeter-totter.

"Good. 'Cause that took a lot of energy," Ty said with obvious amusement. He let his hand slide down Zane's arm, and he took his hand. "Come on. I want to keep you in bed long enough for that pasta to go bad."

Graham stood on the sidewalk, staring wide-eyed at the door. What the *hell* kind of fight were those guys *having*?

He held the envelope between damp fingers. He'd written it quickly. He'd wanted to follow Mr. Garrett and his friend, but he'd missed them leaving the restaurant while he'd been washing dishes. He had been so panicked for a moment he'd almost told Leticia that he needed to go after them, but then he'd overheard Ryan talking about delivering to Mr. Garrett's and realized they had to have his address in the delivery logs. Turned out his place was only a block away, close enough he could walk there on his break, and so he had, shaky but determined.

Graham had to tell someone what Pierce was doing. Who better than an FBI agent who couldn't see his face to identify him?

But now, standing here, listening to what sounded like a violent disagreement inside, Graham was having second thoughts. The door actually rattled as someone pounded on it erratically. Well, the other dude *had* looked awfully angry when they were at Chiapparelli's.

Graham swallowed hard, steeled himself, and gripped the confession in his fist as he stepped up to the door. He wouldn't knock, because there was no way he was going to interrupt whatever epic battle was going on inside, so he smoothed the letter out with shaking hands and slipped it under the door.

It got stuck in the rubber doorstop and wouldn't push all the way under. Graham cussed to himself and shoved it harder. It crinkled up, and he stopped. Another bang and thump against the door followed by what sounded like a shout of pain made him jump back, and he looked up at the door, heart hammering in his throat. The letter wasn't going anywhere, but he sure as hell was.

He turned and jogged to the corner and around the block, back to the restaurant and safety.

CHAPTER NINE

Z ane shifted as he came awake. He was warm, half-wrapped in the
sheet, but something was missing. He frowned and reached out,
his hand catching on the rucked-up quilt before coasting over the cool
sheet beside him. Zane pushed himself up on one elbow as he started
to rub at his eyes. After a moment, he made himself stop. It wasn't like
it was going to help. He still couldn't see anything. His chest clenched
painfully.

"Ty?"

"I'm here," Ty grunted from somewhere near the edge of the bed.
He sounded like his head was down, his voice hoarse.

"You okay?"

"Yeah, just . . . restless," Ty answered, his voice lacking its usual
liveliness, even if he had just woken. "Couldn't sleep."

"You could go for a run," Zane suggested. Sometimes getting Ty
up and moving helped.

"I was thinking about going to the office," Ty countered, sounding
guilty.

Zane frowned. "Thought Mac told you to stay home. If he sees
you, he'll get that pinched look on his face, like he bit into a lemon or
someone twisted his shorts."

"That's how he always looks when he sees me," Ty muttered,
almost under his breath. "I'm sorry. I just can't sit here anymore. I
need to find someone to bully into telling me what's happening."

It had been all of one day. Zane shook his head and made a mental
note to stock up on shiny things to divert Ty the next time they lucked
into vaca—time off from hell together. "Yeah, okay," he said as he
pushed at the sheet to untangle it from his legs.

"Do you want to come?" Ty offered uncertainly. "If I can find Alston, I can blackmail him into giving me something. It won't take long."

"I think I'll pass on actually going in," Zane muttered. He didn't want to be around anyone like this. Not yet. "Blackmail?"

"Long story. Involves a duck and a can of oregano."

"Don't tell it, please."

He felt Ty's hand on his arm, rubbing comfortingly. Ty had been unusually tactile since the hospital, making up for Zane's lack of vision by touching him whenever he was able, as if he somehow knew how much it helped. Zane closed his eyes, grateful for it. He covered Ty's hand and squeezed gently. It was easy to think black thoughts when you were stuck in the dark, and Ty's touch helped him resist it. "Breakfast first?"

"Sure, why not," Ty replied easily. Zane felt him lurch off the bed, and when he spoke again, he sounded like he was stretching. Zane had an immediate vision of Ty's lean, nude body in the dim light of the bedroom, and he flushed with warmth, not really registering the words when Ty said, "I'll go start it up."

He listened as Ty got dressed, probably throwing on his jeans and one of his numerous T-shirts. Zane didn't hear him pad out of the bedroom, but he could hear him banging around in the kitchen, cussing at the tiny, run-down space, talking to the pots and pans. Zane smiled. There were reasons they spent most of their time together at Ty's row house instead of here.

By the time he got up and moving, Zane could hear the bacon sizzling, and the smell of sausage wafting out of the small kitchen area made his mouth water. He could smell the toast, too, and knowing Ty, there would be scrambled eggs. Ty didn't cook a lot, but the man could fix a mean breakfast. Zane made a stop in the bathroom and then sat at the bar that separated the kitchen from the little living area.

"You know what I realized?" Ty asked, picking up the conversation he'd been having with the pots as if Zane had been there for the first half of it. "I don't have a car."

Zane opened his mouth to correct him but caught himself. They'd taken a cab home from the hospital, and the office had sent a car for Ty yesterday. "Where's my truck? You didn't bring it back yesterday?"

They'd walked around the block to the restaurant for dinner last night; Zane had assumed Ty had put the truck in the Little Italy parking garage when he came back from the office.

"That rookie I made drive me to the hospital took the keys. Truck's still parked at the office. That's another reason for me to go in today."

"Maybe one of the guys can pick you up?"

"It's past nine. Everyone's already in. Hell, I'll just take a cab or ride the bus or something." Something about his voice was odd as he stood in Zane's kitchen fixing breakfast, and it took Zane a little thinking to pin it down. Ty didn't sound gruff or hurried. He didn't sound agitated or even all that concerned. He was at ease despite the need to get up and go. It made Zane a little nervous, but in a good way.

"What's wrong?" Ty asked him, apparently picking up on it. "It's not exactly like I'm going to be attacked on the bus."

Zane shook his head, still reconciling the warmth curling in his chest with the idea that Ty might be happy here, just doing something as simple as making breakfast. "I have no idea what the schedule is around here," he said.

"I'll figure something out. Come eat," Ty said, and Zane heard a plate set down on the bar in front of him. "Wonder how a gun on public transportation goes over? Or two guns, for that matter."

Zane slid onto the battered bar stool and had a stroke of inspiration. "You do have another option," he mentioned.

"Oh yeah? You know I can't really sprout wings out of my ass and fly, right?" Ty asked, a smile in his voice.

A smirk pulled at Zane's lips, and he let it show. He loved teasing Ty, and this one always got him riled. "The Valkyrie's out back."

Ty coughed and sputtered, like he was choking on a bite of food.

"Hell, no," he finally said with difficulty. "I'll walk."

Zane chuckled and felt around for the fork he'd heard Ty clank onto the plate. It was mean, but he loved poking Ty about the Valkyrie. He supposed he shouldn't, what with knowing about Deuce and the accident. Ty had taught his younger brother how to ride and left him his bike when he joined the Marines. Deuce had wrecked it not long after, ruining his leg and any chance of following in his brother's footsteps. But Deuce seemed to take it all in stride, so Zane didn't really see the harm in teasing Ty about his absolute hatred of all things with two wheels. "Okay," he said after several mouthfuls of scrambled egg. "Bureau won't reimburse cab fare," he reminded, just to get in one more dig.

"That's okay," Ty assured him in an overly sweet voice. "I've got your wallet."

Zane grinned. "I don't have any cash. When have I been able to go to the bank?" he said reasonably as he munched on a piece of bacon.

"Cabs take credit cards," Ty reminded.

Zane wrinkled his nose. "Fine," he said on a sigh. "Can I have jelly for my toast?" He heard a jar clink down on the bar, and Ty was grumbling. Not really understandably, but obviously irritated now.

"I haven't been on a bike in twenty years," he said, more to himself than to Zane.

"Maybe not a good idea, then," Zane allowed reluctantly. He could *see* Ty on the Valkyrie, and it was a gorgeous vision to think about. But this wasn't a do-or-die situation, like playing chicken with a New York City taxicab. Zane shivered as he momentarily felt his stomach drop just at the memory.

Ty sighed heavily. "I guess it is a better option than walking my happy ass out of the city," he mumbled.

Zane blinked and straightened. "What?"

"Can I borrow your goddamn motorcycle to go to the office?" Ty asked, resigned.

Zane's jaw dropped. "You're not seriously going to take the Valkyrie."

"I could hotwire one of the cars in that parking deck, but they don't take kindly to that sort of thing 'round here," Ty drawled.

"All these months, all the times I've asked you to ride with me, and you're finally getting on the Valkyrie when I *can't see it*?"

"Hey, life's a bitch," Ty told him without a hint of sympathy. He reached out and petted Zane on the top of the head. "You want more?"

"More what?"

"Breakfast."

"No, thank you," Zane muttered, knowing he had another piece of toast and some bacon still to eat. "A drink, though, please."

Ty slid a glass toward him, already poured. "If you don't mind, I'm going to go now so I can catch them unawares and take down the weakest of the herd before they can regroup," he said with a certain sadistic relish. "I need the helmet, jacket, and keys."

Zane sighed. He felt more than a little cheated. "The helmet's on the bike. The jacket's wherever it fell last night." Ty didn't answer as he moved past. In short order Zane could hear the creak of the leather as he put on the jacket and zipped it up. Zane wished like hell that he could see Ty on the bike. Talk about fuel for jacking off.

He could smell the leather as Ty came closer, hear it moving as he checked the pockets. No doubt it would fit; the jacket had been Ty's originally. Ty stood right in front of him and leaned in to kiss him briefly. "If you're good I'll do this again when you can see," he promised, mischief lacing his words. "Keys?"

Zane blinked. "Really?" He smiled despite the current disappointment. "How good do I have to be?"

"Very," Ty whispered, just a breath away. "You can start by giving me the keys."

Zane let a few heartbeats pass as awareness tore through him, then swallowed as he set both palms on the leather covering Ty's chest. "In the dish on the bookshelf by the door."

"Thank you," Ty murmured with another teasing kiss. Then he moved away again, his footfalls barely there in his Converse sneakers and the leather jacket still creaking. The keys tinkled as he picked them up. "I'll call you when I'm done," Ty said to him as he passed on his way to the back door. "Keep your phone on you in case you need anything. Two hours, tops," he guessed as the door opened.

"I'll be here," Zane said wryly, and then added, "Hey, Ty?"

"Yeah?" Ty responded as the door groaned open. A vision flashed in Zane's mind, what Ty must look like, standing in the open doorway, wearing his beat-up jeans and Western-style shirt and Zane's leather jacket, looking back over his shoulder at Zane expectantly. He probably had one eyebrow raised.

"Be careful. I want that chance to see this again," Zane replied easily.

"Yeah, yeah, love you too," Ty groused flippantly, shocking Zane into silence as the door clicked behind him, and he was gone.

Zane blinked hard several times, realized his mouth was hanging open, and let out a long, slow breath, sitting there until he heard the

Valkyrie start, idle for a minute or two, and then purr away. When he couldn't hear it anymore, he ate the toast and cold bacon automatically, absorbed in thinking about—*feeling* about—what Ty had said so casually, and how he himself hadn't found a way to say it at all.

He was so absorbed in his thoughts that when someone knocked on the front door, he jerked in surprise and sent the dishes sliding, the plate knocking into the glass and crashing to the floor, sending the orange juice splattering across the bar—and him.

"Aw hell," Zane swore, standing up and stepping back carefully. His hands and arms were wet and sticky with juice, and he could feel it soaking through his T-shirt and cutoff sweatpants. He turned his head toward the door at the next knock, and then he thought he heard his name. After sparing a thought for the cruel humor of fate, Zane stripped off his T-shirt, using it to mop off his hands and arms as he walked tentatively to the door and cracked it open, immediately shivering in the February wind.

"Zane? It's Ryan. From Chiapparelli's?"

Zane blinked in surprise and opened the door a little more, though he kept himself behind it. All of a sudden he was very aware of how undressed he was, and it wasn't just because of the cold morning breeze. "Ryan?"

"Hi, I know it's early, but I got to the restaurant to start prep work, and Leticia and I got to talking, and, well, because you don't cook—or don't cook a lot, anyway—we made you a care package. Since you're stuck at home and probably aren't up to dealing with hot pots and pans and knives."

It took Zane a few seconds to parse all that. "A care package?"

"Yeah. Italian cold cuts, some fresh bread already sliced, a crock of minestrone, easy stuff. Oh, and cheesecake, of course."

Zane huffed a laugh, truly surprised. "Wow, uh, well. That's great. Thanks."

He heard Ryan laugh quietly. "You're blushing."

"Must be the cold," Zane said quickly, dragging the sticky T-shirt over his chest and hiding bare-chested behind the door.

"You could let me in and shut the door," Ryan suggested, the repressed laughter all too clear in his voice. "That might help with the cold."

Zane squeezed his eyes shut and said a quick prayer. He really, truly, *honestly* had never given Ryan Morelli a single thought other than that he was a nice guy. Now Zane hoped he was right. "Ah, right, yeah, sorry." He cleared his throat and stepped back, opening the door. Ryan thumped up the steps and walked past him, and Zane shut the door firmly before turning around to face blindly into the apartment.

"I grabbed the mail off the steps too. I'll just put this stuff away . . . ah, I see. Well, that explains it."

"Explains what?" Zane asked.

"Why you're blushing. There's breakfast everywhere. Give me a sec and I'll get it cleaned up." Zane tried to object, but Ryan talked right over him. "It's no problem. Actually, here—"

Zane heard a rustle of fabric, then the sink switching on and off. He straightened as he heard Ryan approach. Then Ryan's fingers touched the top of his hand, and Zane flinched in surprise. The touch disappeared, and Zane was again conscious of being half-dressed, his T-shirt crumpled in his hand. When Ryan spoke, he wasn't even an arm's length away.

"Sorry, didn't mean to startle you. Here, you can clean off," he said, and he draped a damp dishtowel over Zane's wrist. "Thanks," Zane murmured.

"No problem, Zane, really." Footsteps moved back toward the kitchen, and Zane followed as he tried to wipe juice and pulp off his arms.

"So, where's your partner?"

Zane paused in surprise. "What?"

"Your partner? Ty, wasn't it?"

"Oh, yeah, Ty," Zane said with a nod. "He's at work."

"Leaving you all on your own?" Ryan's tone conveyed a slight disapproval.

Zane frowned. "No, he's just checking in. Won't be gone long."

"It was nice to meet him. You two must have different shifts since he's never in the restaurant with you. And now you're hurt and he still has to work. You must miss him."

Zane blinked several times as what the man was saying filtered in. "Ah, no, we work together, actually. He's my partner at the Bureau."

"Really?" Zane could hear the surprise in Ryan's voice. "Huh. I didn't get that at all. You said 'partner', and I just assumed . . ."

Zane tipped his head to one side, turning his face to where he thought Ryan stood. "Assumed what?" he asked carefully.

"Sorry." Now Ryan sounded embarrassed. "You make a handsome couple."

Zane was at a loss. Ryan had seen him and Ty at *one* dinner and had come to that conclusion? Then he laughed in more than slight amazement, and the words came out easy as could be. "No, you're right. We *are* . . . together. Not just at work. 'Partner' just makes me think work first."

"Well, good-looking man like that, I'd say you should think 'together' first and 'work' second."

Zane could hear the smile in Ryan's words. "That's good advice," he agreed.

"I know. Okay. All the cleanup's done, food's in the fridge. Is there anything else I can do to help?"

Zane shook his head, still a little thrown. He'd have to remember to tell Ty about this. Maybe he'd drop his crusade against Chiapparelli's. "Thank you for helping with the mess."

"No problem. When you need more food, just call, and somebody will bring another package over or Ty can pick it up." Ryan moved past him, toward the front door.

"Hopefully it won't last that long," Zane said as the door opened. "We'll keep our fingers crossed. Oh, I put the mail on the end of the island there. Take care, Zane."

The door shut before Zane got out another reply. Bemused, he slid onto a bar stool, then curiously reached out to pat the top of the bar. He occasionally got junk mail and circulars left on the steps out front or half-jammed under his door, and that was what the crumpled stack felt like. A couple of envelopes, one with no stamp, some single-sheet pieces of paper folded in halves or thirds, some large sheets of glossy paper with perforations. Zane set the stack back down to look at—to have Ty look at—later.

Right now he needed a shower or he'd smell like Florida's Natural the rest of the day.

"What have you got?" Ty asked as he walked into the conference room where Scott Alston sat working over stacks of paper.

"You're not on this one, Grady," Alston answered seriously. "Go home."

"I went home."

"Yes, but then you came back."

"Who won the pool?" Ty asked as he shrugged Zane's leather jacket off.

"Lassiter. Damn it," Alston muttered. "I had you for four hours."

Ty snorted as he sat down across from the man to reach for the file he was working on. Alston pulled it away and taunted him with it, waving it just out of Ty's reach.

"You're wearing each other's clothes now?" Alston asked wryly.

"Long story," Ty muttered. He gestured for the folder.

"No," Alston told him firmly. "Boss' orders, man."

"What?" Ty demanded.

"They saw you on that newscast, they blew up your car, they blew up your partner. You cannot be involved in the investigation."

"Give me information or I start making a scene."

"Like that's new," Alston muttered as he held the file protectively to his chest and reached for a phone in the center of the conference table. He picked it up and pressed a button, then said in a deep, mockingly serious voice, "I need backup, Conference Room 4."

It wasn't ten seconds later that Harry Lassiter and Fred Perrimore showed up at the door and looked in at Ty in amusement.

"You need to go see McCoy," Alston said neutrally.

Ty pointed his finger at Alston and waved it threateningly. "Next time you get blown up, don't come whining to me."

Alston smirked crookedly at him. "Game next week is at seven," he reminded as Ty stalked out of the office. "Don't forget you'll need a ride!"

"Kiss my ass, Alston," Ty shot back over his shoulder as he made his way to the Special Agent in Charge's office.

"You might as well come in, Grady. My trouble meter started dinging the minute you stepped in the building," Dan McCoy said before Ty had even darkened his threshold. He sat behind his desk expectantly, smoothing his tie.

Ty's jaw tightened as he bit back the response that immediately came to mind. He breathed out slowly through his nose, then calmly asked, "How long am I being kept out of the loop on this case?"

"As I said, we're considering you a possible target," McCoy said in his deep, gravelly voice, repeating what Alston had said. "You and Garrett were at both locations during the events. Now, I know it could just be coincidence," he added, holding up a hand in a "wait" motion. "But until we know for sure, you're grounded."

"I'm not asking to be part of the investigation," Ty pointed out as he stepped into the office. "I just want to know what we've found. Do we have suspects? Has forensics gone over the components? Was it even the same signature?"

"No, in process, and yes," McCoy rattled back. "Look, Grady. There's not much I can tell you. We're pulling in every single person we can from both scenes to submit reports so we can try to rebuild what happened. But there's precious little to work with right now. And two more banks were hit on the same days, so our agents are worn thin."

"Two more banks?" Ty asked, pulling up short. "That's not weird at all."

"Yes, thank you, Kojak, we've already connected the dots on that one."

"If the bombs are being set solely as distractions so banks can be robbed, then why am I being considered a target?" Ty posed.

"Because you're you—you're always a target."

"That seems unreasonable," Ty muttered disconsolately. "Look, you've got to be stretched to the limit on this."

"We are."

"All the more reason to let me do something."

"The last time you worked a bomb, you ended up blowing something kind of important up. And the last bank robbery you worked, you didn't have any gray hair," McCoy told him.

Ty frowned and looked up as if he could see his own hair. "I have gray hair?"

McCoy laughed at him.

Ty growled in frustration and looked away. Either this was a friend being blunt, or it was his superior being evasive. Either way, he wasn't going to get any information. He sighed. "Fine," he agreed grudgingly. He'd find another way to get some information. Instead he moved on to the other reason he'd come in. "I need to find a rookie that was at the second scene. He drove me to the hospital, then ran off with Garrett's keys."

McCoy frowned. "What rookie?"

"He looked about fifteen. I can't remember his name," Ty admitted as he closed his eyes and tried to visualize the name on the windbreaker the kid had been wearing. "Reece, maybe? Reeves?" he tried.

"Reeves?" Alston asked from behind him.

"Sounds right," Ty told him with a shrug as he turned to look back at him. Apparently he and the others had followed Ty to McCoy's office to watch any fireworks that ensued.

"Ty," Alston said with a frown. "Special Agent Lydia Reeves was inside the building when the bomb went off. She was carried out right before Garrett, hurt pretty bad. She's still in the ICU at UMMC."

Ty stared at him, not quite comprehending what he'd said at first. Then the implications came tumbling down on him so hard he almost physically staggered.

"They'd have a spotter," he said softly. "They'd set the bomb and find some way to watch the response."

"Bomber picked up her windbreaker to get closer?" Alston ventured with a frown. "Wait, did you say he kept Garrett's keys? Where is Garrett now?"

Ty was already pushing past him and sprinting for the stairwell.

"Behind you!" Alston shouted, and Ty knew the man was calling in backup to meet them at Zane's apartment. He took out his own phone and hit the speed dial as he raced down the stairs for the parking deck and the hated Valkyrie.

The phone rang and rang with no answer, and Zane's voice mail picked up, his recorded voice serious and to the point before the beep. Ty cursed as the beep sounded and snapped the phone shut. It wasn't like someone would have to attack Zane to hurt him. All they'd have to do was knock on the door, quietly place a bomb in the house, since Zane couldn't see it to know it was there, and the job was done. A neighbor with chicken soup. A deliveryman with flowers. Zane would never be the wiser.

Ty shoved through the stairwell door and darted across the parking deck. He knew he should wait for Alston and a car and backup, but he also knew deep down he could get there a hell of a lot faster on the stupid freaking motorcycle.

Zane leaned forward against the wall, weight on his forearms and head down as the hot water pounded down on his neck and shoulders, splattering down over his back. He tipped his head from side to side, sighing as he felt the muscles relaxing. He'd gotten rid of the scent of orange juice and the sticky pulp residue, but he was nowhere near brainstorming through all the possible fallout scenarios of telling Ty that Ryan had brought him that care package.

Stewing over it wasn't helping his headache; it was a bad one today. The doctor had said he'd have them. Zane just hadn't expected them to get worse. He groaned and turned around so the water streamed down his back.

Then there was a sound under the noise of the water running, something slamming in the outer room. Zane's head snapped up. It hadn't been two hours for it to be Ty. Maybe one, but certainly not two. He frowned and cocked his head to listen. Another sound followed the first, a door being kicked open and banging against a wall.

Zane's hand curled into a fist. Here he was, wet, naked, unarmed, *blind* . . . and he could be in real trouble. His knives and gun were on the dresser in the bedroom. He couldn't do anything but wait.

He didn't have to wait long. After another tense moment, the door to the bathroom burst open, banging against the sink as someone took two heavy steps into the room.

"Zane?" Ty called out over the rush of the water.

Zane let out a shaky breath, and his shoulders thumped back against the tile wall. "Yeah?"

Ty cursed softly as another voice from somewhere in the apartment called out, "Clear!" followed by a reply of the same. "What?" Zane asked, confused. "What the hell's going on?"

"Why the fuck aren't you answering your phone?" Ty demanded. The shower curtain was noisily yanked back, and cold air assaulted him.

"I'm in the fucking shower," Zane snapped. "What's going on?"

Ty reached past him and turned off the water. Once it stopped running, Zane could hear the sound of several more people milling about outside the bathroom. "Get dressed," Ty muttered, sounding angry and stressed and not the least bit apologetic.

Then he was gone, and the bathroom door clicked shut.

Zane growled as he carefully got out of the shower and set one hand on the counter. He didn't have any clothes in here. With an aggravated huff, he grabbed one of the extra-large bath sheets and wrapped it around his waist, tucking in the end. "He'd better have a good reason for this," Zane said under his breath as he slicked one hand through his wet hair, leaving it to drip onto his shoulders, and he opened the door.

He could hear voices in the kitchen and living room. A lot of voices. At least four, not including Ty's. "Jesus Christ, Grady, where'd you learn to ride a motorcycle like that?" a male voice was saying breathlessly as Zane made his way down the hallway.

"West Virginia," Ty muttered in response.

"I didn't think they had sidewalks in West Virginia." Zane recognized Alston's voice now, tinged with amusement. "You sure as hell were riding on one."

Zane stopped in the doorway to the living room, one hand holding onto the towel, and immediately shuddered. Two open doors made for a frigid February crosswind through his apartment. "And again I say, what the hell is going on?"

Ty cleared his throat somewhere to Zane's right, in the kitchen. "Remember the kid who has your keys?" he asked Zane.

Zane turned his head blindly toward Ty. "Yeah?" he ventured.

"Turns out he ain't a Fed," Ty muttered. "Freddy, call a locksmith, will you?" he added as he turned away from Zane and spoke to someone else in the room. Zane recognized Perrimore's bass tones making the phone call as directed.

Frowning a little, Zane connected that piece of information with the men in the room, and he shook his head. "I never knew I had so many friends."

"You don't," someone called back wryly. Lassiter. Smart-ass.

Great. The whole team was here. Although he hadn't heard Clancy yet.

"Guys, close the doors. It's freezing."

There she was. Great. Zane suppressed a grimace, and then the back door shut, cutting off the wind.

"I want new locks on the doors in the next hour. Sweep the place for devices: bugs, bombs, everything." Ty's voice had carried over the chatter that broke out. "I want the file on the investigation, and I want every suspect name you've got," Ty said in a lower voice, obviously speaking to someone in particular.

"You know I can't do that, Ty," Alston answered seriously.

"You owe me, Scott," Ty whispered.

There was silence in response. Finally, Alston murmured something, and Ty thanked him sincerely. Then Zane heard footsteps stop in front of him.

"We're going to my place," Ty announced without preamble. "'Til we know it's safe."

After bumping into something hard for about the fifth time, Zane sighed and tried to visualize the first level of Ty's house again. It wasn't that complex a layout, being a long, narrow shape, but Zane would have to "learn" his way around, counting steps like he had at his own apartment. And that was frustrating.

He heard something thump upstairs and relaxed. Ty was up there instead of watching Zane embarrass himself. At least there was that.

Zane reached out to touch what was in front of him. It was an end table that stood by the arm of the couch against the wall of the narrow living room. He took a moment to orient himself, and then he turned left and took three steps, which—in theory—should put him close to the overstuffed chair he sat in a lot of the time while over here. When he reached out, his fingers jabbed into the soft fabric, and he cursed under his breath. He was closer than he'd expected. He made an adjustment to the mental map, but before he could strike out in another direction, he thought he heard something odd too close to him, and he stayed in place, trying to identify the noise.

It was silent for a few heartbeats. Then a hand touched his elbow. Zane flinched and inhaled sharply even though a split second later he knew it could only be Ty. A soft whiff of Old Spice confirmed it.

"Sorry!" Ty said quickly as he snatched his hand away. "Didn't mean to scare you," he mumbled as the hand returned to Zane's elbow.

"Weren't you upstairs like . . . thirty seconds ago?" Zane asked in surprise.

"Yeah, I was putting on socks," Ty answered with an almost audible shrug. "Feet are cold. Why, did you need something?"

"No. I just didn't hear you come down." Zane shook his head and crossed his arms, and he caught himself blinking against the utter darkness. His eyes were dry and scratchy, and he reached up to rub at one. The nurse had said it was because the eye could not perceive light to force dilation, so his eyes wouldn't produce protective tears as they normally would.

Ty's hand caught his, pulling it away from his face. He felt Ty move closer, and the callused hand at his cheek moved to cup his face. "Don't do that," Ty chided gently. "You want some more eyedrops?"

Zane nodded, resisting the urge to apologize like he had the first twenty times. "Yeah. They're in that bag from the hospital," he said, resignation swamping him again.

Ty was silent as he moved away. Zane had to wonder whether it was because he didn't know what to say to him now that he was blind. It was possible that Ty had always been relatively quiet the majority of the time and Zane had never noticed it because of the spurts of rampant activity and rambling. He told himself that was just one more thing he was going to pay attention to if he ever got his sight back. There was so much he realized now that he'd taken for granted.

A few moments later, Zane heard the bag rustling, and then Ty pressed the eyedrops into his hand.

"Need anything else?"

Zane felt the childish desire for a kiss and hug, but that was a little much, even for him. He was already becoming a huge drain of Ty's time and patience. "No, thank you," he murmured. "I'm just going to bum around down here if you have something to do."

Ty made a frustrated noise. "You know what, sitting around here being miserable isn't going to do you any good," he said abruptly. He took Zane's hand and gave him a small tug, guiding him over to the couch and unceremoniously shoving him onto it. "Sit here. I'll be right back."

"What—" Zane cut himself off as he bounced on the cushions. There was no point in questioning Ty. It was a little refreshing, actually, to be called on his moping. Zane put some drops in his eyes, then leaned back into the corner of the couch and waited, brooding. He knew he was in a shitty mood, but he also was inclined to think he was justified.

From somewhere in front of him there was a click, followed by soft music wafting from what Zane recognized as Ty's Bose iPod dock. It had been a gift from Deuce, something Ty rarely used, and it sat on one of the shelves along the brick wall of the living room.

Ty's taste in music was eclectic, to say the least. He would blast classic rock and heavy metal in the Bronco when they drove on some days, and on others it would be laid-back country. When he worked out, it was thumping club music, something that would get the adrenaline pumping, but at home on the rare occasions when he listened to music, it was often folksy blues or indie rock, occasionally even something from the Rat Pack days. Zane never knew what to expect out of Ty's sound system.

Now the music was slow and relaxed, with a bittersweet undertone. Then, below the melody, was the unmistakable sound of the coffee table being shoved off the rug onto the hardwood, away from the center of the room.

Ty took his hand and pulled at him. "Come dance with me, Zane," he requested quietly.

Zane's stomach flipped as he got to his feet, his hand folding into Ty's after the gentle tug. He wondered if he looked as surprised as he felt and what expression was on Ty's face right now. He took a few cautious steps after Ty out onto the cleared rug, the surprise melting into a deeply felt curl of pleasure and sparkle of unexpected nerves.

Ty laughed as he pulled Zane to him and they fumbled over where to put their hands and how to hold each other. His breath was warm on Zane's cheek, and for the first time, Zane could feel the way Ty held himself as he prepared to dance, confident and strong. He'd seen it on the cruise ship when Ty had done a damn good tango. When they'd danced at the club, it had been more of a whirling mosh pit. This would be their first *real* dance.

"You lead, I'll follow," Ty offered.

"I'd rather follow you," Zane murmured, absolutely aware of how many meanings those words held right now.

Ty's hand tightened in his, repositioning them, and his other arm wrapped around Zane until they were close enough that Zane could feel Ty's movements deep down. He started with slow, easy steps, a real box step and turn to match the music, not just a graceless shuffle. This Zane could do without thinking about it, Ty's body and the music guiding him. He literally didn't need to see a thing. He draped his free hand over Ty's shoulder and relaxed into Ty's arms, their cheeks brushing with each step. Ty turned his face toward Zane's, touching his nose and lips to Zane's cheek, and he curled Zane's hand between them, holding it against his chest. They swayed gently with the music, but Ty would occasionally pick up the pace and turn Zane in a faster circle as the instrumental chorus picked up. Then he would slow them again, pulling Zane closer, pressing their cheeks together in a gesture that was borderline sensual as the music moved them.

Zane's pulse thrummed as he gave himself over totally into Ty's hands, following his capable direction and floating on the music. His bad mood didn't stand a chance, and Zane could even feel a smile pulling at his lips. He'd thought about this, a slow dance with his lover, not a flashy tango or a writhing clash under a disco ball. But he'd never dreamed he would get one. It was possibly one of the most erotic, most *loving* things Ty had ever done for him.

Neither of them had shaved in a few days; Ty's cheek scratched alongside Zane's. But his lips pressed to the corner of Zane's mouth and stayed there. It wasn't quite a kiss. His movements were relaxed and natural. The way his body moved to the music and was able to lead Zane's would have been gorgeous to see. It was better to feel, though.

The song began to wind down, threatening to end the moment. Zane's hand tightened on Ty's shoulder without conscious thought, and he finally turned his face carefully, skimming their lips together. Ty returned the kiss just as tentatively. They slowed to a stop as the song ended, and Ty kissed him again as they stood in the middle of the living room. The next song started up, similar in tempo, still soulful and brooding like the first. Ty didn't move with the music, though, choosing to hold Zane to him and kiss him instead, and Zane had no desire whatsoever to move from that spot. This was something new and fragile, something more intense and yet more comfortable.

Maybe Ty had chosen this because he knew how much Zane loved to dance and he'd been searching for anything he could think of to divert his cranky partner. Maybe he had wanted to do this as badly as Zane. Whichever it was, Zane didn't care. He gave in to the desire he'd quashed earlier and slowly tried to wind himself tighter around Ty.

Ty let him do as he pleased, indulging in the kiss even as he started their dance again, and Zane felt better than he had since before the accident. The tender kisses kindled a cozy golden glow inside him. With his lips on Ty's, his eyes closed and Ty's arms around him, the world didn't feel dark and foreboding.

They continued like that, swaying languidly to the music, and when their lips finally parted, Zane heard himself whisper, "I love you."

Ty snorted softly, as if the words amused him. He didn't stop the swaying motion of their dance. "You're being seduced," he said in a warm voice. He murmured his words against the corner of Zane's lips.

Zane sighed shakily, a tremor of shock echoing through him. He hadn't realized what he'd said before Ty's reply, and his pulse kicked up as it crashed in. Now he didn't know what to say at all, and he felt flushed all over, still shocked by what had slipped out. He wasn't sure if he was relieved or disappointed that Ty had brushed it off—all he could feel was the swelling ache in his chest. "Seduced?" he managed to get out.

Ty hummed and smiled against his cheek. "I was good at this sort of thing once."

The awareness rippling through him made Zane huff out a quiet laugh as he tried to get ahold of himself and let the panic fade. "You're still good at this sort of thing. You could tell me to do anything right now, and I'd try."

Ty slowed their motions to a stop. He grazed his lips over Zane's, still holding him as if they were dancing. His words were whispered when they parted. "Then I want you to close your eyes and dance with me. Tonight, forget that you can't see."

Zane obeyed, and his eyelids fluttered down as he focused on feeling Ty, absorbing the power and magnetism of his presence, so strong that a warm buzz rippled through Zane, urging him to release his surprise and worry, to simply *be* with Ty.

Ty readjusted his hold, pulling him closer and starting into the slow sway again. He began to hum along with the song, and soon he was singing quietly near Zane's ear. Zane had never heard him sing. He truly did have an incredible speaking voice, deep and soulful with that hint of a growl. His singing voice was no less impressive. It washed through Zane, their bodies melding with the dance, and Zane was hopelessly, helplessly lost in him.

CHAPTER TEN

G raham's parents had been in France for the last two months and would be there for another week, so Pierce's crew had been using his house as a home base. Graham sat at the kitchen table, one leg bouncing furiously underneath it as he tapped at the laptop in front of him, paging through news articles. Their press coverage increased every day, feeding Pierce's confidence. As if his ego needed any more stroking. Pierce had been on his high horse for days now, ordering them around. Ross seemed happy enough to keep on with Pierce's schemes, but ever since finding out about Mr. Garrett, the great master plan had lost its shine for Graham. He was pretty sure Hannah felt the same way. Every time he saw her, she looked more and more like a scared rabbit.

"So, Ross," Pierce said from his seat at the head of the table, chest puffed up with self-assumed authority, "you're going to get those keys so we can get into the gym to plant the bomb. I'm picking up the last of the supplies tomorrow, and then I can start building it. This bomb will be the best yet."

"Sure thing, Pierce," Ross agreed, tapping out his orders on the iPad in front of him.

"What gym?" Hannah asked.

"We can't get into a cop gym. They're, like, guarded or in the bottom of the station, aren't they?"

"We got into their baseball diamond, didn't we? Anyway, we're not going after a cop gym. We're planting it at the Y on Druid Hill," Pierce said.

"The Y?" Hannah's voice edged up. "I thought we were only blowing up places with cops. That we weren't going to go after regular people. The mall was bad enough."

"The mall was our best hit yet! And it was because there were civilians there. And the press. The pigs are more likely to fuck things up if they're showing off for the fucking media," Pierce snapped. "Besides, the web site says the gym is closed for renovation. No one will get hurt that doesn't deserve it."

Hannah looked down, frowning faintly as she poked at one of the bank bags in front of her.

"They raised over a million dollars to build that new gym," Pierce said, sounding far too pleased with himself. Graham didn't know why. The Y was a charity, wasn't it? It wasn't like blowing up some million-dollar store. *Didn't the other bombs do enough damage?*

"Why do we need a better bomb?" Graham couldn't help but ask. "The others didn't do enough damage?"

"No, they didn't," Pierce said flatly.

"A bomb is a bomb, isn't it?" Hannah asked tentatively. "It's just supposed to keep them away from the banks."

Pierce smacked his hand on the tabletop, and Hannah cringed. "It needs to be a better bomb because I said so."

Graham's stomach began to roil. He hoped that Mr. Garrett had found that note by now. It was okay, robbing banks. It was kind of cool, kind of badass, and fuck the banks anyway. It's not like they ever did anything good for anyone. He had heard his dad grumbling about all the money they'd lost when . . . well, Graham didn't really understand that part, and half of it had to do with politics anyway and who cared about that, but it had been fun, going after something everyone seemed to think was so big and powerful. Plus, if they got enough money Graham could quit his crappy restaurant job his father had made him get to teach him "fiscal responsibility."

But Pierce was getting scary. It wasn't about the money to him anymore, and Graham didn't know when—or if—he'd stop. They'd been lucky more people hadn't been hurt at the mall.

"Pierce, we're really hurting people—"

"Just the fucking cops!" Pierce yelled.

"So which one are we hitting next?" Ross asked, looking so eager that the acid started inching up through Graham's gullet.

"'We' aren't," Pierce said with a smug smile. "Hannah is."

Hannah went totally white. "What? Me?"

"It's about time you did something besides making phone calls," Pierce ordered. "Time to earn your part of the take. You're going to rob the bank this time."

"B-b-but I don't know how!" Hannah wailed, wringing her hands.

"Suck it up, Hannah," Pierce said harshly. "You want your money so you can get away from Stepmommy Dearest, you'll do what I tell you. You hear me?"

"Yes," Hannah mewled, slumping in on herself.

"So what are we doing while Hannah's hitting the bank?" Ross asked.

"Graham's going to have the car nearby to get Hannah when she comes out. You and I are going to take care of those two piece of shit pigs who called us out on TV," Pierce said with such relish that Graham had to swallow hard on his gorge.

"Do you know who they are yet?"

"The loudmouth's name is Grady. I can't find his address, but I'm going to follow him home from the FBI one day."

"Why didn't you just take care of him when you had him in the car that time?" Ross asked.

Pierce's face reddened. He'd talked a lot of talk, but Graham had seen the size of the FBI agent. He knew exactly why Pierce hadn't "taken care" of him. Agent Grady would tear Pierce's arms off like a pit bull playing with a kitten.

"I want to make him suffer first!" Pierce shouted.

Ross raised his hands in a placating gesture, and suddenly Pierce was fine again.

"So Graham, you have to find a getaway car."

"We can use that kickass truck," Ross suggested.

"That Fed won't be needing it," Pierce said smugly, pulling out a ring of keys and twirling it on his finger.

"I'm not driving a truck you stole from a Fed!" Graham said, feeling his stomach flip unpleasantly.

"Then you better come up with something of your own," Pierce snapped. "You don't like the truck, then I'll drive it. I've already replaced the plate."

Graham slumped down into his chair under the sense of impending doom that hung in the air.

Pierce stood up and leaned over, planting his hands on top of the mess of schematics and maps. "We keep going. No one's getting hurt who doesn't deserve it." He reached out to the middle of the kitchen table and plucked up the pink ceramic piggy bank he'd set there the day he first laid out his plans. "We're gonna split this city wide open," he said, smirking before deliberately dropping the pig to the table and watching it crack right through the middle.

"Ty, you need a break," Zane said as he walked slowly into the living room. He was almost certain Ty was in the kitchen on the other side of the bar. He'd heard glass bottles clanking in the refrigerator.

It wasn't even the weekend yet, and Zane knew the babysitter role had to be chafing. While Ty had been good as gold in the two days since moving Zane to his row house, it couldn't last much longer. Zane didn't *want* it to last; it was starting to freak him out. He almost wanted to pick a fight just to hear Ty rant so it would vault him back out of *The Twilight Zone*.

"What?" Ty asked in a muffled voice, as if he was kneeling below the level of the kitchen counter.

Zane frowned as he reached out in front of him, certain the bar should be there. "I said you need a break. What are you doing? You sound like you're in a hole."

He felt more than heard Ty stand quickly, right in front of him. "Nothing."

Zane tipped his head to the side, trying to remember what Ty kept in the cabinets under the bar. He didn't believe Ty for an instant, but since he couldn't hear anything ticking, he let it go. "Nothing," he stated. "Yeah, that's the problem. You need a *break*," he stated for the third time.

"I wasn't doing anything," Ty insisted in his most innocent voice. It turned more suspicious as he kept talking. "A break from what?"

Now Zane was sure he didn't want to know what Ty had been doing. "A break from your babysitting duties."

"Oh," Ty said with a huff. "Why do you say that? I haven't set fire to anything lately."

Normally, Zane would just give Ty a *look*, deeming the just-spoken words bullshit. But since he couldn't see Ty to focus on him, that wasn't going to work. "But you have the matches in hand," Zane said knowingly.

Ty cleared his throat. "What would you suggest, then, since you can't be left to your own incompetent devices?"

"I think I can manage for a while," Zane said seriously. "Go out. Do something. You've been fluttering like your mom. Not that I don't enjoy it, but I can hear you twitching."

"Fluttering like my mom?" Ty repeated with special emphasis on the words that insulted him, meaning all of them. Zane heard him throw something that flopped like heavy paper onto the counter. "You are an ungrateful jackass," Ty said slowly.

"Ty, I don't think I could be more grateful. I just don't want you to resent helping me."

"You told me I flutter like my mom!"

"To me, that's a hell of a compliment. It means you care enough to stick around and take care of me even when it's driving you crazy," Zane tried to explain. This wasn't how he'd expected Ty to react. He'd figured Ty would have been off like a shot. Not in a bad way, just in a golden-retriever-shut-up-in-the-house-way-too-fucking-long way.

Ty snorted like a bull, and even though Zane couldn't see him, he instinctively knew Ty's head was down. "Well, what about you?" Ty countered, his voice obstinate. "You feeling the need to climb out the window too?"

"Absolutely. But the overwhelming fear of free fall is a definite deterrent," Zane replied, setting both hands on the bar as he shifted his weight. "So I'm sticking with iTunes on the couch for now. You can download a new book for me. That'll keep me amused for hours."

Ty hummed unhappily. "I don't like the idea of leaving you alone. And not just because you could catch a toe on the carpet and go plummeting down the steps."

"You don't have carpet on the steps."

"Not the point."

"We have to try it sometime," Zane said quietly. "As much as the idea appeals, you can't be within shouting distance forever."

"You getting tired of me?" Ty posed in the same tone.

"No." Zane also had a more florid answer, but he didn't think making Ty guffaw would really help this discussion. He'd be a happy man if he had Ty within arm's reach at all times.

"Okay. So. A couple days apart so we don't kill each other, is that what we're talking about?" Ty asked as he started moving around behind the counter.

Zane hadn't really been thinking in terms of *days*. He'd simply been hoping to get Ty out of the house for a couple of *hours*. He really had no idea how he'd cope by himself for days, but to keep Ty from fraying around the edges, he'd get through it. "Sure," he tried to answer confidently.

"I'm not comfortable with you being alone, Zane," Ty told him with the sort of blunt honesty for which most people disliked him. "So give me an alternative, or killing each other is what we've got."

Zane turned in place as Ty moved past him, and he kept his hands behind him, gripping the edge of the bar. "I could hire a nurse to sit here and read to me," he offered, hoping for a laugh.

"Sponge baths are a no. Even I have my limits as to what I'll let you get away with," Ty muttered irritably. He might or might not have been joking, but it was the second time he'd alluded to the concept of jealousy on his part in the last week, and Zane felt a mild wave of surprise. Ty went on talking as if he'd never touched the subject. "We could call in reinforcements. Maybe Deacon could come down for a few days, get your head on straight again."

"I like Deuce, but I don't need a shrink for this. Anyone in their right mind would be scared out of it in this situation," Zane pointed out, trying to keep his calm. Both of them yelling would end with either slamming doors or a furious fuck, neither of which would resolve the problem for any longer than an hour. He could feel Ty pacing around the small dining area that divided the lower level of the row house. The image of a caged tiger came to mind.

"Then how about this, Zane? Either come up with a viable alternative or fucking stop telling me I need a break!" Ty growled at him dangerously as he moved into the living room. "How about I call Shannon back? She offered to come stay with you, and Elaina—" A sudden pounding on the front door interrupted him and made Zane jump.

"Hold that thought," Ty grumbled. Zane heard him draw a gun from somewhere and head for the door.

In a solitary moment of optimism, Ty allowed himself to hope it was one of the field agents working the case at the door, standing on the front stoop, having magically found Zane's keys, explaining it had all been a mistake and Zane was safe.

He peered through the peephole and cursed emphatically when he saw who really stood out there. Four men, all with identical duffel bags in various stages of wear and tear, all peering down the street at the inconspicuous FBI sedan that civilians shouldn't have been able to spot parked a block away from Ty's door.

Marine Force Recon Team Sidewinder. All four of them. As soon as he laid eyes on them, he knew why they were there.

"Shit, shit, shit," Ty muttered as he flipped the deadbolt and pulled open the door. They all turned to look at him with smiles, but he stood in the doorway with his mouth open, ready to offer an apology. He must have looked more surprised than he thought, though, because Nick O'Flaherty rolled his eyes and groaned.

"You forgot," he said accusingly.

"Yes," Ty admitted immediately. The other three men groaned as well and began a running commentary worthy of any peanut gallery.

Ty looked to Nick and shrugged helplessly. Nick was nearly his height, with dark reddish-blond hair and every earmark of a sturdy Irishman from Boston. His eyes were bright green and usually filled with the same sort of mischief as Ty's. He was a kindred spirit in every sense of the word. They'd shared a seat on the bus to Parris Island and risen through the ranks together. Nick was, for all intents and purposes, Ty's best and oldest friend.

"It's been a hell of a week," Ty tried to explain.

"Who is it?" Zane asked curiously from behind him.

Ty turned sideways to look back at him, giving the four men on the stoop a clear view of his partner.

"Uh . . . guys, this is Zane Garrett, my partner," he said as he tried to decide how best to handle the sudden overflow of guests, especially when four of them were going to be irritated as hell. He looked back at them. "Stop loitering in my front door and get your asses in here."

They filed in obediently, and with six big men standing in the living room, the house was suddenly very small. As soon as Ty shut the door, he gestured at Zane again. "He lost his vision in an explosion a few days ago. He's staying with me until he gets it back or we catch the guy. Zane, this is . . . my Recon team."

"What remains of it, anyway. Team Sidewinder, at your service," Nick provided with more than a hint of pride.

Zane stayed in place at the foot of the stairs, hands in his pockets. "A surprise visit from the whole team?" His voice was a little flat, and Ty knew he had to be uncomfortable.

"Not technically a surprise," Nick answered before Ty could open his mouth.

Ty cleared his throat. "I forgot," he said again, for Zane's benefit and theirs. "Zane, this is Nick O'Flaherty. Boston accent. Owen Johns, upstate New York. Kelly Abbott, Colorado. And Digger, deep Bayou." His name was actually Duruand Garrigou, but since none of them had ever been able to pronounce his name to his satisfaction, he'd been Digger since he'd joined the team.

They each offered mumbled hellos in turn, looking at Ty oddly as they did so.

After a short awkward silence, Zane spoke up. "So there's a planned something going on? The thing you forgot?" he prompted Ty.

Ty held his breath, looking from Zane to the other four uncomfortably. They all looked at him expectantly. "I'm sorry!" he finally blurted. "It's been a rough week, okay? They blew up my Bronco, then they blew up my partner, and I got a little distracted."

Kelly and Digger looked at each other pointedly. "Revenge kick," Kelly decided.

"No doubt," Digger agreed.

Ty gave them both a disgusted grunt.

"Hey, don't worry about it," Nick offered easily. He looked over at Zane. "We'd planned to go out in the woods and play some paintball this weekend," he explained for Zane's benefit. "We do it every few months. It was Grady's turn to host."

"Sounds fun," Zane said, a little more energy in his voice this time. He must have been listening to who was standing where, because he turned his head toward Ty. "You should go."

"We *just* had this conversation, Garrett," Ty said in frustration. "I'm not leaving you alone until you can see or they've caught the bomber."

"This sounds pretty heavy," Nick commented drily.

"Welcome to my fucking life," Ty snapped. Nick merely laughed at him.

"We don't have to go anywhere. If we stick around Grady, we can probably shoot real guns eventually," Kelly offered as he sat down on the couch behind him. He had been their Navy corpsman, the medical officer. He'd gone through the same training they had and then some. He was slim and wiry, with unremarkable brown hair and eyes a variable color between blue and gray. His manner was unassuming and affable, but he was the only member of their six-man team who'd been undefeated in sparring matches. He was hell on wheels with or without a weapon.

"I flew from fucking San Diego. I'm shooting something," Owen announced irritably.

"I hear that," Zane muttered. "Look. They changed the locks at my place. I can go there. I know my way around better there anyway." He was sounding sensible, in front of witnesses, and Ty wanted to throttle him for it. "You can visit with them and come check on me in the evenings if you want." Zane gave him a ghost of a smile. "I'll have dinner delivered."

"Were you two the targets?" Nick asked.

"No," Ty answered curtly, still glaring at Zane.

"Maybe," Zane corrected.

"It's possible," Ty granted reluctantly. "Look, I can't leave town right now. A bomber's targeting municipal and federal law enforcement and rescue crews, banks are being robbed all over the place, the city's going nuts—"

"Well, aren't you Mr. Doom and Gloom," Digger observed with a smirk. He was a good-looking man, his skin so dark that they'd never had to paint him with grease oil on a mission to hide him in the dark. His accent was deep Louisiana, which meant half the time he wasn't coherent and the other half he was bitching at them for not answering his questions.

"Anything we can do to help?" Nick offered as the others settled onto the couch together. They reminded Ty of the no-evil monkeys, lined up in a row. He frowned at them suspiciously.

"*Please* take him out of the house for at least a few hours and make him burn off some energy," Zane said immediately. "I can hear him bouncing. Go down to Fell's Point or something nearby."

"You'll be bouncing down the stairs, traitor," Ty snapped.

"Okay, then!" Nick said with a laugh. He stepped up and put his arm over Ty's shoulders as if to restrain him. "We'll pass on paintball and just bum around the city for a few days. In case you need us," he said to Ty. The others nodded and murmured in agreement.

"Usually end up with paintball welts on my nads anyway," Owen grumbled as he examined his fingernails with a frown.

"That's 'cause you always bend over and try to kiss your ass goodbye," Kelly told him sensibly. Ty rolled his eyes.

Nick spoke over them, ignoring the running commentary from the couch. "Garrett, why don't you come with us to dinner? We wouldn't mind getting to know Ty's partner, especially since he's gone this long without trading you in or hitting you."

Zane smiled for the first time since the guys had come in. "Well, you're half right." He shrugged. "I'm game. We haven't eaten yet."

"Great!" Nick said as he looked at Ty triumphantly. "We've never met one of Ty's partners. We were starting to think they were just a myth."

The Greene Turtle Sports Bar & Grille attracted a busy crowd in the evenings. It was a popular hangout in Fell's Point, located along the cobblestone roads that lined the harbor, its tables inside and outside always full and busy with a mix of locals and tourists. It took several minutes of waiting before the team plus one could get a table big enough for all of them to spread out. Nick knew it wasn't Ty's favorite hangout. He always took them a few streets over, to a hole-in-the-wall bar called One-Eyed Mike's. He must have brought them here out of consideration for Zane's blindness.

Nick watched as Ty walked Zane in, staying close, holding his elbow. This Zane Garrett seemed to trust Ty a hell of a lot. He hadn't questioned Ty's instructions even once as they walked the few blocks here and wound through the crowd to a table near the TVs in the back. Ty got him seated in the corner where people wouldn't bump into him and thumped down in a chair beside him.

When Ty finally got settled and glanced toward Nick, Nick gave him a questioning look and nodded his head toward Zane. Ty shrugged easily, letting the unspoken question slide off his shoulders in a way only Ty could. Nick was going to have to get his old friend alone soon and interrogate him.

Until then, he slid into the seat next to Ty, leaning over him to look at Zane. "So give us the story," he told them both. "Zane, we need a new supply of embarrassing Grady tales."

Zane grinned, though his eyes remained downcast. He set one hand on the table in front of him, closing his hand around the edge. "Well, there was this time at the Chinese laundry—"

"No," Ty broke in urgently. He raised his hand to call the waitress over, ordering five drinks by holding up five long fingers and then twirling his index finger around the table. Nick's eyes followed the motion, then moved to look at Ty. He looked worn out, not as apt to go spinning toward the ceiling as the Ty Grady Nick knew so well.

"There's six of us, man," Owen interrupted. "Who's not drinking?"

"That would be me," Zane said.

"Forgive me for stating the obvious, but you don't appear to be the designated-driver type right now," Kelly said wryly.

Ty nudged Nick's elbow, and when Nick glanced at him, Ty put his thumb and index finger out like he was holding a shot glass and tipped it toward his mouth. Nick nodded in understanding.

"A drink is the last thing I need right now," Zane said as he leaned back in his chair.

Nick clucked his tongue. So Ty's partner was an alcoholic. That was uncomfortable. He searched for something to say, watching his companions closely. Zane seemed okay with the topic, but Ty's shoulders had tensed, and he was looking at the table devotedly. Nick knew the posture well, had seen Ty assume it many times. He was preparing to defend a friend.

"So," Nick drew out, "Chinese laundry, huh?"

Zane rapped his knuckles on the table. "Three guys and a dog walk into a Chinese laundry—" he started, phrasing it like a joke.

"Dude," Ty interrupted again. "I told them before we went in: that dog was eyeing me funny!"

Nick chuckled as the others started in on Ty. Nick waited until Ty turned his head to look at him, meeting his hazel eyes, then reached out and patted his shoulder consolingly. Only the two of them and the man who'd debriefed them knew why Ty didn't favor dogs.

Zane continued with the story, telling it well and drawing chuckles from the guys and a dirty look from Ty. It was funny as hell, really, and Nick could imagine Ty and a dog both ending up in a vat of suds and fighting over who could scramble out first. Of course, the dog had won. Digger launched into another story right after, and the laughter continued. When drinks were delivered, the waitress brought a Coke, too, and she moved to scoot around the table to put it in front of Zane.

"Thank you, darlin'," Ty drawled. She winked at him and let her hand rest on Zane's arm as she moved away. Zane lifted his head and sent a smile in that direction. Obviously, they came here a lot. Nick watched Ty for a minute longer. Ty rarely went drinking with his co-workers. Zane Garrett was obviously his friend, and a close one at that.

Zane set his hand on the table and shifted it slightly. He didn't even say anything. Ty continued talking to Digger as he moved the glass of Coke against Zane's fingers. The corner of Zane's mouth quirked up as he picked up the drink.

Nick was surprised to find that Ty and Zane reminded him of Ty and . . . him. He was also surprised by the spike of jealousy. Knowing he could watch Zane without being seen as long as Ty was occupied, Nick observed him for a while longer. He was a good-looking guy, perhaps five years older than Ty and himself, maybe more. He had his head cocked to one side, the one ear turned toward Ty, and a small smile played on his lips as Ty talked about something there was no way Zane knew anything about, since it was an old line from their Recon days.

It had to feel good to be included, being blind and lost. He glanced at Ty and wondered if Ty had gone through the "it could have been me" panic. The Ty he knew wouldn't tolerate the darkness—or the helplessness—well at all, whereas Zane, by all appearances, seemed subdued but in fairly good spirits. At least Nick hoped this was subdued. He couldn't imagine Ty staying with a stick-up-his-ass partner for long.

Nick was lost in thought when he realized Ty had leaned toward him and asked him something. He cleared his throat, looking at Ty with wide eyes. "What?"

"Are you okay?" Ty asked incredulously. "Because Owen's been bitching about the Sox for a solid five minutes, and you ain't drawn down on him yet."

"I left my gun at your place," Nick answered defensively. He set his empty bottle on the table and took Ty's out of his hand. Ty didn't even protest, just held up his hand to order another round.

"Are we for or against the Red Sox?" Zane asked curiously. He had leaned an elbow on the table and shifted forward, head still tipped toward Ty.

A round of jeers came from the others, and Nick had to close his eyes and wave Zane off. "School him."

"O is from Boston," Ty explained to Zane, pointing at Nick. "It's Red Sox or die unless you can prove a deep affiliation with another club or provide a compelling reason to hate the designated hitter. Or kick his ass."

"Preach it, baby," Nick said happily, giving Ty a closed fist in the air.

"Owen is, however, a Yankees fan, and they both carried extra ammunition on missions for 'accidents,'" Ty went on, using his fingers to accentuate the sarcasm.

"I grew up watching ballgames in Arlington," Zane said, sounding greatly amused. "Affiliation doesn't get any deeper than being born and bred Texan."

"Rangers, huh?" Nick said, rolling the word around as if giving them thought. "Sure, I guess they're harmless enough."

Owen gave them both a raspberry.

Ty groaned softly and raised his hand to stop them. "Can we avoid this tonight?"

"Grady's become a pacifist," Digger observed, clearly disapproving.

"He just lost his balls, is all," Owen corrected.

"Don't you remember holding them for me?" Ty asked him without skipping a beat.

"The Rangers are actually looking good this season," Zane said. He was looking up, and though his eyes were unfocused, he had the look about him of someone deliberately feeding the fire. Nick liked that in a man.

"God, Zane, please," Ty tried. Nick reached out and slid his arm around Ty's shoulders, squeezing his arm hard. He wouldn't start a baseball-induced brawl in the middle of dinner. Again.

Zane smiled and laughed, and it sounded real, not put on. Nick thought Zane might not be too bad a guy, if he enjoyed getting a rise out of Ty as much as the rest of the team did. But Ty didn't react to Zane's ribbing the same way he reacted to theirs. He didn't growl or bring out that rapier wit Nick knew was so deft. He merely looked sideways at Zane and huffed, then went back to his bottle of beer.

Interesting.

After four more rounds of beer, some appetizers, several stories, and a lot of friendly squabbling, Digger stopped the pretty waitress to ask where the best place to leave his shoes was.

"Oh God, here we go," Owen muttered.

"What's going on?" Zane asked, directing the question toward Ty.

Ty just shook his head. He was leaning back on his bar stool, propped against the wall behind him. He rubbed at his eyes as if the beer was having its way with him, which was unusual in Nick's vast experience. He must have really been working hard if he couldn't make it past half a dozen rounds. He had obviously forgotten that Zane couldn't see him.

"They don't intend to go home tonight, Zane," Nick answered for him.

"What's your name, baby girl?" Digger asked the waitress.

She was smiling, taking the attention of a table of drunken idiots fairly well. "Caroline. Do we need another round, or are we done for the night?"

Ty made a pained sound as soon as she told them her name, and Nick began to grin.

Zane turned his head, apparently trying to follow the conversation. "Which one is Caroline?" he asked Ty.

"Blonde, smells like sandalwood," Ty answered. Zane nodded.

Yeah. They came here a lot. Nick elbowed Ty in the ribs, and Ty folded up and grunted at him as he set his beer on the table. But he was already grinning, so Nick knew they were going to get him to do it. After six beers, convincing Ty to sing was easy as pie. After ten, it was getting him to stop that was the problem.

Across the table, Kelly and Owen were already providing the melody by humming and drumming their fingers on the table. Caroline narrowed her eyes at them but was still smiling.

"What's all this about?" she asked suspiciously.

"I'm so sorry," Ty told her, smiling even as he apologized. "Please don't ban us after this."

Nick kicked back his stool and stood before Ty could stop him, and he began to sing the first few lines to "Sweet Caroline," the song that Fenway Park in Boston had made its unofficial anthem. Nick had an okay singing voice, enough that people didn't complain when he started.

Zane looked like he was torn between laughing and frowning. "Ty . . . ?"

Ty glanced sideways at him but didn't answer. Instead he held his beer bottle up as if toasting the poor laughing waitress, and he joined Nick as soon as they reached the chorus. The sound of Ty's pure, beautiful singing voice never failed to send shivers up and down Nick's spine.

Caroline blushed prettily and laughed, looking around the bar with her hand over her mouth as they serenaded her, and a lot of the conversation around them died down as people watched, agape.

And then the inevitable happened. Nearly the entire bar joined in. But nothing could drown out Ty's voice from Nick's ear. He put his arm around his oldest and dearest friend as they sang, trying not to think about why a melancholy feeling was settling in his chest.

Zane pulled on the old T-shirt and sweats before feeling his way along the edge of the bed. It was Ty's room, and he was more than a little uncertain if he should stay there or go up to the futon in the third- floor guestroom. Ty hadn't said anything about any of the guys staying over, but they were his friends. An invitation to stay might be assumed. And Zane certainly knew it wouldn't go over well if they saw him sleeping in Ty's bed. There was only so much that could be explained away as "helping" your blinded partner. Zane huffed and rubbed his hands over his face.

He slowly walked toward the bathroom door on the staircase landing, trailing his fingers along the wall. Bare feet touched cold tile, eliciting a wince, and Zane was about to close the bathroom door when he heard Ty's voice. He could pick it out anywhere.

"I can't believe you made me do that," he was saying, his voice a low, hoarse groan, the type that came with either too much alcohol or when Zane was about to get laid. "I'll never be able to go back there again."

"I can't believe you don't still sing, man. What a fucking waste." That was the Boston accent. Nick. When Zane had stood near him, Nick's voice hadn't been quite at ear level, so Nick was shorter than six five, but Zane had nothing else to work with besides the very few details Ty had shared in the course of conversation.

"Leave him the fuck alone, O. It's his God-given talent, he can waste it if he wants to," one of the others said. Kelly, perhaps. Zane wasn't sure he could tell Owen and Kelly apart. The accents were both unremarkable.

"Cab's here," Digger announced, the words barely discernible. He'd probably been standing by the window, but the deep drawl and heavy accent of his voice was unmistakably Cajun.

Ty's answer was lost in the sounds of movement and the front door complaining as it was swung open. Zane frowned and stepped out of the bathroom, moving closer to the stairs. Yeah, eavesdroppers never heard anything good about themselves, but Zane figured he'd be better off knowing which room to go sleep in.

There was a lot of shuffling and movement, saying goodbye, see you later, who's got the cab fare, shut the hell up before I duct tape your tongue to your nose. Fairly typical for the type of people Zane expected to be Ty's friends. After it all died down and the door closed, there was a stretch of silence.

Then Ty cleared his throat. "Water? Beer?"

"Yeah, beer," Nick answered as they both moved past the base of the stairs into the kitchen. So Nick apparently was staying.

Zane frowned, again trying to decide what to do. Listening to Ty talk to an old friend while sitting there with them was one thing. Skulking at the top of the stairs was another. He'd catch certain hell from Ty if he were caught, and that was enough to have Zane moving back toward the bathroom, albeit reluctantly.

"You look like hell, man," he heard Nick say. His tone of voice now, when they were away from the others, was different somehow. More serious and sincere, less teasing. Zane hesitated to call it intimate.

Ty didn't respond to the observation with a smart-ass remark or try to deflect it. He didn't respond verbally at all, not that Zane could hear. Zane stood at the bathroom door, gripping the doorjamb, wondering if Ty would admit to Nick what he'd tried to deny to Zane, that he was exhausted, scared, stressed, and uncertain.

Ty finally just laughed softly.

"Are you sleeping?" Nick asked. It was the same question Ty always asked Zane when he knew the answer already.

"Some. I know I look like warmed-over crap, man. I feel like it too," Ty answered, his voice hoarse but managing to sound flippant anyway. "It's fine. You didn't stay because Owen kicks in his sleep. Or to ask me about my sleep."

"No," Nick admitted readily. "You two work well together?"

"Zane?" Ty asked. He laughed again. "You wouldn't think so from the outside, would you?"

"He doesn't appear the type you usually get on board with, no. He sort of reminds me of that DOD guy—what was his name?"

"Pike?" Ty responded, uncertainty lacing his voice.

"Yeah! Ramrod straight, Ray-Bans, always holding a file."

"No, man, Pike was an officious dick. Zane's a good guy. He's stellar. I trust him."

"Good," Nick said, so softly Zane almost didn't hear it. He was silent for almost a minute, then added, "Was Pike the one we hung over the railing?"

Ty burst into laughter, the sound clear as a bell as it reached Zane's ears. Nick's laughter joined it. "Oh God, that was funny," Ty murmured contentedly. "The screams."

"Almost got the brig for it."

"Worth it," Ty acknowledged.

There was another long silence, almost enough for Zane to retreat to the bathroom again. But Nick's next question, seemingly out of nowhere, arrested his retreat.

"You still dreaming?" Nick asked, his voice lowered reverently like that of a man in church. Or a man with a secret.

Ty remained silent for several heartbeats. "Mostly it's just the desert," he finally answered, sounding somewhat troubled. "But it's not bad, I'm just there. Don't know which way is up, which way is safety, which way goes . . . back. I wake up tasting sand instead of blood, now. They're not like they used to be."

Zane was intimately familiar with the results of some of Ty's dreams and nightmares, and he knew about the desert. He snorted softly. He'd never asked Ty to tell him, and Ty had never offered. "Don't know which way is up" described his own situation pretty damn well right now. Lost. Lost in the dark instead of the sand. Maybe Ty really did understand, just a little bit.

He knew Ty and Nick had been close, very close, close born of blood and beer and sweat and tears and all of that clichéd *Band of Brothers* shit that really *was* true. Zane just wondered if they were still that close and how it was possible he didn't know about it after practically living in Ty's pocket for almost half a year.

"How about you?" Ty asked. "You still dream?"

"Every once in a while," Nick answered. He sounded almost haunted. "I still wake up screaming your name, man. Just like you never came back."

"But I did," Ty answered calmly.

Zane heard Nick snort. "And I dream about that damn table."

"Me too," Ty admitted, the whispered words painful and drawn. Shifting uncomfortably, Zane laid his cheek against the cool wood of the doorframe. Something had happened to them, to Ty and Nick, something like how New York City and a serial killer had happened to

Ty and Zane. Something horrible enough to make Ty sound like that when he spoke of it.

The silence below felt heavy with the past, and Zane's mind strayed toward painful memories of his own before Nick pulled his attention back.

"Anyone but you, man, and I'd have died out there," Nick said, his voice harsh and laid bare.

"We both would have," Ty responded, his voice calm again, in stark contrast. "It's back there, Nick. Stay right here." Zane heard his knuckles rap the wooden table. "Come on," he finally said gently, and Zane heard a chair being pushed back against the hardwood floor. "You can take the pullout. I'll bunk with Garrett."

"Hey, Ty? I may be drunk and I may be Irish, but I'm not stupid," Nick drawled, letting the words run into each other almost insolently. "I remember what on the brink looked like, and it had your eyes."

Zane opened his eyes even though it was to complete darkness. He ought to get into the bedroom now while he had the chance, ought to at least shut the bathroom door, ought to know better . . . but *on the brink* . . . of what?

"Talk to me, Grady," Nick urged, and after a moment of silence, he added, "I mean, Jesus, after what we've been through, if you can't tell me, who can you tell?"

"There's nothing wrong, O," Ty insisted, his voice remarkably calm and honest. "I promise."

"Okay," Nick murmured, giving in and sounding unhappy about it.

Zane could hear Ty moving, steps slow and measured and not nearly as quiet as when he was sober. "Good night," Ty said to Nick, the tone of the words effectively saying "don't ask me again."

Zane stepped inside the bathroom and pushed the door shut with a quiet snick, figuring Ty would be on his way up the stairs. Better for him to come out of the bathroom and be told where to sleep rather than picking the wrong place to be. He leaned back against the closed door, wondering about the tone of Ty's voice. He sighed, wishing he hadn't listened. He hadn't heard anything inappropriate. In fact, he'd heard Ty say some pretty damn nice things about him. But it just raised more questions he couldn't get answers to. Shaking his head, he turned in place and reopened the door.

The impact with Ty's body was almost immediate. Ty whuffed and wrapped his arms around Zane to catch his balance. "Slow down, Hoss," Ty murmured. Zane could sense a smile there, but there was also lingering discomfort or annoyance. And a lot of beer on his breath. "You going up?"

"I . . . I wasn't sure where to go," Zane mumbled, not knowing if Nick was right there or not.

Ty's hands came up to cover his cheeks, fingers pressed against the beard growing in after five days without shaving. He could feel Ty's breath on his neck as he whispered, "I know I smell like beer. But I'd rather have you in my bed tonight than the Irish."

Zane shivered. No Nick, then. "You smell like you, mostly," he said.

Ty kissed him without another word. It was a quick, almost furtive kiss, but there was heat behind it, too, and the sour tang of the beer was fainter on Ty's lips than Zane had expected. The steps below creaked, and Ty pulled away from him and gave his shoulders a turn, heading him in the general direction of the bedroom. A moment later Nick was murmuring goodnight to them both as he passed on to the third-floor stairs, and Ty shut the door to his bedroom behind them.

"Won't he think this is weird?" Zane asked, keeping his voice down.

"There's only two beds in the house. He usually sleeps with me, the others fight over the couches. I told him you needed to be within stumbling distance of the bathroom, less stairs." Ty's hand found its way to Zane's lower back. "Would you rather he sleep here and you go upstairs?"

"Hell no," Zane swore under his breath. "It's just . . . he's your friend and all. A Marine. I didn't know if you had . . . in the past . . . does he know that you . . ." Zane paused for a breath. "Never mind. I'm tired and you're drunk. Time to sleep."

"Are you asking if Nick and I have fucked?" Ty asked, plowing through all the gentle euphemisms he could have used, getting right to the point.

Something inside Zane curled awkwardly, and he flinched, aware of being silent for too long. "I actually hadn't gotten that far in thinking about the 'friends through thick and thin.' More along the lines of would he have any reason to think we might be more than work partners." But now he also wanted to know the answer to the question Ty had thrown out there.

"If you're uncomfortable, I can sleep on the couch," Ty offered, voice low and soothing, just like it had been for most of Zane's blindness. It was the same tone he'd adopted with Nick, telling him to stay in the present instead of dwelling on trauma of the past. Zane had never consciously noticed Ty had that ability, to calm and reassure with his voice, or even that he'd been doing it to him all week, until now. Zane remembered abruptly that Ty did have a degree in psychology, and he wondered if he was really that easily manipulated. Although Ty wouldn't even have to try, not really.

Zane frowned. "No. No, I'm not uncomfortable." He wasn't sure he could explain this well enough to get through the filter of beer, stress, and exhaustion. "He doesn't know about us, right? I'm just trying to be careful."

"He doesn't know," Ty affirmed. Zane could hear the rustle of clothing as Ty got undressed.

He'd never actually answered the other question. Zane didn't feel right asking, though he knew it would bother him now. He took a steadying breath, pulled his T-shirt over his head, and dropped it to the floor. He made it to the bed and under the covers, leaving on his sweats. A moment later Ty crawled in next to him, his skin warm against Zane's, the smell of the bar just faint enough to be slightly arousing instead of nauseating.

Ty pulled him close and kissed him carefully. "He's never been anything more than my best friend, Zane," he whispered. "Stop worrying."

Zane didn't realize he'd tensed up until he relaxed after Ty's words, and he set his forehead against Ty's with another sigh. "You know me pretty well, huh."

"Not as well as I'd like," Ty replied, voice barely there. He kissed Zane again, letting his lips drag across Zane's. Then he sighed heavily and rolled onto his back, his movements restless and slightly inebriated. Zane let him sprawl, knowing that trying to hold onto Ty in this state would just make him squirm more.

He was fairly confident there wasn't anything he wouldn't tell Ty, besides some few select experiences better left buried. But it was a discussion they'd had before, and Zane didn't expect a reply, so he turned away and onto his side, pulling the pillow up against his chest.

A moment later Ty tossed an arm and a leg over him, snuggling up to him like Zane was his pillow. He nuzzled his face into the back of Zane's neck, pressing his hips against him. Zane could tell from the way Ty touched him, the way he couldn't quite keep still, that if Nick hadn't been in the house, they would already be fucking.

Awareness and arousal ripped through Zane like lightning. It was a toss-up whether they'd be able to do it quietly, especially with Ty drunk.

Ty made a frustrated grumbling sound, obviously thinking along the same lines. "Give him a few minutes to go to sleep," he told Zane. His hand slid down Zane's body, strong fingers gripping Zane's hip to pull him back against him.

Zane closed his eyes and smiled, reaching to take Ty's hand in his. "You saying your Recon buddy upstairs sleeps like a baby?"

Ty pushed himself up on one elbow, his knee sliding up Zane's inner thigh. Zane could feel Ty hardening against him, and his own body responded accordingly. It was wild having sex with Ty when all his senses were working. But when he had to rely on the others to make up for what he couldn't see, Zane found that he responded faster than usual. Especially smell: the heady cachets of forbidden beer, forsaken cigarettes, and Old Spice, natural earthy musk layered just underneath that, they all combined with the scent of sweat on Ty's skin, and every time Zane caught a whiff, it went right to his gut.

Ty shifted away and pushed Zane onto his back before moving to cover him, muscles tensed and fingers dragging over Zane's skin. The sound of Ty's breathing, slow and careful, filled Zane's ears.

Zane exhaled carefully. *Fuck*, how he wanted Ty right now. He wondered distantly if he'd ever get enough of him.

Ty's hands moved to cup his face. "Shh," he requested quietly. Then he lowered his head and licked at Zane's lips. Zane hummed a negative and parted his lips, inviting a kiss as he nipped at Ty's tongue.

Ty propped himself up on his elbows and ran his fingers over Zane's hair, holding his head still as he kissed Zane hungrily. The moan deep in Zane's throat surprised him.

"Am I going to have to gag you?" Ty asked in a gruff voice as he began kissing down the line of Zane's jaw.

"I'll be quieter than the bed," Zane murmured, pointing to the headboard against the wall. He almost laughed as he suddenly remembered the last time they'd done something like this—in Ty's childhood bedroom at his parents' home in Bluefield, West Virginia.

Ty began making his way down Zane's body instead of commenting, kissing and nipping at sensitive parts. Zane stiffened for a moment, wishing he could see. *Damn*, he loved to watch Ty do this! Ty pushed his sweats down, fighting against the sheets and the mattress to do it. Zane instinctively moved his hands to slide them into Ty's short hair as he breathed, "Oh fuck..."

Ty hummed cheekily, kissing at Zane's hip as he slid his hands under the backs of Zane's thighs. Zane laughed weakly and shivered all over just thinking about what was coming. Without a word of warning, Ty ducked his head and took Zane's cock into his mouth, running his tongue around the head and sucking.

Zane hissed, hips snapping up toward the wet heat of Ty's mouth. His fingers clenched in Ty's hair for a moment until he made himself relax. When Ty started sucking, Zane actually whimpered. Ty hummed again in response to the pitiful sounds.

Zane didn't necessarily enjoy sex with Ty more when Ty was drunk, but it definitely changed the game. Ty was looser, more apt to be rough and manhandle him, more likely to do things to Zane that Zane would have to Google to know what to call them. He couldn't form enough coherent thought to even think about objecting to this tonight, with company in the house.

Ty hummed again, rising up onto his hands and knees and tugging Zane further down the bed in an animal display of possessiveness. Zane scrabbled a little on the sheets—the first pull of Ty's hands sent a blast of pure hot desire through him.

Zane swallowed, breaths already coming fast. He had no idea what to anticipate from his lover, and he realized the uncertainty was fueling the fire. Great, another kink he didn't need.

But damn, he wanted this. Even better, *Ty* wanted this, wanted him, even blind, and the unadulterated joy Zane derived from that thought was overwhelming. He reached up to cup Ty's cheek, kissing him for all he was worth. Ty responded to his desire, and he supported his weight with one hand, practically devouring Zane as he slipped his other hand between Zane's legs.

Zane clutched at Ty's shoulders and moaned under the onslaught of Ty's sinful mouth. His hips rocked helplessly, and he gasped when he felt the first touch of Ty's fingers.

"Shhh," Ty urged as he pushed one slick finger into Zane's grasping body. Zane bit his bottom lip and his eyes rolled back as he huffed and then relaxed, although his hands clenched in the sheets.

Ty kissed him harder, rocking into him demandingly as he curled his finger inside him. Zane cried out into his mouth and jerked as Ty stroked just right after a few tries. Then he was moving thoughtlessly, lifting up against Ty's body and hand insistently, physically begging for more. Ty hummed in approval and continued to move his finger inside him. Soon he had added another and was sucking at the tender skin under Zane's ear.

Zane couldn't help but arch his back as the tingling turned to taut thrumming that echoed through his body, and he gasped out soft sounds of pleasure and encouragement, turned wanton by Ty's mouth and hands. A long finger rubbed him just right again, and Zane bit off another cry. "Ty . . . oh *fuck*," he choked out.

"You want it?" Ty asked in a rough, harsh voice as Zane writhed beneath him.

"Yes, fuck yes," Zane begged.

Ty moved ever so slowly as he removed his fingers and stole another, slower kiss. Zane sighed longingly against Ty's lips and shifted his legs, pulling up his knees. "Want to feel you, baby," he whispered, sucking Ty's lower lip between his teeth and worrying at it. Ty gave a low growl and complied, pushing against Zane and rocking just inside him.

Gritting his teeth for a moment and squeezing his eyes shut, Zane moaned as the stretch of Ty's cock just inside him started out feeling full and reached the edge of painful, and he arched his back against it, sucking in a breath that made him shiver all over. Ty curled his back and bent to kiss him, letting his body provide the friction that would edge the pain over into pleasure.

The slow, calming kiss did the trick, and Zane relaxed, the even rocking turning the sharp digging into a dull push and heat that bloomed into pleasure. He moaned soundlessly as he tried moving against Ty. Gently, for now. The twisting hunger was still there, only temporarily banked by the transitory pain. Ty groaned against Zane's lips, pushing into him and shuddering as pleasure rippled through them. He murmured nonsense and slid his hand under Zane's hips to lift him higher.

"Yes, oh yes," Zane hissed, raising his hands above his head to grasp the tangled quilt, curling his fingers through it. Ty buried his face against Zane's neck and began to rock his hips steadily, cock sliding with the bare amount of slick Ty had used, and he breathed open- mouthed against Zane's skin.

Zane's exhales shook, and he lowered one arm to curl around Ty and hold him close as they moved together. It was hot and smooth and mind-blowing, the slow slide something entirely different than hot, pounding thrusts.

"God, you feel good," Ty murmured, his movements becoming jerky and almost tortured, the need in them straining what little control Zane had.

"Took the words right out of my mouth," Zane gasped, raising one leg to wrap it over the back of Ty's thigh. He bit his own lip as he felt the tension in his gut threaten to explode. "Ty, I'm gonna lose it," he whispered shakily.

"Do it," Ty urged, either not caring if Nick heard them or forgetting the need for silence.

"Oh hell," Zane ground out, his entire body straining and tensing for another too-short minute until he threw back his head, jaw clenched to hold back a sharp yell. He clenched his fingers in the quilt and flinched with each shot of come against Ty's belly and chest. Finally he couldn't hold back a broken, half-smothered cry of mindless pleasure.

"Zane," Ty breathed pleadingly as he pushed harder into him.

As his body continued to squeeze convulsively around Ty, Zane moved both hands to clasp his face, wishing he could see Ty's passion-glazed eyes. "Baby," he rasped before kissing him like there would be no tomorrow. Ty groaned into his mouth, nails digging into the back of Zane's thigh.

"C'mon . . . fuck me," Zane ordered against Ty's ear in between harsh breaths.

"God," Ty groaned, shuddering again and starting to slam into Zane mercilessly. Choking off a throaty cry, Zane curled around him as the thrusts reverberated through him, feeding the fire still crackling in him. Zane distantly heard the creak of the heavy bedframe.

The shudder through Ty's body and the sounds escaping from his lips told Zane when Ty climaxed, and Zane held even tighter to his lover, chest still heaving. He knew already he'd be feeling Ty for some time tomorrow. Just the thought made his cock twitch in a useless plea for more.

Ty panted above him, hands digging into Zane's hips as he physically wavered. He started to pull out of Zane slowly, gasping at what had to be overstimulation, and he kissed Zane roughly as he did so. The mash of their lips and teeth was enough to draw another whimper from Zane. It was both pleasurable and painful. His low gasp grew into a long groan as Ty slid out, leaving behind an aching hollowness.

Ty crawled up Zane's body to kiss him again, slow and languid, before flopping over to his side with a groan to lie next to him, replete and sweaty. Left gasping, Zane squeezed his eyes shut, feeling like he'd lost his mind while erratic jolts of sensation continued to shoot through him.

"Why don't you go get us a towel, huh?" Ty teased in the darkness.

Zane quietly shushed him, soaking in the aftermath of the major explosion. *Damn.* When had Ty last fucked him so well? He bit his lip and pressed his cheek against the sheet, relaxing that last little bit and just breathing. It still terrified him, the way Ty could make him feel, the way need could become utter desperation.

"Hmph." Ty moved, bouncing the mattress as he rolled away and flattened out in what had to be a sulk.

The disgruntled sound made Zane smile. He sat up and scooted over, right up against Ty, hands on him to find him. Zane leaned over and kissed the corner of Ty's mouth.

"Better," Ty purred as he turned his head into it.

Zane smiled wryly and leaned over again, this time pressing his lips to the very corner of Ty's eye, then nuzzling at his temple. With a sigh, he lay back down and rolled to his side, and Ty followed to wrap around him from behind like it was choreographed. If they stayed like that long enough, their bodies pressed together, the smell of sex permeating the sheets, Zane knew they'd be fucking again.

Not that he was complaining.

But he heard Ty exhale contentedly, and in mere seconds Ty's breathing evened out, his body relaxed, and he fell asleep with Zane neatly folded up in his arms.

Before drifting off himself, Zane lay there, consciously savoring the embrace and idly entertaining thoughts of how he was more than happy to be right there in Ty's arms, every night.

CHAPTER ELEVEN

Ty sat and watched Nick and Digger argue over the dartboard, his chin held in his hand as he leaned on the table. He was smiling crookedly without caring he was doing it. This was the playbook they usually followed. Go out, start drinking in some nice, respectable dive, then get into a meaningless argument over something stupid that would create chaos and mayhem around them and eventually get them kicked out.

Right now the debate was whether the tip of the dart had hit the green or the red. Of course the dart had been yanked out several minutes ago, so it was a pointless argument and both Digger and Nick knew it. They were both grinning as they called each other creative names and pointed their darts in each other's faces.

Ty smiled wider as he watched them. The waitress brushed his shoulder and set a basket full of hot wings down on the table. He looked up at her and nodded. "Thank you," he murmured.

She smiled and put a hand on his shoulder. "You boys need anything else?" she asked, keeping her hand there as she moved behind him.

Ty arched an eyebrow as he looked across the table at Owen and Kelly. They both answered the waitress with shakes of their heads and muttered "no, ma'ams." Ty shook his head as well and craned his neck to look up at her. "Thank you, darlin'," he said softly.

"Any time, sweetie," she answered, the flirtatious undertone to the words hard to miss. She smiled as she let her hand slide off his shoulder and moved away. The touch felt good, and Ty let himself enjoy the attention. He didn't respond to it like he would have a year ago, though.

Nick whistled low as he pulled out his chair and sat with a thump beside Ty. "And you're waiting for *what*?" he asked Ty as he watched the pretty little waitress move away.

Ty cocked his head at her appreciatively as she moved through the crowded bar, then sighed and turned back to the table, propping his elbows on the scarred wooden top and reaching for a stick of celery out of the wing basket. "I guess I've slowed down in my old age," he told them wryly before crunching down on the celery.

Nick raised a disbelieving eyebrow as he leaned closer. Ty glanced at him and looked away quickly before the man could read anything in his face. Nick knew him all too well, though. He knew when to call bullshit.

"Tell us," Nick ordered with a wide grin.

Ty glanced at him, trying to judge his mood. This was the perfect opportunity to tell Nick and the others the truth. He'd come close to confessing to his best friends dozens of times over the years, telling them he was bi or even that as he grew older, he was beginning to realize that he definitely preferred men over women. The fear of being exposed and kicked out of the military and then simply the fear of losing them, especially Nick, had always stopped him. But the military was behind him, and if they were the men Ty thought they were, they wouldn't care. Ty reminded himself that if he could tell Zane he loved him, he could do just about anything.

"Grady? What aren't you telling us?" Nick asked quietly.

Ty winced. "I never was good at hiding much from you," he said in resignation. Nick laughed, shaking his head. Ty held his breath and glanced at the others.

"Garrett and I . . ." Ty put his palm to his chin and swiped at it, glancing down at the table nervously and then looking up at Nick as he tried desperately not to back out. Nick's green eyes were on him, watching him with a mixture of confusion and concern. "We're a little bit more than partners."

Nick shook his head, frown lines deepening. "I don't understand, man. What does that mean?"

Ty took in a shaky breath and turned the beer bottle in his hands compulsively as he tried to decide how to word his response.

"You saying you're . . . what, he's working black ops with you now?" Kelly asked.

Ty came up short. "How do you know about that?"

"Know about what?" Kelly countered with an innocuous blink.

"Ty, focus," Nick muttered.

Ty shook his head and tried to swallow. His mouth had gone completely dry. Kelly and Digger laughed, taking his silence as being sly rather than being sick with nerves.

Nick snorted. "Ty, come on. I'm too buzzed to read your mind tonight."

Ty closed his eyes and smiled, just stepping off that ledge like he'd always done. "We're fucking," he said frankly, not surprised when the public admission caused his stomach to roil even harder with nerves. He looked at the other three, then at Nick, breathless as he waited for their reactions.

They were all staring at him, agog. "Are you shitting me? 'Cause that's not funny," Nick blurted.

Ty swallowed hard and his jaw tightened. A cold dread began to settle in his chest. If Nick didn't handle this well, Ty didn't know what he would do. The others would follow Nick's lead. He shook his head minutely. "Dead serious," he murmured, voice going just a little cooler.

"What're you . . . are you saying you're gay?" Digger asked slowly, as if trying to come to terms with information he didn't quite understand.

Ty swallowed with difficulty and wet his lips. His gut was churning as if he truly were in free-fall. He leaned forward. He couldn't read any of them, and that alone made Ty more than a little worried. He nodded anyway. "Yeah. That's what I'm saying."

He held his breath as he waited for any of them to react, and they took their sweet time.

Nick watched Ty for a full minute before he finally looked away. "Well," he said slowly, obviously still thinking about how to respond. "I'm a little surprised," he finally decided with an uncomfortable laugh. He jerked his hand over his shoulder, pointing his thumb in the vague direction of Ty's row house. "And he's the best you can do?" he asked with a growing smirk as he looked sideways at Ty.

Ty stared at him, shocked by the relatively easy acceptance.

"Bullshit," Owen said suddenly. He didn't look surprised at all, merely angry.

Ty lowered his chin and looked across the table at him, waiting for the reaction he'd dreaded and known at least one of them would have.

"Owen," Nick said with a slight laugh. He held his hand out across the table. "What's it matter, man?" he asked good-naturedly.

"It's bullshit," Owen repeated with a shake of his head.

"No," Ty said quietly.

"All those years in the field and you knew this?" Owen asked angrily.

Ty cocked his head, narrowing his eyes at Owen without saying a word. Nothing he said or did would make it better if Owen was pissed. He was surprised it was only Owen, in fact.

"Owen, man, it's not like it's catching or anything," Kelly said quietly as he sat back in his chair. Ty glanced at him in mild surprise, then back at Owen as the man stood up suddenly.

"You telling us all those fucking years you were supposed to have our backs you knew you were queer and didn't tell us?" Owen growled.

Heads began to turn.

"Jesus Christ," Digger said angrily as he stood and grabbed at Owen's collar. "What's your problem, jackass? This is Grady you're talking to!"

Ty merely sighed and began rubbing at a spot of tension in the back of his neck. It had been there for a solid week now.

"Let him go," Nick told Digger calmly. Digger turned to look at him, scowling mutinously, but he released Owen's shirt, giving him a small shove just to make himself feel better.

"I'm outta here, man," Owen snarled as he grabbed his coat off the back of the chair, tipping the chair backward. It crashed to the floor as Owen turned on his heel and stalked out of the bar.

They watched him go in stunned silence.

"What a fucking prick," Kelly finally said in a shocked voice.

"Don't worry about him," Nick said to Ty softly.

Ty gave him a weak smile and nodded. "Handled it better than I thought he would," he admitted.

"Fucking asshole," Digger muttered as he picked up the chair and righted it, then sat back down heavily, still watching the door where Owen had disappeared.

"Forget it," Nick said with authority. Ty glanced at him, and Nick actually smiled at him and leaned toward him. "Grady, nothing you can tell us after all this time will truly surprise me," he whispered seriously, though he was still smiling. He held out his hand to Ty, palm facing his chest in the same manner he had thousands of times before. Ty reached out and pressed his palm to Nick's, grasping his hand and crossing their wrists. It pulled their faces closer together, a position they'd been in many times over the years as they'd reminded each other not to get shot during a mission.

Nick's voice was low and warm when he spoke. "I can see the fear in your eyes. But I don't give a damn if you're queer, man. And you owe me an apology for thinking I would."

Ty felt like crying in relief, but he managed to just smile and shake his head at the audacity. "You're right," he conceded in a whisper. "I'm sorry for thinking you might be a prick."

Nick patted him on the shoulder with his beer bottle, then let go of his hand and leaned back. He propped one foot up on the chair Owen had vacated and tossed back the bottle, taking a long gulp. "So. I mean, really, is he the best you can do?" he asked again, teasing.

Ty rolled his eyes and took his time drinking a few swigs of beer. "I love him," he finally answered, giving it to him straight. He looked at Nick and nodded, lips pressed tightly together.

"Seriously?" Nick asked in honest surprise. "Like, with-the-heart love or with-the-dick love?"

Ty snorted. "To be honest, it's a little of both."

"He knows, right? You said you're fucking, so I assume it's a relationship?" Kelly asked.

"Yeah. He knows." His chest tightened. It was a relief to be able to talk about Zane with someone besides Deuce. He bit his lip and finally looked up to meet Kelly's eyes.

"But?" Kelly prompted.

"I told him I loved him after the last UC case we worked," Ty admitted with a slight flush.

"Wow," Nick offered.

"Couldn't help it."

"But?" Kelly repeated with a deeper frown.

"When I told him, he didn't really say anything."

His three friends gave him a chorus of pained noises in response.

"Shit, man," Digger practically shouted. "Go pick that waitress up and make yourself feel better!"

Ty laughed out loud and closed his eyes, rubbing at his forehead with the heel of his hand.

"Jackass," Digger grumbled disconsolately.

"At least he didn't say thank you," Kelly pointed out wryly.

Ty laughed before putting his bottle to his lips and taking a long, relieved gulp of his beer. This had gone better than he'd ever imagined it would.

"So, he doesn't feel the same?" Nick asked, confused.

"No," Ty answered, shaking his head. "No, he *does*. I'm just not sure he knows it yet."

"You can't do anything easy, can you?" Kelly asked, laughing.

"Bet that waitress would be," Digger grumbled.

The others began laughing and talking once more, drowning the silence.

But Nick watched him, still frowning in confusion. Ty waited for him to comment, unconsciously holding his breath.

"You love him. You think he loves you, but he hasn't said it," Nick finally laid out.

Ty shrugged and nodded.

"What if you're wrong?"

"Then I'll get to throw his shit off my balcony. Should be fun." Nick snorted, staring at him in wonder. "How do you live life without looking back or forward? God, I envy that."

Ty merely smiled enigmatically at him. It wasn't the first time he'd heard that. Not many people—not even Nick, who'd lived through his past with him, or Zane, who woke up to his nightmares—knew just how hard it was for Ty to shake off the past and the future and just live in the here and now.

"So it's been like two months, and he still hasn't manned up and decided if he loves you, right? But you're still fucking."

Ty just stared at him, trying to decide if that was an accurate statement. They didn't know Zane like he did. Ty knew his partner had to take the issue from every angle, analyze it to death, resurrect it, and then study its dead, rotting body to see the results. Yeah, it might take Zane four months to decide if he loved someone, and then more to decide if that was a *good idea*.

Ty didn't mind waiting.

"What a prick," Nick muttered as he put his bottle to his lips and looked out over the barroom with a disturbed frown.

Ty didn't comment. He leaned back in his chair and put his feet up on the chair beside Nick's, crossing them at the ankles. One foot rocked slowly as they drank in silence.

"So are you the guy or the girl?" Digger asked abruptly.

Ty barked another laugh, almost snorting beer up his nose. "It doesn't really work that way," he managed to answer.

"So how does it work?" Kelly asked in his typical soft, amused voice.

Ty stared at them for a moment, surprised that not only had they accepted the news fairly easily but seemed to be showing genuine interest.

He shrugged. "We're still dealing with the dynamics," he said vaguely. He had never been a kiss-and-tell type of guy, regardless of who he'd been with. They knew that. They weren't asking about sex. They were asking about the relationship itself in the only way they knew how, and Ty had no answers for them.

"He seems like the 'get on your knees, bitch' type of guy," Digger grumbled under his breath.

Ty nearly snorted beer up his nose again. He coughed and sputtered as Nick smacked his back repeatedly, laughing heartily. Ty closed his eyes and felt himself blushing as they continued on with the conversation. Did it bother him that they now knew he liked to get on his knees and be fucked until he screamed? A little. He had always been their go-to guy, the brawn on point, the guy they knew they could throw at anything and he'd go in swinging. Why did his being gay have to mar that tough-guy personality?

Ty didn't know. But in his mind, it did, to an extent. He supposed that was his own problem, though. Or society's problem. He shook his head, concentrating instead on the flood of relief. Not only was it a relief that his closest friends had, for the most part, accepted the news with grace and ease, it was also a relief simply to have told them. To this point, the only people who'd known he was bisexual and leaned toward favoring men were his brother and any man he happened to be fucking. It was an intense relief to just say the words. Come out, as it were.

Nick's hand stayed on Ty's shoulder, as if silently offering support. Ty glanced at him, meeting his eyes briefly and nodding in thanks. How Nick knew it was difficult for him to do, Ty couldn't guess.

The conversation soon turned back to darts, beer, and the pretty little waitress they were intent on *someone* banging before the night was over. But despite the easy acceptance of three of his oldest buddies, Ty couldn't shake the ache of betrayal he'd felt when Owen had stormed out the door. It had hurt, as Ty had known it would. That pain and the unreasonable embarrassment were two reasons he'd kept it under wraps for so long even after being discharged from the Corps.

Digger and Kelly got up to go for one more round of darts, and Nick scooted his chair closer to Ty, leaning toward him to speak in low tones. "Tell me about Garrett," he requested as he leaned his arms on the table.

Ty shrugged uncomfortably. "You met him," he responded defensively.

"Yeah. And I gotta say, Ty, I thought you had better taste," Nick whispered disapprovingly. "He better be a phenomenal lay."

Ty snorted and shook his head. Zane hadn't made much of an impression on these boys, mostly because he'd been sedate and blind and having a spectacularly shitty week. But then, they hadn't been looking at him as a man, plain and simple. They had been judging him as someone who had to watch Ty's back. They were judging him from the eyes of Recon. Man versus Recon—the two were entirely different categories. Just because Ty trusted Zane implicitly didn't mean they did or ever would.

"He's a good guy," Ty found himself saying. "He's having a rough month."

"Yeah, the blind thing," Nick said dubiously.

Ty looked at him and tried to tell himself not to get defensive. He was not responsible for Zane's behavior, nor was he responsible for how other people thought of him.

He found himself fiddling with the USMC signet ring on his finger.

"So let me get this straight. You told the guy you loved him, and he didn't say *anything* in response?" Nick asked, offended, as he saw that Ty was growing twitchy. "He just . . . blew it off?"

"Pretty much," Ty said under his breath. He took a gulp of his beer to cover his gut reaction to the memory. He couldn't help but blush and wince. He'd made such a damn fool of himself. He'd been sure Zane wasn't in love with him when he said it. He'd been sure he wouldn't get a response in kind. At the time he'd have preferred Zane laugh in his face than just let it slide. It wasn't until weeks later that Ty had realized that Zane was still just processing and analyzing, his brain churning to catch up with his heart and what his actions were already saying loud and clear.

"So is he just fucking around with you?" Nick asked curiously. "In it 'cause you're a well-practiced screw?"

Ty glanced at him and shook his head. Zane had never made any secret of the fact that he was in it at least partially for the sex. At first they both had been. "Quit being nosy, O'Flaherty," he chastised, hating that the questions made him uncomfortable. He muttered under his breath. "Irish bastard."

"That's a yes," Nick huffed as he sat back. "Is it monogamous on his part?"

Ty licked his lips and glanced at Nick again, wondering just how much his friend really wanted to know. "Yeah. At least I hope it is, because we've been going without condoms for months."

"Oh God, Ty," Nick groaned as he ran his hand through his hair.

Ty closed his eyes and let his head fall back with a sigh, but he couldn't help but smile. "I know." It really was a departure from anything he'd ever done, trusting someone so much. It was a step to a new person, a step Ty didn't mind taking. But sitting here with Nick, it brought into stark contrast the differences in the person he had been and the person he was now. Sometimes he missed the man he'd been ten years ago. That Ty had been an utter badass. But that was about the only good thing that could be said for the man he'd been then.

"You're just hanging around, hoping he falls for you?" Nick asked, a combination of pity and amazement in his voice.

Ty nodded, unashamed, spinning his ring over and over around his finger. He didn't even have to think about his answer, although it wasn't exactly accurate. Zane had already fallen. Ty was just waiting until Zane was done running all the scenarios and crunching all the numbers.

Nick sat back with a small sigh. "Well, I'm sort of happy for you," he hedged. He reached out and petted Ty on the head for lack of anything better to do, and they both laughed and clinked their glasses together at the absurdity of it.

Ty was down to his last mouthful of beer when Nick finally spoke again. "You're a big ol' screaming bottom, aren't you?" he asked Ty with certainty.

Ty choked on the beer he'd been drinking. He lurched out of his seat to lean over the table and spit the mouthful of beer onto the floor before it went up his nose. Nick was laughing at him as he coughed and sputtered. He slapped Ty on the back and they both began laughing raucously.

"I'll get you another beer," Nick told him, snickering as he headed toward the bar.

"Christ," Ty hissed as he ran his hand over his face. Nick knew him far too well.

A couple of hours later, Nick was well into double digits, and Digger and Kelly had already stumbled off to find a cab and possibly kill Owen if they could find him. Ty was going slower, mostly because he wanted to be able to walk home tonight, but also because the more Nick talked, the angrier Nick got. And Ty was thinking he might have to drag him out and tie him down to keep him from violence before the night was over.

"Why'd it take you so long to tell me?" Nick asked him after a random ten-minute rant about the Red Sox that almost caused a fight with some guy in an Orioles T-shirt.

Ty glanced at him in surprise. He felt foolish now for keeping it a secret all these years, but no one could predict how a loved one would react to such a surprise. He tried to think of a way to put it in terms Nick could understand while blazed.

"Imagine if . . . I had told you I was a closet Yankees fan," he told Nick with a smile. "How would you have reacted?"

"That shit's not funny, Ty. You're not serious, right? I thought you grew up on Atlanta! How do you go over to the dark side just out of the blue!" Nick asked in true horror.

Ty laughed. "See? There was always the chance you might react that way," he said as he finished the last beer he planned to drink tonight. "It was a scary prospect."

Nick stared at him for a long moment. "But you're not really a Yankees fan, right?" he finally asked carefully.

Ty smiled and shook his head.

"Shit, man," Nick muttered. He threw back his bottle, emptying it and setting it down on the table between them with a loud clank. "Don't scare me like that."

Ty grinned and rested his head on his hand.

"You haven't told anyone else, have you?" Nick asked him suddenly.

Ty glanced at him, only to find Nick looking at him sadly. Ty shook his head.

Nick slammed his hand down on the table, rattling the bottles and causing one to tip over and roll toward the edge. Ty grabbed for it but missed it as it fell to the floor. It bounced noisily but didn't shatter. Nick didn't even bother trying to be discreet as he stood up.

"That's not fucking right, Ty," he railed angrily. "You shouldn't have to be afraid to tell anyone who you are or who you're in love with."

"O, calm down," Ty urged quietly as he stood and put one hand on Nick's shoulder.

"You know what? You fought and almost died for your country," Nick continued, undaunted. "What they did to us out there? What happened to us when that helo went down was—"

"Okay, we're leaving," Ty said firmly. He took the beer from Nick's hand and dug around for his wallet.

"You put away killers every day for a living," Nick continued with a point of his finger in Ty's face. Ty resisted the urge to reach up and grab his hand so he wouldn't get poked in the eye. "If you have to hide who you are from your closest friends, then fuck the world, man. It's not fair," Nick spat with a wave of his hand that almost turned into a backhand as Ty quickly leaned away.

"You are a hot mess, man. How many have you had?" Ty asked with a snort as he reached out and grabbed Nick's elbow to steady him. He slapped a few bills on the table and waved at the waitress to let her know they were leaving.

"And you know what else?" Nick went on without answering. Ty began to lead him toward the door, his arm around him to guide him. "This Garrett character? He's lucky to have a guy like you for a partner, much less have you in love with him. He can't find it in himself to return the feeling? Can't even fucking fake it for you? Well, fuck him too!"

Ty cleared his throat and tightened his grip on Nick's shoulders, pulling him closer in case he decided to continue ranting and get louder. They didn't want any trouble from the irate Orioles fans. "I think we need to take a little walk home," he muttered as they stepped out the door into a brisk wind off the harbor. They turned toward Fleet Street, cursing at the cold. But it was only a four-block walk, and Ty wasn't exactly worried about the two of them being mugged.

He stuffed his hands in his pockets and tried hard not to think about anything as he and Nick started off. He wasn't sure what bothered him more, that Owen was so utterly disgusted and pissed off because he was in love with a guy, or that his talk with Nick had left his best friend with all this anger and worry over his relationship with Zane. Nick wasn't the first person to question it. Deuce had repeatedly expressed his concerns: what would happen when one or both of them got tired of the other, what would happen when someone got their heart broken? Except Deuce had been worried about Zane's heartbreak. Nick seemed to think it would be Ty's, in the end.

As they were passing the darkened side of the Broadway Market building, Nick suddenly reached out and took Ty's shoulder. "Ty," he said urgently.

Ty turned to look at him in bemusement, expecting more drunken rambling. Or, God forbid, another near-breach of national security. But despite the ranting, Nick's green eyes were clear and his voice sounded steady. Ty realized he wasn't sloppy drunk, after all. Not impossibly so, anyway. But Ty couldn't quite decipher the look in his friend's eyes. There was sadness there, and anger. And something else he didn't think he'd ever seen. Longing.

"I wish you'd trusted me with this earlier," Nick muttered to him. "If I'd known, all those years . . ."

He opened his mouth to say more, then closed it again with a frustrated sigh. Before Ty really registered what was happening, Nick had taken his shoulders in both hands and was kissing him soundly, right there on the street in the middle of Fell's Point.

Ty flailed, gripping Nick's elbows for lack of a better place to put his hands. His natural instinct was to pull him closer and deepen the kiss, but this was Nick! This was perhaps his oldest and dearest friend, kissing him without a hint of warning. The most disconcerting thing of all, though, was that it wasn't Zane pressed against him. Ty found himself returning the kiss tentatively, regardless, as Nick held him tightly and pushed him against the brick wall behind him. Guilt and shock warred for priority over the pleasure of a really amazing kiss in the brief seconds it took for it to end.

Nick abruptly stepped away from him, inhaling sharply. Ty found himself gaping at the man, unsteady as he leaned against the wall and unable to speak or even breathe.

"You ever get tired of waiting for him to come to his senses, you know where to find me," Nick told him breathlessly.

"Nick," Ty whispered in supreme confusion.

"I'm sorry. That was a shitty thing to do," Nick muttered. He put his head down and started walking.

Ty stared after him for a moment before lurching forward to go after him.

"I should probably go back to the hotel instead of . . . you know, home with you," Nick said as soon as Ty caught up to him. He was holding out a hand at the row of taxis waiting to take people home when the bars closed down. One of them turned on its lights and began rolling forward.

"O, wait," Ty pleaded as he grabbed at Nick's elbow. Nick turned and pulled him closer, kissing him again before Ty could anticipate it. He could feel his body reacting, though, whether he wanted it to or not. Nick delved into Ty's mouth with a swipe of his tongue before yanking away violently.

Nick pushed him away and put out his hand to stop Ty from coming closer. "God! We never were good at self-control." He wouldn't look Ty in the eye. "Just let me go."

"Okay," Ty agreed in a stricken voice.

Nick reached for the door of the cab and yanked it open almost angrily. "Oorah, Grady," he said with a sad smile before he disappeared into the dark car. Ty was left standing alone on the street as the taillights faded off into the night.

Ty tried to tell himself he didn't need to go home to Zane tonight. It was cruel to have alcohol on his breath around Zane, and he'd already done it once this week. His other choices were a hotel or Zane's apartment, but Ty had been drinking, so he couldn't drive, and he didn't want to have to catch a cab. Mostly, he really didn't need Zane to hear the guilt and confusion and myriad of other emotions Ty knew he wouldn't be able to keep out of his voice. He should just call Zane, tell him he and the guys were crashing at a hotel, hole up for the night, and pretend nothing had happened when he woke up hungover.

But he knew he couldn't do that.

When he got home, he was still warring with himself over whether he should even tell Zane about what had happened tonight. He'd outed not only himself, but Zane as well, without truly thinking it through. And then there was the kiss.

It wasn't like Ty had ever been celibate. Zane knew he'd gotten around and wasn't shy about sex. But Ty had never been with anyone he'd hidden from Zane, and since they'd been partnered permanently, Ty hadn't been with anyone else, period. Ty knew it was just a simple kiss, but for him there was no gray area when it came to sex. Either you cheated or you didn't.

He didn't believe Zane was fucking anyone else, but just the thought made Ty cringe. It seemed so unlikely, since they were together so much . . . but really they *weren't*. Obstacles and commitments separated them every day: different projects at work, the softball league, AA meetings, Ty's running and Zane's weightlifting, various and sundry other off-hours pursuits. Throw in the very necessary secrecy that shrouded their relationship, and it was kind of amazing that they were still together at all. But they were, every night that work allowed, despite everything that tried to divide them.

Ty didn't know if Zane wanted his loyalty, but he had it nonetheless. *Semper Fi.*

The real question Ty found himself grappling over was how Zane would take it when he told him about tonight. Would he see it as a threat? Emotional blackmail? Ty didn't think so, but he'd found there were still times he couldn't predict how Zane would react.

It was dark and quiet in the house. Zane must have gone to bed. A wave of desperate relief washed over Ty, and within minutes he was sitting on the back step with a cheap cigar and a couple of bottles to help extend the buzz and ward off the winter chill.

Uncounted minutes later, his entire body still pinged pleasantly, courtesy the two hard lemonades on top of the beer he'd had at the bar. He was just drunk enough that he didn't have to think too hard about what had happened tonight anymore. He held the cheap cigar in his fingers, puffing on it occasionally and blowing smoke rings into the dark. He didn't like to smoke the good ones when he was drunk. It seemed a waste.

The door behind him creaked open, drawing Ty's attention, and he closed his eyes as Zane stepped out onto the stoop. Nerves assaulted him all over again.

"Ty?" Zane asked hesitantly.

"Yeah, I'm here," he answered immediately, not even entertaining the idea of not doing so. He had yet to take advantage of his partner's inability to see, even for fun and games. He wasn't about to start now.

Zane stepped just outside the door. "I smelled the cigar. You guys have a good time?"

Ty lowered his head as another wave of guilt and anger and regret and desire coursed through him. It was such a wash of confusing emotions he wasn't quite sure how to deal with it, and the alcohol wasn't helping. He looked back up and took another drag of the cigar, holding in the fragrant smoke and then exhaling heavily. Smoke billowed out in front of him. "I outed myself tonight," he told Zane in a marginally surprised voice.

Zane's eyes widened as his unfocused gaze shifted in Ty's direction. "What?"

"I told them," Ty said in the same shocked voice as he looked up at Zane. "About us. There was this pretty little waitress and . . ." He shook his head and looked off to the side, as if trying to figure out how it had happened. "I told them I wasn't interested," he tried to explain before putting the cigar to his lips again. He looked down, embarrassed to have to say it again. "They called me on it, and I told them I was in love."

Zane shifted uncomfortably as he slid his hands into his pockets. He didn't have a jacket on, just a thin, long-sleeved Henley. "How'd they take it?"

Ty shook his head, looking at the cigar with a heavy feeling that settled deep in his chest. He couldn't shake the memory of the look of disgust and anger on Owen's face.

"Owen stormed out of the bar," he answered in a hoarse voice, pushing those feelings away for another day. "Apparently being gay makes you incapable of having someone's back in a fight," he said bitterly. Zane's shoulders stiffened, and he frowned deeply, his lips pressing together hard. Ty nodded, flushing and looking away from Zane again. "The others took it pretty well," he went on, swallowing heavily. "Kelly was . . . very interested in the logistics of it all."

He took another long drag. He didn't plan on telling Zane what the other men thought of him. He knew Zane hadn't been in top form when they'd met him. He knew that wasn't the real Zane they'd seen, the Zane that Ty loved.

He closed his eyes, heat coursing through him once more as he remembered the way Nick's lips had felt against his. The embrace had felt right, in a way, at the same time as it felt so very wrong to be kissing anyone but Zane.

But two years ago, if Nick had kissed him like that . . .

Ty shook his head to push away that line of thought. He could torture himself endlessly with uncertainties and questions. Should he tell Zane what had happened? Would it sound like a threat? Would it seem like Ty was giving him an ultimatum? *Tell me you love me, too, or I'm leaving*?

Ty didn't want that, and he would never do that. But not telling Zane about the kiss felt just as wrong. It felt like . . . cheating.

"Nick kissed me," he blurted to Zane as he looked up at him.

Zane froze utterly, like he did when he was very upset . . . or very angry. Then he tipped his head just a bit, the motion indicating he wanted Ty to keep talking.

Ty shook his head, still in slight disbelief over the tale he was relating. He was sure he wouldn't have been able to do it if Zane could actually see him. "We were walking home because he was sort of . . . I thought he was drunk, but . . ." He trailed off and shook his head again, unable to meet Zane's sightless eyes as his cheeks flushed. "One minute he was ranting about risking your life for your country and being able to tell your friends the truth, and the next he was looking at me . . . and he kissed me," he rambled helplessly, telling the story with a variety of hand motions and numb, helpless looks up at Zane.

"And then?" Zane asked softly.

Ty stared at Zane's blank face, wondering at the emotionless reaction. It was like he was just relating another night on the town to his partner, instead of telling his lover about a kiss shared with someone else. He knew closing off like this was how Zane reacted to being devastated, but it still hurt Ty deeply. Why did Zane still have to hide from him?

It took him a long, painful moment to push the twisting sensation in his gut back down.

Somewhere out there Nick O'Flaherty was lying in a hotel bed alone, wondering if he'd done the right thing, hoping Ty would call him, hoping Ty *wouldn't* call him, thinking about what might have happened if they'd just told each other the truth eight years ago when they'd been discharged. Somewhere out there was a man Ty didn't have to put up a front of strength for. Someone he didn't have to fight with day in and day out. Someone he'd always liked and respected. Someone he didn't love but could surely fuck until sunup every night and no doubt be happy and angst-free with for the rest of his life. Nick and Zane were as different as the sun and the moon.

Ty put the cigar to his lips and inhaled slowly, his eyes losing focus as he stared out at the lights of the city. He couldn't tell Zane what Nick had actually said. When Ty got tired of waiting for Zane. It revealed too much about Ty and how well he knew his plodding partner, how long he would just hang around and wait. Zane should be allowed the delusion that he still had secrets, right?

He looked up at Zane guardedly. His cheeks flushed, and a wave of inexplicable loneliness coursed through him. "He just said I knew where to find him."

When Zane flinched, Ty caught a glimpse of emotion flashing across his face. It could have been pain, but it could just as easily have been anger. Or jealousy. Or Ty's own drunken imagination. It didn't make Ty feel any better.

"You've been friends a long time," Zane finally said, his voice noncommittal.

Ty hung his head, his eyes closed as he puffed on the cheap cigar. He had agonized over whether to tell him, and Zane didn't really seem to care one way or the other. That, or he was hiding his emotions behind that same damn mask, and what was the point? Would he ever get to a point where he could just *be* with Ty and not hide anything?

"Yes, we have," he finally murmured sadly.

Ty stayed where he was, sitting on the lower step with his head hanging, afraid to move or open his mouth again for fear of what he might do or say. He had put so much of himself on the line these last few weeks, getting so little in return. Less than nothing, really, since he'd lost an old friend and gained a myriad of new problems.

When Zane shifted his weight and pulled the screen door open so he could walk back inside, leaving Ty alone on the stoop, Ty couldn't let him go. Damn it, he needed someone to let him be weak just once, someone to let him break down.

"Zane?" Ty said shakily, his voice agonized and miserable. He breathed in deeply, trying to regain control of his emotions. One thing he did know for certain: he would get on his knees and beg Zane not to leave him alone tonight. He let out a gust of air, and when he spoke, his voice was calm. "I know I smell like cheap beer and cigar smoke," he told Zane as he stared out into the night. "But I just . . ."

He lowered his head and closed his eyes in embarrassment, unable to finish the request.

For a moment there was silence, and then the creak and snap of the screen door shutting. Zane's shoes scraped on the concrete of the stoop. He stood there, waiting. "You just what?" he asked, his voice rough in the still night air.

Ty turned his head, breath catching. His buzz was long gone, and his body was left trembling with nerves and emotions that he usually ignored or avoided. He could feel his breathing, uneven and difficult, and he knew his heart was absolutely pounding. He thought maybe Zane would be able to feel his racing pulse if he got any closer.

So many times he'd held his tongue, embarrassed to open up to Zane. So many times he'd chosen to be the hardass, the one who supposedly didn't feel anything, the rock for Zane's more volatile mood swings. It had worked for them. It had worked for him. Now it seemed like the house of cards was crashing down around him, and he was just as tired of hiding himself as he was of Zane doing it.

He closed his eyes and took one deep, calming breath, then stood and turned to look at his partner. "I really need a friend tonight, Garrett," he said roughly, determined to keep himself from breaking down, at least for tonight. At least until Zane's sight was back and they could put this chapter behind them. "You think you can handle that for me?"

After a moment's pause in the silence, Zane took a step to the side, pulled the screen door open, and held out his hand.

They lay curled on their sides, Zane behind Ty with his arm over Ty's waist as he waited for his breathing to slow and his pulse to calm. Ty had shocked him tonight. Scared him.

Coming out to his Recon team—and then admitting he was in love—Zane couldn't even imagine what kind of pressure Ty had felt. And on top of that, admitting *who* he loved? Zane was sure that hadn't gone quite as well as Ty had glossed over. They were his best friends, but he'd kept a pretty major secret from them for a long time, and the man he said he loved was a stranger to them. Not the best of situations.

And Nick. Nick, who'd invited him to dinner with the rest of the Recon team. Nick, who had been Ty's best friend since boot camp, who understood what Ty had lived and how to deal with him. Who had heard about Zane and made his own move to give Ty an alternative.

Zane knew why. As he tightened his arms around Ty and pressed his forehead to Ty's shoulder, he knew why.

Zane had wanted Ty since he'd met him, and every time chaos had crashed down on them—separation after the Tri-State case, Ty's near-death experience in the mountains, the danger on the cruise ship, even Ty telling Zane that he loved him—that attachment had grown more intense, despite every doubt and fear and weakness Zane took into consideration.

But Nick's attachment to Ty might be even stronger.

Zane didn't think he could bear to lose Ty now. He loved Ty. Painfully. Desperately. But now wasn't the time to finally get his head out of his ass and admit it, not after what Ty had said tonight. Ty would see it as a reaction to external pressure, not an honest feeling from the heart, and Zane's words would be set aside like the first time he had said them, slow dancing in Ty's arms.

As his unseeing eyes burned, Zane thought very seriously he might cry.

CHAPTER TWELVE

The next morning was a Sunday, and Ty headed to the hotel to say goodbye to Nick and the others. It was time for them to leave, and though Ty hadn't been able to spend much time with them, there was just too much going on for him to feel good about them staying in town. Not to mention the ramifications of his confession. Owen wouldn't speak to him, avoiding him under the auspices of last minute packing. Ty'd had trouble looking Nick in the eye, but he had forced himself to do it, recognizing the same awkwardness in his best friend.

"Ty," Nick said uncomfortably when he pulled Ty aside. "I'm sorry. What I did, it was shitty and selfish, and I wish I could take it back."

"Don't worry about it," Ty told him, wishing Nick would just pretend it had never happened, like so many of the other things they never spoke of.

Nick shook his head. "I just—I need . . . to tell you this, okay?"

Ty nodded with trepidation, wondering what could be harder for Nick to say than anything that had happened last night.

"I've loved you since the day you sat next to me on the bus to Parris Island," Nick blurted.

Ty blinked at him, unable to do anything more.

"And I was going to tell you when we finished our last tour. I planned it out every night in my head." Ty started to speak, but Nick stopped him. "But then the helo went down. And . . . what happened to us . . ."

Ty closed his eyes, immediately assaulted with memories he'd spent years repressing. They hit him like a physical blow. Flashes of chains and dull instruments, peeling plaster in a dark cell, making marks on a ceiling so low he didn't have to stand to reach it.

Nick stopped talking.

Ty opened his eyes to find the same haunted look in Nick's eyes that he could feel seeping through himself.

"I will always be your friend, Ty," Nick practically gasped. They hugged, a tremble going through both of them before they let each other go.

What they had been through together—there was nothing that could break that bond. There was also nothing that could turn that bond into something else, and in that moment, they both knew it.

When it was time for them to catch the shuttle to the airport, they all shook hands and hugged, Owen saying a stiff goodbye instead, and Ty saw them off with a sinking feeling in the pit of his stomach. Nothing was resolved there, but Ty knew he would have to deal with it later. Just one or three more personal problems he had to push to the back burner because of his job.

Zane seemed down and didn't have much to say when Ty got home, and for the first time, Ty was too tired to try to reach into his darkness and pull him out. He went to bed early, asleep before Zane fumbled his way under the sheet and wrapped around him.

The next day he headed back to work, something he dreaded for the first time since Jimmy Hathaway's funeral years before.

"Grady, welcome back. I hope you stayed out of trouble—and the press—over the long weekend?" McCoy said as Ty stopped in his office doorway.

Ty nodded, sedate. A bad week had only gotten worse, and he was in no mood to be witty on a Monday morning.

"We've been through all the evidence we could get our hands on, and there's all kinds of paperwork to be done. I had Clancy leave some on your desk. Exciting stuff to come back to, I know," McCoy said, his voice apologetic. "We're having another meeting with Financial Crimes this afternoon to touch base on leads for the combined crimes, and then I have a consult with a team from Counterterrorism."

"Great," Ty said without enthusiasm. He was finding it hard to concentrate or care about work. His partner was still out of commission, and the more time that passed, the more Ty began to fear Zane's blindness might be permanent. On top of that, Ty didn't like to be on the periphery of an investigation that directly involved him. It was stressful to have his fate in someone else's hands, no matter how good they were at their jobs. And then Nick had traipsed in and fucking kissed him, dredging up things he only thought of in his nightmares.

Ty ran his hand through his hair and turned to head for his desk. Maybe paperwork would actually be good for him today.

"Hi, Ty. Mac had me put some . . . files . . . Are you okay?" Michelle Clancy asked once he got to the team's pod of desks where she sat with Perrimore, Alston, and Lassiter.

"Yeah," he answered with a curt nod. He sat with a thump and gave the chair a moment to protest being used, then leaned back and rubbed hard at his face.

Clancy paused in his peripheral vision, but thankfully she sat at her desk and got to work instead of keeping after him. "Mac set me up as the liaison with Financial Crimes instead of having them call all over the office, horning in," she said.

"My condolences," Ty grunted.

"He's still trying to keep you and Garrett out of the spotlight. Have you heard from Zane? How is he?" Clancy asked in clear concern.

"He's blind," Ty answered in an almost cruel voice. He looked up at her, not wanting to be nasty to her but knowing he would be if she kept talking. He didn't need the reminder.

Clancy met his eyes, her lips thinned with displeasure, but either she felt the impending meltdown emanating from ten feet away or decided she just didn't want to know. She went back to her paperwork without another word.

The pod worked in heavy silence, unspoken questions hanging heavy in the air and one teammate conspicuously absent. It was a good two hours later, with Ty well into the reams of paperwork, when the call came in.

"We've had another detonation at the Inner Harbor!" McCoy's voice snapped through the quiet room. "Activate bank response protocol!"

The two teams of agents and other support personnel, about thirteen of twenty in the office accounted for, erupted into movement with a purpose. Ty grabbed his windbreaker and shrugged into it as he headed for the stairs with everyone else. The office wasn't really set up for emergency responses like this, but they managed. Vans in the basement were stocked with weapons, tactical gear, and all that fun stuff that usually got people killed. They piled into three vans, heading for three separate banks that had been pinpointed as the most likely targets. All far away from the Inner Harbor.

The bank robbers were trying to divide and conquer like the Allies had in World War II, forcing Germany to fight on two fronts. Any military mind knew that a two-front war was almost impossible to win, and that was what the Baltimore authorities had been fighting.

McCoy had devised a plan of his own in response. He had volunteered members of his own Criminal division team, members not involved in either the emergency response to a bomb threat or to the scene of a bank robbery, and he had formed five special task forces in cooperation with the Maryland Joint Terrorism Task Force, supported by the Baltimore Division's Field Intelligence Group.

The proper response to the next bomb scare would still be seen, but those special teams, made up of a mishmash of agents and cops from different agencies, would respond to pre-selected targets based on where the bomb was.

They got updates about the bombing on the way. Two more stores blown to pieces, several with collateral damage. No warning, no evacuation. Uncounted injuries, and they all held their breath with each announcement, waiting to hear about casualties.

Ty closed his eyes and lowered his head. He'd promised himself and all of Baltimore that they would stop these monsters, but all he'd done was get embroiled in it, making himself a target, making Zane a target, egging the bombers on, and seemingly making the attacks more personal and the attackers more bold.

He couldn't shake the feeling that this was on his shoulders.

The van careened to a stop, sending the agent next to him tumbling against his side. Neither one of them acknowledged it, instead hurrying to open the door and spill out to surround the entrance to the bank.

Following the predetermined plan of action, they fanned out to cover the two entrances and check all vehicles present, and one of the assistant SAICs made the call inside to touch base with the manager before a team moved inside.

The call wasn't answered. It was some kind of miracle, but the team had found the right bank.

Ty knelt behind the wheel of a police cruiser, a city cop beside him, listening over his earpiece for instructions. There was a sudden burst of chatter, and Ty turned, pointing his gun with its scope over the hood of the car at the entrance to the bank. A skinny man in a cheesecloth hood exited the bank, a woman held hostage in front of him, a gun held to her head. The cops surrounding him shouted, but Ty was hearing the words in his ear instead.

"Yellow, do you have a shot?"

"Negative."

"Green?"

"No line of sight."

"Red?"

"Nothing clean."

"Blue?"

Ty squeezed one eye closed, looking down the scope at the bank robber. Looking at the man's trigger finger in his scope. It was resting on the trigger guard. He brought the scope up, checking line of sight to the target's head.

"Affirmative," he murmured in answer.

"Take the shot."

Ty breathed out carefully, taking a moment to ask for forgiveness. Then he squeezed the trigger.

The hooded man's body snapped backward as the bullet struck the shoulder of his gun arm. There was no danger of him squeezing off a shot with his finger on the guard, and they wanted him taken alive. A gruesome spray of blood painted the glass doors behind him, and the bullet impacted the glass, sending tendrils of splintered bulletproof glass outward. The man let out a high-pitched shriek as he bounced on the concrete. The hostage yanked free and ran, leaving the cops and agents with clear shots. If the hooded man raised that gun so much as a millimeter, Ty would take his head off.

But the gun clattered to the ground as the man rolled around on his back, still howling and clutching at his shoulder.

Ty raised his head and watched as agents and police officers surrounded the man. The cop beside Ty gave his shoulder a pat. "Nice shot, brother."

Ty nodded at him, standing to watch as the man was dragged toward the police line to be questioned and unmasked. A call was put in to the bank and was answered immediately. There was no one else in there, they were told. Only one bank robber had been there.

Surely all this wasn't the work of one man? There had been reports of two to three in each robbery, and with the bomb spotter, they had the group pegged for up to four. Ty moved closer to the ambulance, his gun over his shoulder as people parted to let him through. The man was on a stretcher, crying out in pain, a scream so feminine that it sounded almost like a child. The mask was ripped off to reveal his face, and Ty stared in shock.

It was a woman. No, a *girl*, a goddamn *kid*, eighteen if she was a day. And she wasn't taking the injury well, sobbing and red-faced, saying over and over that it hurt, calling for her mother.

"Get this," a city cop said, stopping next to Ty. He had the girl's weapon in hand. "It's not even loaded."

"What the hell was she thinking?" the first cop said in disgusted wonder.

Ty shook his head, speechless. Shooting a teenage girl through a sniper's scope had not been on his bucket list. His stomach curled, threatening to send his lunch back up.

"It's a clean shot," the EMT announced. "She'll be fine, but we need to get her moving." They lifted the would-be bank robber up and headed for the ambulance, two cops alongside for the ride.

"Hey," the assistant SAIC said as he stopped at Ty's side. "It was a good shot. Saved her life."

Ty nodded, but he still had to swallow against being sick. He took a step after the stretcher. "Hey," he called to the paramedics. They stopped, looking at him expectantly. The assistant SAIC nodded for them to let him closer. He stepped up to the stretcher and looked down at the girl. Her face was streaked with tears, her blonde hair mussed and bloody from the spray after the high-velocity round hitting her.

"You're that guy from TV," she stuttered at him, still sobbing.

"No. I'm the guy who just shot you," Ty told her, voice hard with anger.

"You aren't supposed to be here," she sobbed hysterically. "You're supposed to be at the other place!"

The paramedics ended the interview before Ty could ask her anything, citing her vitals as too dangerous to continue with the stress. They carted her off as Ty frowned after them, trying to decide what other place she'd meant.

"They got Hannah," Graham told Pierce and Ross as soon as the two boys walked through the door. "They shot her, man."

"Good," Pierce responded succinctly.

"*What*?"

"She was a dead weight, man. Why do you think I sent her alone?"

Graham stared at his former friend, not believing it. "What about the agents?" he asked, heart in his throat.

Pierce just shook his head, not intending to explain what had happened.

"Pierce! What about your white whale?"

"I said forget him. He's not worth it."

"You said he was Moby Dick."

"Yeah, well, now he's just a dick, and I'm done with him."

"Why?" Graham needled.

"Dude, just drop it," Ross grunted, irritated.

Pierce whirled on him. "We didn't go after those douchebags. We were watching at the bank, okay? Moby Dick is the one who shot Hannah."

Graham frowned as Pierce stormed out. He didn't understand. Pierce had wanted Hannah dead, but he was upset because Agent Grady had been the one to shoot her?

He looked at Ross for some sort of explanation.

"Pierce is scared of him," Ross muttered. "He thinks he had it wrong and he's not Captain Ahab after all."

Graham looked back at the door where Pierce had disappeared. "I think he had it right the first time."

Ty paced through Zane's living room, making figure eights around the coffee table and couch as he kept up a constant undertone of muttering and cursing.

Zane was gone. Just *gone*.

Ty had gone home first. There had been no signs of struggle, which had made Ty feel a little better. But also no note, no phone call, nothing to let Ty know where Zane had gone, who he was with, or if he was okay. So Ty had come over here on the off chance Zane had tried to walk it or gotten someone to drive him by for clothes or something. And again, nothing. Ty was scared and angry. He didn't like worrying like this. He didn't like the abject terror that came with knowing Zane was practically helpless without his sight. And he definitely didn't like knowing that these kids, these stupid, spoiled psychopathic teenagers who were killing people left and right, had it out for him and Zane.

Standing there in the bank lot, Ty had mulled over the girl's words, trying to decide what she'd meant when she'd said "the other place." He would have suspected she was just rambling, referring to the diversionary bomb. But where were the other three? What had they used *her* as a diversion for?

It had struck him that they might have intended to come for him, for him or Zane.

He had called, but Zane hadn't answered. On the torturous drive in a Bureau sedan to his row house, he'd tried to tell himself Zane might be in the shower again. It hadn't eased the vise around his chest or the guilt he felt every time the girl's blue eyes flashed through his mind.

Now, he was no longer worried that Zane had been taken. Even blind, Zane would have made a mess if someone had attacked him. That meant he'd left without considering that Ty might freak the fuck out when he found him gone.

And that was possibly worst of all, that after all the crap he'd put up with in the last week, all of himself he'd given and taken, he didn't even warrant a spare thought or simple note before Zane went skipping out the door.

He steamed and stewed another ten minutes and was just about to go out and do *something* when he heard voices outside the door and then fumbling at the lock.

When the door swung open, Ty stood just off to the side of the door, his gun drawn as he greeted whoever was coming in.

"Jesus!" Special Agent Fred Perrimore swore as he dropped to one knee, one hand going for his gun, his other raised behind him to stop whoever was behind him from crossing the threshold.

"What is it?"

Zane.

"Give me one good reason not to shoot you," Ty growled dangerously to Perrimore.

Perrimore's eyes went big, wide, and white, standing out against his black skin, and he looked over his shoulder and up at Zane, who was frowning. Perrimore returned his eyes to Ty, hands out in front of him in a conciliatory gesture. "Because I run interference with BPD?" he tried.

Ty narrowed his eyes and lowered his gun, holstering it slowly. "Good answer," he offered with a nod. His eyes moved to Zane. "Where the fuck have you been?"

Zane raised an eyebrow, uncannily looking right at him even though his eyes were unfocused. He plucked at the sweaty T-shirt visible under his casual winter jacket. "Freddy took me to the gym."

"What's wrong, Perrimore? You can't leave a damn note?" Ty growled.

Perrimore stood up and edged back out the door. "Garrett didn't mention anything about needing to leave a note," he ventured, looking between the two partners.

"I was only gone two hours, and you're supposed to be at work," Zane pointed out.

"Yeah, well, I'm not."

"It's not like I could have gotten anywhere on my own."

"Has it escaped your attention that there may be someone trying to kill you?" Ty asked through gritted teeth.

Zane's eyes narrowed in what would have been a glare if he could have aimed it. He reached out and touched Perrimore's arm. "Thanks for the ride."

Perrimore shifted his weight nervously. "Yeah, Garrett, sure thing." He glanced at Ty, who snarled at him wordlessly. "Yeah, I'll just be going, then," Perrimore muttered as he turned and made his retreat.

Zane reached out to touch the door jamb and walked inside, shifting to close the door behind him. He tipped his head, listening for something. Ty stood glaring at him, knowing he should get control of his temper but truly not willing to do it. He'd reached the end of his rope.

"Are you going to say something or just glower at me?" Zane asked. "I went out for a couple hours. I was with a friend, a trained agent who carries a gun. The only way I'd have been safer would have been to be with you."

Ty pressed his lips tightly together and closed his eyes, but it wasn't helping. "I don't care where you go or who you're with. I'm not your goddamned babysitter," he said tightly. "But you've got to take this situation seriously! You've got to be where you say you're going to be when you say you're going to be there! Just because you can't fucking see doesn't mean the rest of the world has come to a halt too!"

"Take the situation seriously," Zane repeated flatly.

"We only caught one of them today, did you know that?"

"Take it fucking *seriously*?"

"There's no telling where the others are or who they're after!"

Ty kept ranting over him, both of them talking at each other and not actually hearing what the other was saying. Finally Zane shouted above Ty's voice.

"Did you actually hear what bullshit just came out of your mouth? Believe me, I know really damn well how the world is going on without me!"

"And it doesn't matter that I've been bending over backward trying to help you," Ty said angrily. "Doesn't matter that you disappearing would scare the shit out of me?"

Zane grimaced and rubbed at his temple. "Yes, of course it matters, but—"

"But what you want is more important," Ty finished in disgust. Zane shook his head, and Ty glared at him as he felt the weight of the week crashing down on him. "You know what, Zane? I'm done," he said with a wave of his hand. "You want to reconnect with the fucking world, strike out on your own for independence, go do it. But you're gonna do it without me," he grunted as he grabbed up his jacket from the back of the couch and stalked toward the door.

"What the hell crawled up your ass and died? You are totally overreacting!" Zane protested as he reached out, catching Ty's arm by blind luck.

Ty turned and lashed out, catching him right under the chin. Totally surprised, Zane was knocked off balance, and he collapsed backward against the bookshelves, hitting them hard enough to send several books thunking to the floor as he fell with a hard grunt to the thin carpet.

Ty turned to head for the door, shaking his hand and grumbling.

"Ty," Zane said weakly.

"Go to hell," Ty responded without turning around. He grabbed at the doorknob and yanked the front door open.

"Ty," Zane repeated, a real tinge of desperation in his voice. "I think I can see something."

Ty stopped and turned to look at him, frowning. Zane's face was set in a pained wince. He pressed the heel of one hand to his temple as he blinked over and over. Ty cocked his head and watched him, waiting. When Zane looked up, one of his eyes was totally bloodshot, more red than white. He kept blinking like he was facing a bright light.

"Son of a bitch," Ty muttered as he slammed the door shut and stalked past Zane toward the kitchen.

"Get the fuck back over here, you asshole," Zane ground out. "That fucking *hurt*!"

"I'm calling the doctor," Ty snapped back at him. He snatched up the phone and jabbed at the numbers angrily. Zane didn't growl back; he just held his head in his hands, looking miserable. Ty warred with the instinct to protect that had been in overdrive for a week now and the urge to kick him while he wallowed down there. He wouldn't have placed bets on which instinct would win out.

After some terse snapping, he got one of the doctors on the line, turned back to Zane, and poked him with the end of the phone. "Doctor wants to talk to you," he said in a low voice.

"Bastard," Zane muttered from where he sat on the floor, leaning back against the shelves, covering his eyes with one hand and bracing that arm on his propped-up knee. He fumbled for the receiver. "Yeah," he said into the phone. After a moment he added, "Yeah. I've had a hell of a headache all day, until I went to the gym."

Ty paced, still fuming and unable to stand still.

Apparently the doctor was droning on, explaining what might be happening. "So this is a good thing?" Zane asked after listening. Ty could feel Zane's gaze following him. After a week without it, Ty felt uncomfortably pinned down, and that just made him angrier.

"Okay," Zane said, his tone unsure, and he thumbed off the phone.

"Gonna live?" Ty asked him curtly as he took the phone from him.

Zane turned his head slowly, as if afraid he might be dizzy. "Yeah. Maybe you should have hit me sooner."

"I couldn't agree more." He tossed the phone toward the couch as he moved to the door without another word.

"Ty, wait," Zane called out, his voice pained.

Ty answered by slamming the front door. He thought he should have felt just a little bit guilty. But he didn't.

Zane stalked into his apartment and kicked the door shut behind him. Five hours. Five goddamn hours he'd sat at the hospital for the doctors to look at him for five minutes, a ten-minute CT scan, then a pat on the head and shove out the door. And all he'd been able to stew about was how he'd fucked up so royally with Ty, however unintentional it was.

He shed gear and clothes as he walked through the apartment to the kitchen in his jeans and socks, intent on getting a Coke and then a hot shower. When he yanked open the refrigerator door and saw the untouched boxes and bags from Chiapparelli's, his first instinct was to slam the door shut, yell, and throw . . . *something*. But he swallowed on the anger, and though it was really, really close, he made himself grab a can of soda off the shelf and shut the door carefully. He hadn't been this angry in a long time, and it made his head pound, his eyes sting, and, damn it, his heart ache.

Zane slid onto a bar chair and pressed the cold can to his cheek, then his temple, then his forehead, trying to get some relief as he fought the swell of emotions. Upset and anger, obviously. A healthy dose of utterly pathetic gratitude and frantic joy. An aching regret, and an even deeper hurt. The conflict was about to make his head explode.

With a sigh, Zane set down the Coke, and he was about to get up when he saw the small pile of mail sitting forgotten on the far side of the bar. He reached out and dragged it over. Coupons. A church tract. Generic insurance offers. A flier advertising a nearby car-wash grand opening, another announcing a special couples' dinner night out at one of the other prominent Italian restaurants in the area. He unfolded the last one to find only a sheet of paper with messy handwriting.

But it was clearly his name at the top.

Zane silently read the few short lines, and the emotions started bubbling up again, threatening to choke him.

Mr. Garrett, Pierce Sutton is the reason you're blind. He has your truck too. You have to stop him before he kills somebody. Please.

Four days had passed since the teenage girl had been shot outside the bank, and the whirlwind was still churning. The public was equal parts praising the FBI's dedication to keeping Baltimore safe and crucifying the "trigger-happy monster" who'd taken the shot.

That monster just happened to be the same agent who'd become one of the darlings of the media, but no one knew that. And he was missing in action, sent home to lay low yet again until the case was done. He kept thrusting himself in the middle of all the trouble, and Dan McCoy simply couldn't have him around anymore.

McCoy felt sorry for Ty Grady. Usually he was like a cat: he didn't necessarily always land on his feet, but he had the uncanny ability to twist during the fall and at least land on all fours. He just couldn't seem to win on this one, though. He was on all fours, all right, but McCoy didn't think it was voluntary.

So McCoy had sent him packing, sending a different agent several times a day to check up on him. By all accounts he wasn't handling the shooting of the girl well. One agent reported that Ty had actually uttered the phrase "you kids get off my lawn" when the rookie had knocked on his door. McCoy knew that Ty was either messing around with them for shits and giggles or he was truly traumatized. Truth be told, it was probably a combination of the two.

On the plus side, Zane Garrett had been released to light duty by the Bureau doctor late yesterday and was "officially" back in the office. He'd called in the night of the shooting, having found a letter left at his apartment while he was blind, a letter that gave them a name. Fingerprints were no help; whoever had handled the paper didn't have a record, so there was no way to know how the writer had found Zane's apartment. That still bothered McCoy, as well as Zane's team, who had all volunteered to continue the protection detail.

It would have taken a fight to keep Zane out of the office, doctor's orders or not, so McCoy had Zane brought in—his truck was still MIA—sat him down, put his cyber skills to work dredging some more nontraditional sources of information, and kept a close eye on him.

Pierce Sutton turned out to be a kid and therefore in the wind, not at any address his meager records said he might be using and hard to pin down. The search continued, as did other aspects of the investigation, including the one currently on top of the pile on McCoy's desk.

McCoy pushed a button to call for Zane as he perused the file in front of him.

He got an immediate reply. "Garrett."

"Get in here," McCoy grunted as he flipped a page.

He didn't get a verbal answer, but Zane was in his doorway within a minute. He was dressed down, in black jeans and boots with a nondescript blue button-down, pushing the line of what office dress code strictly allowed, and he still looked pretty haggard, hair ruffled and face scruffy. McCoy ignored the break in protocol and beckoned Zane into his office.

"Sit down. I need your help with something."

Zane hesitated for a beat before moving into the office and taking one of the chairs across from him. McCoy looked at him for a moment, then down at the file spread out across his desk. Ty Grady's file. These two were like lightning rods, and any given day, he wasn't sure which one would draw the most voltage.

"You doing okay, Zane?"

Zane snorted quietly. "Better, anyway."

McCoy nodded, looking Zane over critically. Zane's eyes were still bloodshot enough that he could see the red in them from seven feet away, but he decided the answer would do for now. "Have you heard from Grady?"

Zane sat up straighter in his chair and made eye contact. "Not for a few days."

"Neither have I. I've gotten word he's not handling the situation very well. Has his phone off, letting everything go to voice mail. You've heard that he was the one to take the shot at the bank, yes?"

Zane went still. He did that sometimes, McCoy had noticed in the past, usually because it was such a contrast to Ty's incessant twitching. "No," Zane replied, his tone flat. "I only heard they took one person into custody."

McCoy nodded and pushed the file around. "Got her with a sniper rifle. It was an impressive shot, disarmed her but didn't kill her. Still, he's not really okay with shooting a kid, from what my agents are telling me. Anyway, that's not why I brought you in here." He turned the file around on his desk. The pages were covered with thick black ink, lines and lines of redacted information.

"Her?" Zane was now frowning deeply. "A kid?" He glanced down at the file, then back up at McCoy.

McCoy looked at him with some surprise. "You haven't heard any of it? She was seventeen. All we've gotten from her is the ringleader isn't much older than she is and she doesn't know why he's so intent on killing so many people, but he is and she was scared of him. She also hinted to us as she was being wheeled away that he might have it out for you and Ty because you've become the figureheads of the pursuit, so to speak. I'm surprised Grady didn't tell you all this. As soon as he figured it out, he went tearing off to find you, make sure you weren't a collateral target during all the chaos."

Zane looked away, toward McCoy's window. To McCoy's eyes, he looked uncomfortable, which was unusual for the ultra-controlled Zane Garrett. But he'd had a shitty week too. Going blind would throw anyone's emotional equanimity.

"We didn't talk long," Zane finally said. "He had things to do, and I had to go back to UMMC."

McCoy nodded, satisfied with the answer. Who the hell knew what Ty was ever thinking, anyway?

He tapped his finger on the blacked-out file. "I'm trying to see if anything in Grady's file might connect him to this kid, but as you can see, his file is mostly crap. I wanted to ask you if you knew anything that might be relevant."

Zane looked back to the mostly blacked-out paperwork, then up to McCoy. "If that's Grady's file, I don't know that I'll be much more help."

McCoy's brow knitted. "You've never seen his file?"

Zane shook his head just slightly, winced, and stopped the movement with a touch to his temple. "No."

"Huh. Well, you should take it and read up, Garrett. Grady's got to be a damn minefield to walk through without an inkling of what's back there," McCoy grunted as he closed the file and handed it to Zane. "Nothing in there's going to help this investigation."

Zane looked at the file in his hand like he wasn't sure what to do with it, then dropped it lightly on the edge of McCoy's desk. "So there are more of them out there, and they know us. Me and Grady. Possibly where we live. And they're likely out to get us specifically," he summed up, face grim.

"I'd wager if they weren't before, they are now," McCoy told him bluntly.

Zane tipped his head to one side, eyes going unfocused as he thought hard about something. McCoy had seen the man pull together details from disparate case files to create legitimate leads in critical investigations; he wondered just what Zane was chewing on now.

"Where's Grady?" Zane ask abruptly.

McCoy couldn't hide his surprise and confusion. "I don't know. At home, probably. We have someone going around every few hours to keep an eye on him. The last team we tried to sit on him, he actually threatened to shoot them."

"He would," Zane muttered. He stood up. "I need to get up to speed on the contingencies, but I won't last long," he said, waving a hand at his head. "Killer headache."

McCoy nodded, watching Zane curiously. "Don't push yourself. Go on home. I'll have someone come around to check up on you too."

Zane hesitated, apparently choosing his words before saying, "I'm going to stop by and see Ty. We've both had the week from hell."

"Might be a good idea. Maybe you can ease his mind some. It was a clean shot. No one knew she was a kid."

"He did what he had to. What was right," Zane said quietly. "Doesn't mean it doesn't hurt." With that he left the room and, McCoy noticed belatedly, Ty's personnel file.

McCoy grunted as he frowned at the folder. In his opinion, Ty had more on his conscience than the shot he'd taken four days ago. A lot more.

He reached for the file and stowed it in the bottom drawer of his desk, locking it away.

CHAPTER THIRTEEN

As he stood outside the row house door, Zane realized how nervous he was. Not scared, not angry. Nervous. He hadn't seen or heard from Ty since the day Ty had decked him. Four long, lonely, and miserable days that had driven home to Zane just how very important Ty was to him. Every night, lying alone in a cold bed with a lamp on so he wouldn't be in the dark, Zane had struggled to accept that however unintentionally, he'd scared Ty badly and needed to apologize. He'd wrangled even more with the possibility that Ty wouldn't give him the chance, which had only fed Zane's irrational fear of losing him altogether.

Zane had seen Ty easily forgive and let something go—it was one of the most prominent aspects of Ty's unusual personality. But Zane had never seen Ty angry enough to literally walk away. Even when Zane had been drunk on the cruise ship, Ty had dragged him to the pool to sober him up instead of telling him he was done. Then today, the news about Ty and the girl—it had almost knocked Zane over as he realized just what exactly Ty had been dealing with that day.

Zane would get down on his knees and beg to get back into Ty's good graces, if that was what it took.

But first things first. He rapped hard on the door.

It took a full minute before the lock on the door turned. When Ty swung the door open, he wore nothing but a towel, rivulets of water still running down his chest and arms.

"Garrett," he said in surprise.

At the sight of all that glorious skin, heat slashed through Zane so fast that he lost track of what he had carefully planned to say. Instead he reached out, grabbed Ty by the back of the neck, and yanked him a step closer so he could kiss him messily.

Ty flailed and struggled to keep his balance. Zane distantly realized that Ty had his gun in his hand. When Zane pulled back, he glanced at the weapon—pointed away, luckily—and then at Ty for a split second before doing what he'd come to do in the first place.

He slugged Ty.

Ty reeled back, too surprised by the double-edged assault to keep his feet. The gun went skittering across the hardwood, and Ty wound up flat on his back, the towel miraculously still wrapped around his hips.

Zane stood in the doorway, yanked his Wayfarers off, and took a couple of heartbeats to admire the sight. "Didn't see that coming, did you?" he asked as he set his hands on his hips.

Ty shook his head violently, as if trying to clear it, and he pushed up onto his elbows. "What the hell, Zane?" he said in a hoarse, angry voice. "Is there a car out there? People are watching me!"

"Of course there's not a car, I checked. They stopped watching you after your death threat," Zane retorted, stepping inside and kicking the door shut. "You—you spent all that time taking care of me, and then you just took off!" Zane accused with a pointed finger.

"You—!"

"*And* you chewed the hell out of my ass and then didn't even give me a chance to apologize for being a jerk," Zane finished, feeling the frustration starting to ebb. Just being with Ty made a difference. "But mostly? Hitting me while I was blind was a low blow, even if I did deserve it." He offered his hand to help Ty up.

Ty looked at his hand and then back up at him incredulously. "Is that supposed to be an apology? God, you're such a dick!"

Zane stared down at him, all too aware of how thankful he was he could see Ty's face again. He'd dreamed about it every night. "No, that wasn't an apology." He went down on one knee next to Ty and took a deep breath. "But this is: I am *sorry* that I scared you. I didn't think it through, and I'm sorry that after all that time you spent supporting me, you were the one who got let down. I know I can't change it, but I'm willing to do whatever it takes to make it up to you."

Ty blinked at him, obviously surprised by the real apology. He pushed himself up to sit, looking up at Zane grimly. "That was better," he commented with a curt nod. "Did it hurt?"

"Being hit, hitting you, or apologizing?" Zane asked tentatively. Ty snorted and shook his head, looking out the front window. "I hope all of it hurt," he muttered, disgruntled. He reached out and gripped Zane's shoulder, using him to pull himself to his feet. "How'd you get here? And why are you here, besides the urgent need to deliver a knuckle sandwich?" Ty asked as he turned away from him and began walking through the long row house toward the kitchen at the back. His voice was low and controlled, almost devoid of emotion. That meant he was trying to hide that he was angry or hurt.

Zane just punching him in the face aside, if Ty was still angry at him after four days, Zane had no idea what he could do about it. "Came from the office," he answered as he got to his feet. "I heard about what happened at the bank."

Ty stopped at the kitchen counter, placing his hands flat on the countertop, his back still to Zane. He was tense, the muscles in his back and shoulders jumping as he gripped the counter top. The towel was losing its battle with gravity, though, and that was a distraction Zane was determined to ignore. For now.

He slowly approached, not trying to muffle his footsteps on the hardwood, until he stood barely a foot behind Ty. After a moment's deliberation, he reached out to gently lay a hand on each of Ty's shoulders. He was taut as a bowstring beneath Zane's fingers. Giving Ty time to react, Zane slowly took that last step to hold Ty against his chest and carefully close his arms around him. He didn't have anything to say. He knew words wouldn't help.

Ty lowered his head, reaching one hand up to place it over Zane's. The tension invested in him began to ebb, and he slumped.

Zane tightened his hold and pressed a gentle kiss to Ty's ear. "I've got you," he whispered.

"Took you long enough," Ty answered in a hard voice. He turned his head, his cheek brushing Zane's lips.

Pain jabbed Zane's chest. "I'm sorry," he breathed, arms tightening even more. He wanted to ask why Ty hadn't said anything, why he hadn't called, but they were stupid questions and wouldn't make a difference now. Ty had gone looking for him, and Zane hadn't been there. That was the bottom line. He needed to be thinking about Ty right now, not himself.

Ty shook his head, either rejecting the apology or telling Zane he didn't have to apologize again.

"I'm here now," Zane said, drawing courage from the fact Ty hadn't pushed him away.

"They keep flashing her picture on the news," Ty said in a low rumble. "I had to unplug the TV. Cut off the phone."

For a moment, Zane was lost, but then it clicked. "Was it bad?" he asked quietly, setting his chin on Ty's shoulder.

"I took her through the shoulder joint. I was trying to make certain her arm went down so she couldn't pull the trigger. They told me it destroyed the ball and socket—she'll never use the arm again."

"But she's alive," Zane pointed out gently.

Ty nodded jerkily. He was looking at the counter devotedly. Zane felt him tense again. "What the hell are these fucking kids doing?"

Zane shook his head, knowing Ty would be able to feel it. "I tried calling you."

"Turned off my phone. Mac kicked me out, Sidewinder went home," Ty muttered.

Zane didn't ask if there were more reasons, reasons that included him. "We got a line on the ringleader. He pretty much matches the sketch you had drawn. We spent the last couple of days trying to run him down. He's not anywhere his records say he could be, so no luck yet. Mac said the girl was afraid of him, didn't know why he wanted to hurt people."

Zane could feel Ty coiling like a snake about to strike. It was painfully obvious that anger and frustration and guilt and probably a myriad of other emotions had been building inside him the last few days, possibly weeks. He raised his head and breathed out slowly, resting his head against Zane's shoulder as the tension inexplicably ebbed.

He rubbed a hand over his face and turned in Zane's arms.

"It's not like you to bottle up like this," Zane said, taking in the unusually dark circles under Ty's eyes.

Ty met his gaze silently for a long moment, then snaked his arms up around Zane's neck and hugged him, burrowing his face under Zane's chin. Zane held him tight, feeling his eyes prickle, determined not to move from this spot until Ty was ready.

When Ty finally spoke, his voice was muffled, with a wry twist to it. "I'm sorry I went ballistic on you."

Zane wrinkled his nose. "Could've been worse. Some good did come of it," he replied, opening his eyes, the flood of relief at being able to see still fresh.

"You deserved it."

"Not arguing."

Ty raised his head to look at him, finally releasing him and leaning back against the counter. He looked spent, physically and emotionally. "Are you really better?" he asked in sincere concern. "Your eyes?"

Zane relaxed, though the worry for his lover's state of mind still loomed large. "Still a little bleary, but almost back to normal. Doctor said not to be surprised if there was a little more bleeding or blurring." He shrugged as he lifted one hand to cup Ty's cheek. "More than anything, I needed to see you again," he whispered.

Ty rewarded the honesty with a melancholy smile. "I missed you too. Jerk," he tacked on, smile growing.

"Yeah, I deserve that," Zane murmured as he stroked his fingers along Ty's cheekbone. "I might have left a bruise here."

Ty rolled his eyes. "Of course you did."

Zane leaned down and brushed his lips gently over the abused cheek. Ty's eyes fluttered shut, and Zane felt the shiver run through his body.

"That's better," Ty whispered, voice gone rough.

"Will you let me stay?" Zane murmured, lips brushing Ty's skin.

"I don't *let* you do anything, Zane," Ty answered, voice low and dry. His fingers slid into Zane's hair. "But I'd really love it if you stayed."

Zane tipped his head to one side. "As long as you want."

Amusement flashed through Ty's eyes. "You're practically groveling."

Zane hummed in agreement. "Is it working?"

"I *am* finding you oddly attractive," Ty deadpanned. "What can I do to make myself irresistibly attractive?"

Ty glanced up like he was pondering the question. Then he started shaking his head. "No, too many memories of horrible puns."

Zane huffed, feeling a little more of the tension in the air ease. He almost threw back a flippant answer, but instead he said, "I'll give them up, if you want."

"No you won't," Ty said with a bark of laughter.

"I'd try," Zane insisted, lowering his arms to curl them around Ty's waist.

Ty rolled his eyes again, grinning now and shaking his head in exasperation. "Christ, Zane, just kiss me already."

Zane did, thankfully, earnestly, letting it soak in that Ty had forgiven him. The unresolved danger still hung over their heads, but for now, Zane had Ty in his arms and wasn't being sent away or left behind.

Ty seemed willing to cooperate, returning the languid kiss as his hands moved under Zane's jacket. It didn't last nearly long enough before he pulled away and patted Zane's hip. "Let me make a phone call, okay?"

Zane nodded and let go, though reluctantly, as Ty sidestepped away from him, going around the counter to the corner of the kitchen where he kept his phone charger. He unplugged the cell phone and turned it on, then dialed and watched Zane as he waited for an answer. It was hard to read Ty's expression, and Zane suffered a moment's uncertainty, struck with the feeling that he still needed to make amends for something.

Ty's conversation was short. "Hey, man. I need to bail on you today." He looked down as he spoke. "No, everything's fine. I just need to take care of something. I'll catch up with you later, okay? Okay. Bye."

When he ended the call, he plugged the phone back in, then leaned on the counter to look at Zane expectantly.

Zane resisted the urge to fidget. "Should I . . . be apologizing again?"

Ty shook his head. "Deuce," he explained without looking away. "He's been in town for some shrink thing."

Though Zane was surprised and pleased to hear that Ty's brother was in town, he didn't really care at that exact moment. "I don't want to talk about your brother," he managed to get out, though not quite evenly.

"No?" Ty asked innocently. Finally, that flash of mischief appeared in his eyes. True to form, he was enjoying these last moments of Zane's torture for revenge. He forgave easily, but he didn't exactly forget. "I just cleared my whole day, Garrett. What do you want to talk about?"

Zane knew he was being needled. "Baby," he pleaded.

"Oh, you're pitiful. Fine," Ty muttered, rolling his eyes as he made his way around the counter. "Let me go find some pants," he said. He patted Zane's hip on the way to the stairs.

Zane followed close behind, reaching out to pluck at the towel as they climbed the stairs. "You don't need pants," Zane said, starting to smile. "In fact, you don't even need this."

Ty turned to look down at him, standing naked on the steps, unruffled. He raised one eyebrow, obviously trying not to smile. "Is that so?"

"That is so," Zane acknowledged, stopping and smoothing his palm over Ty's ass before patting it and nodding up the stairs.

Ty huffed at him stubbornly. "Fine. I'm sick of weird furniture imprints on my ass, anyway," he said with a crooked, impish smile. He turned and headed up the steps as he spoke. "There are still people who would like very much to kill us, you know. And co-workers randomly dropping by to make sure we're alive."

Zane shook his head as he followed Ty. "Right now all I care about is you."

Ty stopped at the top of the stairs and turned to look down at him. He stayed there until Zane was just a step below him. "You should try saying that more often."

Zane looked up to meet his eyes seriously. "I will."

Ty reached out to tug on his hair, then turned and headed for the bedroom. Zane took that as approval of what he'd said and smiled, then followed right behind him, not stopping until he stood on the threshold. Leaning there, he watched the lithe flow of his lover's body as Ty yanked the curtains on the balcony doors closed and then turned to Zane in the dimmed room, wearing that smile of his again. Zane figured it could either bode well for him . . . or *very* well for him. With a smirk of his own, he knelt and started unlacing one of his boots.

Ty moved around the bed, messing with the covers, digging into the bedside drawer. He certainly didn't have any clothes to get rid of, and Zane caught himself watching instead of unlacing. He jerked one boot off and tossed it aside, then switched knees and started on the other. Maybe he'd wear his cross-trainers and start driving the truck a little more, once he got it back, instead of riding the Valkyrie and wearing boots. He knew Ty would approve. Zane glanced up, and Ty raised an eyebrow at him. He was standing beside the bed, waiting patiently. So patiently, in fact, that it was almost suspicious.

Distracted by watching him, Zane slowed as he pulled off the other boot and let it thump to the carpet. "What?"

Ty shook his head. "Just waiting for you, Christmas."

Instead of getting up, Zane waved Ty over. "C'mere." The bed was handy—Ty could sit and be somewhat in one place, and Zane was on his knees and would be able to touch and watch all he wanted. If Ty cooperated.

Ty moved to stand in front of him and ran one hand into Zane's hair affectionately. Zane smiled and reached up to slide his hands around the backs of Ty's thighs. "You watched over me for over a week. Why don't you let me pay attention to you for a while?"

Ty cocked his head and looked down at Zane in bemusement. "I was imagining less talking and more being tackled to the bed when we came up here," he said wryly as he twirled a lock of Zane's hair around his finger. "What'd you have in mind?"

Zane decided he'd rather show than tell. Still grasping Ty's legs, he leaned forward and licked a long swath up Ty's inner thigh, dragging his tongue along the side of Ty's cock to the soft skin in the crease of his leg.

Ty's hand tightened in his hair, and he made a soft whuffing sound as his body tensed. Encouraged, Zane dropped his head and repeated the movement on the other side, this time angling further between Ty's legs and nosing against him gently. He heard Ty catch his breath, and it helped bolster the nerves fluttering in his stomach. This was the first time he'd ever attempted this. When Ty's hand tightened further in his hair, Zane could tell that he was trying desperately to hold still.

Zane tried not to smile. "Want to sit down?" he asked, glancing up the length of Ty's body as he mouthed along the side of Ty's thickening erection. Ty nodded jerkily, but he didn't move. "I promise I won't stop," Zane said as he leaned back before pushing slightly at Ty's hips. The bed was just two small steps behind him.

Ty took one big step back and sat down heavily. His trademark grin was long gone. Zane thought he might have caught a glimmer of concern in Ty's eyes, but it was hard to tell. Apparently Ty—or Ty's body, at least—approved of Zane's choice of attentions: he was rock hard, and there was a slight tremor to his hands.

"Relax," Zane said as he shifted to kneel between Ty's knees. "You don't need to do this," Ty whispered to him with a shake of his head.

Zane propped one arm across Ty's knee and met his eyes. "I want to," he said simply. And he did. He'd thought about it several times, and it had turned into almost something of a craving. A craving that now got Zane hard whenever he thought of it. He *wanted* to be on his knees for Ty.

Ty lay back on his elbows, his eyes still locked on Zane's. Zane took care not to break that eye contact as he lowered his head, took Ty in hand, and licked around the swollen head of Ty's cock, slow and deliberate. His stomach cramped with a jumble of nerves and need and desire and excitement.

Ty caught his breath and lifted his chin, his eyes drifting shut. Zane could feel the muscles in his thighs tense as he tried to restrain his movements. Zane used his free hand to stroke along Ty's leg and up his belly as he closed his mouth over Ty and suckled tentatively. Ty seemed a lot bigger when he was between Zane's lips. It was an odd feeling, the head of Ty's cock on his tongue. But he liked it. He liked the way it filled his mouth and the way the skin was soft against his lips. He even liked the way he could taste Ty leaking onto the tip of his tongue.

Ty's hand slid into his hair again, his fist tightening but not actually moving Zane's head. It was reassuring, and Zane settled in to figure out what he could and couldn't handle, what he liked, and most importantly, what made Ty shudder under his hands. It was warm and wet and more than a mouthful, and the sensation of Ty twitching on his tongue almost did Zane in. Feeling Ty's reactions had Zane so aroused that he was hurting, and he dropped one hand to unbutton his jeans for some relief.

Ty cursed under his breath, lifting his hips just slightly as he writhed. Zane groaned in reaction and clutched at himself as he moved his other hand to splay over Ty's abdomen, riding the movements.

"Fuck, Zane," Ty gasped, his voice strained. The muscles under Zane's palm tightened as Ty moved again. He might have been doing everything he could not to move his hips, but it was becoming obvious that it was a losing battle.

Zane pulled off of Ty and had to wipe his mouth with the back of his hand. "Go ahead and move. I'm not going to let you choke me," he added before wrapping his hand around the shaft of Ty's cock and using his mouth to cover the head. He could taste Ty more now, that odd spiciness on his tongue, and he moaned. He thought he might like it if Ty came in his mouth, but he wasn't that brave. Yet. Ty echoed the sound he made, slightly more desperate. He reached down to grasp at Zane with his other hand, his fingers dragging against Zane's shoulder as he lifted his hips off the bed. Zane looked up to see him—Zane wanted to see it, wanted to see all of it.

Ty had his head back on the bed, his chin jutting upward as his lips parted on a groan. Every muscle in his body was tense. He breathed out sharply and looked down at Zane when he felt him move. He reached down and pressed his palm against Zane's cheek.

Zane turned his face into Ty's hand, rubbing, and after another few moments, he slowly let Ty slide out of his mouth and then licked his lips as he started pumping his fist over Ty's cock, just how he knew Ty liked.

Ty groaned plaintively and grabbed Zane's hair again, yanking his head back as he sat up. "Come here," he said, his voice low and gruff. Zane let go of him and pushed himself up with a wince, unfolded from the floor, and crawled carefully up over his lover.

Ty's hands slid up his sides, under his shirt, pushing it up as his callused hands dragged along Zane's skin. He was watching Zane's face unerringly, his lips still parted as if anticipating a kiss. It was more than Zane wanted to resist. He leaned down to kiss Ty slowly and thoroughly as he pressed his groin against Ty's hard-muscled thigh.

The pressure forced another groan out of Zane, and he gasped against Ty's lips.

Ty pulled at his shirt, trying to get it off him but reluctant to break the kiss. He growled in frustration. "Get this off," he ordered as he pushed at Zane's jeans. "I told you to stop wearing so many damn clothes."

Zane huffed and crawled backward off Ty and the bed just long enough to yank his shirt off and shove his jeans and briefs down. Then he was right back on top of Ty, hot skin snagging and tugging all over.

Ty wrapped around him, the slide of their bodies so familiar and natural. He hummed against the kiss, rewarding Zane with a grateful sigh. Zane moaned happily. It felt so good. He'd been growing more accustomed to the buoyant happiness, the sheer . . . contentment that spread through him whenever he was close to Ty—sex or not. And every touch made Zane that much more determined to never let go.

"Baby," he breathed. "I need you."

"I know," Ty murmured. He kissed Zane messily while one hand fumbled around beside them on the bed, seeking that little tube of lubricant he'd gotten out earlier.

Zane took several slow, deep breaths, trying to calm down. He wasn't sure if he had a lot of time or almost none before he lost control. He groaned and dropped his forehead to Ty's shoulder. Ty's arms wrapped around him, and then he began pushing Zane sideways, trying to roll them over as he muttered something incoherent. Zane let the momentum move him and landed on the mattress on his side, legs tangling with Ty's.

"Fuck," Zane bit off as their cocks slid together, and he was ready to grab hold right then and there and jack them until he and Ty came screaming. Ty did reach between them, his fingers sliding over them before he gripped Zane's hip as Zane sucked in a sharp breath. Ty tossed his leg over Zane's thigh, flexing his hips.

"We're not going to make it to the lube, are we?" Ty asked in a rough, amused voice as he pressed his nose to Zane's and let their lips drag together.

"Round two," Zane promised as he dragged his fingers down Ty's chest to palm his lover's cock. "Please," he begged as he hitched himself closer.

Ty groaned against his lips and kissed him again. He worked one hand under Zane's neck, curling it around to pull Zane closer. The other hand slid between their bodies again, fingers stroking, palm sliding up and down Zane and between his legs. Zane shivered as he touched Ty the same way, and the electricity of Ty's touch spidered through him, making him twitch and gasp as he stiffened, right on the edge.

"Come on, baby," Ty rasped at him, kissing him hastily as he jacked him harder. A yell wrenched its way out of Zane before he could bite it back. The sudden contact of Ty's hard body against his aching cock was too much to handle, and Zane curled his fists against Ty's back and cried out wordlessly as he spurted into Ty's hand. Ty continued relentlessly, stroking him as his fingers dragged against Zane's abs. Zane barely registered it when Ty pushed him to his back, kissing him just as enthusiastically. He tried to kiss, too, but he was shaking too hard to hold his hands still.

Ty's fingers were on his cheek again. He was holding Zane's head as he kissed him, pushing down and against his body, his kisses more frantic and breathless than they had been. Zane was swept up in it, giving himself over to Ty, dizzy with his orgasm and overheated by the press of their bodies. It took him too long to realize that Ty was actually speaking in between the almost frenzied meetings of their lips. What he was saying Zane couldn't decipher, but he knew he heard the words "missed you" and "love" among them, and suddenly his eyes prickled and his chest tightened. Throat choking up, Zane reached out to wrap his arms around Ty to pull him closer.

Ty actually growled. He rutted against Zane, using the hard muscle over Zane's hip for friction. He slid both hands under Zane's arms, under his body, and gripped the backs of his shoulders again. It was a position they'd found themselves in plenty of times before, and their bodies melded well. Of course, usually Ty was buried to the hilt inside Zane at this point, and the feel of his cock sliding instead against the curve of his groin was both exciting and erotic, like Ty wanted him too badly to take more care in how they both came. Ty bit at Zane's lower lip, thrusting his tongue into Zane's mouth the same way he probably wanted to thrust something else into him.

It filtered through the passion that Zane felt wanted and needed and loved, and it pulled another groan from him. "Ty," he moaned once their mouths broke apart.

Ty ducked his head and pressed his cheek against Zane's, ceasing the frantic movements for a moment as the world moved a little slower around them. Then Ty gasped against Zane's ear and moved over him, their bodies sliding together. Zane tried to focus on what Ty was doing, but he was still woozy and weak. He managed to spread his legs, giving Ty more room between them.

Ty turned his head again, laughing breathlessly. "I wouldn't make it five seconds if I fucked you right now," he told Zane tightly.

"I totally understand," Zane said on a half laugh. "Let me help, baby."

Ty pushed up, then rolled them instead, and he pulled Zane with him until they both lay on their sides again. Zane reached out to press both palms to Ty's chest, feeling its rise and fall.

Ty threw his leg over Zane's hip again, thrusting himself hard against Zane's body.

"Yes," Zane hissed, gripping Ty's thigh and adding a little push to his hips.

"Christ, Zane," Ty gasped out desperately. His fingers dug into Zane's back, his blunt fingernails scratching their way down one side as he sought release. Ty had never been one to cause pain intentionally in bed; he had to be so far gone into the pleasure he didn't know he was doing it. Zane squeezed his eyes shut and shuddered. The sting easily blended with the thrill still lapping through him. He felt himself going hard again, and he groaned aloud and clutched at Ty, trying to twist to get more stimulation, even if nothing would come of it. This time, anyway.

Ty arched his back, and the movement of his hips became more erratic. His cock slid against Zane, hard and demanding. He pulled Zane closer, kissing him possessively, his fingers digging in. He broke the kiss with a sharp gasp and groaned loudly, the sound almost desperate, as Zane felt the warm come spreading against his belly. Zane kissed along Ty's jaw and throat, silently awed by how incredible they were together.

Zane pushed his face into the sweaty skin at the crook of Ty's neck and held on tight.

Ty was still breathing hard, shivers running through his body as he hugged Zane to him. They stayed that way for what seemed like a long time, long enough for Ty to get his breathing under control again and for the cool air to become noticeable on their bare skin.

Finally, Ty moved, but only enough to shift his arm into a more comfortable position and pull Zane closer. "What brought that on?" he asked quietly.

Zane wasn't sure he could vocalize the words that were whizzing through his mind like a Tilt-A-Whirl. "Missed you," he got out. But then he tacked on, in a bare whisper, "Afraid of losing you."

Ty sighed heavily, his shoulders slumping as his grip on Zane loosened. "We're too naked to argue right now, but we're definitely having a talk about the sexual-favors-to-keep-my-interest issue," he mumbled. His words were teasing, but the tone was decidedly less cheerful.

"Wasn't all about apologizing or keeping your interest," Zane tried to offer in his defense. "I'd gotten so riled up just thinking about what it would be like to suck your dick that I could hardly stand it anymore."

Ty was silent, not even breathing as he apparently mulled over what Zane had said. After a few tense moments, he let the air out in a rush and laughed. "Hell, Zane, why didn't you say so? I could have helped you out earlier."

Zane wrinkled his nose and shrugged slightly under Ty's weight. "Took me a while to work myself up to the idea. For some reason it's more . . . I don't know. Intimate, I guess. Even than fucking."

Ty turned his head, looking at Zane thoughtfully. He just nodded minutely and reached up to run his fingers through Zane's hair. It felt like the place for "I love you" again. Zane suspected that was what Ty wanted to say.

So now, that left the words to Zane. It was time. He'd thought it to death, tried to reason out if he was right or wrong, worked to let go of the past and live in the now, chewed over his fears about being worthy of Ty. Zane swallowed hard, taking a quick breath to quell the rush of adrenaline. Fight or flight, he thought distantly, his pulse roaring in his ears.

"You okay?" Ty asked, reading him well.

Zane squeezed his eyes shut for a second, then blinked them open and started to nod, but he stopped and gave a half-shrug. "I'm a little . . . overwhelmed," he rasped.

Ty reached up and ran his fingers lightly over Zane's face, trailing them gently around his eyes. "Have you been sleeping?" he asked grimly, as if he already knew the answer.

Zane turned his cheek into Ty's hand, seeking more contact. Ty knew him very well, better than Zane knew Ty by far. "Not really," Zane admitted. "Too anxious to relax, I guess."

"I figured," Ty responded with a slow nod. He pushed himself up, pulling his arm out from under Zane, and he sat up. "Stay," he told Zane as he got up and headed out of the bedroom.

Zane lay back against the pillows and closed his eyes. He could practically hear his heart beating, it was thumping so hard. He turned his face into the pillow and breathed in Ty's familiar scent. Nerves still sparked through him, and he knew he'd have to deal with the panic soon. The intense relief from the momentary reprieve was tinged with an odd disappointment, and he found he wanted to grasp at the moment and bring it back, do it differently.

Zane didn't open his eyes until a towel flopped onto his belly. "You have that look," Ty observed as he stood at the edge of the bed and looked down at Zane in concern.

Zane fought the reflex urge to wipe his emotions off his face and offered a small smile. "Do I?"

But Ty didn't return the smile. He sat down instead, then stretched out beside Zane on the bed. "You look like you're about to cut and run," he observed in an almost offhand manner.

This time Zane did clamp down on his outward reaction. "I'm the one who came here looking for you, remember?"

It was nearly impossible to decipher what Ty was thinking as he took in Zane's features, and Zane felt a moment's frustration that Ty could block him out so easily. Ty sat up suddenly, bending and stretching to the end of the bed where he always kept a spare quilt folded up. He shook it out and lay back with it, pulling it up over them as he turned toward Zane and rested his head on Zane's shoulder.

Unsure of what to do or say, Zane simply closed his arms around Ty. He turned his head and pressed a kiss to the crown of his lover's head. Suddenly there were all sorts of words crowding on Zane's tongue, and he couldn't get a single one out, much less three that would prove he knew the best thing to happen to him in his entire life lay right there in his arms.

CHAPTER FOURTEEN

"**T**his is WBAL TV 11 News at 6, and I'm Alicia Harrison. Good evening."

A mugshot of a rather attractive young blonde woman with a neat bob haircut appeared over the reporter's shoulder. "Baltimore FBI Special Agent Lydia Reeves has died at age twenty-seven. Reeves was one of six law enforcement agents injured in the first shopping-complex bomb at the Inner Harbor just over a week ago. After eight days in a coma in the University of Maryland Medical Center ICU, she passed away last night as a result of her injuries. She is survived by her husband."

The video cut to a shot of a somber-looking man in a brown suit. The titles labeled him as *FBI Spokesman*. "Agent Reeves was a fine example of the FBI and law enforcement," the man said with a flash of bright white teeth. "Her service to the city is to be commended, and she will be greatly missed."

The reporter reappeared. "Reeves is the third death in the as-of-yet unexplained string of bombings terrorizing Baltimore. Police now suspect that a recent, unsuccessful bank robbery may be related to the bombings."

The shot changed to display the Baltimore police chief. "We are pursuing all leads, and the possibility of the perps using divide and conquer tactics won't be ruled out."

"So the recent rash of bank robberies and the bombings might be connected?" the reporter asked.

"We're not ruling anything out at this time," the chief repeated with worn patience. "Contingency plans for emergency response remain in place."

"What do you mean by divide and conquer tactics?"

"It's quite simple," the police chief replied. "By dividing our response, they're hoping to get away with their crimes."

The video returned to the studio shot. "Following this most recent tragedy, local, state, and federal officials announced that every available resource is being diverted to find the source of the bombs."

The FBI spokesman appeared again. "We're doing everything we can to protect all the men, women, and children of Baltimore by stopping this threat. And we won't rest until we do. We owe that to Baltimore, and we owe that to Lydia Reeves."

The final shot of the reporter displayed an American flag flying over her shoulder. "The funeral for fallen FBI agent Lydia Reeves is at noon tomorrow at Green Mount Cemetery. It will be closed to the public."

With a soft grunt of frustration, Zane undid the tie he was trying to knot for the third time and started over. He'd been a little off all morning, but he wasn't surprised he was shaky, shaky enough that he'd simply trimmed up his beard and mustache instead of getting rid of it altogether. Funerals did that to people, even when you weren't close to the deceased. In his case, it resurrected memories he wished would stay buried, memories of another woman's funeral in the unseasonably cold and wet Texas fall. The fact this morning had dawned cool and gloomy, with the potential bite of sleet or snow in the air, definitely didn't help. Lydia Reeves' funeral was in two hours, and it would be a long, uncomfortable, emotional day.

Zane gave up on the tie when he heard a steady knock and walked out of the small bathroom and through the living room. He picked up his Glock from the bookshelf before opening the door. They still didn't know how the note writer had found him.

A Marine stood on the stoop. A white cover with a black brim bearing the golden eagle, globe, and anchor shadowed his eyes. Bright-red piping on the high-necked midnight-blue blouse stood out against clean-shaven skin, and round gold buttons ran down the front seam. A stack of ribbons hung over his heart, and a red patch on each of his arms displayed three gold chevrons and one rocker above two hash marks. He wore pristine white gloves that disappeared into the long jacket sleeves. The jacket extended to hip length, close-fitted and cinched by a spotless white belt with a gold buckle bearing the branch insignia. The trousers' brighter blue, a royal blue, contrasted with a long scarlet stripe down the outside of his legs, and his black shoes showed a high shine.

Zane stared for all he was worth. Ty Grady in dress blues was a glorious sight to behold.

"Damn," Zane said in sincere appreciation.

Ty cocked his head, the barest smirk twitching his lips. "Morning," he offered, his eyes taking in the mangled knot of Zane's tie.

Zane's gaze followed his, and with a huff he yanked the tie off and stepped back, waving Ty inside.

"Need some help?" Ty asked as he stepped over the threshold, shutting the door behind himself. He swept the cover off his head and tucked it under one arm, a motion Zane had seen many times before but never appreciated to its fullest until now.

"Apparently," Zane agreed as he shut the door. "But not with this one." He meant to turn to the second bedroom to get another tie, but he couldn't make himself look away just yet. The last time Zane had seen dress blues had been on the groom at his sister's wedding. He knew enough about chevrons and rockers to identify Ty's rank as Staff Sergeant, but he didn't know what any of the impressive stack of ribbons stood for aside from the recognizable Purple Heart ribbon on the top row. Zane reached up to cautiously ghost his fingers over it.

Ty smiled gently, letting him touch. "Flashy, aren't they?" he said wryly. He didn't sound like he was boasting.

"No medals?" Zane asked. He knew most of the ribbons had corresponding medals, though not why servicemen wore one or the other or both.

"They're at home. The ribbons don't clink."

Zane nodded. "Looking sharp, Marine," he complimented with a small smile. "Any rules about getting kissed in uniform?"

"Not that I'm aware of," Ty answered, smiling wider.

Zane chuckled and leaned down to kiss Ty carefully, not wanting to get snagged on the ribbons or buttons. He could feel Ty smiling against his lips, and Ty pulled him closer. Zane hummed in appreciation and wrapped his arms around Ty loosely. The wool of the jacket was smooth under Zane's fingers, the embroidery of the patches less so, but Ty's lips were still warm and soft against his.

"You look pretty good yourself," Ty murmured against his lips.

Zane kissed him again as a thank-you. It was just a nice suit, but one he didn't wear often, being an intense black—so much so it almost picked up a midnight blue or indigo sheen in the right light—and more closely tailored than he preferred for work. He'd chosen a soft gray dress shirt and had been messing with an understated silver tie.

Ty smoothed his hand over Zane's chest and hummed. "I know which one will work." He handed Zane his cover and stepped aside, heading for Zane's bedroom.

Zane spun the cover between his hands as he watched Ty move into the next room. He walked differently, Zane noted. Taller, his shoulders more squared, steps more measured, with a gravity Ty normally shrugged off. It was more than a subtle change, one that oddly seemed to suit him.

Some people were born to be Marines. Ty was one of them. Suddenly it struck Zane as a tragedy that Ty was no longer in the Corps. The hint of melancholy he had noticed in Ty's eyes upon occasion made perfect sense now, and the realization settled unhappily in the pit of Zane's stomach. Ty had been happy in the Marines. He had to miss it.

Ty came back a moment later, holding a narrow black tie with silver squares and charcoal gray lines between them. It was one of Ty's, and the corners of Zane's mouth curled up, because he probably had ten or twelve different ties of his own in the drawer. At least one a month got ruined between work and Ty's lack of patience at the end of a long workday. "Okay," he agreed, holding out one hand.

Ty shook his head, sliding his fingers down the expensive silk of the tie. Ty didn't dress to impress all that often, but when he did, he went for broke. He raised the tie and wrapped it around Zane's neck, looking him in the eye with a smile. "Turn around. I'll tie it."

Zane half rolled his eyes but turned around as instructed, facing the island countertop. He loved it when Ty did this. Ty slid his hands under Zane's arms, having to press hard against his back to reach the tie. His fingers were quick and sure as he tied it, and Zane could feel his nose and chin pressing down against the back of his shoulder. When he had it tied, he stepped back and tugged at Zane to turn, then smoothed the tie out and straightened it. Finally he gave a nod of satisfaction.

"Do I pass inspection?" Zane asked.

"It'll do," Ty answered as he looked Zane up and down. He took his cover from Zane and tucked it back under his arm. "You ready?"

"No," Zane said honestly. "But it's time to go anyway."

Ty patted his cheek sympathetically. The entire department was in mourning, but Zane had been the last person to see Reeves conscious, in the store just before the bomb went off. It had left Zane shaken once he'd remembered.

The funeral was going to be a huge public spectacle: the big Bureau and law enforcement turnout, the irresistible PR opportunity, and—because there was no realistic way to keep the press out— cameras everywhere. Zane was trying not to think too much about the very real possibility of the funeral itself being a target.

"Let's get this over with, then," Ty muttered. His eyes were a deep green, trending toward blue today, and though the uniform seemed to do something spectacular to his bearing, the air around him felt worn thin and stretched. Not for the first time, Zane found himself worrying about Ty's general well-being.

His partner wasn't right, and Zane didn't know what to do to help him.

He turned and headed for the door while Zane shrugged into his heavy woolen coat. Zane double-checked his wallet, badge, phone, and firearm, and followed Ty out.

The gravesite lay beneath a copse of giant oak trees. It would be well shaded in the summer, but for now the bare branches reached up to the heavily clouded sky. Green Mount was a beautiful cemetery of great historical significance, filled with monuments and mausoleums that lent a solemn air to that beauty. Even now, in the dead of winter, the grass was green and wet, shining dully against the uneven paths of gray pavers. Tombstones and statues too numerous to count stood vigil over the graves, marble and weathered rock figures that peopled the cemetery when no other living soul was present.

The pallbearers moved silently into the crowd after carefully setting Lydia Reeves' flag-draped casket just so, and the minister began speaking. Zane noted distantly that the man had a good speaking voice; it carried out over the tidy gravesite to the family under the green awning as well as the crowd standing in small clusters amidst the other headstones and monuments. He estimated at least a hundred present, many from the Bureau, and then assorted friends and family who gathered closer to the family for the service. The press had been surprisingly considerate so far, not approaching the family or any attendees, standing to the side, only a couple of digital video cameras running silently.

The minister didn't speak long. He nodded to a woman standing nearby, she read the twenty-third Psalm, and then the gathered lowered their heads for a final prayer. At the amen, the bagpipes, positioned discreetly to the far side of the crowd, wheezed to life, and Zane couldn't repress a shiver as the player began the traditional "Amazing Grace." Two servicemen in dress uniforms, agents Zane recognized from work, moved to lift and fold the American flag.

Movement from Ty drew Zane's eyes, and when he glanced to his side at Ty, a sudden and unexpected thrill ran through him. Ty had come to attention, body taut in a smart salute. His jaw was tight and his eyes were unreadable, staring ahead from the shadow of his white cover. He stood straight and tall, every ounce of him perfect and rigid, the bright colors and harsh white of his uniform in sharp contrast to the washed-out sepia of the day. Zane didn't think he'd ever seen anything more incredible and heart-wrenching than Ty right then. The bagpipes played on, a soundtrack to the very picture of self-sacrifice and loyalty.

Zane's thoughts inexplicably landed on Elias Sanchez, a man he'd never met, a member of Ty's Marine Recon team who had also joined the Bureau. Sanchez had died in the line of duty, murdered by a fellow agent turned serial killer. Sanchez would have had a funeral like this, with the honor guard and the gun salute, with men and women in pristine uniforms standing in silent respect for the dead. As Ty stood now. How many times had Ty done this, said goodbye to a fallen comrade in that uniform?

Zane dropped his gaze, giving his partner what modicum of privacy was possible. He didn't need to continue staring. The sight would be forever burned in his memory.

He blinked when movement from his far right caught his attention. He'd been without his sight long enough that he was still overreacting to quick, unexpected movements. This was out of place, hurried, and he turned his chin to look.

A young man, late teens, Zane suspected, with messily styled blond hair, was pushing his way through the crowd, obviously searching for someone in particular. The music covered any noise he was making. The kid stopped to speak to a woman, who looked around, made eye contact with Zane, and pointed right at him. Zane blinked as the kid made a beeline for him. He was fairly sure he'd never seen the young man before.

Zane was aware of a change in Ty, as if he'd sensed Zane's attention, but he didn't move, still saluting the flag as it was folded. Zane glanced at him, then watched the kid fumble toward them.

He walked right up to Zane like he knew him. Zane had to lean over a little to hear him over the bagpipes and the people who had started singing. "You have to get everyone out of here. Pierce is crazy," the kid said, practically hyperventilating, "and he's coming with a bomb."

Zane stared at him hard for a few heartbeats, then turned to see if Ty had heard. Ty met his eyes, hand dropping as if in slow motion, body already tensing and gears already turning—he was trying to decide the best way to sound the alarm without causing a mass panic, and Zane wasn't sure it would be possible.

"Do you know where he is?" Zane asked the boy. If this kid knew Zane and had a connection to Pierce, the chance of this being legit was way too high.

"No, I got out just before him. I couldn't let him do it." The kid looked about to break into tears. "But I couldn't stop him. I was afraid." Zane grasped his shoulder for a moment before turning to Ty.

"The families?" Zane bit off, noting that the agents gathered around them had focused on the disturbance.

Ty turned and whispered to the man beside him, then moved to speak to another, trying to get word around quickly. Then a commotion broke out on the other side of the crowd.

"It's him," the kid said, pointing, voice high with terror.

With his height, Zane saw over crowds better than most, and he zeroed in on a person pushing through the civilians gathered by the family under the awning. Zane didn't wait.

"Bomb! Down!" he yelled harshly, trying to shove through the crowd while pulling his Glock and focusing on the young man he recognized as Pierce Sutton.

His words were met with complete stasis. For crucial seconds, no one moved. No one seemed to comprehend. Then time kicked into fast forward, and the panic and comprehension crashed through the crowd on a wave as agents pulled their weapons and people hit the ground.

Zane stopped and raised his gun. Pierce bulled his way toward the casket, clambered up on the side rail to snatch the tightly folded American flag in one hand, and he waved it around, his face twisted into a snarl, before throwing it to the ground and jumping off the casket to land on it with two booted feet.

"Son of a bitch!" Ty growled from beside Zane.

Zane saw his chance as Pierce deliberately reached into his trenchcoat: the civilians had cleared out, the minister ducked behind a nearby oak tree, and he had a few seconds for a clear shot.

He wasn't the only one who took it.

A volley of bullets tore into Pierce Sutton before he could utter a word, sending his body jerking like a puppet on slashed strings to the ground.

Time slowed. Silence reigned again. Several heartbeats, and then the frozen tableau broke. Civilians milled about in confusion, and Bureau agents fanned out and around the gravesite, checking for further threats as the family gathered together, most of them sobbing angrily.

As another agent needlessly checked for a pulse, Zane stopped to stand next to the body of the young man who had masterminded bank robberies amounting to hundreds of thousands of dollars in losses, deliberately promoted ill will and hatred in the city, and caused tens of millions of dollars in damages and destroyed property in four separate bombings that had also resulted in scores of injuries and three deaths.

When Lydia Reeves had died, Pierce Sutton had become a dead man walking.

Zane holstered his gun as people started drifting closer. The cacophony that utterly destroyed the quiet peace of the cemetery was giving him a headache. He'd noticed that being blind had by necessity sharpened his hearing, and now he was paying for it. Children sobbing, raised and nervous voices chattering, law enforcement vehicles arriving with sirens on, Bureau agents yelling out perimeter checks, and to top it off, an unexpected boom of thunder echoing from the roiling clouds overhead.

Ty stopped beside him, then bent down to pluck the flag from under the dead kid's foot.

"Crime scene, Grady," someone reminded breathlessly.

"Don't care," Ty shot back as he saved the flag.

Zane was pinching the bridge of his nose, trying to ward off the pain, when he heard a nagging sound that didn't fit. Frowning, he looked around for a cart or machine nearby. He wasn't wearing a watch. But he could just barely hear a measured clicking.

Zane's chest seized, and he looked down at the body as Ty rescued the flag. A flash of metal mostly covered by the trenchcoat caught his eye, and a streak of pure fear burned through him as he saw a wireless timing mechanism with a tiny red blinking light in Pierce's lifeless hand.

Ticking. Zane could hear ticking.

He dropped to one knee, yanked at the coat to uncover the hand holding the timer, then hurriedly patted down the trench until his fingers hit something hard, a bulge at the waistband. He jerked the thick sweatshirt up. For once, Zane didn't stop to consider his options or think through scenarios or figure the percentages.

He grabbed the ticking bomb, yanking it from its duct tape, and ran.

People and tombstones alike created an obstacle course as Zane tried to get away from the gravesite, weaving through the gathered, shoving some aside, almost ramming into a monument taller and wider than he was as he dodged a small child. There, maybe thirty yards away, stood an ancient mausoleum, its stone walls heavy and thick, hopefully enough to contain the blast from the welded and duct tape-wrapped box he clutched against his chest. Finally he broke free of the crowd and, distantly aware of people calling after him, charged the mausoleum doors, ramming into one with his shoulder. He practically slid inside on the pavers smoothed by almost two centuries of foot traffic.

Zane didn't know how much time he had. But as he ran through the deeply shadowed building, past marble crypts and statues, he spared a prayer of thanks that he had at least gotten away from the families and children.

He skidded to a stop and turned into a small room at the back of the mausoleum. Without any traction, he thudded painfully into a wall, but he shoved the box behind the last stone coffin and turned on his heel, his heart thundering in his ears as he slung himself through the doorway and ran.

The dim gray light seeping in from the front doors beckoned to him, and he was a few rooms away—a bare thirty yards—when a shadow rammed into him from the side, sending him sprawling painfully hard into a marble sarcophagus and down to the floor.

Ty grunted his name and held up the flashing red device, then began dragging Zane by his collar across the smooth stone floor until they huddled behind a substantial stone vault. Ty shook against him, adrenaline obviously fueling him, and he held the flashing thing up again.

0:01.

0:00.

Zane covered his head and Ty's as the explosion echoed through the mausoleum. It wasn't a loud, crashing cacophony. It was more a thud deep in their chests and a rush of fetid air from the depths of the mausoleum. The air reverberated with the blast; then all was silent.

Ty raised his head and looked around. "That wasn't so bad," he gasped out.

A deep rumbling answered his words. From the back of the mausoleum came another rush of air, and all around them, the structure trembled and groaned. A stone lintel crashed to the floor, followed by another. Then another.

Zane grabbed Ty's arm and pulled him down again, covering their heads as the collapse sent broken stone flying and blew out the archways, showering them with a hard rain of driving sand and jagged chunks of marble. The light was snuffed out as the ancient building foundered and collapsed around them.

Ty kept his eyes closed for a long time after the deafening roar of collapsing stone had ended. It was stiflingly silent, the only sounds being Zane's harsh breaths and the occasional shift and trickle of rocks.

Ty opened his eyes and lifted his head. He'd expected pitch black, or at least a pretty angel with a harp telling him he was in the wrong place. But there was light coming from somewhere, and the stone vault they'd hidden behind had provided some reprieve from the fallen stone walls that hemmed them in. He looked down at his partner.

"You okay?"

Zane groaned and pushed himself up, but there wasn't much room for him to move. Part of a stone wall had fallen right next to him, shifted to the side by the vault that sheltered them. Otherwise Zane might have been *under* that wall. "Yeah, I think so."

Ty jabbed him hard in the stomach, unable to put any more force behind it due to the confined space. "Stupid jackass!"

Zane yelped, hissed in pain, and swatted at his hand. "What the hell?"

"Exactly, what the hell! You see a ticking bomb, so your first instinct is grab it and fucking run?" A miniature avalanche of pebbles and rocky debris slid down the shelf of stone above them.

"It was me run or try to get a hundred people to run," Zane bit off as he held up a hand to protect his face. There was already a thin dark line of blood wending down his cheek from a cut below his eye.

Ty continued to mutter and curse under his breath, trying to move his body off Zane's in the tight space. "You're a dick, you know that? Scared the shit out of me. Made me run. Got me dirty. I lost my cover! Now I'm trapped in a crypt with a dumbass."

"I'm sorry," Zane muttered. He even sounded sincere.

Ty could only manage to slide off him and sit in the rubble next to him, legs drawn up against his chest. He had to hunch his shoulders and duck his head. He could still hear the rock shifting and groaning ominously as it settled. One thing was obvious: Zane never would have made it out alive if he'd still been running for the door. The entire structure had collapsed in on itself, save for the areas where stone slabs from the ceilings and walls had fallen against the stone sarcophagi in the corners.

"Fuck, Garrett."

"Maybe later."

Ty looked around at the heavy stone bearing down on them both. He swallowed hard as he recognized a cold panic beginning to form in his gut. The stone was too close, too thick. "Might be our last chance," he replied, trying to sound wry but falling flat.

Zane shifted, turning enough to put his back to the fallen wall so he faced Ty. "We'll get out of here. Too many people saw me—us— run in for them not to dig us out."

Ty shook his head as he peered at Zane in the dim light. He could just make out Zane's outline, and he was only three feet away. "What were you thinking?"

"I was thinking . . . get the bomb away from the kids."

Ty sighed heavily. He couldn't bitch at Zane for that. He could feel the stone brushing the top of his head as he sat, and he could only just stretch his legs out in front of him. If he turned the other way, he could lie flat, which didn't go a long way toward calming him. He could feel the stone looming overhead, feel the press of the darkness and the swell of burgeoning panic. His chest tightened, making it hard to breathe, and his fingers still trembled from the adrenaline of his headlong flight across the cemetery after his partner.

He'd watched Zane take off, understanding taking a few seconds to settle in, and he'd grabbed the device from the dead kid's hand, recognizing it for what it was. It was counting down the seconds until that bomb went off. Then he'd run after his stupid fucking partner so he could save his sorry ass before he got blown up. Again.

"Well. What now?"

Zane dug into his jacket pocket, pulled out his cell phone, then cursed under his breath. "Screen's busted. Maybe if we—"

Without warning, the stone groaned again, and Ty pushed himself back against the shelter of the vault as another wall fell toward them and shattered, sending stone fragments cascading across them. Ty heard a last, loud crunch, and when he carefully opened his eyes, it was to complete darkness.

"Oh God," Ty groaned. The panic began to billow. He couldn't take enclosed spaces. He just couldn't do it. The air in their little pocket of space was growing warmer.

"Ty." Zane's low voice was followed by the touch of his hand and a firm tug that shifted Ty closer to his partner, and after another tug, Zane pulled Ty practically onto his lap and against his chest, then wrapped his arms around him securely. "I've got you, baby. I'm here."

Ty struggled against the cuddling. "Quit touching me, Zane," he hissed stubbornly.

"Stop it," Zane said firmly, though his arms loosened enough to led Ty slide down. "Stop it and close your eyes. Listen to my voice."

Ty put both hands over his face and rested his head in Zane's lap. His breaths were shallow and erratic against his hands. "I should have just let you get squished."

"You'd never do that, baby, and we both know it." Zane's hand settled on Ty's head, stroking gently. "Who else would pun you to death?"

"At least I'd finally be taller than you."

"I thought you liked me being taller than you."

Ty tried to answer, but the thought of being tall enough to brush his head on the ceiling while sitting made his stomach turn, and he managed only a ragged breath. The panic was sharp and overwhelming, filling his limbs with a tingling sensation as his gut churned.

"Ty." Zane's voice sharpened. "Stay with me. Come on. Talk."

"Shut up. If I could go anywhere, I'd leave you here in a heartbeat," Ty managed to strangle out. He reached up, horrified when his fingertips brushed cold stone. He'd been trapped in small dark places before, which was why he had such a negative reaction to them now. But the very real knowledge that the walls were closing in, literally and not just in his mind, made him want to cry.

All the while, Zane's fingers carded gently through his hair. "I know what it's like to be totally in the dark," he said, his voice calm.

"But I wouldn't go anywhere even if I could. I'd rather be here with you than somewhere else alone."

Ty reached up and gripped his hand, trying to grasp a thread to keep him from truly panicking. He would hurt them both if he lost control. Zane's fingers curled around his in a firm grip.

"Can I tell you a secret?" he asked Zane, voice low and threadbare.

"Yeah."

"You ever get gut feelings? Like you see something and you just *know*?" Ty asked, feeling stupid but not caring. He felt Zane squeeze his hand. "First time I saw you, after I got over hating you, I knew ... I knew we'd die together. I could just feel it deep down. Never felt that before."

Zane exhaled heavily. "Not today. And not tomorrow. And not for a long time to come, Ty Grady. You hear me? A hell of a long time."

Ty nodded jerkily. "Do me a favor?" He reached out and grabbed at Zane's other hand in the pitch black. He shoved it upward, trying to get Zane to raise his arm. "Hold up the ceiling, okay?"

Zane let Ty move his hand to touch the stone, which inexplicably made Ty feel a modicum better, but he kept his other linked with Ty's. Several heartbeats of quiet passed before Zane spoke. "First time I saw you, after I got over hating you, I knew," he said, echoing Ty's words, "I knew I'd fall in love with you."

Ty shivered all over, torn between the comforting warmth of Zane's words and the cold terror of impending crush injuries. He couldn't get in any air to speak.

"I laughed at myself," Zane continued, a hint of pleading in his voice, "and then I denied it, and then I did everything I could to prove myself wrong, but it didn't work."

"I know, Zane," Ty whispered, though he had to admit the words brought a certain level of relief he hadn't realized he'd needed.

"Ty." Zane's even, soothing tones finally broke on the short gasp of his name. "I love you and I'm scared I'll lose you. Please don't leave me alone in the dark."

Ty closed his eyes, trying to push back the weight of the tons and tons of stone that sat precariously above them. He smiled weakly with Zane's words. "Now was that really so hard to say?" he tried to tease, but it came out sounding desperate.

"Yes?" Zane answered, forlorn. "Jesus, Ty, come here, *please.*"

Just the thought of moving made Ty begin to tremble. He squeezed his eyes closed, gritted his teeth. He reached blindly for Zane, his hand glancing off Zane's shoulder, and Zane did the rest, moving close enough to embrace him in the tight space.

Zane lifted one hand to cup Ty's face. "Do you have any idea how brave you are?" he asked, the sounds ragged and perhaps even a little choked.

"Tell me when I'm not about to freak out, okay?" Ty requested hollowly. The trembles skittered through his body and into Zane's.

"Tell me about the ribbons," Zane requested abruptly, his voice again calm and soothing.

Ty knew what he was doing, trying to take Ty's mind off their impending doom any way he could. He shook his head. "The two on top are the Bronze Star and a Purple Heart," he started breathlessly.

"Bronze Star?" Zane repeated, sounding surprised.

"The country's fourth highest medal," Ty rattled off desperately, trying to find distraction from the realization that he couldn't breathe. He was about to have a full-fledged panic attack. "Awarded to any person who, while serving in any capacity with the Armed Forces of the United States, distinguishes him or herself by heroic or meritorious achievement or service while engaged in an action against an enemy of the United States, in military operations involving conflict with an opposing foreign force, or while serving with friendly foreign forces engaged in an armed conflict against an opposing armed force in which the United States is not a belligerent party."

"Damn, Ty, are you reciting military guidelines?" Zane asked, sounding both impressed and horrified.

"Yes, shut up. It's helping. Accomplishment or performance of duty above that normally expected, and sufficient to distinguish the individual among those performing comparable duties is required."

Zane snorted softly. "What'd you do to earn it?"

Ty breathed in deeply, the air shuddering out of him just as quickly. "I killed a whole lot of people."

Zane was silent for a moment, then shifted against Ty to hold him more securely. "Tell me about the rest."

Ty shook his head and strained his eyes to find light. When he could make out nothing in the blackness, he reached up for the ceiling. If Zane wouldn't hold it up, maybe he could.

He touched the cold stone, and he felt Zane raise his arms to help.

"I'll hold up my end, if you'll hold up yours," Zane said.

"Don't humor me, Garrett. Just hold up the ceiling for me, okay?" Ty snapped, but he was laughing at his own words.

"Yes, Staff Sergeant," Zane said smartly.

A deep rumble and a shiver in the stones interrupted Ty's stinging retort, and Zane grabbed him and yanked him down, covering his head as the stones started to shift and fall again. The shrieking of the rock shearing filled Ty's ears, and just as he thought his heart might stop, just as everything around them shook violently, several large stones behind Zane toppled in the opposite direction, giving them a little more room and letting in shockingly bright dull-gray light.

Ty stared at the shaft of light as if he could actually use it to pull them out of hell. His arms tightened around Zane, fingers digging in reflexively as he fought down the stark terror. It wasn't something he could really control; it was ingrained in him to fear the darkness and spaces that closed in when he couldn't see. Even this hint of light and Zane's arms around him couldn't fight back the impending panic attack for much longer. He was surprised he'd staved it off for this long. He firmly believed it was Zane's doing, him saying the right things at the right time.

Another stone fell away, then another, and as the hole got bigger, Zane literally dragged Ty over his lap and shoved him toward the opening. Voices started to echo around them, their names bouncing off the stone as people called.

Ty crouched at the narrow opening, trying to fight through the haze of panic to judge if he could make it through. He didn't think he could, and forcing the wrong stone to shift could bring the whole thing down. He didn't try it, instead calling out to the rescuers and sliding back into the darkness to sit with Zane. His hand trembled, but he reached for Zane's and gripped it hard anyway as he met his lover's eyes. "You asked me not to leave you alone in the dark."

Zane didn't reply, but he pulled Ty's hand close and pressed his lips gently to Ty's knuckles.

"You two look like shit."

Zane stopped on the threshold to Dan McCoy's office and scowled as Ty pushed past him. "Worse than that," Zane disagreed. His headache still raged, his eyes still felt swollen and full of the rock particle dust that had been kicked up into his face numerous times, and he could just *feel* the bruises coming up all over.

Better than the alternative.

"You okay?" McCoy asked, looking back and forth between the two partners.

Zane still wore his ruined suit, now almost gray from the sand and stone ground into the fabric and boasting a few split seams, and several red scrapes scored one side of his face. Ty's dress blues had suffered as well, but Ty had insisted on changing immediately, even when that meant into the spare running shorts and T-shirt stuffed in his locker downstairs. It was a scarlet-red T-shirt, with a dancing rock, a quivering piece of paper, and an awkward pair of scissors standing in a rough circle, all with guns in both hands and aiming at each other.

Despite their ordeal, Ty had managed to come out looking like an action hero at the end of the movie, hair perfectly mussed, a delicate smudge on one cheek, the appropriate amount of dirt to make him look rugged instead of a wreck. Zane sort of wanted to hate him.

"You ever been buried under several metric tons of stone, Mac? Well, I have. Three times now!" Ty snapped as he eased himself into one of the chairs in front of McCoy's desk.

McCoy frowned but didn't take the bait, for which Zane was grateful. If they could get through this, he and Ty could get out of here.

"All right, Garrett, you sit too. You did your debriefs, so you know we found your truck intact. We'll get it back to you in a few days. Go ahead and check out a car for the rest of the week. You can drive your partner around, since his truck is toast."

"About that—"

"It's being filed with Bureau insurance as a work-related personal property casualty," McCoy said, talking right over Ty. "I'm sure there will be all kinds of paperwork for you."

Ty grimaced but didn't say anything. Zane figured he was still grieving for the valiant Bronco.

"I'll be reviewing all the intel later this week as we deconstruct the case," McCoy announced as he handed each of them a file folder. "But in the meantime, I thought you'd at least like a few answers.

"His name was Walter Pierson Sutton, son of Clarence and Mitzi Sutton," McCoy began. "Father's a doctor; mother's in interior design."

"Upper crust, huh?" Ty muttered distractedly as he licked his thumb and scrubbed at a spot on his arm, checking to see if it was a bruise or dirt.

"The Suttons live in Roland Park, lots of money flowing. Pierce attended the Gilman School." He paused to check for comprehension. Zane was still new to Baltimore and shrugged.

"More-money-than-sense type of place, patches on the uniform, schoolgirl socks," Ty said tiredly.

"It's a boys-only school," McCoy specified. Ty shrugged as if that didn't matter.

"That's where Sutton met Ross Tanger and, through Gilman's elective program, Hannah Myles at Bryn Mawr School and Graham Lewis at Mount Saint Joseph," McCoy explained.

"So they basically all went to school together. White-bread kids with access to money and nothing to do," Zane concluded.

"On the nose," McCoy said with a nod. "The Suttons gave that kid anything and everything he wanted. The other kids had reasons for wanting money that didn't come from Mommy and Daddy. Not good ones, but reasons nonetheless: oppressive stepmother, forced responsibilities, boredom."

"So what went wrong?" Zane asked, turning the pages in the file as he skimmed.

"There's no way to really know what set him off," McCoy said, sounding frustrated as he leaned back in his chair and dragged both hands through his thinning hair. "What we've been able to discover so far is he had a recent fascination with anti-authoritarianism, anarchy, and misplaced social rebellion. The principal at Gilman said he had a terrible attitude with authority figures. And although he didn't have to work, Pierce drifted through several jobs at places in the Inner Harbor—including the aquarium—over the course of the past two years."

"Doing recon," Ty said, almost under his breath. The false alarm at the aquarium suddenly made sense.

McCoy nodded soberly. "Now we can see it as groundwork laid. We've got a warrant to get at his personal effects, computer, and phone, but now that he's out of the picture . . ." He shrugged. The case was closed. More research would be academic.

"He was an angry kid who just . . . decided to kill people," Zane said, having a hard time believing it could happen even though it had come within mere seconds of killing *him*.

"The banks weren't the goal. They were the diversion," Ty murmured sadly.

"This was one pissed-off young man," McCoy said. His exhaustion was clear in the deep lines and shadows on his face. "Initial profile says that by Sutton's reckoning, the world needed to crash and burn and be rebuilt. And the other kids have told interrogators that he zeroed in on Grady after the aquarium. Called you his white whale."

"That . . . makes no sense," Ty muttered.

"He's talking about Moby Dick," Zane said.

"I know what it means, Garrett!" Ty snapped.

Zane shrugged and looked at his partner askance, but he didn't pick up the looming argument. He closed the file and let it fall to his lap, then reached up to rub the back of his neck as it twinged painfully.

"What about the others?" Ty asked abruptly. Zane suspected he wanted to know about Hannah Myles.

"It's clear from interviews with the other three kids that Sutton became increasingly unstable over the past year. Erratic, angry, hateful, but at the same time extravagant and wild. They didn't want him to take his temper out on them, so they went along with his plans," McCoy concluded.

"What's the US District Attorney going to do?" Zane asked quietly, thinking about the sheer terror on Graham's face.

"They'll likely go with our recommendations," McCoy said. "Probably extended time in a minimum-security jail for Ross Tanger, assignment to a low-security women's facility for Hannah Myles, and possibly just probation for Graham Lewis, considering his choice to turn Sutton in and the fact he wasn't personally involved in any robberies."

"So it's over," Zane said slowly.

McCoy raised one shoulder. "For now. This time."

"I'm going to go get drunk," Ty stated, pushing himself up out of his chair.

Zane stood as well, tapping the file folder on his other palm. "You coming to the wake, Mac?"

"I'll drop by," McCoy said. "At least make an appearance and then bow out so the real drinking can begin. You two go on. And you, Garrett, have a drink yourself. That was a dumbshit thing to do, but you're the hero of the hour."

"Yeah, he's a real fucking hero," Ty grumbled as he walked out of the office, but Zane could hear the undertone of pride in his voice.

Then Zane grimaced. "I'm going to be on TV again, aren't I," he said, dread building.

"Running for the end zone," McCoy confirmed. "We're going to have a talk about your newfound popularity next week. But for now, go on. Get out of here. I'll see you two later."

"I've got Garrett's first drink," Perrimore announced as Zane walked into the pub the Bureau had taken over for the night. "He's damn well earned it." Applause broke out, and Zane felt his cheeks heat—he was glad he'd decided not to shave off the beard. He hadn't planned to be a hero.

"He's also our DD, so make it a Coke," Clancy answered as she pulled Zane by the elbow around some tables to join the rest of the crew.

"Hell, I'll buy whatever drinks Garrett wants all night if it means I don't have to drive home," Alston said, toasting Zane with his bottle of beer.

Zane shrugged out of his jacket and sat down next to Lassiter, who bumped their shoulders together companionably.

"Good one, Zane," Lassiter said seriously, holding out his hand.

"Thanks, Harry," Zane replied as he shook it.

"Where's your partner, Garrett?" Alston asked.

"Went home to change," Zane said, frowning a little. "I figured he'd beat me here. He was more than ready for a drink after this afternoon."

"Amen to that," Perrimore added as he set a tall glass bottle of Coke in front of Zane.

Zane smiled his thanks. "They practically had to cuff him to a chair to keep him still long enough to debrief."

Everyone who had ever tried to keep Ty focused on something in the office for more than an hour laughed, and the table dissolved into meaningless chatter. They talked about work, mostly, because to a group of FBI agents, there wasn't much else, and because they'd all worked with Lydia Reeves in some way. But they also talked about softball, their kids, their spouses, their exes, the Ravens winning and the Orioles losing, about the weird smell that had been emanating from the third-floor supply room for a week now, and anything else that would fill the companionable silence.

They were on their second round when Alston sat up straighter and waved at someone who'd just come into the crowded bar. When Zane turned, he saw Ty making his way through the standing-room-only floor toward them. Ty smiled and nodded as he pardoned his way past people, sliding his hand down one woman's arm as he squeezed by her, patting someone on the shoulder and smiling like he knew the guy as he slipped past.

He waved two fingers at the bartender he probably did know very well, since they were just a block or two from his house, and he stepped up to the table to put his arms around Alston and Clancy.

"What'd I miss?"

"You're two rounds behind, Grady," Alston announced.

"What took you so long?" Clancy asked practically on top of Alston's words. "And why didn't you keep the uniform on?"

Zane just watched his partner, again feeling the rush of thankfulness for being able to see. Ty was, as the cliché went, a sight for sore eyes, and Zane wished they were anywhere but a bar crowded with their friends and co-workers. He swallowed hard, feeling his pulse pick up as the same thoughts that had been racing in circles in his head the past few hours started right back up again.

He'd told Ty that he loved him, no ifs, ands, or buts. There was no going back now, and Zane wouldn't if he had the chance. But damn, they *had* to call some kind of moratorium on important declarations during life-threatening situations.

Ty gave them all his trademark crooked grin, either oblivious to Zane's gaze on him or ignoring it like he often did when they were together in a crowd. "I had to change and take everything to the cleaners before the burnt smell settled in," Ty told them just as the bartender called out his name.

Ty turned and stretched across the bar to take the two beers he'd ordered. He stood right there at the bar and gulped down one bottle as the others heckled him. He slammed the empty on the bar, nodded to the girl cheekily, and then brought his other bottle to the table with him. He sat on the edge of Clancy's stool, the two of them using each other as backrests. Ty's knee brushed Zane's as he settled in, and when Zane caught himself watching his partner, he was glad it was fairly dark in the pub's interior but for the colored light of the beer signs and the several LCD TVs mounted on the walls.

Zane could see how very tired Ty was in every move he made, when he'd stare blankly at nothing and then shake it off, how he was so still. He'd been through the emotional wringer today, and the whole past week certainly hadn't been a cakewalk. Zane was even more concerned now than he had been earlier.

When they'd spoken briefly before leaving the office, Zane had honestly thought Ty might drop on the spot, and he'd suggested they just skip the wake. But Ty had insisted he wanted to go, so Zane had relented. They'd stay until the party started to break up; then Zane would drive people home and take Ty home with him. Maybe now, finally, they'd be able to sleep one night in peace, without dreading the coming day. More than anything else, he wanted to hold Ty through the night and know he'd be there in the morning, safe and sound.

"We thought Mac locked you up somewhere," Alston said. "They about had Garrett shackled to the table all evening for the debrief."

Ty had his bottle to his mouth. He looked from Alston to Zane and nodded, still drinking. After he set the bottle down, he reached out and patted Zane's knee. "My partner did all the heavy lifting. They didn't have too many questions for me, just the basics. Do you like risking your life for your stupid partner, do you have suicidal tendencies, does the dark still make you piss yourself?"

"Oh, par for the course, then," Perrimore egged.

Zane didn't try to hold back the chuckle. "Now, now, Freddy, don't get him all riled up when we finally get to relax."

Ty just gave him a raspberry and continued drinking his beer, wearing a decent enough approximation of a smile. The whole table laughed, and Zane soaked in the unusual feeling of camaraderie as the group fell into casual talk again.

The chatter was interrupted when one of the assistant SAICs stood on a chair and yelled to get everyone's attention. The whole pub calmed, and Dan McCoy stood up, drink in hand.

"Okay, I think everybody's here who's coming. It's been an absolute hell of a day, more for some than others, and I want to tell you how proud I am that you all stuck with it through this mess. It would have been way too easy to knuckle under when the public turned on us and the bombs kept coming. But we all did our jobs, even when we knew we'd get nothing but shit for it." McCoy lifted his bottle. "To Lydia Reeves, who died in the line of duty. God bless her memory."

"Hear, hear," Alston said, just loud enough for the table to catch. Zane and the others echoed the sentiment as everyone raised their drinks in a toast to their fallen comrade.

A few moments of expectant silence later, the hairs on Zane's arms rose as Ty began to sing the first few lines to "Amazing Grace." When he reached the second verse, no one joined in with him, all of them either too stunned or too entranced by his voice to do anything but listen as they mourned.

Sunlight glowed buttery yellow as it beamed through the open curtains in Zane's bedroom. His eyes just barely open, he sleepily admired the light, soaking it in, a quiet joy filling him simply because he could see it. He lay still in the mussed bed for long minutes, waking up slowly and savoring it.

Finally he yawned and shifted in the sheets, smiling despite the impressive array of aches and pains from the bruising all over his body.

Ty hadn't added to the bruises last night. They'd both been so tired that all they could do was strip and collapse into bed, where Ty had burrowed into Zane's arms, wrapped around him like a limpet, and kissed him gently over and over between their whispers of achingly tender words that were so difficult to say in the light of day, until they'd drifted off to sleep.

Zane hummed and rolled to his back, reaching out for Ty only to feel cool sheets. Frowning, Zane sat up, and as the sheet pooled across his lap, he heard a soft crinkle. He picked up the sheet of paper and unfolded it to read two short lines written in Ty's messy scrawl that brought Zane's happy morning crashing down around him.

I'm sorry. Walls are closing in and I need to go.
Love you.

Explore more of the *Cut & Run* series at:
riptidepublishing.com/collections/cut-run

THE SERIES

ABIGAIL
ROUX

Dear Reader,

Thank you for reading Abigail Roux's *Divide & Conquer*!

We know your time is precious and you have many, many entertainment options, so it means a lot that you've chosen to spend your time reading. We really hope you enjoyed it.

We'd be honored if you'd consider posting a review—good or bad—on sites like **Amazon, Barnes & Noble, Kobo, Goodreads, Twitter, Facebook, Tumblr,** and your blog or website. We'd also be honored if you told your friends and family about this book. Word of mouth is a book's lifeblood!

For more information on upcoming releases, author interviews, blog tours, contests, giveaways, and more, please sign up for our weekly, spam-free newsletter and visit us around the web:

Newsletter: riptidepublishing.com/newsletter
Twitter: twitter.com/RiptideBooks
Facebook: facebook.com/RiptidePublishing
Goodreads: tinyurl.com/RiptideOnGoodreads
Tumblr: riptidepublishing.tumblr.com

Thank you so much for Reading the Rainbow!

RiptidePublishing.com

ALSO BY ABIGAIL ROUX

ABOUT
THE AUTHOR

Abigail Roux was born and raised in North Carolina. A past volleyball star who specializes in sarcasm and painful historical accuracy, she currently spends her time coaching high school volleyball and investigating the mysteries of single motherhood. Any spare time is spent living and dying with every Atlanta Braves and Carolina Panthers game of the year. Abigail has a daughter, Little Roux, who is the light of her life, a boxer, four rescued cats who play an ongoing live-action variation of Call of Duty throughout the house, one evil Ragdoll, a certifiable extended family down the road, and a cast of thousands in her head.

Enjoy more stories like
Divide & Conquer
at RiptidePublishing.com!

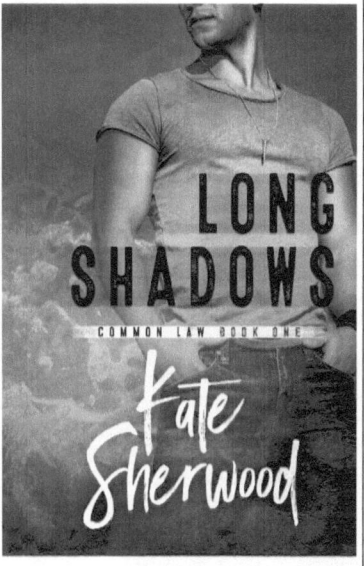

Assassins: Discord

When you're a teen thief and assassin, staying alive gets tricky.

ISBN: 978-1-62649-422-0

Anyone But You

Murder is one hell of a drag.

ISBN: 978-1-62649-891-4